TO G,

FOR ALL HIS PATIENCE AND ASSISTANCE.

FAIRYTALES DON'T COME TRUE

Volume 1 of the *Criminal Conversation* trilogy

Laura Lyndhurst

Imprint: Independently published.

Cover design by: Alice Alinari

ISBN-13: 979-8-701-49006-0

CONTENTS

1: AN ODD HOUSEHOLD

Just because nursing is a respectable profession, mused Dora Stuart-Frazer, doesn't mean that all the clients you treat are necessarily respectable. Take the case she was on her way to now, for example; a good area, leafy and suburban, on the outskirts of a Cathedral city in the South, and a bizarrely-mismatched household consisting of one female university lecturer, the householder, Dora gathered, one rather common middle-aged Irish woman who appeared to be her cleaner, the latter's daughter, a nursing student at the lecturer's university, a little girl, of about three to four years old, presumably the student's child, and a relatively young ex-prostitute.

She wouldn't have known that her patient had been a prostitute, because it was she for whom Dora was providing care, except that the woman hadn't tried to hide the fact when passing the time talking to her nurse while Dora attended to her needs. And not just a prostitute, but one who'd been in prison, released early on compassionate grounds because she didn't have long to live. Thereafter Dora had been slightly distant in manner, her disapproval obvious, although she herself was unaware of the fact until the young woman had issued a gentle reproof. *I can ask them to send someone else if you like; I'm afraid it's clear you're not happy having to deal with me.* Dora had denied the charge, blustering something about feeling a little off-colour, and then reproached herself rather more harshly when on her way home. *For heaven's sake, Dora, try to get a hold on yourself; you're supposed to be a nurse, and a Christian, where's your compassion?* She'd never had any such issues before, so why now?

Perhaps it was because the girl, for to be fair she

1

was a girl, she must be under thirty even with the ravages the cervical cancer had made on her, didn't fit the profile of a prostitute which Dora had firmly fixed in her mind. She was gentle, polite and self-effacing to a fault; almost humble, in fact, as though she was sorry to be such a bother as to need Dora's very-much-in-demand nursing skills. Not common either, not like the Irish woman, the cleaner, who had a rather raucous way with her; well-spoken, cultured, even. In sum, she troubled Dora because she wasn't the hard-faced, brassy tart (to use the harsh and unsympathetic words which went through Dora's mind) that their respectable social sisters like Dora usually pictured prostitutes to be; and Dora was nothing if not respectable.

In truth it wasn't totally her fault, her disapproval; she'd been raised by a strict mother, a midwife and an upstanding member of the Church, who always reminded her daughter that it was necessary to try even harder and to be ultra-respectable, because they were black in a majority-white country. There would always be some of the native population to hold their skin colour against them, even more so if they showed just the least divergence from what was expected in this society. Therefore it was necessary to work hard, uphold and obey the law, show a clean house exterior to those who passed by and observe clean behaviour both outside and inside of that house.

It wasn't quite what I was expecting when I came over here from Jamaica, she told her daughter; some of these people who throw casual racist comments around would do well to remember that it may have been these black hands, or others like them (extending her work-worn and still very capable arms before her) which brought them into the world. It amused her, she said, to think of this at times when she felt under racial pressure, but she lived by the doctrine of necessity she'd expounded to her daughter, and Dora in her turn had followed suit.

Dora was proud of what she'd achieved in her

forty-eight years. A successful career in nursing, currently for a charity which provided care for the terminally-ill; although she found it oddly noteworthy that while her mother had given her skills to bringing new lives into the world, Dora now used hers to help suffering lives out of it with as little pain and as much dignity as possible. Her husband, Desmond, was expecting another promotion at any time now for his hard work in management. She had met him through the Church; he was from a family similar to her own, immigrants from Jamaica, Baptists with the same beliefs and values, so it seemed meant to be when they hit it off at a church youth club gathering one weekend.

Dora had been rather shocked by the event; some of the young people present, including Desmond, had turned on a portable radio to a music channel, and begun to dance. Dora couldn't conceal her thoughts; We're Baptists, she exclaimed, we don't dance! We're black, countered a smiling Des, as he danced up to her and took her by the hand, we've got rhythm in our blood; white Baptists don't dance, but we sure do. And he whirled her out onto the floor where, captivated by his wide smile and laughing eyes, Dora had given up on her apparently misplaced principles and allowed him to show her how to do it.

She hadn't needed much coaching, as it happened, she had rhythm in her blood, the same as the others, it seemed, and she enjoyed dancing; with Des that is. They made a good couple, and when he asked her to make it a permanent arrangement off the dance floor, she hadn't hesitated to say Yes; they'd even hyphenated their surnames, Dora Stuart and Desmond Frazer. It had been a good life with him, they'd had fun when young and yes, even a good sex life; within the bounds of respectability, of course, nothing weird or kinky going on here, healthy missionary-position sexual activity with children born as a result. Two children, a son and a daughter, successfully

3

supported through university by Des and Dora to the point that they were now working as a doctor and a dentist respectively.

Now, of course, the parents being middle-aged, the sexual side of things was on the decline, for Dora, at least; an early hysterectomy due to endometriosis had lessened her sex drive, although that had been rather low in the first place. Des was still keen, but he was a man of course and they had naturally-higher sex drives, Dora thought. She usually put off his requests with humour, A man of your age, We ought to be past that sort of thing by now, We both have an early start tomorrow, and so forth; and he usually desisted with a good grace, if rather ruefully. And now Dora disapproved of prostitutes even more than she had before, if that were possible, because just by existing they were a reminder of the constant temptation available through women, any women, to men; not her man, though, not her Des, of course there was no latent worry in her mind that he just might be tempted to go that route, one of these days.

Or was there? Des was used to getting home first in the evening, Dora's working day frequently going on well into the evening, or even taking the form of a night shift, due to the varying needs of her patients; but recently he'd taken to going out drinking with a few work colleagues on the occasional evening. Nothing heavy, he assured her, just a couple of drinks and wind-down-from-work talk in a relaxed social setting; nevertheless, it had set Dora wondering. Why now, after all these years of coming straight home? Who were these colleagues? Male only? Male and female? If some of the latter were of the party, Dora wasn't sure she wanted her Des talking and laughing with them in a pub; work was work, but this was something else. Colleagues saw each other differently outside the workplace, after a few drinks; look how notorious office Christmas parties had become.

She knew she was being ridiculously old-fashioned but she couldn't help it; Des was only human, and what if he took a fancy to one of these women, what if he had an affair? Not that he would, of course, she was sure, but just supposing, for argument's sake? It would have to be divorce, of course, there was no other option; and Dora didn't believe in divorce, didn't want a divorce, she liked her life the way it was, orderly and wholesome and respectable.

So her current patient, Ms Magdalena Mystry, was an unwelcome reminder of the very existence of illicit sex, just waiting to pounce on Dora's husband, in the persons of prostitutes or other women no better than these; the result being that the compassion which Dora was supposed to feel for her patients, and had never had any problem in feeling previously, was sadly lacking in this case. But, Come on, she told herself, you're better than this. By her very name this girl should remind you of Mary Madgalen, who was supposed to be a reformed prostitute, even if there's a lot of doubt about that now. Christ forgave, and so should you. So she made a great effort to be not just civil but even friendly to the woman; outwardly, at least, and although that was all that was required really, Dora told herself, she still felt awkward and in the wrong.

One evening, as she bent over the patient, the gold cross which she always wore around her neck slipped beyond the bounds of her uniform neckline and dangled before the face of the girl, who commented; You're a Christian? Thank you, then, for working on a Saturday, when Dora nodded an affirmative to the question. The nurse brushed her thanks aside as misplaced, ignorant, even; because although the majority of people these days didn't seem to care in the slightest about respecting the Lord's day, most of them knew it to be Sunday, not Saturday, for Christians. And Dora would work on the Sabbath, because people who needed nurses couldn't be conveniently ill from Monday to Saturday only. She'd known that when she trained to nurse, and as she was doing the Lord's work, he'd understand, she was sure.

The girl apologised; I'm sorry, I presumed you to be a Seventh Day Adventist, I understand that to be one of the major sects in Jamaica; and their Sabbath, I was told, happens on Saturday. Not so ignorant, then, conceded Dora to herself, rather better-informed than most, in fact; but outwardly she corrected the girl. Oh no, I'm a Baptist; and, curious despite herself, asked, You seem to know something about it. Did you have a religious upbringing yourself? And, as she tucked her cross back inside her neckline, she glanced automatically at the girl's neck; no cross there though, but a gold chain with a letter 'H' pendant upon it. Strange, she thought, as the patient's name was Magdalena; but it was none of her business, the girl would tell her if she wanted to. Which she was now doing, replying to Dora's question; Oh yes, I was raised as a Christian; my parents lived for their faith, and were very strict in passing it on to me.

Dora was perturbed; How then could the girl have landed in such a profession? In her opinion, anyone raised correctly in the path of righteousness shouldn't end up as this one had. But she seemed to understand Dora's line of thought, and to want to explain herself. I'm afraid the religion didn't have a good effect on me, and I lost belief quite early on. It was a very restricted life with my parents; they didn't give me the type of upbringing other children had. I didn't go to school, because they didn't approve of much that was taught in the state system. They held very straight-laced religious views and rather narrow views of the world in general, it seemed to me, as I got older. My father had been a teacher, before he went into the Church full-time, so he taught me at home; the basics, reading, writing, English and maths, plus whatever else he considered safe.

But I wanted to break free, to go out and experience the wider world, and go to university, to begin with. They didn't want that, though, they opposed it; they wanted me to stay at home and marry a young man they approved of within the church community. I had to fight them, and eventually they agreed, although reluctantly, to let me attend university; but they stopped their financial support after the first year and I had to find a way to support myself.

Dora was disturbed by this; she thought of her own mother, Rose, working extra hours to finance her daughter's nursing training, her father Les doing likewise on the London underground. There hadn't been exorbitant fees to pay back then, of course, but her wise parents had known that even with a grant from the government their daughter would need more support from them. Then she thought of her own Ruth and Matthew, who'd been subject to fees and taken part-time work to help pay their way; and how she and Des had gladly helped, so that the children wouldn't compromise their studies through too much time away from them. There had been much extra work for both Dora and Des, plus a good deal of scrimping and scraping on household costs, but the children had made their way through university to emerge debt-free, with a solid understanding of the value of money, to take up their respective careers. How would we all have managed without that parental support, both moral and financial? She didn't approve of the road Magdalena had taken, and surely the situation she'd found herself in wasn't so bad as to have sent her down it so soon in life.

She found herself wanting to understand further; hearing the girl's story might help to awaken in Dora the sympathy which had so far been lacking. So, How did you manage to get to university? It must have been difficult, given that you were taught at home. Magdalena nodded; I was helped by a librarian, but it's a bit complicated and I don't want to bore you. Oh no, Dora insisted, I wouldn't be bored; I'd like to hear, and I have the time. Well then, the girl continued, when Dora had helped prop her up on pillows for comfort, My father included literature in what he taught me, although only those books he thought suitable, which weren't many; and on condition that I accepted his warning that it was all fiction and not get carried away by it. I agreed, because I enjoyed study, and not just because I'd got little else to occupy me. I wanted to find out as much about the world as I could; and a greater experience of this when I was grown and away from my parents would either prove or disprove his ideas, I thought.

As I wasn't allowed to watch TV or use a computer, and as we didn't possess these, anyway, in line with my parents' views, books were about all that was available to me. My parents accepted that I needed to get out sometimes, and the public library they felt to be relatively safe; so I was taken to the library on weekdays, while other children were in school. It was quieter then, and the librarians agreed to keep an eye on me, as long as I was no trouble; and of course, they soon found that I wasn't.

I was allowed to stay and read for a couple of hours before one of my parents collected me, and I read as many books as I could, after my father had vetted them first. I say that, but the fact was that I read much of which he wouldn't approve. Being a child and inquisitive, and left alone, I found other books and, having glanced through them, started to read them. But as I couldn't take them home to read, I began hiding them behind or on top of the bookshelves, where others couldn't find them and borrow them, so I could continue with them the next time.

Of course, a librarian discovered me one day; Why are you doing this? after she'd ascertained that I was hiding a book. Because I'm not allowed to take it home; my parents don't approve of many of the books in here. She examined the text in her hand with surprise, presumably thinking it harmless for a child of my age; then looked at me and the plea in my eyes before apparently deciding that I needed to be encouraged. Here's what we'll do; you give me the book you're reading when you finish each day, and I'll keep it under the desk for you. You can ask me for it the next time you're in; as long as you don't take too long to read the books, I can't keep them for you indefinitely, you know.

I assured her I wouldn't, which was true; I devoured books, and the knowledge contained within them which seemed a window onto the wider world for me. Magdalena sighed then, looking back; I must've been an odd sight, perched at the library table and reading avidly, the child with the very short white-blonde hair, and only the dress I wore to identify me as female. In an attempt to discourage the sin of vanity in me, you see, my hair, which had been considered beautiful, had been shorn by my mother, with the proverbial basin over my head. It had the opposite effect, though, because since the day she allowed it to grow again (when I was around eleven or twelve years old, and judged on the verge of puberty, the time to attract a potential husband) I never had it cut, apart from a trim occasionally to keep it neat; and look at me now!

She smiled ruefully, and Dora made sympathetic noises over the brutal loss of hair brought about by the chemoradiation therapy the girl had undergone. Magdalena shrugged, and returned to the main story. Over time, like my hair, my arrangement with the librarian Mrs Cardinal (that was her name) grew to include her colleagues, so I was always assured of continuing where I'd left off in my reading. That's how she came to be my accomplice in my getting to university. I showed so much promise in my studies, as well as discrimination in what I read (as he thought) that my father allowed me to study as a private candidate for GCSEs and A levels; in subjects of which he approved, of course. I realised later that it was only meant to keep me busy, because I couldn't spend all day doing housework with my mother, until such time as they found me a husband.

I sat the exams at a college approved by the examination board; my grades were good, easily enough to get me into university, but my parents refused to let me apply. When I told Mrs Cardinal she obtained the correct UCAS forms, and helped me to complete and submit them; I was no longer a child, she said, and it was my right to choose my own future. Well, I received more than one offer of a place to study English and European Literature, but then I had to fight for the right to take one of them up, because my parents weren't happy that I'd applied behind their backs and more opposed than ever to the idea.

Her face contracted with some pain then, and Could you please? she indicated a need to Dora, who realised with shame that in listening to the story she'd been neglecting her duties to the patient telling it. She hastened to provide what was needed and, when the girl was more comfortable, said goodbye for the night; she was off home to Des, and a late supper, and didn't want to keep him waiting. Magdalena smiled, in a light-headed way brought on by the administration of morphine; Of course, you mustn't be late; thank you for everything, and for listening. It's been interesting, looking back. Well, you don't have much to look forward to, Dora thought inadvertently as she let herself out, and then reproached herself; Of course the girl did, her sins would be forgiven, if she was repentant, which Dora was sure she was; but of what, exactly? The nurse resolved to find out.

2: BEGINNING

Arriving at her usual early-evening time the next day, she found her patient sitting with the cleaner, named Celia, apparently, and laughing over a joke the latter was just finishing telling. Dora took silent umbrage, having heard enough to gather that the thing included bad language and was told at the expense of nuns; and in her opinion religion was not suitable material for coarse humour.

Celia left the room then, and Dora smiled tightly through partly-pursed lips as she passed, receiving in return a knowing grin which she interpreted as the woman reading her thoughts and mocking them. All this was noticed by Magdalena, who hastened to appease her nurse. Please don't be offended, Celia was raised as a Catholic but had a rough time when she was young and lost her belief because the Church didn't help her. She's bitter about that, so it makes her feel better to poke fun at it. I understand, because I lost my faith too.

How did that happen? Dora wanted to know; and as she went about making her comfortable the girl told her. I suppose my relationship with religion was on the wane before I arrived at university, but I suppose the thing that really finished it happened not long after I got there. I was feeling a bit lonely when a girl in one of my seminar groups was asking all of us if we'd like to go to a special Sunday evening service at her church, about three miles from campus.

Well, some old habits die hard, and she'd a car and offered to take me there and bring me back again, as I was the only one to take her up on the offer. So I went with her, but it turned out that she'd got a boyfriend there, and he'd other ideas for the evening; so she disappeared with him and so did the lift back she'd promised me. I'd insufficient money for bus fare, even had there been any buses at that time on a Sunday night, and no other members of the congregation would go out of their way to give me a lift and see that I got back safely, despite being made aware of my problem by the minister. So, with an ironic comment to the effect that I supposed Jesus was walking me home (which they found very witty) I set off to walk in the dark and the rain. And maybe he did walk with me, because I got back safely; but I'd learned that there's a difference between a Christian and a Churchgoer, and the knowledge put paid to my already damaged faith.

Dora had to concede that the girl had a point; there were some people who attended church but didn't seem to apply its teachings to their life outside the building. But it clearly hadn't been this incident alone which had caused her to lose faith, so, How had it become damaged already? she enquired. Part of the problem, Magdalena told her, was what my parents and their beliefs deemed suitable for a girl. A rather Victorian angel-in-the-house doctrine it was, housekeeping and making a safe haven from the world without for the menfolk within; or one man, a husband, more precisely. I wasn't necessarily opposed to the idea of marriage, I just thought I ought to have the greater say about who I married, and when; and I felt I wanted to experience more of the world before I settled to it, if I did at all; it should be my choice. University I believed would help me in this, although my parents weren't inclined to agree; and just as we reached an impasse the issue became critical, because a young man came to my parents' notice.

He was the son of other members of their church, about the same age as me, and on those grounds deemed a suitable potential husband for me. He and I used to see each other at the church anyway, and at the youth group gatherings, but now we were given an extra degree of freedom to get to know each other. We did get on well, there was some attraction on both sides, and things got physical, unbeknown to both sets of parents. Now, of course, I realise that what went on between us was perfectly normal for inquisitive teenagers, but I knew little if anything at the time about sexual matters. My parents had fudged the issue, teaching me that 'intimate behaviour' (she put little quotation marks around the words with her fingers) was to be avoided until I was married, but they hadn't told me what that was, exactly.

Anyway, the boy and I apparently went too far, as he told me, further observing that I could be pregnant already; guilt-fuelled panic set in, but fortunately my period started a few days later. I was confused by it all, especially by the sex, which had been disappointing and seemed very little, given the fuss that's made about it; and paranoia set in after another incident seemed to prove to me that I'd sinned gravely.

Dora cast her mind back to times she'd spent with Des at the church youth group, and afterwards, when he'd walked her home in the dark and kissed her, suggesting other things they could do if she cared to go somewhere more private with him. She did care, and was sorely tempted, but she'd resisted with all her strength; only because she'd been fully informed about the facts of life by her midwife-mother though, and exactly what she ought not to do before marriage. This girl, it appeared, had been left ignorant of those things, and also lacked school friends to bring her up to speed, children having a way of finding things out before they were supposed to know them. What else then was to be expected? And apparently what happened had left Magdalena cold, where even Dora of the low libido had experienced almost irresistible sensations when Des had kissed and caressed her.

We had a social day for young people at the church community centre, Magdalena continued, smiling ruefully at the memory, and at one point we played a sort of 'piggy in the middle' game. We all sat in a circle, one person blindfolded in the centre, and were given a card each with the name of a railway station on it. The youth leader would call out, for example 'Derby change with Exeter', and those two would have to run across the circle to change places and 'It' would try to catch one of them. If caught, that person would become the new 'It' and give his or her card to the old one, to play as that station. Simple enough, but the trouble began for me when I was issued my station name; Maidenhead. I panicked internally, while trying to remain cool externally; I knew God was on to me, pointing the finger of irony at me, and that I was a 'fallen woman'. Guilty, guilty, guilty, unless I married the boy responsible; who I knew was very willing.

But my rebellious and independent streak asserted itself; I didn't want to get married yet, maybe never, to him or anyone else. My parents, not knowing of our foray into the arena of sex, nevertheless tried to force the issue; and I suppose I do resent them, because if they'd told me the facts of life and I'd known what to expect I would've realised that nothing very much had happened and wouldn't have worried about it so. And maybe I wouldn't then have thought of myself as 'fallen' and got into the situation which shaped my life and took me down the path I've followed since.

But that'll have to wait for next time, she concluded, as a knock at the door announced the arrival of Laura, the lecturer-householder, with a cup of tea and a request to know whether Mags could manage anything to eat? At which Dora realised she'd almost exceeded her time and needed to get moving. She carried out the necessary tasks for her patient and left the two women together, wondering about their relationship as she drove slowly through the late-evening traffic. She'd noted the affectionate diminutive version of the girl's name which the older woman had used; Mags, she called her, it seemed.

Mother and daughter, perhaps? Laura was certainly old enough for that to be feasible, she had to be in her late fifties at least, or even her sixties.

But No, Dora dismissed the idea, she didn't fit the picture of the old-fashioned and strictly religious mother which Mags had painted and, if she'd been that person, would she have had her 'fallen' daughter back to live with her? Not that Mags had said a great deal about her mother, whose life appeared to have been dedicated to serving the father; which wasn't the impression Laura gave, even had the father been around, which he wasn't. So they weren't linked by blood, unless Mags had other relations whom she hadn't mentioned, but Dora didn't think so. What, then? It was the oddest household, all-female, comprised of four, maybe five, generations. She resolved to find out what linked them all, as tactfully as possible.

3: ARRIVING

She got the opportunity the following evening, when Laura let her in and ushered her into the kitchen for a quick word, she said, before Dora went in to Mags. She's been a bit low this afternoon, Laura volunteered as, having offered tea and Dora having accepted, she busied herself with kettle and cups. Old memories, you know? I don't know exactly what's getting her down, some things she's told me but a lot she hasn't; so I've just been trying to talk about positive things and maybe you could do the same? She smiled weakly as she took two mugs herself and indicated the third to Dora, Could you please? as she went to precede the nurse to the girl's room.

Dora couldn't resist fishing; I know how difficult it must be, believe me, for a mother to have to see her child suffering like this. But Laura shook her head and smiled again; Oh, no, I'm not her mother, I never had children; my ex-partner wanted to have one, but I was so busy looking after my own mother, when I wasn't working, that I didn't think it would be fair to the child. And by the time my mother passed away Yvonne had long-since become tired of waiting, and she'd left me. And with a regretful sigh she passed down the hallway, Dora following her.

So her attempt to establish the relationship between Mags and Laura had disclosed another piece of information which left her mentally reeling; a lesbian! She hadn't been ready for that, and she didn't approve, before even considering the other issue which now raised its head; Were they lovers then, these two? Her thoughts were apparently confirmed as she followed Laura into the room where Mags, dozing, opened her eyes and then her arms, into which Laura went, after depositing the tea mugs on the bedside table, for a deeply affectionate hug which had the effect of softening even Dora's disapproval. I'm sorry I've been such a misery all day, the girl was saying, I'm feeling a bit better now, I'll try to be happier. No, don't apologise, from Laura, we all have down-days and you've every right; and then more affectionate talk in the same vein passed between the two.

Dora excused herself to visit the bathroom while Laura was with Mags; she'd been stuck in traffic for longer than was ideal. As she washed her hands she considered the notion of these two as a lesbian couple. She'd heard somewhere, some gossip in a staff room once, of the notion of prostitutes turning to other women, presumably in disgust at what they experienced from men on a daily, or nightly, basis. Only natural, when you think about it, the person giving the information had said; but there was little less natural, as far as Dora was concerned. The affection between these two was touching, but anything more ... her thoughts were happily prevented from going down that route as she re-entered the bedroom; She's all yours, she was told by Laura, who took her her mug of tea and left nurse and patient together.

Dora couldn't resist the urge to continue probing, as she went about her duties of attending to her patient's needs and making her as comfortable as possible. She's clearly devoted to you, she observed, not looking at Mags directly but focussing on the task in hand; Have you been together for long? The girl answered immediately; Oh, no, I've only been living here since I was released because, you know ... Dora did know this part of her patient's history; she'd been in prison, released early on compassionate grounds for her last few months of life. I didn't know her that well before, Mags went on, I hadn't seen her for some years, then she came to visit me in prison and offered me a home here until ... She trailed off again, and Dora nodded; then, as though to round things off, Mags continued. She was one of my university lecturers, and my personal tutor, originally; she felt responsible for the way my life went off the rails, which was silly of her, really, it was all my own fault.

Dora felt relief; fortunately the girl hadn't taken her meaning, and it seemed that the relationship between tutor and former student wasn't an intimate one. To move things on, in case Mags realised belatedly what her nurse had been getting at, she said the first thing that came into her head; So how was university, once you got there? You had a bit of a fight with your parents over it, I think you said yesterday? The girl nodded; They'd have had to let me go when I was eighteen anyway, so I pointed this out to them and stood my ground. I can be very stubborn when I want to be; unfortunately I haven't wanted to be often enough for my own good.

Enough of that, though; she put the melancholy thoughts aside and made an effort to focus on the positive, as Dora sat down to listen. I loved university; I enjoyed my studies, but also adored being free of the restraints of my parents' home and lifestyle. There were so many people, so many new experiences; music groups, sports, there was even a small theatre on the campus, where local amateur groups performed, and professionals on tour, not to mention the university drama students putting on productions to practice their intended profession. I even enjoyed the jobs I took, waiting tables at campus cafés and bars, working in shops, because I got to talk to people of my own age, which'd been mostly lacking in my life before.

I avoided close relationships though, mainly because I'd been used to being alone and found I preferred it like that; I suppose I was still rather shy, I needed to get used to people slowly, in manageable chunks, you might say. I was able to socialise with other girls in general, but the kind of close relationships where clothes and secrets about boyfriends are shared, weren't yet for me. I couldn't have spoken about boyfriends in any case, because my experience with the young man before university had put me off, frightened me; so despite the relationships of young people I observed all around me, boyfriends and girlfriends, I couldn't face the idea of doing anything like that again. There were young men who tried, some quite pleasant, but not enough to tempt me to go there again.

Dora felt sympathy for this; she'd been lucky, finding the right man straight off, not having to go through all the teenage angst other girls less fortunate suffered. She'd comforted Ruth through enough instances of heartbreak, and her daughter still hadn't found the right one. Dora felt guilt also because, having found her Des so soon, she had a feeling that she didn't fully appreciate him; but she pushed that thought aside, and concentrated on Mags. *We have a good life, better than many, and that ought to be enough,* she told herself.

It was halfway through my second year when things got difficult, the girl was saying. My parents had helped me out in the first, and through living as cheaply as possible I'd managed not to get into debt. But in the second year they made it clear it was up to me to pay my own way; hoping, I was sure, that I wouldn't be able to and return to their home and the marriage awaiting me, as they thought. I was determined to do no such thing, but it wasn't going to be easy. For one thing, I'd had to move out of campus accommodation, which was limited and reserved for first-year students who needed to get used to living away from home gradually. So I incurred the higher costs involved in living in a local house, even though I shared it with five other students.

I found not one but two jobs, with more hours available than I was able to work, but I needed time to study and sleep, not to mention my social life, which was becoming largely non-existent. I needed some advice and I had an interview arranged with my tutor-mentor, Laura Hogarth; Laura, whose house we're in now, she clarified for

Dora. She was a user-friendly lecturer; her manner invited you to confide in her if you wanted to, but equally she respected your privacy. It was a routine progress check I had with her, how I was getting on both academically, socially and so forth, so I decided to ask for her help.

When I knocked at her office door she invited me in, then offered me a coffee, as she was making, and we got down to the nitty-gritty of how she could help me. I told her finance was becoming an issue, because my parents wouldn't help me any more, and so costs were mounting. I don't want to leave here buried under a mountain of debt, I told her, so I'm working as much as I can. I've a weekend shop job and an evening shift in an on-campus café, but I've obviously got less time for study because of this.

I remember how she seemed exasperated about the whole fees-for-study thing, and the fact that the majority of young people are encouraged to go to university now, whether they have academic ability or not. She thought that most students leave university drowning in debt, or compromise their studies because they want to avoid that by working to pay their way as they go along. So too many were leaving with degrees at low grades, either because they couldn't study enough due to working in a shop or bar or whatever, or because it's not really what they're cut out to do; and they're all in debt to some extent anyway.

Well, I certainly wanted to avoid that, so and I asked her please to give me an extension on my essay deadline to take some of the pressure off. I didn't get the answer I wanted, though. I'm so sorry, Mags, she told me, I can't do it; not on those grounds, and even if you were the first, rather than the fourth, who's been in here asking me for exactly the same thing today. Look around you, it's as I just said, the place is full of students burning the midnight oil studying because they're working their backsides off for money so they don't leave here with a debt which outweighs the value of their degree. They're working in shops, bars, waiting tables, and I don't even want to think what some of them are doing in the sex industry.

I didn't know what she was talking about then and said so; she told me that there was apparently a significant proportion of students doing strip-a-grams, topless modelling and who knows what else to get by. Her point was that if she gave me an extension because my work and study conflicted, she'd have to give one to all her students, and they'd tell others, so other lecturers would have to do the same, and the whole thing would just snowball and marking deadlines would get pushed back across the board, and so on and so forth; basically, it was impossible. She was very apologetic, but I was going to have to find another way to make it work.

I remember feeling really disappointed as I left her office; I had a shift in the café due to begin in about an hour, so there was no point in trying to study. I went straight to the café instead to see if anyone I knew was there. I saw Simon and Anna, who I knew from one of my seminar groups, but they were busy preparing for a presentation they had to give in half an hour so weren't available to talk. There was also an older girl I knew to a certain extent, and I ended up speaking to her about the learning-versus-earning problem. Liz Needham; she was a Business Studies student so she wasn't doing any of my courses, but she shared a house with someone who was, and we'd met sometimes via our mutual acquaintance. She was in her final year, and she'd managed to keep her debt level relatively low; at some cost to her study, true, but she was doing better than I was, from what I'd heard her say previously, so any advice would be gratefully received.

The trick is, she told me, to get the maximum money for the least amount of work; which sounds obvious, but where to find these high-paying jobs? Well, I've worked at darts tournaments, and at lower-level motor racing circuits, you know, scantily-clad nymphet holding a placard? I didn't know, but I nodded anyway because I thought she wouldn't help me get the work if she didn't think I was experienced enough for it. But there's nothing doing in those at the moment, she continued, although there's one annual gig I've been doing for the last couple of years, and it's coming up again soon. All of £150 in your pocket for about six hours' work, plus taxi fare both ways, but it's not everybody's thing; you need a strong stomach and nerves of iron. I was excited; about £25 an hour! I thought of my minimum wage jobs, which netted me not much more than that for six hours all told; so, Give me an idea and I'll see, I told her.

It was a charity dinner, apparently, to be held at a swish hotel, men-only, those rich and influential types who're patrons of various charities and other worthy causes. Hostesses were required to look after them, escort them to their designated tables and sit at the tables with them, two or three girls to each table. They were to talk to the men, encourage them to drink and get the drinks when required, help them to relax and have a good time. It gets a bad press from those who've worked it and disliked it, Liz said, on the grounds of supposedly getting pestered, sexually-harassed, call it what you like; but if they'd checked it out properly they could've seen going in that it wasn't going to be easy.

But if you can do it the money's good, plus, who knows? You could meet a well-off guy who might do a lot for you. There was a girl, Angie, in the year above me here; it was she who first put me onto it. She'd been working it for a couple of years and in the third she found a man, a bit older than she might've liked, true, but loaded, absolutely loaded; he paid her fees here for the rest of her time, and her living costs, and the debts she'd already run up. Obviously she had to sleep with him, regularly, while she was still here, but it seems it worked and she left uni debt-free.

I thought about what Liz was saying; What happened with the man when she finished here? She shrugged; I don't know, maybe they carried on, maybe not; but it was all worked out legally, she got a contract and everything, so maybe that was covered in the details. The point is, if you're going to meet anyone who could do you some good that's where you'll do it; how many rich guys are we going to meet in this place? She swept her arm around the café, full of students and staff, all none-too-well-off, and they looked it.

The disapproval on Dora's face was obvious to Mags; she shrugged apologetically. I know, it doesn't sound good, and maybe it was wrong to do it. I hadn't considered looking for a rich man to fund me until Liz mentioned it, and it didn't seem like such a bad idea, the way she put it. I mean, I'd be using him, wouldn't I? I'd be an in-control woman, a modern woman, in charge of my own life and using what I'd got to get what I wanted and serve my own requirements. I wasn't supposed to fall in love, like the heroine of a cheap novel. I took bad advice from Liz because I was naïve, and I'm not making any excuses. But I can't regret it, because it was how I met Teddy, and I loved him so much, even if it did go disastrously wrong; and I'd still be with him if I'd the chance to do it again.

Her hands were playing with the 'H' at her throat now, Dora noticed, and she trailed off, dreamily, looking off into the distant past with a gentle smile on her face; which could of course have been the morphine, but Dora didn't think so this time. Who was Teddy? she wanted to know. We'll get to him; the girl dragged herself back into the present; If you've time, that is? Dora did, and she wasn't going anywhere, she said, until they had gotten to Teddy.

So I considered what Liz had said, Mags continued, and asked her to talk me through the negative side of the thing, because I thought I might as well go prepared, if I went at all. For the record, she told me, I personally don't have a problem because I knew going in what it could be like. 'Men only' tells its own story, if you know what the male of the species can be like, left to himself; men behaving badly, adolescent boys in supposedly adult bodies, lads at what's basically a high-class stag do, let's be honest. So I'm always in control, and anyone who goes in there and comes out shocked is naïve to say the least; they need to wise-up on life or they're going to get themselves in deep trouble. Sexual harassment? Maybe; but it's pretty clear from the outset, the signs are there for anyone to see, if only they'd think it through.

Firstly; the agency in charge of hiring advertises for 'hostesses' who are to be 'slim and pretty' young women; no young men, you notice, plus they're requested to wear black underclothes. Now, apart from when talking about air hostesses (glorified waitresses, if you ask me) the word 'hostess' has been known to have sleazy overtones for a very long time. Think nightclub hostesses, one example of which would be the Hugh Hefner empire, Bunny girls; Google it, she said, when I looked blank and shook my head. Back in the nineteen-sixties and seventies, the Playboy Club, the name tells the story; the girls wore very little, bunny ears and fluffy tails on skimpy satin body suits. They served drinks, ran gambling tables and went to parties for club members at Hefner's home, the Playboy Mansion, with an implication that they might in certain circumstances serve more than drinks.

So anyone considering applying for this dinner ought to have been hearing alarm bells. 'Slim and pretty' says very clearly they're being hired for their looks; cue alarm bell number two, and it shouldn't take a genius to work out that the request for underclothes to be black says fairly clearly that they'll be on show. As in, worn under skimpy, revealing clothing, which in the event is what's been and will continue to be provided for us to wear. Cue the third alarm bell, and anyone who didn't like this ought never to have applied.

Liz was well into her stride now, Mags commented,

and I was in awe of her by this time; she was so worldly-wise and knowing for her age, and I felt like a baby beside her as she continued. Next, she said, those girls who were hired were asked to sign a contract, a non-disclosure agreement which we weren't allowed to read or take a copy of. Well, I'll admit an important rule of self-preservation is never to put your name to anything you haven't read. Did I tell you that Laura Hogarth called in a girl I know in one of her modules for plagiarism? The idiot had signed the cover sheet to say she'd referenced all her sources, but she hadn't, actually, she'd used loads from one particular secondary text without footnoting or adding it to her bibliography, so that it looked like her own ideas; and it was her bad luck that Laura knew that particular text inside out and backwards. The silly bitch was in tears, claimed she didn't know it was that important; well, why do they attach a page for you to sign if it's not that important? But, to get back to the point, it was her own fault and she needs to wise up.

Having said that, though, Liz conceded, I'll put my hands up to having signed without reading for this dinner; but if I'd insisted on reading and copying they'd never have let me through the door, and I needed the money. I figured I'd been in enough situations while working the darts tournaments, the racetracks, and the car shows to be able to look after myself here. The doors weren't locked and there had to be fire exits, legally; and this was a five-star hotel, not some dive with non-existent health and safety, after all. So a rapid departure in a worse-case scenario was possible; which incidentally was what anyone who wasn't happy about this was perfectly free to do at this point.

Mags paused for breath; she was beginning to tire, but apparently determined to initiate Dora into the mystery of Teddy before the nurse left for the night. We were warned, Liz continued, that the men might be 'irritating'; well they're going to be drinking the whole evening and you're scantily-clad, so you shouldn't to be shocked at the form the 'irritation' takes and you ought to be able to handle yourself when it happens; not 'if', because it's bound to. Once at work in the room we were allowed supervised comfort breaks of a limited amount of time and refused these if they became too frequent.

Supervised comfort breaks? I queried; *The Handmaid's Tale*? 'Jezebel's'? Liz prompted me. I remembered then; I had, I'd done it on one of my English modules. D'you know it? she asked Dora here and the latter shook her head. Well, Mags informed her, suffice to say there's a scene in an exclusive brothel where the girls aren't there willingly; and if they try to avoid working by going to the loo too much they're in trouble. There's no doubt what those women were there for, and this dinner was similar; we were being paid to be out there talking to the men, not hiding in the loo. Dora got the point, and Mags returned to Liz and her advice.

Ditch any illusions you might have and go for it, Liz told me, that's if you've a strong enough stomach. Those are my words of wisdom on the subject, she concluded; think it over, but don't take too long because you need to apply pronto. So I said I'd sleep on it and let her know in the morning; then I went to work my shift and return to my digs afterwards in deep thought and apparently ever-deepening debt unless I could find some other sources of cash, and fast.

The worst outcome, I decided, was that I could work the dinner, get some hassle from the men present, meet no-one to help me out in the longer term, but get paid £150 and taxi fare. First prize, however, was that I find someone as Liz's friend Angie had; and the unknowns were any range of things that could happen in between these two. The most important thing now was, could I handle it, whatever happened? As to any harassment, the thing took place in a hall full of other people, so as long as I stayed close to the crowd I ought to be alright; oughtn't I? As to meeting someone, for one night or a longer relationship? My one experience of sex had left me cold, but not traumatized; it didn't seem the worst thing in the world, and if I were to meet someone bearable it might be possible.

Having considered the Could I? of the situation, I considered the moral part, the Should I? As far as whoever-up-there it may've been who'd taunted me with the Maidenhead thing was concerned, I was already a fallen woman anyway. Not that this was a problem any more, because I'd got rid of the religious viewpoint on my 'lost virtue', as my parents would call it; so I decided I might as well give the dinner thing a go because I couldn't see that I'd anything left to lose. I tried to rationalize my decision with my mother's idea of the only thing a woman need do is to 'get a man', and that would be what in effect I was doing were I to find Mr Right. Not as permanent fix, though, not a husband, although the old-fashioned issue of having no virginity to bring to him no longer applied; but an arrangement with a man who'd be prepared to sponsor me financially in return for my companionship, as it were, as the next best thing. That way I could get my debts and remaining fees paid, then get out into the world, get a career and take control of my life as an independent woman; or so I thought, naïve as I was.

The next morning, in the cold light of day, I woke up in more than the literal sense. Did I really expect to find this mythical sponsor who'd take away all my financial worries? That'd be too much like one of the fairy-tales I'd been studying; goose girl gets prince, or whatever. But the rent was due, and I liked to eat at least once a day, so £150 in my hand sounded good, and I decided to risk it for that. I was straight onto Liz as soon as I decently could be, made the application before I lost my nerve, and was accepted to work as a hostess at the dinner. I was nervous for the next few weeks, until the appointed day arrived, but managed to immerse myself in my various types of work and not think about it any more than I could help.

I'm sorry, she said at this point, but I'm afraid that Teddy's going to have to wait after all; I'm feeling very tired now and I'd like to sleep. This was no problem for Dora, time was getting on anyway and, although she was interested in hearing the girl's story, getting home and spending what was left of the evening with Des was more important to her. She did all she could to make Mags comfortable, then made her way home and thought on the way about what she'd heard.

It was no understatement to say that the girl had been given bad advice; if it had been her Ruth, Dora would have locked her in the house rather than let her take part in any such affair. But of course, Ruth would have been at university, and Dora would have had no way of knowing what she was up to; she could have taken work at this dinner, or another like it, given that she hadn't studied near home, for all her mother knew. But Dora dismissed the idea out of hand; Ruth would never have given the time of day to such an idea, she knew what was right and what was wrong, she'd been brought up properly, in a good, God-fearing household. But then so had Mags, she told herself.

She put the problem out of her mind as she arrived home, and frowned at the sight of the darkened windows; Des wasn't there, apparently. A note on the kitchen table informed her that he'd made dinner, put hers in the oven to keep warm, then eaten his own and gone for a drink with his work colleagues. Dora was perturbed; going for a drink on the way home was one thing, but coming home and then going out again was something else. Had he gone to see someone? Some other woman, perhaps? Of course not, she told herself harshly, then made the best of things, spending a lonely couple of hours before taking herself along to bed. She hadn't been hungry, despite not having eaten since lunchtime, but had forced herself to eat, her sensible nature telling her that she needed food, hungry or not.

She couldn't sleep, and heard Des when he came in; it was the right side of midnight, the clock on the bedside table told her, and he didn't try to sneak in unheard, which Dora took for a good sign. But she feigned sleep when he came to bed, because she couldn't face an inquest into where he'd been, and with whom; and Des, finding her apparently asleep, didn't try to wake her but turned his back to her and was asleep very quickly. Dora, however, lay still in her misery and felt the tears come to her eyes and roll off her cheeks onto the sheets before she eventually fell into a fitful sleep in the small hours.

4: KEEPING I

She felt better the next morning, although only slightly so, not having slept soundly until it was getting light; she'd then been awoken too soon by Des, showered and dressed and bearing a cup of tea. He was apologetic about not having been there on the previous evening; he'd initially turned down the invitation to go to the pub, apparently, but once he'd eaten he was restless, with no Dora for company, and there was nothing on TV, so he'd thought Why not? and gone. Dora accepted his version of events because it was easier to do so and she didn't feel up to discussing the matter in any more depth than he was offering.

When he'd gone to work, she dawdled over her breakfast, most unlike her usual efficient self, and pondered the situation. She had time, having few appointments today, or so she thought; because the situation then got worse, courtesy of a phone call from Ms Mystry's district nurse. Mags had requested a change to her visits; she found that she was sleeping more during the day, and lying awake for most of the night. It made sense therefore for Laura, Celia and Vivie to see to her in the evening, and for Dora to come in for the night shift.

Dora was taken aback; she'd been working night shifts up until last week, with Mrs Briggs, who'd slipped away one evening. The poor woman had been in constant pain, and it was a mercy for her to be out of it, but Dora had been looking forward to spending her nights at home, and not just for the sleep. What of Des? It had already occurred to her that he'd be able to be out all night also. If he wanted to be, that was, and Dora thought that he didn't want, really, but she couldn't be sure; her confidence on that score was at a low ebb. In terms of work, she seemed to be building up a relationship with Mags in a strange sort of way, and didn't want to let her down. It was unusual for the same nurse to attend to the same patient all the time, but demand wasn't too high at present, which was why Dora had been with Mrs Briggs regularly for a month. But it made it difficult for her to find a reason not to work through the night, leaving Des continuing to be alone and to his own, possibly questionable, devices. So with a heavy heart she let her correct side take charge and accepted the request to provide through-the-night care for Mags.

Des was surprised; Dora had said herself that she'd like some time before taking on another patient to fill the slot Mrs Briggs had vacated, so she could be home at night for a while. But now she seemed keen to dive straight back in, without any break at all. If I didn't know you better I'd think you were having an affair, he joked; and, although she laughed with him, Dora wasn't sure how she felt about that. It was good to be respectable, yes, but to be so predictable, so ... boring? Or was Des just saying that to distract her from any idea that he was in fact the one having an affair? She was depressed by the thought.

Her new shift pattern commenced that evening at nine pm, meaning she had time to prepare dinner and eat with Des if he came home at a reasonable time and didn't go to the pub on the way. This was the good part of her new working pattern, but the bad was that there was nothing to stop him going out again once Dora had gone to work. He arrived at a reasonable time, though, no pub visit tonight, and settled down in front of the TV with a cup of tea as Dora prepared herself and left for work. Would he stay there? She put the question aside as best she could and concentrated on driving.

When she arrived, Mags had the little girl, Katie, on her lap, telling her a bed-time story; not quite what Dora had expected, but Mags was surprisingly good at story-telling, putting on different voices and roaring so

31

convincingly that Katie appeared convinced that she was the monster. The little girl seemed to like it, though, and was reluctant to leave when Vivie came to take her and put her to bed. Too late for a child that young, in Dora's view, but the loving hug that passed between her and Mags before she left the room made it clear that Katie was not lacking in love; just some sleep, perhaps.

When they were left alone together, Mags thanked Dora for changing her shift pattern at such short notice; I suppose I'm used to sleeping during the day and working nights, she explained, apologetically, and Dora, for some reason which she didn't understand, felt the need to lessen the impact of the blatantly-obvious reason for this. I work nights frequently too, she offered with a smile; It feels a bit exciting, somehow, sleeping when most other people are awake and then spending the night awake while they sleep. She didn't add that it had also been a good method of fending off sexual requests by Des, at least until recently, before he started socialising and Dora had started worrying about what other form than going to the pub that might take.

Mags nodded; I thought, too, that it'd be a good time for me to talk, to tell you things about my life, as I've been doing; that's if you're interested, of course. Oh, yes, Dora assured her, and she meant it; maybe hearing the life-story of this girl would help the nurse to understand, and feel some sympathy for her and others like her. Because she already felt something, the ice was starting to break, as she experienced the person rather than the profession. So, having ascertained that her patient was comfortable, and OK with being on her own for five minutes, Dora went and made them both a cup of tea. Are you sitting comfortably? Mags joked, when she returned; Then I'll begin.

It's a bit like that woman in the old story, Dora said, before Mags could do so, and the latter looked at her quizzically; You know, Dora continued, the Arabian Nights, it was, telling stories through the night to delay her husband from executing her as he'd done all his previous wives. Yes, of course, Mags agreed, I studied it at university; Shahrazade, that was her name, in the Thousand and One Nights. He couldn't sleep, he was a deeply-troubled man because his first wife'd been unfaithful, as had his brother's, and other women they encountered when they went on a journey to get over their bad marriages. So Shahriyar (that was his name) started marrying women and killing them the morning after the wedding night; but Shahrazade married him on a mission to save any more women from that fate. She provided him with therapy through her stories, occupying his mind during his wakeful nights and leaving him on cliff-hangers so that he'd have to let her live to hear the end of the story. In my case, I guess, I'm giving myself therapy, evaluating my life to try to make sense of it. Anyway, Shahrazade stayed alive long enough to have three children by Shahriyar and for him to have got so used to her, and even love her, that he wasn't angry any more; and of course they lived happily ever after.

Which I won't, she said stoically with a shrug, and Dora, who'd been wondering if Des knew any married women who'd be up to behaving like those unfaithful wives in the story, quickly asked Mags to tell her about Teddy, to divert her own thoughts into something more positive.

Well, the evening came, the girl commenced, and I'd arrived at the stag dinner. Liz and I had shared a taxi to the hotel, saving one-half of a return taxi fare to be shared between us, and she charmed the cabbie into giving us separate receipts so we could both claim. I took comfort from her all-knowing company during the journey and the registration process, which turned out to be everything she'd said it'd be. When we were dressed in our uniform of the evening, and we'd been given the pep talk, we were moved off to our designated tables. We weren't together, which would've been too much to hope for, so we parted, with Liz telling me, You're on your own now, good luck, see you back at campus if not before. We'd agreed to make our separate ways back afterwards, given that we didn't know what chance and fortune might send us.

I managed to put aside the qualms I felt, despite Liz's helpful briefing, about not having read the contract, and of wearing such revealing clothing; I concentrated on the event, which wasn't too bad at first. There were two other girls working on my table, both of whom had worked at this dinner in previous years, so I had expert help on hand. We were kept busy initially escorting the guests to their places, including helping those who managed to be at the wrong table to find the right one. Thereafter it was all about fetching drinks and making conversation with the men on my table, which wasn't difficult, because even before they had a drink or two on board they were only too ready to talk to me. All I really had to do by way of initiating conversation was to check they were comfortable, did they need another drink and did they have everything they needed? I tried re-wording that last question after a suggestion that my company on his lap was needed by one man, but it was difficult to avoid the sexually-suggestive comments they made; I could see what Liz had meant, it was going to be a long night.

But as more men arrived they began speaking to each other to a great extent, business cards were being exchanged all over the place and dinner of course was being served and eaten. Then came the speeches by the great and the good of the charity running the show, and directions to the bathroom were in great demand, of course, after all that drinking; in some cases it was necessary to take the man in need into the corridor and point the way. It wasn't exactly rocket science to find the Gents, the route was well-signed, but many of them predictably enjoyed following a scantily-clad hostess rather than finding their own way.

After dinner people began to get really loosened-up, and it all started to get a bit out of hand to say the least. I'd learned, along with much else since I came out into the world, that men, even when they haven't had too much to drink, are frequently trying to chat-up women, both when the latter are fully-clothed and definitely in the outfit we were almost-wearing there; I'd seen enough of it at university, although the young men there had nothing like the confidence of this older and experienced lot.

Are you alright? This she directed to Dora, who suddenly looked so uneasy that Mags couldn't help being concerned, But the nurse nodded; Yes, I'm fine, as she put aside the unwelcome thought that maybe her Des was doing exactly that while she sat here, and concentrated on the story before her.

So I wasn't totally surprised when one very drunk man, Peter something from my table, confronted me in the corridor as I was on my way back from directing someone else to the men's room. He was the one who'd suggested I sit on his lap early on, and I'd avoided him as much as possible ever since. He was clearly still stalking me, but the hand full-on to my leg, and moving rapidly upward, together with his proposition, threw me into a panic just long enough for him to back me against the wall. His hands were everywhere, it was like being smothered by an octopus, but I just froze, I couldn't defend myself; and then a voice interposed.

She paused for a few moments, lost in her recollection of the moment, and her hands were busy with the 'H'; then she spoke again. Are you having a problem there, my dear? That voice; I'd heard it at the table, honey poured over caramel poured over gravel. Smooth and very appealing in a way I couldn't quite identify. She sat quietly for a moment then, thinking back again, and the smile that appeared on her face was like the sunshine; then she sighed and continued. I couldn't think of a cool and worldly answer, and a lame Yes, was all I could manage; but he'd already taken command of the situation. Peter, old boy, I think it's time you went home and slept it off, don't you? Your wife would probably prefer that. Peter, who'd frozen himself on first hearing the voice, backed-off muttering something which seemed to be agreement, albeit grudgingly-given. Then he departed hurriedly, warily edging around his opponent, who emitted a sense of lazy, understated power, which I found an added attraction to that given off by the voice.

I looked at him more closely, now that my Peter-shaped problem had gone, and remembered him from earlier. He'd never seemed to enter into the boozy revels that quickly got underway, but sat quietly, drinking slowly and listening to the speeches, speaking to those on either side of him whilst slowly examining the others at the table with a calm yet somehow interrogative gaze. It was only when I'd felt his eyes on me – further inspection now revealed them to be a deep, dark brown – and returned his look briefly that I realised I'd been under scrutiny, and thereafter became aware of his watching everyone else. Calm and controlled I think best describes him, but with a sense of something dangerous firmly leashed underneath; and yet despite this I was attracted to him.

I tried to salvage some dignity in his eyes and erase the impression of a scared rabbit-in-headlights which I felt I'd given; I told him that I'd had the situation under control, really, but thanked him anyway. His voice was amused; Of course, I do apologise, but I'm used to taking charge. He was laughing at me, but I couldn't think of anything to counter with; so I smiled and shrugged and put my hands up to let him see he'd won. He was gracious in victory; Would you like a drink? I suspect you could use one. I took his proffered arm to hold and we proceeded to the bar.

He ordered champagne without consulting me; taking charge, as he'd done in the corridor, and I didn't mind that. Not to mention the champagne, which I adored; such a change for a girl from a teetotal background, and I drank it far too fast as we assessed each other. I saw an older man, in his fifties I'd guess, well-groomed beard and hair, both dark and going grey around the edges; the former short, but the latter wavy and longer. It suggested distinguished style, with a hint of wildness. He must've been over six feet tall, with not a hint of spare flesh, yet not exactly slender; the double-breasted dinner jacket suggested a broad chest. I was interested and excited in a way I'd never experienced before, and I never even thought about whether or not I could get to like him, or even tolerate him, at worst, for the next eighteen months if he was the older, well-off man who'd fund my degree fees and living expenses. I was attracted to him as a woman to a man and all such considerations were secondary to that most basic instinct.

And what did he see? I was sure he'd assessed me already, at the table back in the hall, before I was aware of him, so whatever impression he'd formed came from there, now augmented by our encounter in the corridor. Before him was a young woman dressed in the regulation uniform of black; basque, laced up the front and back and pushing bosoms skywards, wide belt imitating a skirt, with elastic-and-lace-topped hold-up stockings. We'd been given the choice of these latter or garter belts and suspenders, and on Liz's advice I'd chosen these over the others, as she'd said those were much more suggestive and sure to get us into trouble; and I'd gotten into trouble enough just wearing these.

What was I thinking? Mags broke off then, with a laugh; naïve doesn't cover it, no wonder those men thought we were a bunch of tarts. Dora smiled in sympathy, and then wondered at herself as the girl took up her tale again. Anyway, this rather provocative ensemble was finished by black stiletto heels, as worn by all the other hostesses there. Not the classiest clothes, very cheap-looking, especially as every expense had apparently been spared in the manufacture. But as they'd obviously been decreed for all the girls my knight in shining armour must've realised that it wasn't necessarily my personal taste; I hoped so, anyway. My only possible distinguishing features were my deep blue eyes and long, impossibly-curly white-blonde hair, which fortunately stood out from the crowd of other blonde girls working the dinner. So, apart from the hair and eyes, it was all down to whatever he may've sensed below the surface.

I should've been engaging him in conversation, as instructed in the pep-talk earlier, but by the mutual consent of our eyes we seemed to have got past that point. He broke his gaze first and looked around the bar, which was descending into even more riotous behaviour all around. One of the girls was dancing on a table, I remember, with a ring of men trying to look up her skirt, which oughtn't to have been difficult but they were all very drunk and one fell as he bent over too far. Elsewhere couples were dancing on the floor, getting close, too close in some places, and one man had his face resoundingly slapped. Another man, falling-down drunk, staggered past me and did a double-take; Get your coat, you've pulled, isn't what they say round here? He roared at his own humour but his audience wasn't impressed. Yes, she has, but you're a couple of hundred of miles out in your vernacular; now do go away.

My hero sounded bored but looked daggers and the drunk held up his hands in that 'No offence intended' way and left as fast as his staggering and weaving condition would allow him to. My host (because, in an odd sort of reverse of situations, I'd become his guest by now) exhibited disapproval in his tone: There's supposed to be a party afterwards, but from the state of this place it's started already and I'm not sure it's quite me. I nodded agreement as he continued; I'm afraid it sounds a bit obvious, but what would you say to a quieter private party of our own?

Should I? I was aware from what I'd heard in the Ladies during my comfort breaks that propositions had been made and accepted between others during the evening, with financial considerations also offered and accepted, but I sensed that a request for this latter by me would change the nature of whatever attraction was there between us and what might develop from it. In any case, I'd forgotten about money by then, because I was strongly attracted to him, drawn to his aura of whatever it was he exuded, and as far as I was concerned I'd finished work for the night. I'd done what I'd been paid to do and this was my own time to spend as I wished. So I threw caution, and my nerves, to the winds; Yes please, I'd like that. And I went upstairs with him to his room.

She lay back in her chair then; I just need ten minutes, do you fancy a tea, or coffee? And would you mind making me one also, when Dora replied Yes, and there are some cakes, coconut macaroons, do get us some of those, please. Dora went to get the refreshments; it was well past ten o'clock by now, closer to eleven, and she wondered briefly what Des was doing before returning to Mags. The girl munched luxuriously on the cakes; I love coconut, my favourite comfort food. Teddy always used to give me coconut cake and hot chocolate when I needed comfort; when I got my period, times like that, you know? When she'd had enough, she wiped her mouth with a tissue and recommenced fiddling with the letter around her neck as she continued:

I wasn't exactly sure what to expect from Teddy; my pet name for him, because I subsequently found him to be named Edward du Cain, a businessman. I also wondered why I'd wanted a university education, because I got the foundation course of a different type of education that night, with Teddy as educator-in-chief. She stopped playing with her pendant here, clasping her hands in front of her as she spoke. It all nearly went horribly wrong, though, and I still squirm with embarrassment to think about it. I thought I knew about sex, you see, and I know it sounds incredible in this day and age of sex education and openness and technology, that a teenage girl could be so ignorant about sexual matters. But I hadn't been to a traditional school, and when I had my isolated sexual incident with the boy at the youth group I had little if any idea of what constituted sex. It began tentatively, some kissing, touching, teenage experimentation, you know, but it got a bit out-of-hand one evening and we went all the way. Or we thought we did, because the boy was a beginner too; I've told you this already? She looked at Dora, who nodded, and with her attention momentarily on the nurse, Mags remembered something.

Do you mind me talking about sex in detail? This to Dora, who inwardly thought Yes, I do, but outwardly was a nurse so shouldn't really have a problem with it; so, No, go ahead, she encouraged Mags, who did so with a measure of embarrassment strange in one who'd lived as she had. I believed that the boy touching what I later realised was his only partially operational organ against the outer lips of my own, with (sorry) a dribble of liquid, was the culmination of the sexual act. Her cheeks were bright red, and she took a moment to recover herself before continuing: If he knew otherwise he wasn't about to tell me and admit his own inadequacy.

Well, my instinctive sexual sense had been disappointed by this experience; Is that all it is? I'd thought and, deciding that it was, I consigned it to my file of things learned, mastered and there to be used in the future if necessary. Which is probably why I was so confident I could cope with exposure to potential harassment at this dinner. If that was the most I'd got to fear, what was the problem of flaunting my assets for immediate financial gain and the potential for dating men who might be of further help to me? I felt that I'd moved into the twenty-first century; it was my sexuality, and I could use it as I wished, inside or outside of marriage. How much I'd got to learn.

So when I found myself alone with the all-knowing and super-sexually-sophisticated Edward du Cain, it wasn't a level playing-field, so to speak. I just expected to lay there and hold him and kiss him and have him behave like the boy I'd known, which of course was a joke; their experience levels were polar opposites. I let him undress me, and didn't object to his leaving on my stockings; I repaid him the compliment, leaving on his underwear. Nor did I have any problem with the kissing and caressing that led us to the bed, in fact I couldn't get enough of it. But then he sat down on the side of the bed and took my hands, pulling me towards him and encouraging me to Kneel down, darling. I was wary, because this was unexpected, but I knelt anyway, and he gently pushed me backwards, so that I was sitting on my haunches and looking at his hip level.

Well, then he removed his briefs and exposed himself; large, and alarmingly-hardened, as I found when he took one of my hands and placed it there, and nothing like that of the boy I'd known. He put his other hand behind my head and pulled my face gently towards this part of him which was totally alien to me; the attraction I felt for him gave way to fear as I instinctively jerked away both my body and my hand from a scenario that was outside my woefully inadequate experience. I panicked and backed away from him, scrambling backwards until the wall behind me made any further retreat impossible. There I froze, exactly as I'd been when confronted with the drunken Peter in the corridor, but far more frightened.

He drew back, surprised at my reaction but still kind; What's the matter, my dear? I didn't know what to say, how to answer him; clearly I'd totally blown the cool and knowing image I'd wanted to project through not understanding what he wanted of me. I turned away and curled up on the floor in misery, any future I'd hoped for with him disappearing rapidly before my eyes. He put on the light; Do you want me to pay you? Because you ought to have said so before coming up here. The kindness had gone now, and I heard irritation, boredom even, in his voice, and saw a hint of ice in his eyes to match that in his voice as he continued; The first rule, if you want to go down that particular career path, is to get paid first. He reached for his shirt and began to put it on, clearly finished with me; I shook my head and tried to get the words out; I don't … I'm not … and I burst into floods of tears.

This display of honest innocence, rather than my air of false sophistication, must've convinced him, because his whole manner changed. He walked across the room, helped me up off of the floor and sat us both down on the bed, with his arm around me. He turned my face towards him, stroking it where the tears had streaked it, searching for something and, finding it, spoke to me in a gentle and much kinder tone of voice. Don't cry, Baby, I'm not cross with you; but I suspect you haven't done this much before, have you?

So I just let it all out and told him the exact limits of my previous experience. A few questions from him, to make sure he'd got it right, and he laughed softly, not at me but at the situation. My dear, you're still a virgin; how wonderful. I didn't think so; my inexperience had made me look foolish in his eyes and I said so; You must think me such a stupid, childish girl. And wasn't I just? she laughed at the memory, her hands on her pendant again, but No, no, of course not, he told me, and Don't cry, because I was welling up again. He held me close then, and he was kissing and caressing me gently.

She shivered at the memory; I remember it all, every detail. This makes it so much better for both of us, he told me, I'll have to take over your education, won't I? I'll be your first lover, I'll initiate you, make you a woman. Let's start again, shall we? Then he carefully helped me under the quilt; Keep the stockings on darling, you're freezing and they'll help warm you, I remember he said, then he put the light off, snuggled down with me and held me in his arms like a little child. Then he shushed and soothed and stroked me until I slept for a while. And when I woke he started over with me, from the very beginning, slowly and gently and patiently; so that, by the time I left him the next day, I'd shed my virginity and was in thrall to the sexual satisfaction he could give me. And I was also totally in love with him.

She stopped then, lost in contemplation of her memories, and Dora was silent also. She was shocked at the sexual confidences which had just been disclosed to her, and more besides. She didn't like the sound of Edward du Cain one little bit; a man in his fifties, playing around with a girl easily young enough to be his daughter; his granddaughter even, depending on where in his fifties he was exactly. And the girl didn't seem to mind, even thought she was in love with him, if she even knew what that meant. Dora had to restrain herself from snorting in disgust, as she would have done had she been at home, on her own time; but she wasn't. She had to remind herself that she was here to make the last days of this girl, her patient, as painless and dignified as possible; and if that meant she had to listen to these things, which clearly gave Mags some comfort to recall, well, it wasn't the worst thing in the world.

She roused herself and, to bring her patient out of her reverie, asked if she needed anything; food, drink, a trip to the bathroom? The latter was requested, and Dora waited outside the door just in case her assistance was needed; it wasn't, so she helped Mags back to her room, made her comfortable in her bed, and continued to listen as the girl started to speak again, her hands in action upon her pendant.

He was an awesome lover, my Teddy, completely in control, and physically not what the greying hair and suit suggested. Naked, there was no spare flesh, just well-exercised muscles in a wide-chested physique that many a much younger man would've envied. He was strong, too; as my education at his hands progressed, and we moved into the realms of somewhat less-gentle love-making, I realised just how restrained and self-controlled he'd been with me initially and was grateful for that. I could've been put off for life, if he'd just used me selfishly to satisfy his own desires, but thanks to him I was developing an appetite for and enjoyment of the sensual pleasures he introduced me to. He was happy to feed this appetite too, as well as to take over the more prosaic task of feeding me with food and drink and my more formal, academic education for the next couple of years.

On the Sunday morning after the Saturday night, as we lay exploring each other in the daylight, he asked me, So, my darling, how did an innocent little baby like you find your way into this den of iniquity? And as I'd finally done on the previous evening, I was totally honest with him, which seemed to be the thing that worked best. I was a student, I told him, with no parental support any more, working and earning some money but still getting into debt and behind with my studies, and I'd come to work at the dinner for the money but also in the hope of perhaps finding a sponsor for the rest of my degree course. And you found him, was his brief and straightforward reply. No condemnation of my course of action, just those simple words which, if I hadn't already fallen as deeply in love with him as it was possible to be, would probably have clinched the matter.

Around mid-morning he had to leave, Things to do, my baby; but he made sure that I had a hot shower and a good breakfast, during which he made some calls and had my own clothing reclaimed from wherever the organisers of the dinner had stored it and brought to his room. He then delivered me back to my digs; in his chauffeur-driven car, of course, which impressed me no end. I've a lot on for the next couple of days, but dinner on Tuesday? Shine here will collect you, at four-thirty, shall we say? And I'll get my solicitor onto the contract. Then he was gone, and I spent the rest of the afternoon in daydreaming about him, about what'd happened and what was still to come.

I got through the next couple of days in a blur. I attended my lectures and seminars on Monday and Tuesday, but I wasn't really there, as Laura had occasion to tell me in no uncertain terms on Tuesday morning. By the evening I was in a fever of excitement, worried that even my best clothes would look shabby compared to my well-groomed date; was that the correct word to describe him? My lover, I decided, remembering that he'd used the word, with a little thrill at the idea; I have a lover and he's everything to me. I couldn't believe how my life'd changed in just a few short days.

I was watching at the window and out the door so fast when the Bentley (as I subsequently discovered his car to be) arrived outside and Shine got out; he was going to open the back door for me, but I indicated the front passenger door and he didn't quibble. I felt it'd look better if any of my housemates were watching, although I hoped they weren't, because it'd look very odd for them to see me get in the back. This way I could pretend that Shine was my boyfriend if they asked questions, and they'd be sure to. I'd had difficulties with seeing Liz after the dinner and getting away with telling her as little as possible, because of course she wanted to know how I'd fared. I'd ignored her texts on Sunday, but couldn't avoid her for ever so had to meet with her on Monday. She'd struck out on any deal over and above the wage for the evening, she said; Just a couple of scabby one-night offers from total sleaze-buckets, can you believe it? One of them had the grace to ask for my phone number, but I suspect I won't be hearing from him any time soon. And that's the last time I'll work it, too, this time next year I'll be out in the big world of work. Oh well, nothing ventured, nothing gained.

She was philosophical, but intrigued as to my

fortunes, which I concealed from her as much as I could. I didn't want to share this thing that'd happened to me, which I somehow felt would tarnish it; I just wanted to hug it to myself for as long as possible. So I made up a story for Liz of having a few drinks with some guy afterwards and giving him my phone number, for future reference, before taking a taxi back to my digs. I'm not sure she was convinced, but I didn't really care. I did let her have the taxi fare we'd saved on the way to the dinner, so as least she made a little extra on the engagement; but this probably deepened her suspicions, given that I was in it for the money too.

But now my chauffeur-driven journey, albeit in the front rather than the back of the car, delivered me to Teddy's home, which turned out to be the penthouse of a very swish apartment block on the South Bank, overlooking the river; I felt absolutely like the little goose girl who gets the prince. Teddy nodded as he looked at my best outfit of black leggings and long black boots, teamed with a purple wool tunic and my blonde hair left loose. Very nice, darling, but maybe not quite the thing for where we're going tonight. I've had Harvey's bring over a few things, maybe you could choose something?

Indicating a doorway, he led me through into a palatial room which turned out to be a dressing-room, where there was indeed a selection of extremely good-quality clothes, far above and beyond those I was wearing, awaiting my choice. I hope there's something you like, I picked what I thought from what they initially bought, in a couple of sizes which I thought might come close to yours; but I'm not the best at dressing women, he told me with a strange sort of modesty. But you're very good at undressing them, I countered, and I was all over him like a puppy, which he enjoyed very much. Something I liked! Was he joking? I liked it all, loved it all, and like a child in a sweetshop I didn't know what to try first.

Teddy was very good, suggesting what he thought

might be best, and I was happy to be guided by him into a simple but tasteful little royal-blue velvet frock (Goes so well with your hair, Baby), with matching high-heeled shoes (They show off your stunning legs, darling) and gold and pearl ear-studs and necklace; real gold and pearls, I'd no doubt by now. Keep the rest too, if you like it, darling, or the bits that fit, or whatever, I'm sure it will come in handy. And we'll have to get you some good lingerie as well, Baby, although it will be strictly for when we go out; nothing of the kind allowed when we're home together. I was overwhelmed by his easy generosity and overflowing with gratitude and love.

I don't know how long it took to drive to the restaurant because I was once more in a daze; I feared midnight coming and my turning back into a run-of-the-mill student and having to run away leaving one royal-blue velvet slipper in the car. The restaurant was everything I might by now have expected it to be, given the tastes of this man, my lover, to which I'd been exposed so far. The food, chosen by Teddy for us both, naturally, was pate de foie gras and fillet steak, with an excellent red wine; he was educating my palate as well as my sexual appetite. I wasn't sure I could eat much, over-awed as I was, but he encouraged me; Eat up, darling, you must be hungry and I want to see your appetite for food and wine, to see if it measures up to your other appetite. So I blushed, and he laughed, and after dinner we went back to his apartment and to bed, where he made slow, gentle love to me before we slept.

In the morning I awoke early, and just lay there, looking at Teddy sleeping by my side, and the room, and listening to the faint sound of the world waking up far below us. Then I dozed again, and woke again, and then Teddy was awake also. Well, darling, we'd better get moving to get you back to your studies; and me, shy suddenly and thrown by his brisk manner. Don't you …? I couldn't get the words out. What, darling? Don't you want me again before I go? That laugh, so smooth and exciting; Of course I do, Baby, but the weekend must have been a lot for you to take in, and I didn't want to rush you … So I smiled lazily myself, and rubbed my body up against him and stroked that part of him which I was so frightened by on Saturday, and he laughed again and it was quite a while before I was ready to get up and go back to my studies. Or before he'd let me. But it's alright I told him, I don't have any lectures or seminars on Wednesdays; which information he stored for future reference.

Before I was delivered back to my digs we arranged that I'd go to him for the weekend, Shine being sent to collect me on Friday evening; which would become a regular pattern for our future together. Teddy, having spoken to his solicitor on Monday, had arranged for one of the partners to come over on Saturday afternoon to go through the draft contract with us and finalize the details (To keep everything clear, above-board and legal, darling). When he told me I expressed amusement, because I was beginning to get the idea of how things worked in Teddy's world; I didn't know that solicitors made house calls, the associates, never mind the partners, or that they worked weekends. And he said exactly what I'd thought he'd say; My solicitor works when and where I want him to, Baby. So I said, to tease him, You ought to make sure that the contract stipulates 'exclusive' mistress; aren't you worried about all those boys on campus? He wasn't phased in the slightest; I never even considered it, my dear, should I be concerned? No, I laughed and put my arms round his neck, What do I want with a bunch of schoolboys? I've got the Headmaster.

And sure enough, on Saturday at two in the afternoon, Mr Nicholas Michaels of Michaels, Owen and Baldwin, legal representatives to Edward du Cain, arrived complete with draft contract. I was rather shy, when it came to the point; it was one thing to find Teddy, and have him agree to my plan, but to have a professional third party involved in going over and legalising the details of such a very personal and intimate arrangement raised feelings of shame in me that I was hoping I'd been cured of. Teddy knew what was going on in my head, and teased me about it later. You'll have to learn not to care what people think of you, Baby, it isn't important. Nicholas is paid for his legal skill, not his opinion, unless I ask for it.

Nevertheless, at the time he left me alone with Nicholas (as I was invited to call him) for a while to help me feel comfortable with him. He was very discreet; I draw up pre-nuptial agreements all the time, Ms Manville (my original name; I made up Mystry later), and so many people do without the actual nuptials these days. This is just another contract of the same kind; I have one myself. With wife or mistress? I wondered, but kept that to myself. Anyway, working out the details wasn't too difficult, because he obviously had great experience of the kind of things that could become an issue and raised these for discussion.

When it seemed we'd worked it out, Nicholas promised to have the finalised contract put together and ready for our signatures by Wednesday. Teddy had me collected by Shine, we read the copy which Nicholas had e-mailed to Teddy to be sure we were happy with it, and one of his practice associates, a notary public, accompanied by his PA, came round with paper copies and witnessed our signatures. So by mid-afternoon on Wednesday, less than two weeks after I'd met Teddy, I'd become his 'Contract Courtesan', providing my exclusive and unlimited services as his mistress in return for his undertaking the entire financial burden of living costs and study fees for the duration of my university studies; the contract to be renegotiable on completion of the same.

And that's how you become a kept woman, Dora; Mags rounded off the episode in an amused tone. Top level, top class in the profession, the crème de la crème of the trade; the negative side, of course, is that from there the only way is down. But of course I didn't think about that at the time; my life'd taken such a turn-around, I was in love with the most wonderful man in the world, I felt, and I'd have done anything for him. Which ultimately I did, but that's for another night; right now, I feel unusually tired.

She stretched her arms over her head, flexing her shoulders as if to work off stiffness, and lay down, helped by Dora into a comfortable position. She slept then, and Dora kept watch over her through the small hours. She looked like a child in her sleep, so innocent, a newborn baby even, given the lack of hair, and Dora felt curiously maternal towards her. She thought about the story of the girl's life so far and wondered where it was going, although clearly it'd gone wrong. Had du Cain a wife somewhere, even children, perhaps, that he was keeping quiet about? Then Dora thought about Des, about her own husband, and wondered what he was doing right now; was he still at home, in his own bed? She considered phoning to check, but rejected that as undignified, beneath her; and she hardened her heart against Mags and all women like her.

5: KEEPING II

When Dora arrived home the following morning, Des had gone to work. He'd aired the bedroom, made the bed and cleaned out the shower after he'd used it. He'd also left crockery and cutlery out for her to make breakfast, before she went to bed. All, in fact, as was usual when she worked nights, and she couldn't fault him. He was very considerate as men go, or people in general for that matter; she'd worked in enough messy and dirty houses to be able to turn a blind eye when necessary, and wipe her feet on the way out, as Des had joked once when she'd told him about this. He was so clean in his personal habits, and in general; would he really make a mess of his marriage for a temporary infatuation?

But men did, she reminded herself, and women like Mags were there as proof of this. Ashamed, Dora found herself checking the bed sheets for any tell-tale indications; make-up, perfume, perhaps? No; but what am I doing, she asked herself, am I suggesting that he'd bring some other woman here, to our bed? She went to the utility room; his shirt, socks and underwear were in the laundry basket; but no scent or lipstick or other signs were to be found there either. Disgusted at her own suspicions she showered, had a fast breakfast, went to bed and slept until mid-afternoon.

She couldn't be bothered to get up straight away; there were some chores to be done, but she didn't feel like doing them today, which was unusual for her. She got up, eventually, treated herself to hot chocolate and crumpets for tea, the kind of thing that Mags ate, she realised, as she sat enjoying them in her dressing gown in front of the television. Eventually she stirred herself and, when Des arrived home, promptly at his usual time, she was washed and dressed and ready to eat with him the dinner she'd prepared. He was pleased to see her, interested in what she'd been doing, affectionate; too affectionate, perhaps? Dora hated herself for these unworthy jealous thoughts, but couldn't stop them. She was glad when it was time to leave behind her domestic issues and go to work, where she could focus on her patient's needs; if only she could forget her patient's previous profession.

The door was opened for her by Celia, her least-favourite member of the household; but the woman was polite, pleasant even, as she informed Dora that she'd got the kettle on, and would she be making a cup for the nurse also? Yes, please; and Dora went about making Mags comfortable, before sitting herself down with the tea brought by Celia and tuning in to the latest instalment of the girl's story. There was a change tonight, however, for it became clear that Celia was staying with them, for a while at least. It's good for me, Mags explained, going over it all again, and it's what you're supposed to do at this time, isn't it? Before, you know... anyway, thanks for listening. But it's going to get a bit more personal, more explicit, and I don't want to embarrass you or make you feel uncomfortable; any more than I've done already, anyway. So Celia's going to sit with me for a while, because nothing can shock her, she's seen it all and she's heard already how I met Teddy; and she smiled at Celia, while the Irish woman squeezed her hand with an obvious affection that redeemed her somewhat in Dora's opinion. So, Mags continued, please do some work on your laptop if you want to, or even have a sleep; I know you're not supposed to, but if it's OK by me then it oughtn't to be a problem, and Celia can wake you if I need you.

Dora thought that was a good idea; some of what she'd heard already was bad enough, and she wasn't sure that she wanted to listen to the even-bluer memories of an ex-prostitute. So she thanked the girl, although she declined the offer of sleep; better to play by the rules, she thought; but she took out her laptop and started on some training reading, while Mags addressed her story to Celia.

In my excitement at the wonderful turn my life'd taken, she recommenced, I counted the hours each day and every week until the evenings on Tuesdays and Fridays, cutting lectures to prepare myself for the time ahead, and waiting shivering in anticipation for the moment when I arrived in Teddy's apartment and, more importantly, in his arms. Because having spent several nights under his tutelage, I'd become addicted to sex with him (although I preferred to call it love-making, of course) and couldn't get enough of what he had to offer. He took full advantage of my enthusiasm; he told me, in a lazily amused way, You're a natural, darling, you love it, don't you? And I love giving it to you. And give it to me he did, in any number of positions and scenarios over the next few years; and I loved every one, or convinced myself that I did, even more so because he enjoyed them.

Dora, while trying to filter out the sound of the girl's voice, couldn't help herself from listening anyway, and felt the hot blood of embarrassment in her cheeks at this point. Thank goodness it doesn't show on black skin as much as it does on white, she thought. And she tried, but failed miserably, to concentrate on her work rather than the tale being told; to which the unshockable Celia, she noted, was smiling knowingly and squeezing one hand of the storyteller, while the girl's other, Dora noted, was as usual at play with her pendant.

Having gotten Teddy's foundation course under my belt, so to speak, my sexual degree studies under him became the most important thing in my life; I'm the Bachelor and the Master, darling, and you're the Master's Mistress, he'd joke. I was for throwing up the whole university thing; I'd won first prize in Teddy, why did I need a degree anyway, now I'd got a rich and apparently powerful man for my lover? Madness, considering I'd gone out to find someone to sponsor my studies; but love is a form of madness, I think. I remembered being shocked to find there were girls at uni just to find a husband, a university-educated professional who could support them, even in this day and age; and now I was one of them, it seemed.

Teddy, however, insisted that I complete my academic degree on the grounds that I learn the value of going all the way through whatever I'd taken on, adding, You never know, darling, it may be of use to you in the future; and I can't be with you all the time, I have my business to see to, and you need something to occupy you. So I kept up my studies, and my student accommodation, while Teddy attended to his business during the week, spending the weekends at his apartment, with some Tuesday evenings and Wednesdays thrown in, his business commitments allowing. He'd send Shine to collect me on Friday evenings, or Saturday mornings if he had business that over-ran from Friday, and he'd drive me back himself on Sunday evenings.

And of course, that was only during term-time; in the holidays I was available all the time, although of course Teddy still had to attend to business; but I could study while he did that. I didn't have to work in shops or bars any more, and my housemates and other fellow students gradually noticed. But I'd never become that close to any of them that I'd discussed my finances with them, so I managed to suggest to them in a vague way, without actually lying, that I'd got support from elsewhere now; and left it to them to conclude that my parents were probably providing for me.

On the one hand, oddly, I didn't really care what they thought; but on the other I didn't want them to know about Teddy. It was my life and my business and I didn't care to share it; and people, I'd noticed, could be so nosy, my housemates included. They did notice Shine collecting me on Fridays, and sometimes Tuesday evenings, and returning me on Wednesday afternoons, and assumed that he was my boyfriend, obviously with money because he drove a Bentley, which to them explained my not working, and I didn't disillusion them. He didn't wear any kind of uniform or hat, just a smart suit, and his appearance worked; early to mid-thirties, I judged him to be, and very good-looking with black hair and eyes and fine cheek bones. All of this made the deception easier, and my housemates fell for it. Where did you find him? some of the girls would ask, jealously, and they'd sometimes tease me because he never kissed me, just formally let me into or out of the car. What would they say if I told them I'm the contracted mistress of a rich man who pays my fees, I thought; mistress? Or whore? The negative word came to me unbidden, and I thought it better not to tell them.

When Teddy brought me back on Sundays I made him drop me further down the road and I'd walk the rest of the way. He was amused, as ever, at my inability to not care what others thought, but he realised I had to live with these people and feel comfortable with them for somewhat longer, so he complied with my wishes in this. But he insisted on waiting and having me call him when I got to the front door so he'd know I'd arrived back safely before he left. My housemates didn't ask about this; I think they'd realised I preferred to keep my private life exactly that, and stopped questioning me; we shared a house, but I was withdrawing from their company and isolating myself, the better to be available for Teddy whenever he wanted me.

The interior of his penthouse apartment was so different from the worn-out décor of my digs; very modern, light and airy, chrome and glass with big squashy sofas and soft carpeting in tasteful neutral tones. He always had the heating up very high (except when the weather was hot in the summer), so high that it was easy to walk around wearing nothing, or next-to-nothing, which was the case most of the time when I was there. There was a huge terrace with a magnificent view over the city; A penthouse with no roof garden? I teased him at first. No, darling, even if the English weather was warmer, there are so many helicopters over London we'd have little by way of privacy. The terrace had awnings, though, and large potted plants, so it was possible to be as private as Teddy wanted out there. He had staff to clean and do his laundry and so forth, but I never saw them when I was there, and I was grateful for the privacy, being it seemed incurably sensitive about other people and their opinions of me.

Teddy usually had catered food sent in on Friday evenings, easy-to-eat things like cocktail sandwiches and pastries, filled with smoked salmon, crab, or lobster; things we could eat easily, washed down with bubbly or white wine, while lounging on a sofa or in bed. We'd get up late on Saturday, and go for brunch somewhere in town before going to a matinee, the theatre or opera, or to a gallery if there was a new exhibition and Teddy could get a private viewing arranged. Because he didn't just undertake my sexual education, but my cultural one also; theatre, opera, ballet, galleries, you name it, we went there. He enjoyed taking me and teaching me; he was a well-educated man of refined tastes. The first time there was a performance he thought would be good for me, he asked me to organise tickets for a suitable date, but I tried and it was sold out; so he made a call to someone, somewhere, and we got tickets just like that. I've since wondered if he was showing off his obvious clout for my benefit, because thereafter his PA made all the bookings for him, and presumably she had no problem; Mrs Markham calling for Mr Edward du Cain and there were no problems, tickets were always available.

Teddy liked to go to the residents' gym on the ground floor of the apartment building, and apparently went very early in the morning on most days of the week. But he hated to get up and leave me at the weekend, so he'd skip

Saturdays (You're a bad influence, darling, I'll get unfit and fat and then you'll leave me, he'd say), but get up and go at about nine o'clock on Sundays, leaving me in bed, like a lazy slut, he said, with amusement. Then we'd shower together when he returned and go for a walk by the river before a brunch, or lunch, and then go back to cuddle up and listen to music, or watch a film, before he gave me tea and cake and took me back to my digs.

She paused here, and Celia commented on how well she'd done for herself, finding Teddy, while Dora felt some relief that the subject-matter appeared to have changed course into a less-explicit track; but she was wrong, and had to concentrate very hard on her computer screen during what followed, as Mags didn't hold back.

It was a hedonistic lifestyle, she recounted, and I entered into it enthusiastically, especially my continuing sexual education at Teddy's hands. She looked off into space for a moment, then laughed. The first time we experimented with what some would call sadomasochism was very mild. Teddy loved my backside; It's beautiful, he'd say, like a big, juicy peach, it's gorgeous, I want to squeeze it and bite it, but I don't want to hurt you or mark you. So he'd nuzzle his cheeks down against it, kiss it and stroke it, squeeze it, anything that occurred to him. One night he couldn't help but slap one of my cheeks; not too hard, play-slapping, and I jumped and we both laughed, but he did it some more. Maybe I ought to beat you on the bottom sometimes, he mused; not hard, maybe I could get a little whip, just light silken strands, which would stroke you just a little. And I'd do it to punish you for being a bad girl; because you are a very bad girl. Very good in bed, hopefully, I countered, but you wouldn't want me to be a good girl in general, would you? True, Baby, what would I do with a good girl? Good Girls go to Heaven, I told him, repeating something I'd seen on a poster in a bar at uni, Bad Girls go Everywhere. Exactly the point, darling; I want you to be bad, but I don't want you going everywhere. So I think you need to be disciplined regularly for being a wanton little slut who probably wants to take her big luscious arse everywhere.

And the next weekend he'd gotten a whip, which was more like a toy, actually; silk, or something similar, with very fine strands knotted to inflict nothing harder than a light stroking sensation. I wasn't sure about it, but he promised he wouldn't hurt me, and I trusted him because he'd always kept his word to me. So I lay face down on the bed and he gave me a few light strokes; so light I could barely feel them, and then he kissed where they had fallen, not that there were any marks. But the effect on him was profound; he took me more vigorously than he had previously, and I enjoyed it, tremendously, and wanted it like that again and again. And if the price for such enjoyment was to have Teddy whip me a little, then I liked that too; so my education continued, into the realms of kinkier sex.

By now, Dora felt that even her dark skin couldn't hide the deep flush of embarrassment which she'd felt creeping up from somewhere below her neck and which she now felt hot all over her face. She managed to get out something about needing the bathroom, and took herself there. She splashed cold water all over her face several times as she tried to come to terms with what she'd been hearing. Did people really do such things? Apparently so; or should she say, Did men do such things? Because it seemed to be du Cain in this scenario who had the perverted desires, Mags going along with them because she'd do anything for him; although she appeared to have enjoyed the whole thing immensely, Dora recollected.

If du Cain had had a wife somewhere, she wondered, would he have asked her to do these things? Maybe, and maybe not, but if the former then it was entirely possible that she'd said No; Dora certainly would have, if

Des had asked such things of her. So du Cain had found Mags to do them with him, and maybe that was the point of women like her. Which begged the question, had Des found another woman to do such things with him? Absolutely not, Dora's sensible side told her; but how could she be sure? Look at all those men at the dinner where Mags had met du Cain; respectable men of business by day, moving into a kind of old boys' club to prey on young and attractive women by night; presumably while their older wives sat at home, alone; or at any rate, with their respectability for cold company. Like mine, she reflected, unhappily.

·   Dora had to remind herself then that she was supposed to be working, and dutifully took herself back into the bedroom; where Celia, yawning and pleading tiredness by now, gave Mags an affectionate hug, said Goodnight, and took herself off, leaving nurse and patient along together. Was Dora alright? Mags wanted to know, adding a request for the nurse to be honest; I know it's all a bit X-rated, but I've got to look back at it, and some parts at least are good memories. Dora, instead of lying politely as she would have done usually, took up the offer for her to be honest. How could you do those things? So … she wanted to say, 'perverted', but changed it to 'kinky', that Mags had used herself and which sounded more fun, somehow. The girl took it in this way, shrugging and smiling; Because I loved him, she said simply, and I enjoyed them, when he did them with me. It'd sound too ingenuous to say that nothing's off limits, in love, but Teddy and I had established limits in our contract; things I didn't like the sound of, and things he didn't like too, for that matter. But the fact is, there were things he'd never ask of me, and I trusted him, and he kept his word on those. Her face darkened here; I didn't realise, though, there were things we hadn't broached that he might, and did, ask of me later.

She thought for a moment; No point in going there now though, and she changed the subject, with a corresponding lift in her tone, and mood. It wasn't just all sex, you know; Teddy could be terribly romantic too. He knew my date of birth, because it was on our contract, for some legal reason; although I didn't know he'd gone looking for it. So when my birthday came around a few months after we'd begun, I didn't think about it much; birthdays were never made much of when I was a child, and I'd told Teddy this in some matter-of-fact conversation we'd had a while before. But now, when he asked me to go over one Tuesday evening, and the following day happened to be my birthday, he pulled out all the stops in surprising me.

He didn't let on when I arrived, just told me to put on something special because we were going out for dinner. So when I went to dress, I found a zipped-up cover on the front of the wardrobe, with a large label saying Something Special for Someone Special; it contained a beautiful gold-fabric sheath dress, floor length, fitted all the way down, with a fish-tail train arrangement. It felt just like an extra skin, and I felt like a mermaid. No undies, darling, it fits too well for any VPL, he told me; and he sat and watched me undress (Not too fast, Baby) and then slip the gold sheath over my body, nude except for a generous spritz from the expensive bottle of perfume he indicated on the dressing table. Isn't it a little too tight? I worried, but No, Baby, no-one who matters except me is going to see you, and I love the way you look in it. I put on the matching gold shoes I could see on the floor, and then Teddy presented me with a red velvet box, containing necklace, bracelet and earrings, gold with little pearls making patterns on them.

What's the occasion? I was startled at so much luxury, even from Teddy. Can't I make a fuss of my Baby sometimes? As if he didn't constantly spoil me. I left my hair loose and flowing, the way he liked it, and we went down to the car; I swear that Shine's face registered something – admiration? - before his usual impassiveness descended. When we pulled up at the quay of the redeveloped docks I realised we were going on the water, but when the boat turned out to be a private charter just for us I couldn't believe it. How much more could my Teddy surprise me? A string quartet, that's how much; which played for us, their own repertoire and our requests, as we had dinner, cruising along the river with the city lights around us. The food and drink were delicious, but I really can't remember quite what we ate; I was in a daze, an overload of happiness. Could it get any better?

It did. I don't remember the car journey back, but I'd had a lot to drink; champagne, naturally. And when we did get back, it was just after midnight; and there waiting for me was a big birthday card, flowers, chocolates and Happy Birthday, Baby. I felt like Cinderella, and told him so; I was in his arms, and he was kissing me, and I him, and then he scooped me up and carried me into the bedroom. He peeled the gold sheath off me with ease, like a snake shedding a skin, and switched on the multi-room audio system. We were surrounded by music, romantic, emotional and beautiful; classical guitar, with orchestra, it was. Arms around each other, we just listened and, when it died away at the end, I had tears in my eyes; and when I turned to Teddy, I swear that he did too. It was probably the most beautiful piece of music I've ever heard, and my voice was shaking when I told him so because I'd got a lump in my throat. I was overwhelmed with the whole experience, and Teddy clicked the repeat button on the control and the music swelled out again. He put his lips on mine and there followed the best part of the night. I later wrote down the full title of the music; I would remember it as part of what I swear was, up until that time, the most beautiful evening ending in the most beautiful moment in our life together.

She sighed then, and returned to the present reality; I'm getting a bit stiff, lying here, and I think I need to go to the bathroom, which should sort the cramp; could you, please? Dora could, and afterwards made hot chocolate for

Mags and tea for herself. The girl looked rather pale and drawn, but the hot drink bought a bit of colour to her cheeks; I just wish I could sleep, though, she exclaimed in some frustration, but I still feel wide awake, although not up to telling much more of my story.

You've heard so much about my life, Dora, she said then, and I know absolutely nothing about yours; tell me about yourself; are you married, do you have children? Tell me something about you, if you wouldn't mind, that is. Dora didn't, so she told her patient about her parents having come over from Jamaica, her nursing training, how she met Des, with his shocking dancing and his comment about white Baptists not dancing but black ones absolutely having to. About their marriage, the births of Matthew and Ruth, the hard work to bring them up well which had culminated successfully in the professional status of both. Not a lot to tell, really, she ended, rather ordinary and boring, nothing outstanding to make the News, but pretty good for ordinary people like us.

It sounded rather good to me, and not at all boring, Mags countered, rather wistfully; I mean, I loved Teddy so much, and I don't regret at all meeting him and living with him. But I would've liked our life to be a bit more boring, somehow, in the way you describe boring as being; without the bad bits, of course. Well, countered Dora, everyone has bad bits; and she thought then of her own, the bits she hadn't told Mags about, her current worries over Des and what he might be getting up to when she wasn't there. Not like my bad bits they don't, Mags countered in her turn, and many of them have a happier ending than this. And I'd have liked to have children, she added, like you did; could you bear to listen to some more? She appeared to have regained some energy now, and spoke quietly. I'd put on the radio, or TV, but I don't want to wake the others, they all have work to do in the morning; at least I can keep my voice low. And Dora having agreed to listen, she recommenced.

If ever Teddy had been going to give me a child, and we could've been like any normal family, I swear it would've been on the birthday night I've just told you about. But it didn't happen. After the first night I spent with him, he'd asked me, As you were so innocent, my Baby, I guess you haven't taken any measures to prevent unwanted consequences? I looked at him blankly. Birth control, darling; I don't need any babies at my time of life, except you, of course. I replied that I hadn't, and felt very silly again; another blow to the cool and know-it-all image I'd wanted to project.

He was very good about it; Never mind, Baby, nothing to do about it now but wait and see, we can deal with it if and when it happens. In the meantime, as you could already be enceinte, no need to do the birth control thing just yet, and you'd look even more angelic with a baby in your arms. He laughed then; All very romantic, I suppose, but giving birth to it would hurt you, and babies can grow into brats, however much you do for them. So, on a balance of the reality outlasting the romantic, I think we're best off without. And on those grounds babies were ruled out as a deal-breaker (or at least a factor for re-negotiation) when we made our contract.

So, when my monthly came, a few weeks into our relationship (on a Monday, thankfully, so our next weekend together wasn't spoiled), Teddy had me see a doctor who set me up with the appropriate pills. I'm ashamed to say I wasn't honest with him about that though; I just pretended to take them, and flushed them down the toilet later. It wasn't that I particularly wanted children; my parents' overwhelming wish to get me married off and breeding as fast as possible had put me off the idea initially. But I allowed that someday I might want them, and I loved Teddy so much that I couldn't imagine wanting any other man, never mind children by him; so it seemed right to take the opportunity while it was there. I felt he loved me too, even if he never said so; he looked after me so well, he gave me so much. Just what he'd done for my birthday was overwhelming, and a man'd have to be dotty about a woman to treat her that way, wouldn't he? So I couldn't imagine that, in the event, even taking what he'd said into account, he'd turn me out alone into the world with our helpless child in my arms; most of the time he saw me as a helpless child myself. So I trusted that he wouldn't abandon me if it ever happened; but it didn't, and eventually I began to take the pill for real.

She stopped speaking abruptly, turned in the bed and knocked on the wall behind her several times with a show of strength which belied her condition. Dora, taken unaware, almost jumped out of her chair, then jumped again less than a minute later when Laura burst unannounced through the door, fastening a robe around her nightie and anxiously eyeing the dying woman on the bed, who spoke the minute her friend was in the room; Could I see Katie, please? Of course; and Laura was out of the room again. Dora, taken aback at the suddenness of it all, didn't think it at all right to drag the sleeping child from her bed; but it was none of her business, so she kept her mouth closed and tried to make her facial expression as neutral as possible when Laura re-appeared several minutes later, the little girl wrapped in a quilt in her arms. She was barely awake, and settled down easily when placed next to Mags in the double-bed, the former snuggling down next to the child, putting her arms around her; and both were asleep very soon afterwards.

Dora closed down her laptop, walked around the room quietly to stretch her legs, then sat back down and contemplated the now peacefully-sleeping pair. Didn't Vivie, who Dora took to be the little girl's mother, mind her child being disturbed and carried here in the middle of the night, just at the whim of Mags? Even if the latter was dying, it seemed rather hard on the child; but, Remember

64

your compassion, Dora, she told herself, it won't be much longer, and the child can sleep all she wants afterwards. Nevertheless, this really was the oddest set-up of a household she'd ever seen, and she'd seen a few in her time. She looked at the sleeping pair before her, and the unwelcome thought came to her that Des could at this moment be sleeping just as peacefully, in the arms of another woman, and there was nothing she could do about it. She felt the tears on her cheeks and brushed them away angrily, then re-opened her laptop and forced herself to concentrate on some training tasks, one eye on those and the other on the bed to make sure no harm came to the little girl. The Devil made work for idle hands, and she was determined to renounce him and all his works.

At around 6am, Celia came in, unbidden, bearing a cup of tea for Dora, who drank it gratefully; she was beginning to warm to the Irishwoman, having noticed that the place was kept spotless by Dora's own exacting standards. And, if Celia was somewhat unprepossessing with her rather coarse facial features and big, raw-boned body, at least she seemed to be good-hearted, generally-speaking. Why don't you get off early? she offered now; I can do what's needed for her, indicating the sleeping Mags, I've seen you do it often enough, and Vivie can do the meds.

For a moment Dora was seriously tempted; but no, even if Celia could do the washing and dressing part there was still the medication to be administered, and Dora would never delegate that to an untrained person or an unqualified student nurse, no matter how skilled the latter was. Vivie was very good, from what Dora had seen of her, but it would be unprofessional, not to mention dangerous, and Dora was a professional to her fingertips; so she thanked Celia kindly, but declined the invitation and stayed until the child, all warm and sleepy still, was carried out and Mags awake and ready for Dora to administer to her needs.

As she drove home, Dora allowed herself to think about her other reason for not wanting to go home early; what would she find there? Des, asleep alone, as he ought to be? Or not there and the bed not slept in, in which case where had he spent the night? Or, worst-case scenario, home but not alone? In the last two cases, action would be needed, action which Dora didn't want to have to take; she'd prefer not to know, therefore. She arrived home to the same scenario as on the previous day; but, worn out with worry, she ignored the shower and breakfast things laid out for her and merely threw off her clothes before taking to the neatly-made bed and sleeping like the dead.

6: DISSATISFACTION

Her arrival at Laura's house that evening found Mags watching an old film on the television which had been installed in the corner of the bedroom for her convenience. I just had to watch this, she told Dora, it was a favourite of mine in the old days; there's only half-an-hour to go, but I warn you, I'll cry buckets at the end. And she certainly did; *Gigi* it was, and Dora had seen it and understood how it could relate to her patient's own situation. It's because he does the right thing, Mags mumbled through a handful of tear-soaked tissues, she loves him and she's prepared to go to him without marriage because of that; but he loves her too, and he realises that nothing less than marriage will do.

She dissolved into her tissues again, so Dora went to get her hot chocolate, and a piece of the cake which was always there as the girl's comfort food; coconut and lime it was today, and Dora cut herself a small piece too, feeling that she deserved some comfort from her own worries. She met Laura in the kitchen and, having been told what Mags had been watching and her current condition, the lecturer hurried to the bedroom and enveloped her friend in a hug, shushing and soothing her until she calmed down and consumed what Dora brought her.

Of course, she said as Dora administered to her needs, it was good to see the film, but it's made me feel down; because I didn't get the happy ending that Gigi did, and why would I? That's just a fantasy, this is reality. Oh, I know, she continued, when Dora made as if to protest, my finding Teddy and my privileged lifestyle with him; it sounds like a fairytale, and I really thought I was in one, but reality didn't take too long to kick in. It started off innocently enough, she continued, well, maybe not innocent at all, actually, by many people's standards. But it seemed fun, and harmless, at the time, and if no-one's being hurt, where's the harm? Dora had no idea what was coming, and partly dreaded hearing it, but she said nothing and let the flow of words continue.

Mags hesitated, then; He shared me with his brother, you see; and Dora had to keep her face impassive, hiding her shock, but Mags knew it was there anyway. I know, it sounds terrible, but it didn't seem so at the time; it seemed very natural, in fact. I suppose if I hadn't been in a reckless mood it mightn't have happened, but I was, and it did, and I can't change it. It was a Friday, you see, and I'd not had the best of weeks; mostly, because I didn't get as good a mark as I wanted on an assignment. It was my own fault, too much thinking about Teddy and being with him, rather than concentrating on the essay in hand. I couldn't blame anyone else, rationally, but irrationally I decided to blame the tutor, which turned into my own personal black cloud covering the entire campus and my old enjoyment of it. But soon I was waiting for Shine to arrive and ferry me to Teddy's arms, and he couldn't get me there fast enough; except that I couldn't decide what to wear. It didn't really matter, it wouldn't stay on long enough anyway, but I liked Teddy to see that I appreciated the gorgeous garments he gave me. Not that I had many of them at my digs, they wouldn't have fitted in with the student side of my life and I didn't need over-inquisitive housemates; so they were mostly kept at Teddy's place, but I kept a few things so I could show up there looking halfway decent.

So I was in my room, trying on every good item in my wardrobe, dressed in nothing apart from lace-topped hold-up stockings (which reminded us both of our first night) and high-heeled shoes, and no lingerie because it was strictly forbidden unless Teddy had a specific reason for me to wear it. I was getting cold, because the heating was on a timer and at that moment was very decidedly switched off;

so I threw on a coat, simple yet chic in Teddy's usual taste, which came to hand. And then I thought, why not just go like this, just in the coat and stockings and shoes? It's not possible to tell I'm wearing nothing else, the coat comes down to my knees, and all I have to do is walk out to the car, sit in it, and then walk across the car park to the apartment block door and, once inside, go up in the lift to Teddy's penthouse. He loves surprises, and this ought to surprise him as I've never done before.

Once in the car, the back rather than the front this time because my housemates were all out, I considered the greeting Teddy was going to get from me, because I hadn't any inhibitions with him, not physically, anyway. After the reserved parental behaviour of my childhood I adored our physical contact; I couldn't get enough of it and didn't hide the fact. I'd seen at university how other people played games in accordance with some kind of code, like the housemate who told me in the kitchen one day that she'd met a new guy and was really into him, but didn't want to seem too keen, so what should she do? You're asking the wrong person, I told her, and sent her to Liz, the all-knowing one. The legal contract I'd got with Teddy removed the need for those kind of games, I'd thought. Our relationship was based around sexual contact; he wanted this from me and I was only too happy to provide it because it was exactly what I wanted too, given that I'd fallen in love with him.

So we played sex games, aimed at our mutual enjoyment; and if I was shy on occasions it was a genuine shyness, and he enjoyed coaxing his little Baby out of it. But sometimes now I was beginning to pretend shyness, so he could enjoy coaxing me some more; I was realising the pleasure of occasionally playing the kind of games I'd thought unnecessary. My open and honest approach was becoming compromised, but at least tonight it was genuine; Teddy wasn't going to know what hit him when he opened the door to me.

As I mused on our meeting, I realised I'd involuntarily lifted and stretched my legs out before crossing them, to relieve the strain of sitting for so long; which meant I might've shown something of what was beneath my coat, which had fallen open, to the chauffeur. This wasn't Teddy's usual car, as I'd gathered from Shine as he held the door open for me; Different car tonight, Miss, the other's in for servicing. He rarely spoke to me, apart from wishing me a good day or evening or night, so this was the most he'd ever said to me. I looked at him sharply, because the tone of his voice seemed to me to change subtly with the last few words. Did that 'in for servicing' apply to me also? I was sensitive about what he might think of me and my relationship with Teddy, given that he was a part of it, in a functionary way, and to any implied criticism he might show of it. But his face wore its usual impassive expression, and stayed that way as he drove; this temporary car didn't have the electric privacy panel that the Bentley had, so I could see him whenever I looked in front of me.

Now my eyes went straight to his face in some alarm, but his were on the road. Had I noticed a swift movement though? Had he been looking down, to where my coat ended and my legs began, in the mirror? I couldn't tell; but then I thought, So what if he sees anything? Give him a thrill, make him need to go in for servicing himself, serve him right. I was still in the reckless mood and wanted to provoke some reaction in him. So I stretched and re-crossed my legs again and didn't look at his face until some minutes later, to find him still focussed on the road. His groin area was hidden by the door when he opened it for me to get out, and I didn't look at his face, just nodded and said Thank you in his general direction. So much for not playing games; but he didn't matter, I thought.

Teddy was certainly surprised when he opened the door, wearing only a silk dressing gown; all the better for my purposes. I was all over him, straight into his arms, mouth on his mouth and tongue inside it as I dragged him towards the bedroom, pushing off his robe and shedding my shoes on the way. I was surprised to find silk boxers under the robe, but got rid of them fast and showed my disapproval by freeing my mouth and tut-tutting momentarily. He wasn't slow to respond; when was he ever? And my coat came off equally fast, with his appreciation of what wasn't underneath it very quickly making itself felt. She giggled at the recollection; Fast and furious action ensued, then You are a constant source of surprise and delight, my darling, as he rolled over and gasped for air. I came up for air myself, and then, unexpectedly, Hello! from the doorway made me freeze momentarily, then look over and remember to cover myself, ludicrously, as it was far too late for my misplaced modesty.

A man in casual shirt and chinos stood, or rather lounged, with one hand on the door frame, a drink in the other and a grin on his face. The whole scenario was like *Four Weddings and a Funeral*, when Hugh Grant was trapped in a hotel room with the bridal couple, unaware of his presence, eagerly consummating their union; Did you see that film? Dora nodded; she wasn't sure whether to be shocked or amused, as Mags clearly was, at the remembrance. He looked a bit like Hugh Grant too, I thought, but then I realised he looked rather like Teddy too. I stared at him, and felt myself blush, but then started to giggle at the silly situation as Teddy sat up with amusement and put his arm around me; Mags, this is my younger brother, James; James, this is Magdalena, about whom I've told you.

Well, she went on, the grin on James's face widened, if that was possible, and his voice was full of laughter; Very glad to hear it, I thought Waitrose was using a new strategy for their deliveries. You know, Blonde Bombshell Delivered Direct to your Dick. Thought I was going to have to start using them instead of Sainsburys; they deliver via a big burly bloke with tattoos, it's not the same. I mean, he might be to some people's taste, but not mine. He mock-shivered to punctuate his words and I laughed; Hello James. If there'd been any ice to break it would've melted fast. Hello Magdalena; Good name, suits you. As long as you're not going to start singing 'I don't know how to love him'; you know, *Jesus Christ Superstar* and all that. I knew what he meant, I'd seen it, because the church organised an outing when it was in the West End, and my parents actually allowed me to go. No, I told him, still laughing, I'm unreformed and unrepentant as yet, and he was Very glad to hear that, too.

Teddy joined in then. Why don't you go and get us a bottle, James, and take a few minutes; and, Right-oh, off he went to the kitchen while I questioned Teddy. What's he doing here on a Friday evening? Why didn't you tell me when I arrived? Darling, he just came by to drop off some papers that wouldn't wait, and, incidentally, neither would you, which is why I couldn't tell you until after you'd ravished me. He was right and I couldn't argue. I thought I liked James though, he was funny, he'd made a potentially awkward situation easier, and I told Teddy as much. He considered, then looked at me with his head on one side; So … maybe then you wouldn't mind if … because it might be fun if … What, Teddy? He wasn't usually hesitant or lost for words. If he joined us. So now I was hesitant; You mean … like those pictures you showed me? Because he had a collection of antique pornographic pictures, Dora, and he'd shown me them to demonstrate the sexual possibilities available, including threesomes.

Dora didn't know what to say, but she didn't have to, because Mags was into her stride. I was suspicious; Is that what he's here for? Did you dream this up before I got here? No, Baby, on my honour, he did actually drop by with those documents; I mean, he called to say he had them, and

I wanted them immediately so told him to come, but he was just going to bring them and have a drink and then go. But as he obviously likes you, and you like him … he trailed off. I like a lot of people, Teddy; that doesn't mean I want to jump into bed with them five minutes after I meet them. Well, I didn't know and like that many people, actually, and I was in bed with Teddy not too much more than five minutes after I met him. But he was too courteous to remind me of this inconvenient fact just then; he liked the idea, and I liked James, and I loved Teddy and wanted to make him happy; so if James liked the idea too, then why not? I didn't stop to consider the possibility that I might be justifying my liking for James through the handy excuse that I was contracted to want whatever Teddy wanted.

I wasn't ready to capitulate just like that though, too easily. I wanted Teddy to persuade me a little more, so I did my shy and uncertain act, to which he responded as desired. Don't be upset, darling, please, taking me in his arms, I didn't want to upset you. But you're so beautiful, so sexual, so sensual, you were made for love-making, I knew it when I first saw you, and it's been such a privilege for me to introduce you to it. I love to make love to you, to see the pleasure you take and the pleasure I take from you. I would like to hold you and touch you and feel you while you're being made love to, and then make love to you myself and show you off and share you, I'm so proud of you. He was kissing me and stroking me, cupping my breasts, stroking them and squeezing the nipples gently. James adores you, I can tell, and I know he has nothing but respect for you; it would make me so happy to make you both happy. You would have twice the love-making and he would have the joy of giving one half of it to you. His voice was as smooth as his hand, stroking my breasts more urgently, and I felt my token resistance melting and my desire growing.

Dora felt the hot flush rising to her face again, but not just from the girl's recollections; she was remembering times with Des, when she was much younger, before they'd had the children, and the good feelings she'd experienced with him. She couldn't have stopped the storyteller now even if she'd wanted to, and Mags probably wouldn't have stopped anyway; she was back in that bedroom, carried away by her memories: Just then James reappeared in the doorway, bottle of bubbly in one hand and three glasses deftly held in the other. He sauntered to the dressing table and proceeded to open the bottle, as Teddy looked the question at me and I nodded slowly. James old man; Mags and I were wondering … if you would care to join us? James turned towards us, lifting his eyebrows and a glass of bubbly simultaneously; Very glad to hear it; of course I would.

He drained his glass, poured one for each of us and passed them to us to drink while he divested himself of his clothes and I examined him more closely. A few years younger than Teddy, I would've said, more slightly built and with finely-chiselled features, less grey of hair but equally distinguished in his own way. I smiled and welcomed his embrace, as he came to bed; he bent over and kissed me gently on the cheek, then looked into my eyes, and I dropped them, genuinely shy suddenly because Teddy was there and I was naked with another man and felt somehow guilty, which was mad of course because the situation was of his choosing.

It was the first time I'd been with a man who wasn't Teddy, and James didn't feel that much different, really; a similar face, slightly slimmer torso and darker hair, but when I closed my eyes there was no real difference to notice. I could feel Teddy watching me, touching me, kissing me, encouraging me and praising me, and I wanted to make him proud of me. I won't embarrass you with the details, Dora, you know how it works. Anyway, James spoke to me afterwards; I'm pleased to finally meet you, Ms Mystery, Teddy's told me all about you. And what has he told you? Oh, you know, the post-coital contract, shagging rights and bragging rights. I could feel myself blush; I was fine with Teddy, but still sensitive to what others thought about my relationship with him. Teddy pulled me over to him, lifted my chin and looked at me with amusement; What a little innocent you look, with that maiden blush on your cheek.

I felt the need to assert myself then; I'm not sure I like you talking about me to others. Why not? James cut in here; I would if it was me, which it should've been had my far-too-fast brother not got in first. I gave him a questioning look; Oh, you've seen me before, I was at the dinner. You showed me to my seat and I thought then, what a stunning girl, you really stood out from the crowd. Unluckily I wasn't on your table but the next one; I was going to try to make a play for you, but unfortunately for me, Teddy got there first.

I've wondered how things might have turned out, if James had got to me first, Mags wondered here; he was younger than Teddy, not as rich, but he'd plenty of money, and I'm sure I'd have accepted him if he'd offered to sponsor me. Yes, Dora, I know it was a very mercenary and immoral way of thinking, but I didn't think so at the time; I wasn't the only girl doing it, and it seemed quite natural. Anyway, she moved back to her story, things turned out as they did, and here I was with both brothers. I'll just say that it was quite a night, and I lost track of time; eventually we settled down under the covers, like a couple preparing to sleep. Except that there were three of us and I was in a man-sandwich; very cosy, really.

Dora could feel the hot blood of a continuing blush in her face; she didn't want this level of detail, but there seemed no way around it. She excused herself, she needed the bathroom, if Mags would be alright alone for a couple of minutes? She would, and when Dora returned she had mercifully reached a less-physically-intimate part of her story.

When I awoke in the morning, James was gone; there were no clothes over the chair, so it looked as if he'd left entirely. There was just Teddy, awake already and looking at me thoughtfully from where he was propped up on his elbow next to me. He leaned over and kissed me gently, smiled, then got down and gathered me in his arms, caressing my hair and skin and murmuring gentle affectionate nonsense. I snuggled down and enjoyed these attentions, which included no sexual advances or any reference to the previous night, including James, for which I was grateful. Between them they'd tactfully managed to spare any embarrassment I might've felt with the daylight recollection of the night before.

Eventually Teddy went to the kitchen, with explicit instructions to me not to move but to stay and relax; not difficult because I was weary from my night-time exertions. He returned shortly with breakfast, hot chocolate and warmed chocolate croissants; comfort food to make me feel comfortable, presumably. He urged me to drink the chocolate, and fed me bits of the pastry as if I was a child, his Baby in actuality. I needed no urging, I was wildly hungry anyway; I must've lost pounds with all the exercise, and we'd never got around to eating on the previous evening. But I was happy to go along with being babied and spoiled; I must've earned it.

Then, as the last piece of pastry was lifted, something shiny and sparkly was disclosed on the plate underneath; Teddy dangled it before me teasingly before he let me wrest it from him. Earrings, gold and diamonds, I swear; How gorgeous, really for me, you're not joking? I couldn't believe it. Of course not, Baby, you deserve them. I like to give you things, to see you happy. He made me sit still while he fixed them into my ears, then showed me the result in a hand mirror from the bedside table. They did look good, even with the heavy, sleepy eyes and mussed been-to-bed-and-then-some hair. I was happy, overwhelmed, and all over him with thanks which turned to hugs and kisses and, inevitably, to love-making, which he said would christen the earrings correctly; slow, gentle love-making, so different from the previous night.

We spent the rest of the day being lazy; Teddy showered himself, but ran a comforting hot bubble-bath for me. Then we curled up on the sofa in bathrobes and watched light nonsense on the TV, dozing lightly when the need took us. We went out in the evening, casually-dressed, just to the Greek on the riverside nearby, and had an early night, sleeping in each other's arms. When it was time for me to leave on Sunday afternoon, Teddy drove me back to my digs himself, as usual. He kissed and hugged me affectionately and said he'd call me and see me again mid-week. I gave him a huge hug and shook my head side to side, the better to jingle my new earrings by way of appreciation. Back in my room, I looked in the mirror; who looked back? Someone who'd experienced yet another first, someone wearing gold and diamond earrings. Did I feel bad about it? Not as bad as I might've; I was being thoroughly corrupted and loving it.

Teddy called mid-week as he'd promised and took me to dinner at another very swish establishment, red velvet seating and discrete lighting. Crab Bisque flamed with brandy, followed by Omelet Arnold Bennett, and a crisp white wine to accompany these. Then a rich coconut cake, my favourite as you know, with a chocolate sauce, and coffee, and liqueurs. But he didn't take me back to his apartment, and he'd said so when he arranged the evening; No bed tonight, Baby, we both have work to do tomorrow. True, but what Teddy wanted he usually got, so I assumed he was tactfully giving me recovery time from the weekend.

I missed spending the night with him, but on the other hand it meant I could really pig-out on the food and drink. I loved them just as much as sex, and Teddy had developed my appetite for them all, but the latter doesn't mix well with too much of the former, so I usually tried to eat lightly when with Teddy. But come the following weekend I was with him from Friday to Sunday and it was business as usual, just me and him and sexual pleasure, although he was undemanding in this; still light duties perhaps? Whatever, I appreciated what I supposed to be his consideration, but encouraged him by being more demanding myself; which he loved, and didn't fail to meet me in.

I've made myself hungry now, she announced then to Dora, with all that talk of food; would you mind very much making me some more hot chocolate, and cake? Some for you too, of course, and could you help me to the bathroom first? Of course Dora could, so they both visited the bathroom, and had another comfort break of hot drinks and cakes; then Mags fell into a light doze for a short while before waking to speak in a different vein.

The next time I spent with James, she stated, more serious of tone now, didn't end as well, I'm afraid; they say there's a positive and a negative side to everything, and that applies in this case. It was one Thursday evening, while I was immersed in study, when Teddy phoned to tell me, Sorry, Baby, I have to go to Amsterdam for the weekend, something's come up business-wise and I have to get it sorted immediately, so I'm on the first flight in the morning. I understood, I had to; business must come first, and if I was disappointed it wouldn't be the first time. I'll see you next weekend, Baby, so sorry to leave you alone on this one. But he offered a small compensation; How would you like to go and play with James on Saturday evening, or would you prefer to stay home and study? He was teasing, but I went along with it; I can study on Saturday during the daytime; do you want me to go to James? It would do you good to get out, darling, too much study could make a boring Baby, and he'd be happy to have you.

So I agreed to go; Shine would pick me up and then collect me to take me back to my digs at ten, Teddy said; and promptly at four I was in the car and on my way. I hadn't dressed up massively, I was sort of smart-casual, and wearing lingerie for a change; but I figured it'd all be coming off fast so there was no need to get too done-up. As several times before, I wondered what impassive Shine the chauffeur thought about it all. I tried to heed Teddy's oft-repeated maxim about not caring what unimportant people thought of me, but it was difficult to break the habit.

James greeted me warmly as I got out of the lift; the place had very efficient security, just like Teddy's block, but it was very polite of him to come and meet me there. I got a big hug and kisses on both cheeks, and then we were in the apartment and he was taking my coat; Kick off your shoes and make yourself at home, darling; but I'd already removed my shoes, being trained to Teddy's liking for order and cleanliness around the place. James ushered me into the kitchen, which I wasn't expecting; I've cooked, darling; I hope you like lasagne? I don't have your number so couldn't check with you. Well, I love it, fortunately, so I was given an aperitif of Prosecco (Not champagne, darling, if we're going Italian) and invited to go and have a look around and get comfortable while he put the food into the oven.

His apartment was a revelation in its absolute difference to Teddy's. It wasn't as big, although still pretty sizeable, and not a penthouse, although still quite high up in a smart South Bank apartment block. But inside, I suppose cosy would be the word to describe it; it felt like a home, rather than the smart and stylish designer interior that Teddy had decreed for his own apartment. Rugs, cushions, drapes and squashy sofas in warm-coloured patterns, as opposed to the neutral tones of Teddy's; his CD collection, which I looked through, James having suggested I put some music on, was also arranged haphazardly, everything just anywhere, unlike Teddy's neat, alphabetically-arranged discs. The whole place was somewhere to really settle down into, as we very quickly did.

James was rather shy with me, which was absurd considering the threesome we'd had with Teddy; but maybe this was more like a traditional date would be? I had no frame of reference by which to judge, apart from my lamentable teenage fiasco and my life in Teddy's world. But James had followed me out of the kitchen, having put the oven on, and we curled up on the sofa; although conversation was slightly awkward, and having got past how lovely it was for him to see me again, and for me to see him, and how had we both been, we arrived at a pregnant pause, so to speak. So I took it upon myself to lean over and kiss him and stroke his cheek, and then we were in familiar territory. When we'd done, we were a mess of undone buttons, breasts pushed out of bra, trousers around knees, like two teenagers on a date, as James said; but the ice was broken, and dinner was ready, so we laughed at ourselves as James suggested bathrobes and we lost our crumpled clothing in favour of these and went to eat in the kitchen.

He cooked well, lasagne washed down with a red wine which was decent, but nothing like the vintage stuff which was always in Teddy's glasses. There was salad, and garlic bread, then a dessert wine and Amaretti biscuits, which James suggested taking to bed with us. He put some music on, not classical as was usually the case with Teddy, but what James referred to as 'classic stuff' by someone named Janis Ian; a concept album, *Between the Lines*. We listened, and discussed the music while we drank our wine; and when a particular track came on, about a bar girl, with the lines 'And if he wants to hold you, If he wants to know you, Honey that's what you're here for', we got down to some more serious fooling around.

I call it this because, despite being only a few years younger than Teddy, James was more like a far younger man in many ways. So sex was interspersed with biscuits and wine, and more wine, which led to spills on the sheets (No problem, darling, they'll wash, he told me, so different to Teddy) and crumbs everywhere, including some interesting parts of our bodies, meaning lots of laughter as they were removed. But eventually we calmed down, and settled down, and James replaced Janis Ian with an album by Roy Orbison. *Mystery Girl*, with 'She's a Mystery to Me', which I'm sure was a reference to when he'd called me Miss Mystery, on our first meeting; and he didn't deny it, when I asked. So we snuggled down and relaxed, as the music played.

At some point, as Roy was singing 'In The Real World' and we were resting, cuddled up and cosy, James checked the time; Half past nine and, as he noted, time to get my sexy arse in the shower to be ready for Shine to collect me at ten. I thought of my shabby student digs, and how my housemates would all be out having fun at this time on a Saturday night. Why couldn't I stay? I wound my arms around him winningly but he wasn't playing. I'm flattered, darling, but if Teddy says you go at ten then go you must. He won't mind, I said, he wouldn't want me to be lonely. James didn't agree; You should know Teddy better, darling, what he wants he gets and we all do what he says.

I tried to prolong matters with various tricks and allurements, but James was having none of it; Artful little puss, but we're out of time and you'll have to shower back at your place, darling; and let's neither of us tell Teddy that you wanted to stay, OK? Bad idea, believe me. I thought he was making too much of the matter, but I let it go; as I had to. So after a big hug and kisses, I just had to throw on my clothes and go as I was, with essence of James all over me and been-to-bed hair. Shine kept his usual impassive face as he let me into the car, but he couldn't have missed my tangled hair and he was close enough to smell raw sex all over me. He must've had some thoughts on my tousled condition, so different to when he'd delivered me a few hours ago.

I soon forgot about Shine and his irrelevant opinions, however, when I was back in the reality of the messy shared bathroom at my digs. I should've showered, but the water wasn't hot and the rapidly-moulding grout around the shower tray, plus the damp marks on the walls, were more than usually off-putting. So I decided that the remnants of my cosy time with James all over my body were preferable, and took myself to bed as I was. I couldn't get straight off to sleep because I was musing over the differences between Teddy and James. The younger brother was certainly more boyish, more fun, and there was laughter in his eyes, which were light brown and the greatest difference he had to Teddy, whose eyes were dark, with a touch of ice in them when he wasn't happy.

I felt I was being disloyal to Teddy with this line of thinking. He did allow food and drink in the bedroom, although he hated for anything to get spilt; so I'd learned to be very careful. But he could be so much fun, and I did love him, but somehow he was always Daddy Teddy, there to cuddle up to. My parents weren't physical types, not demonstrative, and I'd always been discouraged when I instigated physical displays of affection. So Teddy filled that need, albeit as Daddy combined with lover; the two seemed to go together in what I sometimes thought was an unhealthy way. Cuddling, when we were alone anyway, always led to something more intimate; which, healthy or not, worked for us both so I tried not to think too deeply about it. I wished he was with me then, with his arms around me, keeping me warm and comfortable and safe. And on this thought I eventually drifted off to sleep.

On Sunday the bathroom didn't look quite so bad by daylight, so I managed to resign myself and re-adjust to being a student. I spent the day in study and the thought that Teddy would be pleased with me because I was feeling confident I could do well in my forthcoming final exams. He phoned me on Monday; I've just got back from Amsterdam, darling, can you come over tomorrow evening? I missed my Baby at the weekend. Of course I could, I'd been working hard and Teddy was being very good about not disturbing my studies as far as possible; I owed it to him to do as well as I was able. But my confidence about my ability to do well meant I could afford a little time off, and I justified this because it'd be spent in carrying out my contract duties to Teddy, I thought formally, and then laughed at the thought of what that meant in actuality.

So Tuesday evening found me transported to Teddy's apartment, and I was so glad to see him that it wasn't long before we were in bed and getting re-acquainted with each other. And as we rested afterwards, I asked Teddy if he'd like me to tell him a story; the erotic type, to get us back in the mood after having already indulged ourselves, but No, Baby, why don't I tell you one for a change? This was unusual, but I was curious to hear what he came up with, so I nodded and he began. There was once a young woman, a shameless slut, a common whore who plied her lascivious trade in a wanton and promiscuous manner. His tone was hard and he was looking at me, unsmiling; I began to feel uneasy as he continued. James du Cain, for example, confessed that she spent some hours on Saturday last at his apartment, where she performed with him countless acts of fornication in a shameless and brazen fashion, and offered to stay with him until the dawn to continue her lewdness. What has she to say in her defence?

I was hoping he'd smile, that he was making some kind of joke of my evening with James, but his gaze had hardened now, and I could see the ice in his eyes. He knew about my attempt to stay with James, against his wishes, and was challenging me to explain myself. I'd no defence, I'd been taken totally off-guard, but I tried to make light of it; It was only a suggestion, no big deal, I can't believe

83

James bothered you with something so unimportant. But Teddy wasn't going to let me off the hook; You've condemned yourself, Baby, so I'll have to punish you; turn onto your stomach. It felt like one of the games we'd played sometimes, and had it been I'd have been giggling by now; but he was deadly serious so I obeyed, frightened by the chill I could see in his eyes.

He whipped off the covers, exposing my naked bottom, then thrust a small, thin cane before my face; I'd never seen it before; a souvenir of Amsterdam? He used it to push my hair forward over my shoulders, baring my back and bottom, and then he struck. It stung; too hard; I winced and cried out, but he struck again, and again; five times in all, on the bottom, and I felt humiliated, with the indignity of it as well as the stinging pain. I didn't even try to escape, I knew better; What Teddy wants, Teddy gets, and we all do what he wants, went unbidden through my mind.

Then he was holding me, kissing my eyes and mouth, stroking me and talking me round as he well knew how to do. Don't be upset, Baby, you know I don't want to hurt you but I have to punish you if you misbehave. You belong to me, Baby, and if I say you go back to your digs you go. I was resentful, though; James oughtn't to have told, I repeated. But Teddy was ready for that; He didn't, Baby; I bluffed and you fell for it. I tried to take in this new method of manipulation, then tried to get round him as he usually got around me; It's so lonely in my room, and damp, it was just so much more comfy with James.

Teddy examined my face; You like sex too too much, Baby, but you're mine and if Daddy Teddy tells you to control yourself you pack your hot little pussy up and take it back to your chaste bed in your digs; understand? And the coldness was still in his eyes, so I capitulated. I'm sorry, I'll be a better-behaved girl in future, I promise; it wouldn't have happened if you'd been here. The ice in his eyes melted, and amusement took its place; he knew I was being sly and he couldn't resist it. So it's my fault? Yes; I wound my arms around him suggestively but I wasn't in the clear quite yet. I've trained you too well, Baby; most working girls would love a night off, but you wanted to just keep on going. He was stroking me now, in my intimate places, and I was responding as I always did. I've said it before, Baby, you're a natural and you can't help yourself, so I have to help you to help yourself. I've spared the rod and spoiled the child, so in future a few strokes of the cane on a regular basis won't go amiss by way of correction; although you'll probably learn to enjoy it. So now I'm correcting the mistakes in your homework and you'd better enjoy it. And I did, although the slight stinging from my buttocks reminded me, if I needed any reminder, that I stood (or rather, lay) corrected.

The following morning, Teddy gave me a present; something that at first sight seemed better than the new cane (a souvenir of Amsterdam indeed), but turned out to be something more sinister. A necklace, a gold chain to be exact, with a pendant gold letter 'H' dangling from it; and she pulled it out from under the neckline of her nightie and brandished it. And why 'H'? You've been wondering too, haven't you, Dora? The nurse nodded, not sure now that she wanted to know. It couldn't be for my name, the girl continued, I'm 'M' all the way. Teddy knew that; he'd have a reason, that I was sure of, so I looked at him questioningly. 'H' for Harlot, which is exactly you, my little slut; and every letter of that word works for you too. He was amused, but there was serious meaning behind his words. 'H' is for Harlot, Hooker, Whore, allowing for the silent W; 'A' is for Adulteress.

I would've stopped him there, but I hesitated because, although we weren't married, technically, our contract presumably counted as a formalized relationship. I tried it anyway; I haven't committed adultery, I've only done things you asked me to do, or suggested I do, with

James. But he wasn't having it; You tried to move outside the bounds I set, Baby, and disobeyed me. And if you remember your former religion, I believe there's something set down about just looking at someone and wanting them means you've already committed adultery in your heart; look it up, darling.

I gave in, and let him continue. 'R'; hmm, Receptive, to sexual advances, I suppose; 'L' for Loose, as in Women, like you, Baby.'O'; now 'O' is interesting, and you may have covered this at university. I believe, back around the Elizabethan age (I think Shakespeare and his contemporaries used it in their works), 'O' signified woman; her lack of a penis, the gap, the space, the round hole she has instead. Then 'T' is for Tart, Tramp, Trollope, whatever. He was looking at me intently and the chips of ice were back, like diamonds, in his eyes. I want you to wear this always, Baby; like Hester Prynne and her 'A'; I believe you've studied *The Scarlet Letter*?

I had, and recently; seventeenth-century American Puritan community punishes woman taken in adultery by making her wear a scarlet letter 'A', in case you don't know it, Dora, it's not that well-known. I'd studied it with Laura, you know, and I still remember her acid and uncensored comments on Hester's unknown lover; Some man in the community is the father of her child, she said, but he's keeping quiet and letting her take all the flak, the cowardly fuck. Sorry, Dora. Mags put a hand to her mouth and smiled ruefully, but then was serious again.

Teddy could be very sophisticated in his punishments; he took the chain and placed it around my neck, and I bowed my head so he could fasten it behind my neck. He pushed my hair aside and fastened the clasp, and I shivered as his fingers gently brushed my skin; then he turned me around, lifted my chin and inspected the 'H', which felt very cold and chilled my body as Teddy's eyes chilled my mind. The effect of the thing on him was prodigious, I could see; a label, a brand of ownership. He looked at me, and the ice in his eyes was melting and being replaced by something else I knew well and which was usually more welcome to me; desire, because of course we'd christen my new adornment, if it could be called that, in the usual way. But as Teddy caressed me with mounting passion, then laid me down and possessed me, I didn't enjoy it quite as much as I usually did. The act expressed the fact; I was his possession.

She looked bleak then, but her expression was broken by a large yawn and her tone when she spoke was matter-of-fact. That's probably a good place to stop for the night, and I do feel tired now; apparently even telling the bad stuff seems to be good for me; could you, please? So Dora plumped the quilt and pillows, then helped Mags into a comfortable position; she was very quickly asleep and breathing evenly. Left to her own thoughts, Dora didn't know what to think at first, apart from why Mags kept the 'H' pendant, given the cruel reason for its having been given to her, and why she appeared to be so attached to it.

But then she realised she was angry; this young woman had been failed by life, beginning with her parents. Not sending her to school struck the nurse as being like raising a wild animal in captivity, then sending it back to the wild with no preparation; not even that, because its wild instincts would surface at some point. This was more like sending a domestic pet to the wild; it'd be eaten alive by the predators out there, who'd learned their survival skills as they grew. And Mags had fallen into the hands of a singular predator, it appeared; privately, Dora thought that Mr Edward du Cain ought to be strung up by parts of his anatomy she'd rather not mention, even to herself, nurse though she was. She watched the girl sleeping, looking curiously innocent despite the ravages of the condition which was killing her, and marvelled at the softening of her own attitude towards her.

7: KEEPING III

Des had gone to work by the time Dora arrived home the next morning; if he had spent the night at home, she thought with dread. She remembered the things Mags had told her about, censored to some extent though they were out of consideration for the nurse; had Des been getting up to such activities, with some other woman? He'd never done such things with her, it was all strictly respectable with Dora; but maybe she ought to have been ready to experiment a little? She tried not to think about it, as she showered and ate breakfast, but then couldn't sleep so tried reading to focus her mind on something else. But the book she'd chosen, one which Ruth had given her for a Christmas present (It's a best-seller, Mum, everybody's reading it) turned out to be full of sex, pornographic romps amongst the horse-riding community. Ruth really ought to have known better, it was the last thing Dora needed. She threw it aside in frustration and took a sleeping tablet; something she rarely did, but she needed sleep and to be awake and alert for her shift tonight.

She awoke around five in the afternoon, with a heavy head, so staggered to the kitchen to make some tea to wake herself up. Of course she was late in getting dinner on, and of course Des came home before it was ready. He was good-humoured about it though; he'd never been one of those men who expected his meals on the table when he came home, he accepted that they both worked and always did his share, of cooking or housework or whatever needed to be done. So, as he observed that Dora was looking a bit peaky, he insisted that she sit while he finished preparations for their dinner; then he ate with her, did the washing up (Dora wouldn't have a dishwasher, she thought they didn't clean things as well as her own human hands could), and waved her off from the doorway as she backed the car down the drive. The better to see me off before he goes himself? she wondered, but cast the thought aside and concentrated on driving.

Tonight the door was opened by Vivie, the member of the household with whom Dora felt she had the most in common, nursing student as she was. Dora's enquiry as to how her studies were going received a positive response, but How's your little girl? received a blank look, then Oh, you mean Katie; yes she's fine. More mystery; was Katie not Vivie's child then? Dora was dying to ask, but reminded herself that it was none of her business and held her tongue; and when Vivie showed her into the bedroom, there was the little girl, being told a bedtime story once again.

Dora had thought previously that Katie spent time with Mags because she was a comfort to the dying woman; now, however, she considered the possibility that they might be mother and child. Apart from Vivie, Mags was the only other candidate for the mother, Laura being certainly too old and Celia, although just about qualifying, didn't appear to have a man in tow; not that it was an issue, in this day and age, but surely in that case Vivie would have said when Dora had asked that Katie was her little sister, wouldn't she? Dora hoped to find out without having to ask; but it really was the most curiously-constituted household.

After many cuddles and kisses, Vivie removed the little girl, Celia brought them both tea, and Mags recommenced her story. I was telling you about the bad stuff, wasn't I? Teddy wanting to be in control; and I'm afraid it got worse. Some weeks after the night with James, I left the campus on a Saturday evening; usually I'd go on Friday, for the entire weekend, but sometimes Teddy had business which took him away until Saturday afternoon, and this was one of those. Shine collected me, as per the usual arrangement, but also as usual didn't attempt to engage me in conversation. He always just got out, opened the door for me, gave me a respectful (I hoped) 'Good evening' which I'd return, and then ensued a silent drive, which I thought ought to feel awkward but didn't, not totally, anyway. I usually felt relaxed enough in his company, somehow, I suppose I'd gotten used to him, although I had no idea what he thought of me. Why should I care? But I did, which is why I'd teased him with my open-leg flash on the evening of the threesome, and the question of what he thought engaged my curiosity, albeit only occasionally.

As I'd hoped, my housemates thought he was my boyfriend, and I didn't mind that; it kept the boys from making any kind of advance to me and causing awkwardness between us when I rejected them. He was a lot younger than Teddy, and to my eyes good-looking in a dark and brooding sort of way. I sat next to him in the front passenger seat that evening, for the benefit of those housemates who were home, so Shine had to put up with me there, although I got the feeling he'd have preferred me to be in the back. I could feel disapproval coming off him in waves and it bothered me once more.

As soon as I entered the apartment on the penthouse level, which I'd gathered since the first time I went there was the only level tolerable to Teddy, I noticed a difference. The white envelope containing my next fee instalment wasn't on the console table in the lobby, as it invariably was when it became due. Teddy had wanted to make the whole payment in one go, but I'd insisted that, as there was an option to pay via instalments, why not take it and let the rest of the money make some interest in an account somewhere? He was amused at first, his Baby showing money-sense, but he did see my point; and as I still had notions about throwing it all in at some point it would've been a waste to pay all in one go.

He also liked to pay by the old-fashioned method of cheque, which I didn't understand but accepted as one of

Teddy's little idiosyncrasies. I never had to ask him for the money; I'd given him the schedule of payments, dates due and so forth, when he'd offered to take over, and this went to his super-efficient secretary, Imelda Markham, who made out the cheques to the university pay office at the appropriate times. She passed these to Teddy, who'd add a quantity of cash for my living expenses and leave them in an envelope for me to take whenever I wanted during the weekend. It was a tasteful and tactful arrangement, and so typical of him to make it work as smoothly as possible. But apparently there was a glitch this weekend; one I could do without, as this was the final instalment before my exams some months later, and hopefully graduation not too long after that.

I was just wondering about this when Teddy came out to meet me, and I noticed another difference; he was dressed formally, suit and tie and shoes. He gave me a kiss and a hug, as usual, then, There's a change tonight, darling, we're to have a guest, as he lead me through into the lounge. I hesitated; Did I miss something? Am I supposed to be here? He never had anyone else around for the weekends, except for when James had dropped by and become incorporated into the proceedings. No, darling, I want you here, I've missed half the weekend with you already.

He brought me my usual champagne from the waiting ice bucket, and sat me down on the sofa, taking the seat next to me as I waited for some explanation of the change to our normal routine. Usually it was early bed, taking our drinks with us, punctuated at some point by a pre-prepared meal of cold lobster, crab, smoked salmon sandwiches and suchlike, which had been sent in by caterers earlier. Now I noticed there were some light eats already on the coffee table, and I was hungry, which Teddy realised; Do eat up, darling, our guest will be here in about half-an-hour and I wouldn't want you to go without. As I did as he suggested, he continued, He's a very influential man, I need his help with some business affairs; so I invited him over for a social drink, and I need your help with him. He saw you at the embassy drinks party last month and wanted to meet you. The thing is, he paused and continued, I need you to be especially nice to him.

I remembered the party but not the man and, as when things had gone differently to our usual routine with James, I became suspicious. How nice is especially nice, Teddy? And then, partly to tease him, As nice as I was to your brother? Because I knew he didn't mean that, well, I hoped so anyway; but he was deadly serious. Good God no, Baby, nothing like that. The Judge wouldn't be into anything like that, and neither would I, except with James, obviously. No, he's much older, he has issues that maybe go with that; he just needs some help with those issues, and when he sees someone special who looks like they might be able to help … He stopped there and looked me directly in the eye. I was becoming alarmed now; How much older, Teddy? And how can I help him? I don't know exactly his age, darling, about seventy-five, maybe, or a few years more? And his issues …

He went into coaxing mode then, get-round me mode, and it was usually for play, something to get us both excited and ready for love-making, but this wasn't the same. His voice was caressing me, as were his hands, and he was kissing me gently, and I was aware that I was being got around and I was weakening … Did you put something in my wine? The thought hit me suddenly. Of course not, darling, look; and he leaned over lazily and drained my glass. I'd never do something like that to you, you ought to know that by now. He was obviously offended, and I was sorry that I'd suspected him; I said so, and he hugged me. If you don't want to do this then that's OK, but if you do it has to be of your own free will; and it would make me so happy. So I took the route of least resistance and agreed, albeit with some trepidation; what Teddy wants, Teddy gets.

He led me into the bedroom, Do put on something more comfortable, darling; not undressed, but something less formal. So I put on the soft cashmere dress which he chose for me, with black lace undies (unusual, but Teddy's wish, which is what I was here for, after all), lace-topped stockings and soft velvet pumps. He gave me information on what would be especially-pleasing to the Judge, and I asked him, How do you know all this? He's been with women before, darling, and they've kissed and told, so to speak. Women supplied by you? I wondered, but whether or not, they've obviously spoken to you. But I didn't say this, I said, I'm frightened, Teddy, and he squeezed me again. Don't be, my Baby, it will be alright, I promise; I'll look after you, don't I always? Trust me.

Then he went to a drawer and brought out a little silver box, real silver, this being Teddy, of course; I think a little of this will help you. And I knew what the powder was when he opened it, and why he took a banknote out of his pocket. I'd heard of such things at uni, and I'd never wanted to go down that route, but now I was frightened of what Teddy wanted me to do and I'd do anything that might make it less unpleasant than I feared it'd be. He gave me another powder first (Harmless, darling, talcum powder, for practice), so I practised, and I spilt some of it, I was shaking so, and when I managed to snort it I sneezed a few times, but I got the hang of it eventually; and then I took the real thing and waited. And soon the good feelings came, and I felt calm and confident and positive and ready to do what I'd got to.

When the Judge arrived I was welcoming, and smiling, and so happy to make sure he was comfortable, and to make conversation with him; which in fact mostly meant listening to him and saying something admiring every now and then. And when Teddy took a phone call and announced, Apologies, but I have to sort this out now, and went to his den, saying that Magdalena will make sure you have everything you need, I wasn't frightened but surprisingly in control. So when the Judge spilt his drink down my frock, which was because I'd jogged his hand accidentally-on-purpose, I acted like I was upset and said I needed to try to clean it, and he'd have to help me.

I took him into the spare bedroom, with its ambient lighting and non-obvious security cameras, and took off the frock for cleaning with the facial wipes on the dressing table. But the stain wouldn't come out and I got angry with him – more angry than I'd planned to be – because it was his fault, and I said I'd have to punish him. He, meanwhile, had sat down on the edge of the bed and was looking at me, in my silk-and-lace lingerie, with garter belt, stockings and suspenders. He was breathing heavily now, and reached out a hand to stroke me; but I slapped it away, hard, and he kept trying to touch me, but I kept slapping him. I'd never hit anyone in my life before, but I didn't find it difficult. It felt a bit silly at first, in fact, but then I felt angry. I stood in front of him, and took off my bra; I was staring directly into his eyes, challenging him, and he reached out, but Slap, round his face this time, harder than I'd intended but he seemed to like it. So did I, by now, bizarrely; I was punishing him for wanting it, and punishing Teddy too, for wanting me to do it.

Then I slipped out of my panties, and he tried to touch me down there, but his punishment continued until he begged me for mercy; he slid onto the floor and onto his knees and actually begged. So I stopped slapping him, and told him gently that it didn't matter, really, and I let him touch and stroke my naked body; although I stopped him firmly when he tried to feel inside me. Then I helped him remove his clothes, and we lay naked next to each other on the bed and I caressed him also; and although I was revolted by his sagging and liver-spotted flesh, I felt removed from the proceedings, as though I were sitting in a corner, just watching. Then his face went dark, and he put my hand on him and held it there, moving it up and down quickly until he was satisfied; the dribble of white liquid putting me inconveniently in mind of my teenage experience.

When he was ready, I showed him into the en-suite bathroom, and put on a robe myself while I waited for him to freshen up. When he came out he kissed me on the cheek; Thank you, my dear, I'll see you again. Not if I can help it, I thought, as I showed him back to the lounge, where I knew Teddy'd be ready to give him a drink and escort him to the Bentley for Shine to take him back to wherever he came from. Then I went to Teddy's bathroom and took a long, hot shower myself; he hadn't really done anything to me, apart from stroking me gently and having me slap and stroke him, but I felt dirty. I thought of Lady Macbeth and her damned spots of blood.

Teddy came to find me, with a fresh robe, which I hadn't seen before; black lace and silk, and I put it on with relief. I didn't want to put the other on, it felt soiled from my skin where the Judge's hands had touched me. And then I thought, Does Teddy think so too? I felt uncharacteristically angry with him now, because if I was dirty it was he who made me that way; and I said so, I shouted it at him, which shocked him initially, but then I dissolved into tears; and he soothed me, and calmed me, and put me to bed, then brought me hot chocolate with brandy in it. I felt so tired, so weary, it must be the strain, I thought. I can't believe I just did those things, Teddy; tell me I was having a bad dream. No, darling, my clever Baby, you did them, but so well, you might have been a drama student. Because, of course, he'd got the whole thing on film now, and probably watched it back while I was in the shower; it hadn't taken that long in actual fact. Are you pleased, Teddy? Of course, my Baby, I'm always pleased with you. Go to sleep now. And I did.

She spoke as though in a trance, looking down and

not meeting the gaze of Dora, whose overwhelming feeling was of anger; how could this awful man have used her so, and how could she have let him? And getting her onto drugs too, now. But Mags sighed, and then carried on speaking, so Dora had to keep listening.

The following morning I slept in, and Teddy let me; when I woke, he was nowhere in sight, so I went wandering round the apartment in search of him. I found him in his den, which was his office when at home; it was unusual for him to be in there at the weekend, when I was there, anyway. He heard rather than saw me, then looked up, dropped everything and came over, sweeping me up into his arms and carrying me into the lounge, then sitting on a sofa with me on his lap. Sorry, Baby, you were out for the count, and I had to get straight onto something. Our guest from last night has done what was needed; thanks to you.

I was troubled at remembering the events of last night, not just my part in them but Teddy asking me to do them in the first place. Was it really necessary, Teddy? Absolutely; sometimes there's just no other way. Couldn't you have got someone else? Who could I trust but my clever Baby? I looked down, not knowing what to say, and he held me even closer and lifted my chin so that he was looking into my eyes; but I dropped them, away from his gaze, and he lifted my chin higher, very firmly this time, and his gaze forbade me to drop my eyes again. Listen, Baby, I won't lie, I may need you to do something like that again in the future, maybe more than once, if you stay with me.

I looked at him in alarm at this; there'd never before been any suggestion that we wouldn't stay together and, despite my issues over what he'd just had me do for him, I couldn't think of life without him. But, my darling, he continued, I'll always be close by and I will never put you in danger; this guy wasn't dangerous, was he? I shook my head; Well, anyone else, if there is anyone else, will be similar to him; and I will never, never let anyone else make love to you. I looked at him then, the question in my eyes and he answered it directly; James is my brother, he's special to me, as you are, and I don't have a problem with bringing my two special people together with me. But no-one else; never. He stressed this and held me tight, and I clung to him; Maybe it won't happen again, I prayed, but if it does I'll think about it then.

Her hands, which had clasped each other in her lap while recounting the incident of the Judge, were now holding and stroking her pendant as she continued in a calmer tone of voice. We both felt like some fresh air, and as the day was dry and windy, with some sunshine, we walked along the river and had lunch in one of the many restaurants in this fashionable area; Italian, this time. As I lifted my wine glass I saw the new addition to my right hand; a ring, fashioned of yellow, white and red gold, with a little pattern of diamonds set on the front. Teddy'd given it to me when I'd showered and dressed, just before we came out, and I'd got to wear it.

He saw me looking and smiled; I'd like to give you something else, Baby, I'd thought to take you to Paris for a few days, would you like that? Of course I would, I was happy anywhere with Teddy; but I'd never been abroad and the thought was exciting. The thing is, Baby, you don't have a passport, and that'll take a little while to get. Plus you have exams coming up in a few months' time; you need to study, and I don't want to distract you from that. So can we put it off until you've finished the exams?

He was right on both counts, so how could I argue? He was paying for my studies, after all, and the least I could do was get a decent result for him. Speaking of which, when it was time for him to take me back to my digs, the white envelope containing cheque and cash was there, as it hadn't been yesterday evening, sitting on the console table in the lobby by the front door for me to take.

It occurred to me later, when I thought about the events of that weekend, that paying by cheque for my studies was a way for Teddy to exert control over me. If he'd set up a direct debit, or paid by card, I couldn't see the transaction and might just have taken it for granted that Teddy would pay. But if I had to expect a physical cheque I'd be thrown off-balance if it didn't appear when required; as had happened this time.

It wasn't good, was it? She looked at Dora, who really didn't know how to react. But you can see, Mags continued, how Teddy had got the ability to rationalise even the worst things and convince me to do them; while on the other hand he was so loving, so giving, that I didn't find it too difficult to put the bad things behind me and concentrate on the present, which at that time was my forthcoming exams. So, although I wasn't happy with him for what he'd made me do, I have to give him due credit as the force keeping me on the straight and narrow as far as my university studies were concerned.

When I'd first met him, in an overflow of irrational thought stemming from my new-found passion, I was minded to throw over my whole university career; what did I need with a degree, now I'd got Teddy? Then, fortunately, some more realistic reasoning clicked in; I'd only just met him, and we hadn't yet arranged a contract. What if he threw me over the following week? I'd completed half my degree, what a waste if I didn't do the other half; and, of course, wouldn't I be giving in to what my parents had wanted me to do? Forget study, get a man, get married, get pregnant and spend my life being the little woman in the home? There's nothing wrong with doing that, of course, if it's what you want, but it wasn't what I personally wanted.

So I'd kept on with my studies, and Teddy had been meticulous about leaving me alone when I needed to revise at the end of my second year, and now, at the end of my third. He let me take charge of my time, not phoning me in case he disturbed me at the wrong moment, but made it clear he'd always be available if I wanted to call him. I tried not to disturb his working day, but on the few occasions when I did (needing reassurance when studying something I was less than confident about), I found that he'd left instructions with his PA to disturb him whatever he was doing. Supportive was his middle name during this time.

My final exams were a nerve-wracking time, but Teddy was always there when I phoned after sitting one; and I always called him then. Other students went for drinks together, to have a post-mortem on the question paper, compare what they'd given by way of answers and so forth. But by now I'd largely withdrawn from their company, having been drawn into Teddy's world in every aspect of my off-campus life; he was everything to me and I wanted no other company. So I had civil and polite relationships with my housemates and students in my seminar groups, but no close friends, no girlfriends to sound off to when things weren't going well. And I'd no need of them because, the more negative aspects of our relationship notwithstanding, I felt so entirely lucky in my love for Teddy.

This was reinforced on the evening after I'd sat my final exam, when Shine arrived at an appointed time to ferry me to the Thameside apartment and a dinner at the Greek on the waterfront. I felt I'd done well enough to pass today's exam, as I did the others I'd sat, although I wasn't sure I'd done as well as I might; I was honest about this to Teddy, who dismissed my worries; Well, Baby, I'm sure you've done better than you think, but I'll be proud of you whatever.

The thing is, he continued, have you thought about what you want to do next, darling? No, I hadn't; I'd found it exhausting, studying as much as I'd been doing. I enjoyed it but I was conflicted between wanting to study and wanting to be with Teddy. I'd been to a few of the talks and demonstrations that'd been arranged for final-year students, along with the careers fair that'd taken place, to get an idea of what was out there for me to forge a career in, potentially. But as yet nothing appealed, and I'd really got no idea. Teddy was sympathetic; Never mind, Baby, there's plenty of time for that. But on a more immediate practical level, you'll have to get out of your digs soon, so you do need somewhere to live. He was right, of course, and I told him I knew that I had to start looking for somewhere, as of tomorrow.

This exchange took place over coffee at the end of dinner, at which I'd eaten less than usual. I couldn't find the courage to ask Teddy the question that was really on my mind; What about Us, now that we've both fulfilled our respective sides of the contract? What would I do if he didn't want me any more? Strangely, the 'H' around my neck had made a contribution to consolidating our relationship, for me. It wasn't a wedding ring, but it acted in the same way, I felt, being always there as a reminder of and link to him, and I found myself touching it for reassurance whenever I felt the need.

Which was what she did these days, almost continually, Dora realised, but why? Given that du Cain appeared to be out of her life now, she'd have thought Mags would have disposed of the thing, but apparently her reliance on it had become a habit she couldn't break, and continued now alongside her narrative.

But then he was paying the bill for dinner; Come on, Baby, a little walk before we turn in will do us good. We were within easy walking distance of his apartment block; we'd walked here and I assumed we'd be going straight back, but Teddy turned off in the other direction, his arm around me guiding me along with him. A short walk later, he turned off into one of the smart new apartment blocks which had recently gone up in this fashionable area. He apparently had a security code, as he let us in, and into the lift after the security guard had checked him out on the computer; up we went, and out onto the top floor. Another key, and Shoes off, darling, the carpet's new; and I saw that we were in an apartment not unlike that in which Teddy lived already. It was the penthouse, although smaller, obviously newly-carpeted, but otherwise unfurnished as far as I could see; and there was a panoramic view over the city from the picture window leading onto a terrace.

I just looked at Teddy as he put his arms around me; How about this, darling, could you cope with being this much closer to me? Could I? Couldn't I! You still want me? You try keeping me away from you, Baby. I threw my arms around him and was so happy I'd have shown my thanks, physically, there and then, but Teddy wanted to wait. We'll christen it properly when it's furnished, darling, we can have great fun doing that together. So we walked back to his place, arms round each other, and I demonstrated my continuing happiness with him there.

The upshot was that we renegotiated our contract – Good to continue having something formal on paper, darling, he said, and I didn't argue – and I moved from being part-time student, part-time mistress for my sponsor, to being the full-time kept mistress of Edward du Cain, living in a property owned by my lover and myself his property, as I was coming to realise. All my living costs were paid by the man I loved, and I couldn't foresee a time when he might want me to leave or when I might want to leave him. I was as happy as it was possible to be, living in the present.

I was so happy our relationship was to continue, and it was only when I'd accepted his offer to live in the new apartment that it occurred to me; Teddy hadn't asked me to live with him, in his apartment. Before, it'd been the only sensible option for me to carry on living near campus, but now I wondered. I'd asked him once, in some inconsequential conversation in bed, if he'd always lived alone; Far too selfish to live with anyone else, Baby, it's best this way, it suits me to do what I want to do when I want to do it; do you enjoy sharing your student digs? I didn't, I had to agree; my housemates would leave the shared kitchen and bathroom messy, which irritated me, and the only reason I could bear it was because I spent a fair proportion of my time away from there, with Teddy. Now I was glad I'd asked him about it way back then, because to do so now might suggest he ought to be moving me in with him, and I'd feel so humiliated if he said he didn't want to.

But I still wondered about him; had he ever had a wife, children, any family apart from James? Was there a Mrs du Cain out there somewhere, current or ex? But I couldn't ask him, because he never volunteered personal information and my limited questioning of him in the past had shown me that he didn't welcome this. It had occurred to me that I ought to look in the desk in his den, when he was at the gym in the early morning and I was alone; but he always kept it locked when he wasn't in there, and he'd know, anyway, there being security cameras in every room of the apartment. It went against the grain with me, in any case, to snoop on him, plus I'd read Perrault's 'Bluebeard' and Angela Carter's take on this, 'The Bloody Chamber'; do you know the story, Dora? And she had to explain, briefly, the story of the new wife who'd gone searching where her husband had expressly forbidden her to go, and found the bodies of his murdered previous wives, and only narrowly escaped becoming one with them.

Well, I wasn't much like the girl in the story, I really didn't want to go there, didn't want to know; if I didn't know I could pretend it didn't exist. Me too; the thought came involuntarily and unwelcome to Dora, who thrust it aside as Mags continued. I trusted Teddy, and didn't think he'd got any other relationships on the go, as he spent too much of his time with me, in his own apartment or out and about, both nationally and internationally; but who knew? His personal assistant, perhaps? Teddy could do anything in his working day, including an afternoon with another woman in his apartment, or a hotel, or her place even, and I'd never know.

I'd seen her once, his PA, when she bought some documents that wouldn't wait over to Teddy's apartment for signature before despatch. Imelda Markham; in her early forties, I would've said, striking but not pretty, with deep black hair and eyes and a Roman nose. I was slightly curious about the possibility of her and Teddy, so asked some meant-to-be-subtle questions which he saw straight through. Don't be silly, darling, shagging the staff is a definite no-no; if I've got some secretary mooning about being in love with me she's not going to be doing her job properly, is she? Imelda's been with me for a while, she's immensely efficient and totally loyal, but she also has a husband (Scandinavian, an architect, I think) and a couple of children at university. She goes to social events with me on occasion, when I think it necessary, but Shine drives her back home immediately afterwards. So no need to be a jealous Baby. I didn't know what to say, so I just pouted and gave him the big eyes, which made him laugh, shake his head and rumple my hair. Thereafter, I let the status quo continue and trusted him to tell me whatever I needed to know.

When my results arrived, I was only slightly disappointed; not a First, but a 2:1, and that I only scraped. But given how distracted I'd been with my love life I felt that I could've done far worse; and potential employers, should I ever get around to using my degree for a career, don't look at how good or bad a 2:1 it is, they just see a 2:1. It also made me feel I'd given Teddy value for his money, and he was pleased with me; Well done, darling, I'm so proud of my Baby; now how about that trip to Paris I promised you? I wasn't arguing, so the thing was arranged and I had a heavenly time. Flying, my first time ever, in a private jet, no queuing with hordes of others, and an attentive stewardess bringing food and drink on request. A luxurious hotel near the Palais Garnier, and a tour of the Palais itself; there was neither opera nor ballet we wanted to see on there at that time, but we went to the modern opera house at Bastille for a performance of *Faust* instead.

It made me think, and finger the expensive jewels in my ears, and around my wrist and neck (because I was allowed to remove my 'H', to replace it with another piece of jewellery, when Teddy said so) when Marguerite was seduced by the jewels left outside her house by Faust, before he seduced her in actuality. But I didn't really see any likeness between us, and anyway, she ended up going to Heaven, so it was alright really, I thought; and the whirl of enjoying Paris soon erased any negative thoughts I might've had. The view from the Tour d'Eiffel after dark, Steak Tartare followed by Tart Tatin at a smart restaurant on the Place des Vosges, and the pleasures of French patisserie, including macarons in many flavours, which I adored: as I adored being in the City of Love with the man I loved, which was the best bit of it all.

She came back to the present then; How I do go on, your poor ears must be sore. But Dora denied this, claiming that she was happy to listen if Mags wanted to talk. But the patient was feeling tired now, she said, and would try to get some sleep, after she'd been to the bathroom, if Dora could help her, please? Dora could, and did, and when the girl was sleeping, breathing deeply and evenly, she sat and watched her, letting her own thoughts wander through some of what she'd heard tonight; unfortunately, though, it wasn't particularly pleasant. She thought about the 'Bluebeard' story and applied it to her own life. She'd never been curious about what Des might be doing when he wasn't with her. She'd trusted him completely, as he did her, and never even considered that there might be areas of his life from which she was excluded; then why was she so unsure now? Was there a woman somewhere wondering if Des had a wife and children?

You're being ridiculous, she told herself then, Des isn't a rich and powerful man like this du Cain; any woman he meets is going to be at the office, where everyone knows he's married with children. Not that this would necessarily stop a woman who wanted him, or loved him, she thought; but she put that unbearable thought from her, covering it swiftly with another. He doesn't have the money to set another woman up the way du Cain did; we're comfortable now, but no more, and would Des go into debt for the sake of an affair? It had happened to others, Dora thought uneasily, there had been cases on the News in the past; but then she firmly removed her mind from the unpleasant subject, opened her laptop and concentrated on a training exercise; but the thoughts kept coming back to her, hard as she tried to keep them out.

8: COMMON

When Dora arrived the next evening, Laura was sitting by the bed, looking through some old essays which Mags had written and reminiscing with her about the days when they'd been student and lecturer. It had come to mind, Mags said, because she'd been talking to Dora yesterday about her final exams; she'd thought the essays lost, but Laura'd found copies filed on one of her thumb-drives, when Mags had mentioned it to her. They carried on talking, while Dora sorted out medication, then Laura left them alone together for Dora to see to her patient's other needs. When she was clean and comfortable in bed, the girl picked up the thread of her tale from the previous night, along with her eternal pendant.

I was talking about Paris, wasn't I? Well, when we returned I found an e-mail waiting for me with the details of my graduation ceremony. It gave me an unwelcome headache, so much so that I almost decided not to bother, and have the degree certificate mailed to me, which with hindsight would've been the best option. But Teddy thought I ought to do the cap-and-gown thing; You've earned it, Baby, I'm proud of you and I'd like to be there and see it awarded. I wanted him there too; he'd paid for the majority of my studies, and living costs, but my parents had contributed something also, and that was the problem.

No way could I have both Teddy and parents in the same building, and meeting each other. My parents were so stern and self-righteous in their views that I'd feel ashamed to let Teddy meet them; and I knew without doubt they'd totally condemn my relationship with him, and hate him on sight. I'd grown more and more out of touch with them as time went by, to the point that they knew next to nothing about how my life'd developed. So I just decided not to tell them, have the graduation with Teddy present, then contact them later and tell them bluntly what I was doing with my life; then they could get in touch, or have nothing to do with me, whatever suited them. I really didn't care.

In the event, it was a disaster. For one thing, my allocation of two tickets for guests at the ceremony didn't turn up at my digs (where I still had a month or so on my rental agreement), despite an e-mail telling me they'd been sent. I had to go into the office to sort it out, and the clerk still insisted that two tickets had been sent; well, they must've got lost in the post, because I hadn't received them. After much argument she grudgingly agreed to give me duplicates, as long as I promised to destroy the originals if they did show up. She was slightly mollified, though, when I said I only needed one, and that she could give the other to someone else who wanted extras (these things being like gold dust, apparently).

The day went off well, initially, with the conferees being brought in after all the guests were seated, and going up individually after the speeches to receive our certificates. As we sat on the sidelines and waited I looked for Teddy, and saw him at the front. I was surprised, it being unreserved seating and first come, first served, and Teddy always turned up when it suited him; but I expect he bunged someone, Teddy always getting what he wanted. We found each other afterwards, when people were milling around, sons and daughters, mothers and fathers, husbands and wives, kissing each other and throwing mortar-boards into the air. As I ran up to Teddy and into his arms I heard 'Magdalena' in a sharp voice; and there were my parents.

I must've looked shocked, and they looked disapproving, and I don't know how Teddy looked because I didn't dare look at him. I knew I was in trouble right away. I only ever got called 'Maria', my first name, if I was behaving in what my parents thought an appropriate and proper manner; it was more usually 'Magdalena', as now. At least it solved the issue of where my lost tickets had gone. They'd been sent to my parents' address, presumably due to the 'latest technology' university computer system not having been updated, because I'd certainly sent in the contact details for my digs. So my parents, not hearing from me, and not getting a response to the letter they'd sent me, (they didn't do mobile phones, smart or otherwise), decided to use the tickets and come to the ceremony anyway; hopefully to see me and find out what on earth was going on in my life.

My flying leap into Teddy's arms had told them most of the story, and they weren't going to wait around exchanging pleasantries to find out the rest. At the first blunt question from my father, Who is this man?, looking Teddy up and down in the most unfriendly manner possible, I decided I couldn't cope with them both together and asked Teddy to give us a few moments. He was reluctant to go and leave me, but I gave him my extremely rare no-nonsense face and he settled for retiring to a short distance away, from where he could rescue me if things went bad. I'd no issue with sending him away; I knew him fully capable of handling himself, and of coming off best, in any altercation.

Once he'd moved away, my father spoke for both parents, and didn't mince his words; Why is he here?, not waiting for an answer to his first rude question. He's my partner, I replied to both questions, He's been supporting me since you stopped doing so. So we got into What do you mean by that? and, I mean, paying my study fees and living costs. Are you engaged to be married? No, we're not, but I live with him as a wife would. So he went into moral outrage overdrive; I was never likely to be married, now that Teddy'd had what he wanted without that, and He looks older than me, and I'm your father ... Sodom and Gomorrah, Living in sin, Kept woman, Fallen woman, Whore of Babylon ... and so on and so forth.

I was beginning to feel uncomfortable, more because people were beginning to stare at us, rather than with what my father was saying, but then he trailed off and looked unnerved. Glancing in the same direction as he, I saw Teddy, giving him what could only be described as the evil eye with an unwavering gaze. My father looked away first and, for his parting shot, declared that they disowned me, that I should never again use his name or he'd sue me. Then he left in umbrage, dragging my mother (who hadn't said a word) with him.

I went over to Teddy, who looked more than a little concerned for me; Darling ... even he was lost for words, and just put a reassuring arm around me. I think he got the gist, given that my father hadn't troubled to lower his voice, and I didn't feel like going over it again. Of course, Baby, he told me, just remember that I'll always be here for you. So the end of my relationship with my parents cemented Teddy even more closely to me, and I counted them well lost for that.

I wished we'd stayed in Paris, she said reflectively at this point; Teddy did take me abroad again, but nothing was ever as good as Paris. She mused on the idea, seeming rather down, so Dora suggested hot chocolate and cake, which was accepted. When the nurse returned, with a mug of tea for herself for good measure, Mags had perked up. Shall we watch some TV? All this looking back is getting me down a bit, tonight. So the portable in the corner was switched on, the channels flicked through, but there was little of interest, especially at this time of the night, and an art programme chosen as the best to be had.

Art had never been a big deal for Dora, so she let it flow over her while her patient watched with some interest, until Mags captured her attention; Oh, look, look! I've been there, I've seen that; I stood right where the presenter is standing. Dora saw a large picture, modern, unrealistic, almost cartoon-like, of five women, pink and naked and angular, two with distorted faces, one with a dark-skinned face on her pink body, staring out of the canvas in the most unfriendly manner. Dora didn't like it at all, and said so, albeit in the most diplomatic manner she could muster. Don't worry, Mags told her, Picasso's not to everyone's taste; but it seems like even the TV is determined to get me looking back at the bad bits tonight. Do you mind? She indicated that she'd like to turn off the TV, and Dora gave her willing assent.

The thing is, Mags recommenced, Teddy took me to see that picture in New York; and our visit there was good, at first. It was when I'd been in my apartment for about three months; he told me we'd been invited to a drinks party, and would I like to go? We went to this kind of thing on occasions, always with contacts of Teddy, and I liked going anywhere with him, so of course I said yes. It's in New York, darling, he told me then, will that be a problem? He'd do this, to surprise me, and of course I was surprised, and delighted. I'd been to various places in the UK and Europe with him, but now to go to the USA, I'd love it. I thought we might stay a few days, Baby, I have some business to attend to, and this party is connected to that, but I could show you a few of the sights while we're there. I was all over him, You're so good to me, Teddy, and he was happy that I was happy, so it was a date. Flights and hotel were duly arranged, Teddy helped me decide which clothes to take (Although you can buy a few things while we're there, Baby), and off we went.

It was arranged that we'd have a couple of days before the drinks do, which would be on our last night before returning home, and I was very excited about it. I couldn't believe the sheer size of the place, but fortunately I was with someone who'd been there before and knew his way around. We stayed in a very plush hotel on the Upper East Side, and Teddy sent me shopping with a chauffeur-driven car and a professional shopper, Stacey, while he went to his business meetings. Stacey was good company and knew exactly where to go; You absolutely HAVE to go to Macey's and Bloomingdales while you're here, Mags, no shopping trip in New York would be complete without those.

Then she took me to some of the stores on Fifth Avenue, Saks, Armani and so forth, and we walked down Madison Avenue and checked out the windows before I bought the most divine simple-yet-chic cocktail frock in Dolce & Gabbana; I decided to wear it for the drinks party. We lunched at the hotel, which was on Madison and therefore handy, and I rested up for a while before Teddy returned. We had a great evening when he took me to dinner at an offbeat place in Greenwich Village (Everyone just says The Village, darling, it's the only one in this city), where we went down for jazz in the basement after we'd eaten, and then back to the hotel; all in the chauffeur-driven car, of course.

The following morning Teddy had another meeting, so I was despatched once again with Stacey, this time to take the ferry to see the Statue of Liberty, check out Central Park and to lunch in Little Italy. Then in the evening Teddy took me to the Metropolitan Opera to see *La Traviata*, Verdi's kinder version of *La Dame aux Camélias*. At least poor Violetta, who gave it all up for love, was briefly reunited with Alfredo before she died, unlike Marguerite in the book, who dies before Armand can get to her, Dora; but I still cried for her. This amused Teddy, who'd seen it before several times and was desensitised, I told him, but that didn't bother him; You're such a baby, Baby, but you're irresistible with tears in your eyes. So he consoled me back in our hotel suite, and hotel bed, and the following morning he was free, so we spent the day together.

First, the Museum of Modern Art; I wasn't sure about it, but Teddy was keen to try to show me some work of at least one artist, Picasso. We looked at a whole range of pictures, and I couldn't take it all in; I was having a great time in New York, even the jet-lag didn't seem to be affecting me too much (and it didn't seem to affect Teddy at all), but it was a whirlwind tour and I was beginning to suffer from cultural overload. But I did remember *Head of a Sleeping Woman* and a favourite of Teddy's, apparently, *Les demoiselles d'Avignon*, which apparently the artist himself had called *Le Bordel d'Avignon*, that is, The Brothel of Avignon; and that's the one we've just seen on TV, Dora. The stare of those women, the two in the middle specifically, was difficult to lose and difficult to forget. Picasso put a couple of men in it initially, darling, Teddy told me, customers I suppose, but he took them out and let the viewer confront the gaze of the women directly. I appreciated Teddy's interest, and tried to seem interested myself, but I was glad when he suggested we'd done enough and ought to have lunch; a larger one today, as the drinks party would take over the evening, and we'd just get canapés there.

He whisked me off to a very modern restaurant, where we ate in comfortable conditions in the lounge; and I did feel much better after foie gras tart (which reminded me of our first-ever dinner), beef and celeriac, and a strawberry pudding. This was just as well, because, Just one more stop before we go back for a rest, Baby. Then he took me into Tiffany, and presented me with A small token of my appreciation of you, darling; a choker, white diamonds, tiny, so many of them, set in gold. He took it from the box, and fastened it around my neck, his fingers lingering on my skin, and kissed the place where it fastened, while the saleswoman tactfully looked the other way. I kissed him, and hugged him, I was so happy; then he took me back to the hotel and made incredible love to me, so that I felt I was floating up to heaven on a cloud of happiness. I must have fallen asleep in his arms, and when I awoke in them, with Teddy caressing me gently, he spoke; and what he said left me speechless.

Her voice had taken on a negative tone now, and Dora automatically looked at her hands, which had dropped the pendant; and the nurse realised that she'd been expecting this to happen. Positive thoughts of du Cain seemed to trigger her attention to it, negative to cause her to drop it, and her tale took on a darker tone now. I couldn't believe what I'd just heard; and once I'd got my voice back I just about got out, Is this what you bought me here for? And for once he couldn't say anything, because of course he had. Then I got really angry, which I didn't do often; Is this what I am to you? Come to New York, darling, we'll have some fun, Baby, go shopping, see the sights, wining and dining and a simple little diamond choker from Tiffany, oh, and by the way, I want you to fuck some guy for me while we're there, OK? Sorry, Dora, but his eyes widened at the obscenity too; I'd never used bad language until he'd taught it to me, to use in sexual scenarios, but I'd never used it the way I did now, the way other people used it, to make a point; but I was just so angry.

I jumped off the bed and went to the window, looking out at the New York skyline, then turned and glared at him; he looked back at me, seemingly unsure of how to proceed, then, I'm sorry, Baby, I ought to have told you before we came, but I was worried you wouldn't come. Of course I don't want you to have to do this, but sometimes it's necessary and I did warn you, after the Judge, that I might have to ask you to do these things again. I wouldn't ask unless it was absolutely necessary …. He continued in this vein, and I came back to the bed and sat down on the edge, my head in my hands, anger-faded and wearied; then he came and sat beside me and put his arms round me and called me his Baby, and his Darling, and yes, even his Love. It didn't quite equate to saying I Love You, which he'd never said, I'm sure, but it did the trick.

I shrugged him off at first, but then the full impact

of the issue hit me, and I fought it as best I could; Teddy, please, I really don't want to do this, but he was adamant. I know, darling, but I need you to. So there was anger, and then tears and appeals from me and a lot of manipulation from him, but nothing was working on either side, and I brought out my last line of defence. Teddy, you know you were my first and only, apart from the others who were your wish (I didn't want to name James and the Judge), and I know I'm not your wife (I lowered my voice on the word, which I was embarrassed to be using), but if I was, would you ask me to do this? I waited, head lowered, while he presumably digested my words.

At last he spoke, and there was that tone of slight amusement in his voice, which I sometimes loved and sometimes loathed; this time it was the latter. Is this a proposal of marriage? Of course it wasn't, but I stayed silent; then, Do you want me to make an honest woman of you? I looked at him directly; Please don't make fun of me, Teddy. I'm not asking you to marry me, I'm asking you to spare me this humiliation. I know I'm contracted to you, and for what, but I'm also human and it'll break my heart to do this, because I love you, and it'll damage our relationship. Then I lowered my head and waited.

I'd asked him for mercy, but he showed none; Then, for the sake of that love, I need you to do this for me; do you want to see me in prison? And I looked at him; No, of course not, because I didn't; and then I said quietly, so that he had to strain to hear me, OK, I'll do it. Why did I do it? Because I loved him, and didn't want to be without him. End of.

There were tears running down her face now, and Dora felt awkward; she wanted so much to put her arms around the girl, to comfort her, but somehow she couldn't bring herself to do so. Instead, she put out a hand and gently touched her on one arm; I really think you should stop now, you're upsetting yourself, it's too much. But Mags shook

114

her head; No, really, I need to tell it, to get it all out there. I've never really told it to anyone, well, I've told some to Celia, bits and pieces, but not everything. It's a bit like confession, she reasoned, taking herself in hand; you understand that, don't you? It's not a Baptist thing, or of my parents' church, but it's a religious thing. Or like talking to a counsellor; how do you feel, being a psychologist instead of a nurse? Well, I wouldn't mind the increased salary; Dora tried to lighten the mood, and was rewarded with a light laugh from Mags, who wiped her eyes and raised her head; I'll go on, if you don't mind; it's good for me, really. And although Dora doubted that, she continued to listen.

In the evening, after having a lie-down which was anything but restful, and a talk with Teddy about the evening, I got myself ready for the party. My new D&G dress, black, raw silk, with a tasteful little pattern of bling on the left shoulder. Teddy gave me a reassuring hug, It looks stunning with your hair, darling; but all I could think was that I was in mourning for my lost illusions. Without saying anything, he brought out a locally-acquired equivalent of the little silver box, and also without saying anything I set myself up with the courage it gave, putting some in a lip-gloss tin in my handbag for a top-up later, if needed.

The party was in our hotel, in a private suite somewhere, very convenient. The usual business types, trophy girls on their arms, all dressed-up to the nines in the very best available. Waiters bringing round champagne on trays, or Perrier or fruit juice for those teetotal or watching weight, or whisky for the hard drinkers. I took champagne, and managed for the next couple of hours to drink not so much as to look the worse for it, and not so little as to be nervous of what was to come. Make the right conversation, small talk, light froth, humorous comments, make up to the men because Honey, that's what you're here for; bitterly I remembered the Janis Ian album which James had played to me.

And then I was introduced to my man; Maxwell J
H....., fat, balding, much older than Teddy and, to give him
credit, polite and attentive to a fault with me. So we talked
the talk, and eventually walked the walk, all the way back to
his room, after I'd been to the aptly-named powder room,
ostensibly to freshen up but in reality to top up with the
magic white powder that was going to get me through this.
And no-one paid any mind that I arrived with one man and
left with another, because I wasn't the only one. I was in the
company of some of the other well-groomed young women
who'd been talking and drinking and strutting their stuff
around the party we'd just left; and now we'd be using that
stuff for the more private pleasure of the men we did all
those things for, in whatever way they wished.

MJH's way was to stand behind me, arms around
me, rubbing himself against me while he slowly and
carefully undressed me before he turned me to face him and
return the compliment. Janis Ian was with me again,
mocking me this time, I felt; If he wants to hold you, if he
wants to know you, Honey that's what you're here for. As I
peeled the layers off him I averted my gaze from the rolls of
fat, and the bald head, and it was easier to do when I lay
down next to him on the bed, although his hands were going
everywhere before he pulled me on top of him and had me
caress him all over, with particular attention to his groin, in
the hope that something would come up.

But it didn't, despite my ministrations, and I was
relieved I was to be spared this; so the hands had to do, and
I did bring him to a successful conclusion, albeit in a sad
little wet patch on the sheet rather than inside me, which he
would've preferred and I wouldn't. Then he pulled me
down beside him, and kissed me in a rather sweetly-sad
way, and held me close against him and fondled me until he
slept, and I lay there until he let me go and turned away, in
his sleep; so I quietly got up and dressed and returned to the

suite I shared with Teddy.

I didn't know whether he was there or not, I was in too much of a hurry to get into the shower and try to get myself clean, and Lady Macbeth was with me once again. The secret, black and midnight hag that I'd become peeled off the new D&G dress and discarded it on the floor; it was spoiled now, my accomplice in the sordid doings I'd just been a part of, and I'd never wear it again. But hopefully, now that I'd pulled his strings, MJH would pull those that Teddy needed all tied up. I'd never feel clean enough, but when I'd scrubbed myself for some time I was tired, bone weary; I seemed to be developing obsessive tendencies like Teddy's, which was appropriate because it was his work that'd brought me to this.

I finished up and went to bed but sleep didn't come easily, the more so because Teddy wasn't there, neither in the bed nor in the suite. I couldn't think straight, my thoughts were jumbled, and even when I eventually slept I dreamed. The women from the painting were there, Picasso's hard-faced whores of Avignon, looking straight at me with their level and unnerving stare and seeming to talk to me. In your five-star hotel, with your designer clothes and jewellery from Tiffany, you're still selling it, same as us; do you really think you're any better than we are? No, I didn't.

I slept again, and at some point I sensed Teddy getting into bed beside me, and the women of the brothel were still there, and I was with them, in the line-up, so to speak, naked and staring. I saw Teddy before us, braving the brazen gaze and returning it with his own, looking, appraising, and then choosing me and possessing me, taking what he'd paid for. I wasn't totally conscious, nowhere near, but I responded instinctively, automatically. I didn't know what I felt, apart from grateful that he'd chosen me instead of one of the others, rather than leaving me in the line for whoever else might come along to choose. I am chosen, I do not choose, it seems; I could choose to go, but where to? I told myself that I chose Teddy, but my choice would count for nothing if he chose to go elsewhere. These crazy thoughts went round and round in my head, and eventually my over-taxed brain sent me to sleep.

She sighed, and was silent for a while, then; I was glad to get back to my Bankside apartment; I'd slept all the way over on the plane from New York, and now I felt like I wanted to lock the door to keep me in and everyone else out. I wanted to hibernate, and the cold weather outside was an extra incentive. Outside places seemed dangerous; even in Teddy's apartment there was the spectre of the Judge, because although I never really went into the spare bedroom he was still around the place, in the lounge where we'd had drinks beforehand. My own place was inviolate, so far; but what else might Teddy want me to do, possibly in there?

But for the moment it was my safe space, as safe as it got, a warm womb of comfort, and I hunkered down there for the long haul. I turned the heating up, although it was always quite high because Teddy liked it that way, and put on extra layers of clothing. I usually walked around in very little, due to the high temperature and the fact that Teddy could drop in at any time; but now I felt vulnerable like that, so I used clothes to protect myself.

Teddy, strangely, seemed to understand; he'd been serious with me the morning after, apologetic, loving, as usual doing everything he could to make me feel appreciated. And when I was cuddled up close in his arms, illogically feeling protected by the man who'd made me feel threatened in the first place, he risked a reference to MJH which made it clear that he'd known that there was no risk of the man violating that part of me which had only ever known Teddy, and James; I wanted to keep it that way, and I did, until the situation changed, and then it was because I exercised my choice to change it.

So Teddy humoured my need to stay feeling safe

and secure at home; because it was my home, unorthodox as our life together was. He didn't ask me to come to his place, which he usually did about once or twice each week, but just came to me and did cosy, at-home things like other people. So instead of going to plays, or the opera, we watched these on satellite TV channels dedicated to the arts, or from opera houses which allowed the public, via subscription, to access their libraries of past performances on TV. He also bought DVDs, of old films and TV programmes, so one way or another we had plenty of viewing matter, and we would sit and watch these with a bottle of wine and snacks, or sweets, the macarons and coconut creams which I loved particularly. For main meals he'd have food cooked and sent in; he could eat out at business lunches, because of course he still had to go and attend to business during the week, so he didn't feel imprisoned by my need. And when he was with me we'd listen to music, play silly board games like Monopoly (he always won) and Scrabble (I always won), do jigsaw puzzles and of course just be together. Which was what I liked best, of course; just me and him and no-one else, no outside world intruding and spoiling what we had between us.

She stopped then, and suggested putting the radio on; a classical channel, a programme of soothing night music which she liked. Dora obliged, and it wasn't long before Mags was sleeping soundly, curled into a ball like a baby in the womb and breathing peacefully. Alone in the quiet of the night, Dora reflected on all that she'd heard tonight; such sordid goings-on, such abuse of a girl who couldn't protect herself from it and who had nobody else to turn to. So lost was she in thinking about her patient's wrongs that she forgot to think about Des, and what he might be getting up to in her absence.

9: COMMON II

The following night, Mags was asleep when Dora arrived. She's been asleep on and off all day, confided Laura, who opened the door to the nurse; I do hope it's not a sign she's going downhill so soon. Dora reassured the worried woman; Mags had taken to spending a large part of the night in telling her life, re-examining it. She'd naturally be tired in the morning. Laura looked unsure, but accepted what she'd been told anyway.

The girl awoke, if somewhat groggily, when Dora went in, and accepted her medication but nothing else before she was asleep again and didn't stir again until the early hours. Dora watched over her; she didn't feel like doing any work on her laptop, preferring to enjoy the quiet of the night and the deep, regular breathing of her patient. It lulled her into an almost-meditative state, beyond thought, beyond her worries about Des; but after a couple of hours, she was surprised by the door opening, and realised to her shame that she'd been on the verge of falling asleep.

Celia entered, bearing a tray with two mugs of tea and a plate of biscuits, and not missing the yawn which the nurse couldn't suppress. She looked over at the sleeping girl, as if to make sure that she wasn't disturbed, then spoke to Dora, audibly yet quietly at the same time. I thought you'd appreciate a brew; I can't sleep, myself, so I'll sit with you and watch her, if you want to shut your eyes for a bit. Dora thanked her for the tea, and for the offer of sleep, but declined this latter; she wasn't supposed to, it was against regulations, and she apologised for the unsuppressed yawn. Do you want to talk for a bit then, keep you from nodding off? She won't wake, as Dora cast a glance at Mags, I remember it used to take a lot to wake her once she was off for the night. I used to sit and watch over her back then; a surrogate for Vivie, I suppose she was, so childlike, despite all that's happened to her.

When did Celia watch over her in the past? Dora enquired. It sounded like an unusual set-up, but then this household was unusual, and Dora was getting used to the surprises it yielded. Nevertheless, Celia's answer took her off guard; I was her cellie, the Irishwoman volunteered, then, Her cellmate, when Dora looked at her quizzically; we were in prison together. Dora nodded knowingly, hoping she covered her shock in this way, although she was sure she wasn't fooling Celia, who seemed to understand everything. We were in the same profession, the woman volunteered, although I wasn't at the high end, as she was; well, I was never really a looker, plus I didn't come to it as she did. Strange though, although maybe not, we both started out in similar ways; did she tell you about her teens, when she thought she'd lost her virginity but hadn't? Her tone was one of amusement, and Dora nodded; the shock was wearing off, maybe because she was getting used to the ability of this house to never be ordinary, or boring, in the activities of its occupants.

Well, in my case it was true, Celia went on, and I got pregnant; out of wedlock and in my early teens. Even in the time of increased Feminism and relaxed standards that was still a moral outrage to the small village community in Southern Ireland where I lived. But really, what did they expect? I hadn't been told anything about the facts of life, and my ignorance was punished severely. The boy who was the father disappeared, my family didn't want me, so I went to Dublin, and that took some courage, let me tell you; but even there I couldn't get any help. I wasn't thinking about abortion at this stage, you understand, there's still none of that over there, but there was no help to be had for me, and I got to feeling desperate. I thought, If I could get to Dublin I could get to England; and then I did start thinking of a termination. So I got to England, and it was possible, but when it came to the crunch I just couldn't do it. So I had my Vivie, and I've never regretted it, but it was a struggle to raise her. I was working, cleaning, like I do now, taking her with me in a carry-cot, but I still couldn't make ends meet and at a certain point there was no option but the profession to get by.

Are you a mother yourself? she asked Dora then, and as the nurse nodded, Well, you'll appreciate then how a hungry baby, no food in the house and the rent overdue can be a tipping point; you know when it comes to it that you'll do whatever you have to for them. Dora nodded again, politeness seemed to demand it, but internally she was in turmoil. Prostitution? Never, her head said, but her heart disagreed; she'd never had to consider such an option, but if she'd had to? She just couldn't imagine such a scenario, couldn't make that leap, couldn't imagine herself in the situation in which Celia had found herself. Des would never have left her like that, even if she'd forgotten herself and been intimate with him before marriage; and her parents wouldn't have disowned her, she was sure. Lucky, you were lucky, she told herself then, you've been surrounded by supportive people all your life and never appreciated it, never considered that others haven't been as lucky as you. People like Celia, who carried on now after a pause for her own thoughts.

That's how I ended up in prison; her tone was matter-of-fact, her life was what it was and she was used to it. Take me or leave me, had become her attitude to life. It's not illegal, what we were doing, but how you go about it can be. I was living in a small flat with a friend, another working girl, and more than one working from the same residence constitutes a brothel, which is illegal. We were cash-strapped, we'd pooled our resources, which were limited, to live and work in the same flat, and by doing that we broke the law. It should've been OK, because the neighbourhood had a lot of questionable activities going on, and most people minded their own business and looked the other way.

But one neighbour got snotty about the amount of men coming and going at our flat, and contacted the police, so there we were, arrested. My friend was a first-time offender, so she didn't get a custodial sentence, but I'd been in trouble before, and more than once. Persistent loitering to solicit in the same area, despite repeated warnings, advertising by putting cards in telephone boxes. That's all they're used for, these days, she said then, no-one in this day and age uses the phones any more, and they've all been vandalised anyway. If they wanted to stop us they ought to take down the phone boxes; and she laughed at the thought before continuing.

Anyway, as a repeat offender with quite a bit of previous to be taken into consideration I was given three years' custodial, and was out in eighteen months. I started out in another prison, but got re-categorised and moved to the place where I shared with Mags just a couple of months before her. We had about ten months sharing, and when I left I wondered how she'd manage without me to look out for her; she doesn't belong in prison, poor kid.

She sighed; I tried not to think about that; at least I was back with Vivie. She was in her mid-teens by then, a sharp kid, well, she'd had to be, given the life we'd lived; she'd managed to avoid social services by sofa-surfing with a school friend who'd a sympathetic mother. I was going to go back, when I'd got sorted, brave the prison and visit Mags, but in the event she came out and here we are. I was lucky to meet Laura through her, and she's helped me turn my life around; so hopefully that'll have been the last time I go in.

I'm sure it will be; the words came from Mags, who had awoken, unseen by them both, and was stretching her arms above her head and announcing a need for the bathroom. So Dora assisted her, and helpful Celia got hot drinks for nurse and patient, then took herself off to bed and left them to it. Mags, fully-awake now, started to speak of her life once more.

The things I've told you about Teddy, Dora, and what he wanted me to do; it sounds bad, I know, but he wasn't bad, really, he was so loving most of the time. He had problems, like anyone; business problems, I know, and maybe personal ones too, but he never spoke about himself, never really opened up to me, and he was so guarded when I tried to ask him.

I remember one time, a while after New York; I woke in the night and reached across the bed to him, but he wasn't there. My eyes became accustomed to the dark and I saw him, standing by the window, thoughtful, looking out. I got up, silently, and went to stand by him; no robes required, she laughed, because being in the penthouse and not overlooked, we could've lived comfortably as nudists if we'd wished. By now I was feeling more secure, even without clothes, and Teddy was there to protect me. It was a large window, sliding open if needed to give access to a small terrace, with a big view over London. Now, in the small hours, there wasn't too much traffic noise, especially up there, just the lights of the streets and buildings, the gleam of the river and, as it was a clear night, the glow of some stars in the sky. We didn't often see them, because of the city light-pollution; that frustrated Teddy, he was an avid amateur astronomer, and gazed at the stars whenever he had the time and was in a place from where he could see them. So I remarked on their presence then, adding, You can see so much from here; and I felt his arm go around me.

Too much, I sometimes think, he pondered; I feel I could see so much more that's important from somewhere smaller, quieter, simpler. This lot, he indicated the spread of the city below us, it's a distraction. I took up his theme; Out in the countryside, perhaps? But he shook his head; Still too close to all this, it doesn't take long to get back here, or for here to reach us. Maybe an island somewhere? I ventured then, and he squeezed me; Would you like that, Baby? It'd be very different from what you have here.

I didn't have to think before answering him; Yes, but I don't necessarily need all this; I mean, I appreciate it all, you're so good to me, you keep me in absolute luxury. But if I had far less of that and far more of you I think I'd be very happy. And then I thought I sounded ungrateful, as if I was hinting that I wanted something that he didn't have to give, so I trailed off, but I didn't want him to misunderstand me so I tried again. Maybe that's it, Teddy, this over-complicated society we live in makes us over-complicated too; all I'm trying to say, and making a mess of it, is that I love you and you alone would be enough for me. And at this point she resumed her pendant-caressing, which Dora had been expecting.

He nodded and hugged me close; So how would the simple life work on your island? Well, it'd be a very small and quiet island; somewhere warm in the summer, so you could be outdoors working in the fresh air. No business suits, just plain casual shirts and trousers. We'd have a very simple house, whitewashed stone or brick, running water hopefully, or somewhere nearby to draw it from; and electricity if possible, but if not we'd use candles and a wood-fired stove. So you'd have to chop wood most days, for a constant supply to keep us going, but the exercise would be good for you. I was making it up as I went along, but I wasn't finding it difficult; it did sound so different to the lifestyle we were currently living, and I warmed to my theme: We'd keep chickens, and we could grow some vegetables, and maybe you'd go out in a boat and fish sometimes. And in the winter it'd be cold, but not too cold, and we'd shut ourselves in by the fire, and wrap ourselves up and take long walks by the sea on the better days.

I stopped then, and I could feel his smile in his

voice, and something more that I couldn't put my finger on. Baby's dream; he thought about it, then, And what would you be doing in this new Arcadia? Oh, I'd clean, and cook, and sew and mend clothes for us, and keep house generally. We'd sell some eggs and vegetables to make money, so I could go and buy whatever we couldn't produce ourselves, and I'd help you with the outdoor things too. We'd go to bed at sundown, and get up at sunrise, and in between we'd keep each other warm. It'd be a very simple life, but it'd be just you and me. I realised that I really meant it, and I must've sounded wistful, for Teddy continued; And a baby to make three, perhaps?

His tone was amused, and maybe I stiffened involuntarily, thinking of the babies I wasn't having, because his voice softened. Oh darling, I'm so sorry, I'm such an insensitive sod, I wasn't thinking. I squeezed his hand; It doesn't matter, I'm used to it; and I wasn't lying. Does it hurt terribly? No, I told him, there was nothing in my childhood that I'd want to reproduce for a child; and for some people that'd make them want to have children to give them the childhood their parents never had. But I don't feel like that; getting me married and having children as soon as possible was what my parents wanted for me. I've told you how they tried to almost force me into it, so maybe that's why I've turned away from it. But I found the right man – I kissed him here and he reciprocated – and maybe very occasionally I felt it might've been good to have a child with him. But it's not going to happen so there's no point in worrying about it.

I hoped I'd reassured him, because we were so close then, and because he was interested in what I wanted; and as we were on the subject, I wanted to be honest, as I used to pride myself on being. So I began to confess about how I didn't take my contraceptive pills in the early days; but I stopped mid-way, in confusion, because how did he know I couldn't have children? Of course he understood my bewilderment; I know, Baby, I've known for ages. You threw the pills down the loo at my place sometimes, and they didn't always flush away.

He said nothing more, just continued to hold me, and gave me another squeeze, and I wanted to show that I was really sorry. So, I suppose you ought to punish me for that; and I offered to get the rod. But No, he cuddled me against him, that's just a game but this is real; and confession is its own punishment, you know. That sounded deep, like something I ought to've known already; Who said that, and when? I did, Baby, about thirty seconds ago. And he continued to hold me, but I couldn't get over my guilt; But it was wrong of me, what if …? What if it had happened when James …? I couldn't say it, but of course he understood; Then your baby would've had two fathers; a double blessing or double trouble, depending on your viewpoint. We're brothers, we're close, we've shared a great deal so why shouldn't we share fatherhood of a child? He could've said, Especially as we've shared the mother, but he didn't, and I loved him all the more for his attitude in this.

Our joint mood had become more serious, heavy, and Teddy had begun to lift it, but I wanted to lighten it even more; Sometimes I feel almost motherly towards you; when you look tired, or careworn, and I know your business is giving you problems, I want to put my arms around you and protect you and take you away from it all. Silly, really, as you are my protector. His mood lifted; Look, and he indicated the stars in the clear sky. The sun wasn't lighting the horizon yet, so they were still faintly visible. He located and showed me the constellations Ursa Major, the Great Bear, and Ursa Minor, the Little Bear, or where they would be if we weren't in the middle of a city and unable to see much of them.

He told me then the story of the nymph Callisto, seduced by Zeus, the king of the gods, and thrown out of the service of Artemis, the goddess of chastity, when her pregnancy was discovered. Of how she was turned into a bear for her protection, and how her son Arcas when hunting nearly killed his own mother, but how Zeus lifted them both to the sky as these constellations for their protection. He told me there was a star in the Boötes constellation, not visible to us now, but near to both the Ursas, and called Arcturus, or the Bear Watcher, or Bear Guard. So you're the Major, little mother, and I'm the Minor, your son; and most of the time I'm also the star Arcturus, watching and protecting you, but sometimes it's the other way around, with you protecting me; we're linked through them, anyway.

The story pleased me, and Teddy's ideas, and I made sure I remembered the constellations, and how to find the star, or at least its general area, as I wouldn't be near a telescope that often. But mostly I thought that I'd never seen Teddy quite so, I'm not sure of the word I wanted, but genuine, authentic, maybe. And when we went back to bed and just cuddled until he drifted off to sleep again, I lay there and wished that all the bad stuff had never happened. No contracted sex for money, no impotent old men, even no James; just Teddy and me and love, and simplicity like that we'd just shared. It was the closest we'd ever been.

Even though we spent every night of the week together, she said then, reflectively, except when he was away on business and couldn't be there. I suppose that's how I knew it was going wrong, or thought I did; I suppose that's how most people know, if you're together every night and then one of you begins not being there, if you see what I mean. She stopped then, both her story and her pendant-playing, and she must have seen something in the nurse's face because she looked at her with concern. Dora, I'm sorry, I'm going on about this and here you are, working every night, away from home. How do you make it work? Do you have a family you'd rather be with? I've never asked, it's all about me, isn't it?

And Dora insisted, No, of course it wasn't, Dora was here for Mags and the latter had every right to spend the time in any way she wished. But she gave the girl a brief outline of her own life, Ruth and Matthew and Des, and how she always managed to have dinner with him before going on the night shift, and always met him going on his way to work when she got home in the morning. She made that last bit up; she wasn't going to mention her fears about what Des got up to during the nights when she wasn't there.

Mags seemed reassured by this, remarking that Dora appeared to have a healthy relationship with a good, supportive man. Maybe I was over-sensitive about Teddy, she remarked, reverting to her own story, but the difference was very obvious; he went from spending almost every night with me to just one or two nights each week, and when you're the one waiting home alone you've got far too much time to brood about it. And our relationship had started to change, you see; it'd never been quite the same after he punished me for wanting to stay over with James; a minimal change, but still a downturn in my feelings towards him. I still felt resentful about it, and of the occasional meetings Teddy required of me, with various men who needed to be sweetened, or bribed, or blackmailed, which took their toll. I'd stopped asking Teddy not to make me do these things, in case I brought down more punishment on myself, because he'd started getting mean.

I felt it weak and unworthy of me to accept what he dished out, rather than having the guts to stand up to him and, potentially, leave him. But as I couldn't bring myself to do that, and couldn't live with hating myself, I blamed him for my weakness also. My nerves were in constant shreds when he picked on me for some infringement (usually imaginary) of the rules of our contract, and once when I was feeling totally overwrought, with period pains as well as the psychological torture, I actually shouted at him: Why don't you let me go, then, if I'm so unsatisfactory?

He was silent momentarily, and when he spoke it was with apparent amazement which moved rapidly into a tone dripping with sarcasm and sneering emphasis on the words intended to be particularly insulting. Let you go, darling? But where would you go? Back to your parents as the penitent Magdalen? I gathered they aren't as forgiving as the Son of God they claim to revere. And your erstwhile suitor probably wouldn't be quite so keen to marry you now that you're damaged goods; shop-soiled; the demonstration model they sell off cheap when they bring in the brand-new one. Or maybe put your lower-grade degree to some use after all this time? Jump the queue of more recent graduates, or those of your own era who've been putting what they learned to good use? Or peddle your hot little pussy on the streets perhaps? Not right now, of course, the middle of your monthly isn't the optimal time to go on the game. Maybe Baby needs to calm down and cuddle up with a hot-water bottle on the tum till her mood stabilizes.

So, having put himself in the right and me in the wrong by blaming my period, he executed a rapid mood swing of his own and settled me on the sofa, fetching me the said hot-water bottle and hot chocolate and cake himself. I didn't want them at all, but somehow choked them down while he watched me; because, however viciously he may've put it, he was right; I had nowhere else to go and continued to put up with whatever he cared to dish out.

So the crisis had been averted for the time being, however unsatisfactorily, but of course that wasn't the last time Teddy was nasty to me. He went to Amsterdam quite often, although he never took me with him. Coals to Newcastle, darling, he said wearily when I once pointed this out to him, which was uncalled-for and very hurtful. So I said nothing more and took myself into the lounge to sit and stare out of the window and try to get over his meanness.

He came in a while later, bringing me hot chocolate and cake, his usual apology; I'm sorry, Baby, I was horrid, a lot on my mind. Forgive me? Which of course I did, after some Teddy-type getting-round me, and he said he'd take me next time, so we could go to the Rijksmuseum and the Van Gogh Museum, and drink in a coffee-shop and smell other people's legal hash on the air. But it never did happen, because other things happened first.

She stopped then, and the deep furrow which appeared in her brow told Dora that she was thinking about those other things, and they weren't pleasant. I'm cold, she said eventually, when Dora had asked whether she needed anything, I'd like a hot-water bottle, would you get me one please, if you don't mind. Of course Dora didn't and, the required article provided, Mags lay down in the foetal position with it wrapped in her arms and slept until Dora awoke her gently to administer her medication before she left and returned to her own neat and tidy home, with the breakfast things left out and the bed made by Des.

As she ate a lonely breakfast, Dora reflected on the difference between her house and that of Laura. The latter was as clean as the former, courtesy of Celia, and as tidy as any home can be which harbours a small child, yet it felt warmer, cosier, for the love felt and care taken of each other by the residents. The walls seemed to have absorbed it, and reflected it back out, whereas Dora's home felt cold and empty. But there are five of them, including the little girl, Dora justified herself, and just the two of us here now; and she resolved to call Ruth and Matthew later, when she'd slept and woken refreshed.

She wasn't successful; both her children were busy in their surgeries, with full waiting-rooms, Dora had no doubt. She left messages and hoped they'd respond while she herself was at work; we're all too busy working outside it these days, she reflected, to find enough time inside the home with our families. She'd like to see her children, and soon; as well as loving them, she wanted the feeling of security in her achievements which seeing them would give her. In the meantime, she cooked dinner, hoping that Des would be around to eat it with her, which he was. He had no plans for anything except sitting in front of the TV tonight, he told her when he arrived home, to her great relief; and that's where she left him as she made her way to Laura's house and Mags's continuing life-story.

10: DISSATISFACTION II

The girl started without preamble, once Dora had done what was medically-necessary and made her comfortable; she looked tired tonight, but denied feeling sleepy. I'd rather spend the time talking, I'll sleep soon enough; her tone was of grim resignation and fitted what she went on to tell. Teddy'd been changing, withdrawing into himself, and being out on business more and more. I hardly see you these days, I had to say to him one night, but Baby, he excused himself, I have a lot of business going on at present, I can't be around as much as I'd like. I knew that, but I missed him; I wanted to impress on him that he could let me help, confide in me, but he wasn't listening. You sound like a wife, God forbid; you're still with me, aren't you, Baby? I haven't thrown you out or given you away, have I? And I won't. You're mine, Baby, you belong to me and I won't leave you. He put his arms around me and began stroking and kissing me, getting round me as of old and as he so well knew how to. The more pressing business of love took over, and I let the matter drop, but I wasn't reassured when I thought about it later.

Over time he seemed to have been withdrawing himself from me as well as finding increasing fault with me. Sex was still happening, of course, but the cuddles and fun seemed to be disappearing from the process. Even his customary gentleness, when we made love in what I thought of as a normal, loving way was turning into something rougher, less feeling. What's wrong, Teddy? You don't seem to be with me, even though you're here; I feel like a piece of meat. This I was actually emboldened to ask him once, when he'd hurt me and hadn't even seemed to notice when I cried out in pain rather than pleasure. As a rule I didn't intrude on his inner life with such questions, but things were going seriously wrong, I felt. He answered me, though; Business matters, Baby, don't worry your head, I'll be fine when it's sorted out. I'm sorry I hurt you, you know I didn't mean it. But he didn't improve, and not long afterwards he hurt me again, and I bit my lip rather than cry out, because I didn't want to go into the whys and wherefores yet again. I had another theory by now, of what was wrong, and I didn't want to ask because I was afraid of what the answer might be. So when he was sleeping, I lay there and thought it through.

Teddy's tired of me, I thought, that's all it can be now, look at the facts. He used to be in my bed six or seven nights each week, but now I'm lucky if it's one or two; and when he's there physically he's somewhere else, mentally. With someone else, I decided, physically on the nights he wasn't here and mentally when he was. He's had enough of me and has found someone else and doesn't know how to tell me. The idea of Teddy not knowing how to do something was new to me; he always knew what he wanted and how to get it, and other people's feelings didn't enter into it, generally-speaking. But I'd been with him for over four years now, and that must count for something, so maybe he was trying to work out how to soften the blow for me. Because it would be a blow; I'd made him my world, my life. I'd become dependent on him emotionally as well as financially, and I still loved him desperately, even if I didn't like him at times, when he made me do things I'd rather not.

I could feel the tears coming. I didn't want to wake him, and he did wake so easily. So I carefully got out of bed, got my robe from the chair, then took myself into the lounge and curled up on the sofa, feet up and arms around my knees. Then I put my face down to my knees, to muffle any sound, and cried as silently as I could, the tears just running down my face and into my robe. What'd I do if he left me? Hope that he left me with some money to keep me going until I found my feet, and found a life; found a place, found a job, found that I couldn't live without him? I might just as well go out onto the terrace and throw myself off now.

I looked up, and saw the view rather blurred thorough my tear-filled eyes. I wiped them, and saw more clearly; St Paul's, with the Millennium Bridge before it. I remembered how it'd wobbled, when they first built it, because they'd forgotten to do something in the construction, so they had to fix it. My relationship with Teddy now seemed just as unstable, but I couldn't think of a way to fix that, especially if there was someone else. If he loved her, as he didn't love me, he might've moved her into his Thameside apartment, for all I knew; but that was the problem, I didn't know.

He used to have me go over to his place sometimes, if he had too much going on to be far from his den, the domestic nerve-centre of his business empire; but he hadn't had me there for months now. I thought ruefully of how he'd send Shine to collect me, even though it was only a ten-minute walk; There are some bad characters out there, I have to protect my Baby, he'd tell me. Shine would know what, or who, is going on, I thought then, but I rarely saw him now either. Obviously he didn't have to collect me from my uni digs since I moved to Bankside, so I only saw him on those ten-minute drives or when he took me with Teddy for dinner, or to the theatre or opera or wherever. But those trips had dried up also, in the last few months. Not that I'd ask Shine, even if I could; how humiliating would it be, to admit effectively that he knew more about my life than I did myself. I put my head down and cried again.

Then, I don't know how, I became aware of Teddy, standing in the doorway in his silk dressing-gown, watching me quietly. How long had he been there? I'd no idea, but he knew that I'd sensed him now, so he came over and sat next to me, as I tried to brush the wetness out of my eyes and off my cheeks. What's wrong, Baby? He took my hands gently and looked into my face. I'm sorry, Teddy, I didn't mean to wake you; that was all I could get out. That doesn't matter, Baby, but you do; what's going on? So I couldn't avoid the issue any longer, although I was dreading the outcome; I didn't want to sound like a broken record, like a nagging wife with the same old words and phrases, as Teddy had once said in a bad mood. So I tried to do it differently, in my own way, which was probably a strange one but the best I could make up at the time.

Teddy, I know I'm not a government minister, or a captain of industry, or a genius like Stephen Hawking. I'm a kept woman, a mistress, a pampered pet, a toy. I put my hand up to stop him as he tried to interrupt and he allowed me to continue. And I'm not complaining about that, it was my choice and my responsibility. But the thing with toys is, we're here to be played with and we get to expect it; but eventually we become outgrown, and those who played with us previously find new, more exciting toys, and playtime ends, often with us getting thrown out of the pram. So if you've got a new toy, Teddy, and playtime is over for us, and you want to throw me out of your pram, it'd be better if you just did it. And then I looked down and waited for the end.

But it didn't come. He reached out and lifted my chin, and made me look at him; he looked tired, and drained, but there was love, I'm sure it was love, in his eyes. Is that what you thought? I just nodded; I didn't want to revert to the old clichéd script, You're never here, and even when you are you're somewhere else. I let what I'd said stand and left it to him to say what was needed; and he did. Baby, there is no-one else, there never will be anyone else, you're all I need, now and ever and I'll never let you go if I can help it.

He took me into his arms then, and kissed me, and I

was so relieved that I just clung to him and cried some more, and he was apologising and I was telling him that he didn't need to, and he was telling me about business problems, big ones, things that needed most of his time and energy and skill to sort out, but he'd get them sorted, soon, and then things would be back to normal, I promise, my darling. And I was so happy, and touched, and emboldened to say, Let me help; I know I can't do much, but if there's anything I can do, anything at all, let me do it; because I love you and I can't bear to see you weighed down by troubles. And he picked me up, and carried me back to bed, and held me until I slept, like on our first night together; Thank you, Baby, that means the world to me.

Her face darkened then, and her fingers, which had been stroking the pendant steadily during this last part, stopped and stayed stopped when she began again, in a faint voice which Dora had to lean towards her to hear.

Teddy really did try hard to make things better. He stayed with me every night for the next week, bought me a beautiful pair of filigree gold hair slides, and had me wear them when he took me out to dinner one night. It was the Greek on the waterfront, but it could have been a greasy spoon somewhere for all I cared; I'd got my old Teddy back with me. She was looking downwards now, although she had raised her voice to a more audible level. And then, on the seventh night, after making love to me with his old gentleness, he took me in his arms and stroked my hair while looking into the middle distance rather than at me directly. Baby, I do need you to do something for me. I'd heard this before, of course, too many times, and was wary, because it usually preceded a request to entertain one of the old men with whom he apparently did business. But I was aware that he had problems now, and I'd promised to do anything that'd help, and even though I'd hoped it wouldn't be in this way I was prepared to do it, for him.

He was far more serious than on the previous

occasions, and he looked weary. Baby, you know I wouldn't ask you if there was any other way; and yes, he wanted me to meet someone, but this time it was someone I'd met before, and didn't like at all. A Prince someone, from somewhere in the Middle East, very arrogant, very supercilious and very into treating everyone around him like dirt under his feet. He was impotent, like the other men Teddy had asked me to spend time with, but this one was angry about it and very unpleasant to be with on that account. The last time, he'd taken his displeasure out on me as though his inability was my fault. His anger had been expressed through extreme verbal abuse, and treating me as though I were something less than human, with shoves and slaps into the bargain, and I'd left shaking with fear, cocaine notwithstanding.

He was to date the most unpleasant individual I'd ever encountered, and I never wanted to encounter him again. He'd felt dangerous, even though Teddy had promised never to put me in danger, but Teddy had been nearby and I'd had to trust to his protection should things turn really physically nasty. But now the Prince was arriving in the country tomorrow (I've only just been asked, Baby, Teddy told me) and was staying at the country house of one of their mutual associates, a Lord someone-or-other. There was to be a drinks party in the evening, in his honour, to which Teddy (and I, by association) had been invited; and the Prince had requested his host that a woman be sent to him in the hour before this. Not just any woman, but the blonde one from before; meaning myself.

I knew I'd have to do it, but to avoid thinking about it, I suppose, I focussed on the least-important thing; But I'm meant to be at the party with you. You'll have to forget that, Baby, it's immediately beforehand and he wouldn't want you there; and I'm sure you wouldn't want to be there anyway, with him present. I don't want to be with him anywhere, I wanted to say; but instead I just said, OK,

Teddy. And he took me in his arms, Bless you, darling, and held me until I slept.

The next morning dawned and I wished it hadn't. Teddy went out as usual and I just lay in bed, miserable, thinking about it all. I'd nicknamed the Prince 'Sheikspeare' after our last encounter, on account of his wealth of bad language and creative use of it. I wanted to make a joke of him, because you don't fear what you laugh at; but this man was no laughing matter. He'd called me every foul name he could think of, and more, and it wasn't the dirty-talk game I'd played sometimes with Teddy as a prelude to love-making; this was mean and nasty and vicious, befitting such an unpleasant person as he was. The other old men had all called me 'my dear', or something similar, and were courteous to me, kissing me before they left, pleasant and grateful. This one acted as though I were nothing, dirt on the street; he implied that he hated himself also for having to use a thing like me; and I felt the same way about him. I tried to put him out of my mind, but didn't have much luck.

When two in the afternoon came I thought I'd better start making an effort. I knew that if I'd anything about me I'd just leave, put Teddy and doing favours for him behind me and start again. But I'd nowhere to go, and anyway I loved him and preferred to be unhappy with him than without him. So I hated myself for being a pathetic slave to love, and somehow made myself feel a little better by transferring that hate onto Teddy.

I was ready when he came back to check me over and get me on the road, and I tried to be calm, although it was difficult; but I'd made a promise and I'd carry it out, however bad it made me feel. He looked over my outfit with approval, although I noticed he avoided eye contact; he needed to, he wasn't going to be nearby to save me from harm as he'd promised always to be, and he knew he was failing me. But I squeezed his hand, and smiled, if a little tremulously, and he took me in his arms and I knew it would be alright; I hoped so, anyway. Then, before he took me down to the car for Shine to take me to my doom, he produced the box with the magic white dust and a banknote to administer the stated dose; I wouldn't send you there totally unprotected, my darling. And I did feel better, or at least to some extent removed from the proceedings, with my medication on board.

I didn't see Shine on the journey, he was at the wheel already when Teddy helped me into the back of the car. The privacy panel was up, and for once I didn't consider what Shine might think of me; the magic dust was good in that respect also. I didn't look at him as he opened the car door for me on arrival, and pointed me towards the man waiting by a door directly ahead of us. I realised we were at the back of the mansion, the man at the door clearly a member of staff who'd been put on watch to collect and deliver me to the client. Back door, back stairs, I thought; it made sense. I thought of King Charles II, and his Page of the Back Stairs, William Chiffinch, who regularly brought women up to his royal master's bedroom to entertain the king; and led them down again when their work was done. Then I thought, ironically, that there was a cocktail party about to happen here, and the legitimate guests would be arriving soon at the front door. But here was Cinderella, arriving at the back door to get her Prince, who's anything but charming, and have their own party; his cock, her tail, and throw her back onto the streets when he's done. No Happy Ever After to see here.

She was speaking bitterly now, and making no effort to censor what she said out of consideration for Dora, but the nurse understood; the memories were dark, and getting darker, and she was involved now, beyond the hostile feelings which she'd initially felt for Mags, who now checked her tone and tried to make it as neutral as possible, as if to distance herself from the events she was retelling.

I was shown up the back stairs to a bedroom, en-suite of course, which was good because I needed to top up my medication. I'm sure I overdid it, but in the circumstances why wouldn't I? I was careful to leave no traces, although I couldn't see any drugs busts occurring at a Lord's country mansion. I waited in the bedroom, where my Prince duly arrived, arrogant as ever. I'll avoid the unpleasant details of what occurred, apart from that I helped him achieve what he could (which was very little, as before) and escaped mostly physically-unscathed but psychologically-shredded from the high-volume verbal abuse and treatment of me as something lower than human life. He pressed a button before he disappeared into the en-suite, and the same man who'd brought me in opened the door and escorted me back the way I'd come.

I asked him if there was a bathroom I could use; I didn't need a medication top-up, just to wash my hands and face and drink some water, use the loo and try to get my nerves together. He showed me to a room, in silence, and took my arm to propel me briskly down the stairs when I re-emerged; probably keen to get the hooker out of the house before I infected them all. He gave me a smile; supercilious or just plain superior? I couldn't tell, but both were negative options so it didn't really matter. Maybe he'd been waiting outside the room and heard things and imagined more than had actually occurred. Probably hot for it, if so, and considering shoving me up against the wall and giving me a quick one. The righteous gloating over the fallen, I thought, hypocrite, as in *King Lear*; something on the lines of, Beadle, why dost thou lash that whore? Thou knows thou hotly lusts to use her in that kind for which thou whips her. Not an exact quotation, but my head wasn't in the right mode for precision. I was glad to get out of there, back to the streets where he probably thought I belonged. I didn't like the paranoia he made me feel.

It was still light when I came out, which was a

surprise. After the dark deeds I'd been involved in, behind closed curtains, I'd somehow expected it to be later than it was. Shine held the door for me when I got back to the car, and looked at me from the front when he got back in, to make sure I had my belt on and was settled before he started off. He'd got the privacy panel lowered, but when he hit the button to raise the partition between driver and passenger compartments, which was normal procedure, I stopped him and asked if he'd mind leaving it down. I feel a bit alone back here sometimes, I told him by way of apology, my old problem of caring what people thought of me resurfacing.

I got a hint of a smile from him; no fraternising with the hired help allowed by order of Teddy, but that's what I was also. We were both human and I needed to feel some kind of company at this time; I didn't consider that Shine would witness any physical manifestations of my psychological state which might occur. But, No problem, he nodded, and hit the button again so the partition returned back down the way it had come up. As he drove around the front of the house, where guests for the party I was banned from attending were getting out of cars, I clearly saw Teddy, immaculately dressed in a DJ, with a young blonde woman on his arm.

I didn't know whether Shine had seen them also. I caught his eye in the rear-view mirror but he looked away quickly so I was sure he'd seen them, and I felt humiliated by his knowledge. But I couldn't dwell on that because I was too busy trying to take it all in and my mind was going crazy with a whole confused mess of ideas. Was this some sick joke of Teddy's? Spin me all those lines about never leaving me, never having anyone else, to get me to do what he wanted? Laugh behind my back while I was doing it, thinking I was making a noble sacrifice for my faithful lover? Leave the tart you're tired of to do the dirty work and take the new, novel one to the party on your arm to show her off to the boys? Teddy's new totty; What happened to that hot little blonde you used to have in tow, old boy? Went off the boil, old chap, time for something tastier. Well, point her in my direction, I'll soon warm her up again. I could imagine the comments.

Then I remembered a scene from *Dr Zhivago*, an exchange between Zhivago and Komarovsky over Lara, who'd been seduced by the latter; What happens to a girl like that when a man like you has finished with her? Interested? I give her to you. I remembered when Teddy had given me to James, had shared me with him, for the added frisson it would give to his pleasure, I thought now. Bitterly, I imagined a conversation they might've had about me, after the dinner when it'd all begun. Teddy, you lucky sod, you bagged the best bit there, I saw her, I was going to make a play but you got in first. It's better than you think, James old chap, she was a virgin. And James would've groaned, Typical of your luck, the only piece of virgin arse for miles around and you land her. Well, she didn't stay that way for long, obviously, and James would've nodded, ruefully, as Teddy continued; I got that cheap kit off of her, I was just about to give it to her and she almost went through the roof. Well, I thought she was trying it on for money like they all do, little whores, but she was so upset when I accused her, paroxysms of tears and whatnot, and it all came out. She thought she'd had sex already, can you imagine, but it was just a bit of schoolboy fumbling; she was as green as they come, and by God does she come! So I got the lot. You unfroze her assets, in fact? And Teddy would've laughed, I'm showing her the ropes and God, she really loves it, can't get enough of it. And James groaning at what he missed out on; Point her in my direction when you've had enough, would you, there's a good chap? Or before that, I'll make it worth your while. And of course Teddy did, James presumably having provided a sweetener in the form of some dodgy stock trading or whatever, and Teddy not only pointed me in James's direction but managed to control our whole encounter via the threesome he arranged.

And after that, when James disappeared while I was still sleeping, they were probably on the phone to each other while I was in the nice hot bubble bath that Teddy ran for me, before checking his online accounts to see that the deal James had arranged had gone through, and calling James to thank him, and James saying Thank you, old boy, just like being lads again, great piece of arse, we must do it again sometime, maybe just me and her next time? Which of course it was, leading to my punishment by Teddy for wanting to over-run the time scale he'd specified and another downward curve in our relationship. But then I thought, maybe I'm just being paranoid …

No, I thought then, perhaps he'd always had others alongside me, a whole stable of us; some people keep horses in stables, some keep stables of whores. Teddy's acquaintance Hugo Traynor kept both, I remembered him telling me on the way back from Newmarket once. In the past it would've been me arriving at the front door with Teddy, instead of which I'm bundled out the back like dirty laundry, or something else dirty, something not respectable which can't be allowed through the front. Wholesome food goes in one end, shit comes out the other; my paranoia was spiralling out of control and my head was a mess of indistinct thoughts, out of which suddenly rose a memory of when Teddy took me to see *Rigoletto* at the Royal Opera House.

A controversial production, it was, with the first scene staged as an orgy held by the depraved Duke of Mantua. I felt for Gilda, the deluded heroine who dies for love of the undeserving Duke, and my namesake Maddalena, the experienced hooker who lures her brother's intended murder victims and knows all about the cheap chat men use to lure women, but falls for the Duke anyway. But what really stuck in my mind was the young daughter of Monterone, who's been seduced by the Duke. In this production they put her on stage, out of her depth in the middle of the orgy, staggering slightly from alcohol she's not used to and desperately trying to cover her nakedness with a rug she's found. She's sexually-harassed in the scene, humiliated when her father, who's been accused of treason, is led through the hall and witnesses her shame, and then used in a drunken sexual game. She reappears, fully-clothed, in a later scene, where the Duke is clearly tired of her; and is led away by Count Ceprano, with his arm around her shoulders.

What happens to her now? I'd wondered, and I knew. She'd be passed from one courtier to the next, until there were none left, and the last would pass her to his servant; and so she'd descend down a chain of men to the bottom of the pile and die in poverty and misery, hopefully before she was streetwalking or in a brothel. I shivered for her; this might be fiction, but Verdi was trying to depict reality in this opera, and there must've been, and still are, somewhere, others like her.

Her fingers had stopped moving now, and both hands held and tightened over the pendant; Dora could see the whiteness of the knuckles. So, was that what Teddy was doing now? Tired of me and passing me on? I tried to focus. My head was all over the place, and I was coming down fast now from the coke high. Was he passing me around, using me like Maddalena to lure his victims? Maybe he'd allow the next one to go all the way with me, and then he'd be saying to me, so-and-so was really pleased with you, he wants to spend a whole night with you, and I think you ought to let him, but it has to be of your own free will. Then he'd be manipulating me, getting round me as he well knew how to do, so I'd agree, eventually, and the guy would come and spend a night with me and the next thing I knew Teddy'd be gone and it'd be the other one coming each night. And he'd take over the rent agreement on the apartment, or he'd have to move me out because maybe

Teddy owns it and needs it for his new fancy, so I'd be in a smaller, less-expensive place, and I'd be passed from man to man, down the scale, like Monterone's daughter. Because what would I do, where would I go, if Teddy was tired of me? I have nothing, no-one, and I'd be grateful to the next guy for taking me on.

I couldn't imagine Teddy just leaving though, he'd be decent enough to speak to me first, I was sure, well, I wanted to think so. As in, It's been great, my darling, we've had a marvellous time and I'll never forget you, you're so sweet and loving and it's been a privilege for me to start you off in life. The thing is, though, Baby, there's no more I can teach you, you've learned so well and you'll be an exquisite mistress for any man who's lucky enough to win you. So it's time to graduate, take what you've learned and use it with someone else who'll love you for it. We'll both move on, go our own ways with wonderful memories of what we've had. Of course you can keep all the clothes and jewels, they're yours, my dowry to you, if you like. And he'd kiss and caress me, then; But the apartment, well the lease is up soon and I can't really justify renewing it. Now, you've met so-and-so, I think? He really adores you; why don't you let him take you to dinner, I know he wants to, and you could get to know him that way. He'd probably renew the lease on this place, although personally I think a clean break with the past would be better, a fresh start without memories all around you …

Oh, yes, Teddy would know how to persuade me. So I'd go to dinner with the other man, and by the time he brought me back we'd both know that I'd take him, the contract unspoken, unwritten, but signed in spirit anyway. So I'd take him into my bed because I was scared of the future; and he'd stay a couple of hours, maybe, then tell me he'd pick me up tomorrow afternoon, when he'd take me and show me another apartment. Not a penthouse, not in such a good location perhaps, but still good, still high-end.

After all, Teddy bought a virgin and this man is buying another man's cast-off, and they don't command such a high price. Then he'd buy me an early dinner and take me home, stay a while; tomorrow I'd pack and move in, he'd meet me there later and stay over, and it would've begun.

You've made the move, one man to the next, and maybe he'll be as generous as Teddy, maybe not, but it's up to you. Now's the time to use those skills Teddy taught you, and if you're very skilful he'll be very generous. You've got a little nest-egg behind you now, Teddy's dowry, the jewels he bought you, and these are your insurance. It's up to you to add to those, as you make your journey from one man to the next, down through the ranks of the super-rich. Slowly I'd be moved on and on until I was too old, and what then? Age beckons; you've seen *Shirley Valentine*, think Marjorie Majors, her old classmate. If Shirley is forty-two then so is Marjorie, doing very well nevertheless, but not with one man, a high-class hooker with an exclusive band of international clients, one of whom she's flying to Paris to meet when her grown self enters the film. What's out there for her, and for you?

The menopause, ultimately, and that can happen early, as early as the late forties, as Laura can testify; Only forty-eight, and the flushes were uncomfortable, but ultimately I was FREE, thank heavens, and sooner than most, I remember her saying. So use those skills, put into practice what you've been taught and build up that nest-egg, because you're going to need it. Yours is a career for the young, with early retirement, so plan for that. Look after yourself, don't smoke (it gives you lines), don't drink (ditto), exercise, watch your diet; you know it makes sense.

And if one day you're in the bar at a hotel (hopefully you'll still be on the five-star circuit) and you should bump into Teddy, maybe he'll buy you a drink, and maybe you'll talk over old times and what you've both been doing since, or not. Remember *Gigi*, Hermione Gingold and

Maurice Chevalier, 'Ah, yes, I remember it well', except that he clearly doesn't remember a thing. And maybe you'll spend a little time in Teddy's suite, in his bed, for old times' sake, and maybe you won't see pity in his eyes for how you've aged, because, well-preserved or not, you won't be the young girl who gave him her virginity all those years ago. I do remember *Gigi*; I've watched so many old films, passing time until Teddy would come to me with desire in his eyes. I remember Gigi herself, saying something to Gaston like, I understand that I'll go into your bed, and when you finish with me I'll go into another man's bed. She didn't want that, but agreed because she loved him. And I got a large lump in my throat when he did the right thing, and married her, because he loved her too.

I got angry remembering that; How dare Teddy treat me this way? Because he could, because I was totally dependent on him, both emotionally and financially. But I felt despair then, because I couldn't imagine life without him; whatever bad things he'd put me through, the scenarios, the punishments, the men, he was mine and I loved him. But I wasn't Gigi, or Cinderella, or the goose-girl, or any fairytale heroine, and there was to be no happy ever after for me.

It all got too much; I closed my eyes and leaned against the leather upholstery and tried not to think about Teddy and his new girl, or James, or the arrogant Prince, or the superior manservant, or any of the supposedly-fictional misery which men cause women. But I felt my control crumbling and I started crying, just tears in my eyes at first, but they overflowed and ran down my cheeks, and my chest started heaving and my breath came out as sobs, and I dissolved in tears and then my whole body started shaking and I couldn't control it.

And then; Hey, hey … I looked up and saw Shine staring at me in the mirror; You alright? I couldn't answer him, just closed my eyes and carried on crying and shaking as the car carried on. Then we stopped, and I couldn't be sure, I'd lost track of time, but I thought that we hadn't been on the road long enough to be back at Bankside yet. I raised my head and looked out of the window; it was very quiet, and getting dark quickly now, but I could make out foliage, trees and hedges, some kind of woodland?

Then the door opened and Shine got in. I looked at his face, which was registering an emotion this time; Pity, I thought, and I just dissolved again. He spoke, another first apart from his usual mechanical greetings or explanations about some change of schedule or vehicle or whatever; Hey, Angel, what's up? Tell me. And I felt his arms go around me and hold me, and it felt so good to be treated as a human, something higher than a human in fact, after being treated as some kind of spawn of Satan all evening. I asked him, Who am I telling? I don't know what to call you. Call me Steve; and he held me until I calmed down, and I sobbed out what I could, being made to feel like the lowest of lowlife, of being like dirt under people's feet, worse in fact, because people don't think about dirt, it's just there, and about Teddy and his other blonde, but I'm not sure it was that distinct.

When I'd calmed right down to just sobbing, he passed me a handful of tissues and spoke to me as I tried to dry my nose and eyes. But I must've got mascara smeared everywhere, because he took some tissues and wet them with his mouth and then wiped around my eyes till he was satisfied with his work and then just held me again. Don't cry, Angel, I can't bear to see you cry, it breaks me up. You're gorgeous, any guy'd be proud to be seen with you. I fell for you right off, when I used to pick you up from uni and you'd sit in the front next to me. I always wanted to drive out here and park up like this and take you in the back and make love to you. Those legs of yours, those incredible boobs, that long blonde hair and those big come-to-bed eyes looking up at me, you did my head in. I wanted to stroke that hair (he was stroking it now, gently), and look into those eyes, and undress you from the top down and stroke your boobs and bite your nipples. I wanted to see your pussy properly; remember that time you flashed me from the back of the car, not once but twice, to tease me? It was too dark to see much, but I could make out your bush and I had to drive the rest of the way with a massive hard-on and hide it when I opened the door for you. I wanted to see if your bush was as blonde as your head, and finger it gently until you were ready, then bury myself in you and feel those beautiful little legs going round me and you moving under me, and your hips going up and down with me as I moved in and out of you, and feel you really enjoying it till I made you come, and then I'd come, I'd pump you full of my juice and then we'd rest up a bit and do it all over again. I love you, Angel.

He was looking into my eyes as I looked up at him, and he carried on stroking my hair; then he did undress me from the top down, and caress and suck my breasts until I had to stop myself from crying out at my need for him. And he found out that my pussy is as blonde as my head, but he didn't have to finger it to make me ready because he only had to touch it to discover that it was hot and wet and so ready for him. And he slid in easily, Christ, Angel, molten lava, you're a little volcano, and you're so tight. And I did enjoy it, so much, and he enjoyed me, and we did it again, that night and many times after.

She was speaking as if in a trance now, words uncensored, and Dora was taking in every word, unembarrassed and unblushing and unphased by the intimate details and four-letter words that were coming from the girl's mouth. Her prejudices were overtaken by sympathy for what had happened to this girl's life, and her own problems retreated into the background for the time being.

Mags sighed; But before those times there was the

immediate future to face. After what seemed like insufficient time in the car, Steve broke the mood, of necessity; We'd better be getting back, Angel, if you're not there when the boss gets back we'll both be in trouble. But Teddy didn't return until well after I'd showered Steve off my body and was snuggled up in bed, not sleeping but thinking about the love-making I'd enjoyed with him. I'd managed to put aside the horrific time I'd had with the Prince, but then I heard him arrive, Teddy, the agent of my misery, and it all came back to haunt me; including the idea that he'd been in bed with his other blonde, giving her all the cheap words of love-making that he'd given me so often.

I feigned sleep while he undressed and used the bathroom, and as he slid into the sheets and put his arms around me. Are you OK, Baby? I tried to sound loving, but I didn't do a very good job; I'm alive, Teddy, but I'd rather not talk right now. He hesitated; then, The Prince seemed pleased. Good for him; I wish I could feel the same about him. It was like last time, if you have to know, but that's all I'm saying. Baby, my Baby, I'm sorry, please, please forgive me; and he held me and kissed my face. You aren't to blame and neither am I that he's incapable; but I kept my end of the bargain and he has to keep his, so things ought to work out now. We can get back to normal, my darling.

And after holding me and caressing me for a while, he took me with his usual fluid ease, slowly and methodically enjoying me, and why shouldn't he? He'd bought and paid for it, although to be fair he was as usual trying to give me equal pleasure. I covered him with kisses and caresses, while still feeling bitter about what he'd put me through this evening and secretly resenting his invasion of what I now saw as Steve's space. Not to mention feeling jealous of the unknown girl I'd seen him arrive with tonight; maybe we'd both been playing away. Fortunately my body didn't let me down, but reacted automatically to his; but I closed my eyes and imagined it was Steve, and then it was better than it'd been in some time.

Afterwards, when he slept the sleep of the satisfied, I lay and thought about what'd just happened. Teddy hadn't been his usual groomed self when he came to bed; usually he liked being as clean and neat as possible, even when going to sleep for the night. I'd teased him about it in the past; What's the point, you're only going to get all rumpled anyway, why not wait until morning? Although, oddly, he never had any problems about sleeping just as he was after sex; I'd thought it was a sign of the strength of his love for me, but now I considered that maybe he was just too tired to bother, especially as he'd most likely be doing it all again at some point during the night; everyone has their limits. I'd smelled whisky on his breath, and his sexual performance hadn't been the usual polished article, nor had it lasted as long as usual; the whisky, or tired from his other blonde? Or was I now comparing him to Steve? I lay and turned my thoughts from my old lover to my new, and soon slept the sleep of satisfaction myself.

Talking of which, I'm feeling sleepy again now, and that's a good place to stop. She let go of the pendant and stretched her arms over her head; the tension had gone out of her face, the bitterness from her voice, as though she'd exorcised the events of her life through the telling of them. She snuggled down, while Dora helped make her comfortable before sitting and watching over her while the dawn broke outside. Such a chaotic life, she thought, focusing on her patient's issues rather than her own, and it's brought her here. How? Mags had come to this house from prison, that Dora knew, so somehow she'd moved there from Teddy and Steve. Go directly to jail, came automatically to her mind, from the board game she and Des had played with Ruth and Matthew, who had gone directly from home to university and into their respective professions.

That wouldn't have been Mags's route, Dora was sure; and she considered the girl's home life then. True, she'd fallen out with her parents, but what kind of parents were they to behave as they had? Dora appreciated that she'd only heard the daughter's point of view, but she didn't think the girl was lying. I was lucky in my parents, she told herself, and without flattering myself and Des I think Ruth and Matthew were also; I can't imagine treating them the way Mags was treated. She thought then about the phone messages she'd left for her children, and hoped she'd find replies from them when she got home in the morning. A family get-together was badly needed; and as Mags awoke and Dora tended to her needs and administered her medication, she resolved to arrange one, and soon.

11: BREAKING AWAY

There were indeed messages waiting when Dora arrived home, as a late-for-work Des informed her as he rushed around putting papers in his bag with one hand and trying unsuccessfully to fix his tie with the other. Dora stopped him and did the tie for him, as she'd done on previous occasions, while he told her that he'd slept in, which was unusual for him. What had he been up to, she couldn't help wondering, to sleep through the alarm, or even to forget to set it in the first place? And all her worries and insecurities were back with her, not helped by the messages from Ruth and Matthew; they were sorry to have been so out of touch and yes, they really must all get together soon, but it couldn't be this weekend because Matthew was duty-doctor for the weekend out-of-hours emergency clinic at the hospital while Ruth had to attend a conference in Brighton. So maybe the next weekend? Everybody's work allowing, of course.

Frustrated, Dora went to bed and fell asleep surprisingly quickly, given how agitated she felt; she slept right through until 5pm, when she was woken by the ringing of the phone and Des telling her that he wouldn't be home to eat as he was working on to make up for being late that morning. Not to worry about leaving him anything to eat, he told her, he'd pick up a take-away on the way home. Or go to the pub for something, together with a few drinks with your colleagues? Dora wanted to say, but restrained herself. She was glad to get to work, to listen to someone else's troubles and have them take her mind off her own.

Mags was in a reflective mood initially, which Dora decided didn't move her story on but made for interesting hearing. I'm sure it was Steve saying he loved me that clinched matters and took me over to him, she recounted, because Teddy rarely if ever said that. He said he loved to teach me, to instruct me, to watch me ecstatic in the throes of making love; but he never said he loved me, me myself. And I'd never broached the issue because, after all, weren't we a business arrangement when all was said and done? We even had a legally-binding contract, signed by both of us, stored with his solicitor. A contract renegotiated when I graduated from university and Teddy set me up in the apartment where I lived for him alone.

I used to think about my adequate but lacking-in-affection childhood; was that the root of my overwhelming need for love? Whatever caused it, it made me content to stay alone in my apartment while Teddy was out doing whatever he did to fund our lifestyle. Or rather, his lifestyle, because we weren't really a couple in any sense, I told myself now that I'd turned against him. I was one of the perks of a successful man's life, I decided, like the Bentley or the Thameside apartment he lived in. A trophy mistress, set up in another riverside apartment and kept in luxury, to be visited or summoned to visit him, taken around town to show off his possession of me, and on business trips to sweeten the nights. Or loaned to other men at his pleasure, as a bribe or a honeytrap for blackmail. A whore, by any other name, despite the veneer of glamour and luxury which overlay our relationship, and my pathetic need to love and be loved as the reason behind it.

She said these things in a curiously neutral tone, with any bitterness or other emotion ironed out of it, and continued in this vein. Love; the reason why was I so ensnared in Teddy's clutches. I hadn't gone to the charity dinner to look for love, but for a wealthy sponsor to pay my way through university; and I was willing to repay him with my body. Of course, any man willing to pay had to desire me enough to lay out that kind of money, and to keep providing it; and if he loved me as well he'd be ready to keep doing so until he fell out of love. So I'd thought; but Teddy it seemed was attached enough to keep providing for me just through physical desire alone. What I hadn't banked on was my falling in love with him, so quickly and so deeply; and loving him, I couldn't bear the thought of losing him, so I needed to feel he reciprocated my feelings.

But he'd failed me when I most needed him, when I'd laid myself open to him and offered my loving help in whatever form he needed it. And he'd taken that offer and abused it, abused my love and used it against me, by asking me to do probably the worst thing he could ask of me. The old ploy used by lovers against each other since time immemorial; If you really love me you'll prove it by doing this, or that, or whatever. And Steve had been there for me when Teddy ought to've been, and I'd transferred my love to him.

It wasn't too difficult to be together with Steve at my apartment. The whole place was rigged with security cameras, of course, which Teddy could access via tethering to his smartphone through the most up-to-date technology, just to keep an eye on things from time to time. But Steve knew how to disable the link, and reconnect later, and showed me how to do it; so we could be safe from either being recorded or from Teddy's more immediate eyes. Should he tune in and get nothing, he could phone Security at either apartment block, or even phone me directly. But of course I'd tell him that everything was fine and he must just be outside a hot spot.

The cameras in the spare bedroom had another use, of course, when Teddy had me entertain other men, the better to entrap them if necessary in the future, whether I were bribe or reward in the present. But as I didn't particularly like that part of my employment, I was averse to using that room when Steve was with me. I preferred the main bedroom, where I slept both when alone and when with Teddy; it had far more positive memories, even if my relationship with Teddy had gone sour. So I easily reconciled any qualms I might've had about entertaining Steve in the same bed, and sometimes the same sheets, because I was so out of love with my employer, as I now thought of him, by this time.

He rarely if ever came around during the daytime, from Monday to Friday, and if he did he always phoned ahead; I'm on my way over, Baby, why don't you wear … and he'd stipulate what I should be wearing, or not, when he arrived. And of course, if he was on his way over Steve would be driving him, so there was no chance of us being in a compromising situation when Teddy arrived. Additionally, if he didn't need Steve for the morning, or afternoon, or whatever, he'd let him go off duty until a time stipulated; which was perfect for Steve to call and then visit me. There were occasions, though, when Teddy would call and bring his collection time forward, usually necessitating a scramble for Steve to leave in a hurry; which Steve, with unaccustomed wit, described as Getting his gear out of my hot little arse and getting his own arse in gear.

She laughed briefly at this, the first emotion she'd shown today, and then was serious again. Best of all, Teddy made regular business trips overseas; so when Steve had taken him to the airport he knew we'd got all the time available until he had to pick Teddy up on his return. So we had long, hot afternoons in bed which we were able to extend into and through the nights on those occasions.

Teddy hadn't taken me overseas with him for a long time now; but to give him credit, on the morning after that fateful evening of the Prince he'd tried. How would you like to go to Paris, darling? We could take a few days, we didn't get to the Louvre last time. I could get us a view of the Mona Lisa early or late, when the masses aren't around. Oh, and there's a little brasserie in Montmartre you'd love, not to mention a bit of shopping around the Champs Élysées area and a box at the Palais Garnier, after a champagne supper, obviously. What do you think?

I'd got to be careful. I was very confused, because I was sure I loved Steve but I didn't want to lose Teddy, even if I was out of love with him; he was such a big part of my life. I needed time to think, so I put my arms around him and kissed him deeply. That is so sweet of you, Teddy darling, it sounds gorgeous and I'd love to; but could we leave it a while? I'm feeling a bit tired, I haven't been sleeping and my monthly is due (which was true) and I don't think I could do it justice. Maybe in a few weeks?

He looked a little disappointed, but nodded understandingly; Of course, Baby, rest up today and we'll have dinner somewhere special tonight, is that OK? I nodded and smiled and accepted his compromise offer; I knew he was trying, and I didn't want to alienate him. And then of course his business affairs took over and there was always a reason why Paris had to be put off; which suited me fine because I wanted to be at home, where Steve was never far away.

Over the next few months Teddy tried hard to get us back to where we'd been. A spa break (We have to get you back in peak form, Baby), shopping trips, visits to the theatre and opera and meals at all my favourite places with my favourite foods cooked to order if they weren't currently on the menu. Even a few last-minute days in the Channel Islands, when the weather turned hot, so I could just lie in the sun. He'd wanted to take me further away, to guaranteed sunshine in the Caribbean for a week or two, which sounded heavenly; but as with Paris I found excuses not to go, because I wanted to be close to Steve. Besides, I reasoned to myself, why wouldn't it be like New York, me getting all relaxed and suntanned so Teddy could give me to some repulsive old man who needed sweetening? I didn't trust him not to do this, and told myself it was his own fault; which, in fairness to me, it was.

Then, of course, I'd feel terrible about what I was

doing to Teddy. He knew he'd damaged the fabric of our relationship and was trying to repair the tear; and the old me, his soft and in-love Baby, would've cried at how hard he tried. But I wallowed in my resentment of what he'd made me do. I told myself that he'd contracted my body, but not my mind; so my body paid my debt to him but my mind was elsewhere, with Steve. I hardened my heart against Teddy (and her voice hardened accordingly at this point) and, although at face value I accepted all his peace offerings and gradually softened towards him (or at any rate, I acted as though I had), inwardly I took a cruel pleasure in laughing over what he didn't know. Whenever I was in the back of the car with him I'd got the secret thrill of knowing we were sitting on the spot where it'd all started with Steve, where we'd first made love. And I knew that Steve, sitting up front driving, face impassive as usual, albeit hidden from me by the privacy panel, knew what I was thinking and was thinking it too.

There's a saying, Don't bite the hand that feeds you, and another, more graphic, that goes something like, Don't shit on your own doorstep; and maybe they don't exactly fit what was going on here, but they come close, I think. It was wrong of me to let Teddy sit there, all unknowing, but I was so out of love with him at that point that I didn't care. Her voice, which had temporarily softened, hardened again now. It served him right, I told myself, for all the times he'd persuaded me to do things I didn't want to do, or terrorised me, or punished me when I didn't deserve it; so I laughed behind his back and so, I think, did Steve.

She shivered at this point, and thought for a moment, then continued; I couldn't get enough of Steve saying he loved me, and I couldn't get enough of his body either. He was much taller than Teddy and most other men, for that matter, being six foot six in his bare feet, and like Teddy he used the gym and kept in shape. The difference was that he was at least twenty years younger and correspondingly muscled, toned and energised; which wasn't to denigrate Teddy's abilities and energy, which were considerable, but Steve just had more to give.

Oddly, despite the fact that he clearly knew what he was doing, there was something almost prudish about his love-making. When we first got started, he never used any other way than missionary position, which I soon questioned, very tactfully, of course. I'm not here to compete in any sex Olympics, Angel, I love you, he told me, I don't want to treat you like a hooker or a piece of meat. It took a bit of persuasion, although not too much, to convince him that I wouldn't feel degraded if we did it other ways. I love you too, Steve, I want to give you pleasure, like I know you want to give me, and it's great already, but it could be even better. So then he demonstrated that he clearly knew what to do, he'd just been reticent about doing it with me. So things got a bit more adventurous between us and it all just got better and better.

She paused again, thinking back, and Dora took the opportunity to think about how close what Mags had just said came to her own love-life with Des. Was she too unadventurous? Des had never complained, never given any indication that what they did wasn't enough for him; but maybe, like Steve, he loved her and respected her too much to ask those kind of things of her. So, was he doing them with someone else? came unbidden to her mind, but she dismissed the thought firmly. They were still together, still happy as far as Dora knew, but Mags and Steve clearly weren't; she wanted to know their story so listened with interest as Mags continued.

Between bouts of love-making, we'd talk of the numerous times when we'd been in the car, he the driver, me the passenger, wondering what he thought of me; and now he told me. You've got something special and it's there for any red-blooded guy to see. You look like an angel, but there's a little devil in there too, peeping out and teasing us to come on in and find you; and when we do, she's there, sex in person, giving everything she promises and more, and enjoying it all so much it makes it twice as good.

Another time, he asked me, Do you remember your birthday, Angel, when you wore that gold number? So tight, it was almost like it was sprayed on, it showed nothing but it showed everything, if you know what I mean. Christ, I got hard as soon as you came out of the building, so then I had to drive like that and I couldn't keep my attention on the road, I don't know how I didn't kill us all. I imagined peeling it off you later, and then licking you all over where it'd been. If the boss had known the birthday present I wanted to give you that night he'd have fired me on the spot; I was surprised it didn't burst out the front of my trousers. Didn't you save it for me for later? I teased him. You bet, Angel, and he gave it to me there and then, and fortunately Teddy was away for the week, and Steve had to be understanding because it was his fault, really, that I was in no condition to entertain either of them for a few days.

Dora was surprised at herself that she was no longer reacting with shock to the more explicit parts of the story; I've become desensitised, I suppose, she told herself, I've heard so much of it that I've got used to it. She was pleased with herself; she'd found the sympathy which had been lacking when she first came to Mags, rediscovered a part of herself which had gone missing, gone AWOL, when it had no business doing so. What else might she not rediscover? She didn't think this overtly, but there was somehow a feeling of calm within her, even when she thought of her own recent worries; she knew they'd be solved, and for the better rather than the worse, hopefully.

But Mags was remembering, and must be listened to. We had a really close shave one time. It was a hot summer day, and Teddy was having a meeting at his own apartment; so Steve called me and came over. Unfortunately for us, his meeting over prematurely, Teddy had the same idea and in an unprecedented move decided to surprise me. As we lay in bed, he phoned Steve; I've finished early and decided to walk round to Bankside as the weather's so fine; you can collect us from there at around six. Major panic, because it wouldn't take Teddy more than ten minutes to walk here. Steve couldn't find his boxers so left them, speed-dressed in his trousers, shirt and shoes for some level of decency and left carrying the rest of his gear, to put on when he was clear. Via the stairs or the lift? It could be that Teddy, having decided on walking, would use the stairs; or the lift might seem the better option as he'd already had a walk. Then I remembered the service lift, used by housekeeping, deliveries and so forth; Teddy wouldn't use it, so that was Steve's escape route.

I, meanwhile, had time for very little more than a fast shower-off, leaving my hair to get minimal attention with a brush and a generous spritz of perfume. The bed had to remain rumpled, which is how Teddy found it, with me naked and towelling myself off next to it when he arrived. Showering at this time of day, darling? Well, it's so hot; I was lying on the bed with the fan on, thinking about you and getting even hotter, so I had to. I thought I was probably overdoing it as the words came out of my mouth, but I was hoping this would fulfil the dual purpose of getting Teddy in the mood (although he was there already or he wouldn't have been here at that time of day) and explaining any awkward damp patches he might find on the sheets. He was undressing by now, so he seemed to be accepting my explanation and even laughing at it; A shame you did, darling, you know I like you best when you're hot. It was only when I was on my back on the bed, with him buried in me, that I saw Steve's rogue boxers peeping out from under the quilt. So pulling Teddy's head in close with my right arm and moaning passionately, I grabbed the pants with the left and took them over the side and under the bed in one fluid motion.

162

We got away with it that day – just – but even in my out-of-love-with-Teddy frame of mind I felt my appalling behaviour towards him had reached a new low. What'd happened to my much-vaunted honesty? I became brazen in my attitude; serve him right if Steve had been there first, in both the body and the sheets. I even considered not showering if I'd been with Steve in the afternoon before Teddy came to claim his contracted rights in the evening. But he'd know, so I duly washed my lover off before my liege-lord repossessed my body.

One night-time, when Teddy was overseas on business and Steve was staying over, I woke to find him sitting up in bed, awake and looking thoughtful. A penny for them? I asked as I snuggled up against him. Oh, nothing, Angel, I don't know. I just woke up and thought, Where are we going? What's going to happen? I mean, I love you, you know that, but where do we go from here? I didn't want to think about that. Do we have to go anywhere? Can't we just go on as we are? He rumpled my hair, which was already very mussed-up from our earlier activities. You know we can't, Angel, even though you'd like to pretend we can do this indefinitely. We're going to get caught at some point, we've had a few close shaves already. I knew he was right, but I still didn't want to think about it. I thought I didn't love Teddy any more, but I couldn't imagine my life without him in it somewhere. So I persuaded Steve to forget it; Don't think about it now, It'll work itself out. And it did, but not as I would've wished.

She thought for a moment, then requested a visit to the bathroom followed by hot chocolate, which Dora supplied. When she'd drunk it, thoughtful and silent, she continued in a low voice. I'm not sure I should tell you the next part. I mean, I ought to get it out there, but it's bad; it's all bad, actually, but I feel particularly bad about this bit. The distress on her face was unbearable; Dora moved closer, into the chair right next to the bed, and took her hand. If it hurts you too much then don't tell; but if you want to, do. You can tell me anything.

She was surprised at herself, but pleased also; her sympathy had resurfaced and she really meant what she said. She could listen to anything, she was bigger than petty prejudices, especially for this girl, who hadn't stood a chance. She squeezed the girl's hand reassuringly, the hand which so far tonight had been still and calm, rather than fiddling obsessively with the pendant. She smiled, and received an uncertain smile in return before Mags looked downward as she spoke:

I wasn't totally surprised when Teddy arrived one day, mid-week, in the early afternoon. He didn't usually come around at that time of day, but it wasn't unknown, as Steve and I almost found to our cost on the occasion I've just told you about. I acted pleased to see him and waited to see what he'd got in mind; he appeared to be playing an aloof game. He didn't touch me in any way, didn't even kiss me, but again this was a not-unknown scenario. Come into the bedroom, darling, and get undressed for Daddy. I obliged, as he watched me intently, and I noticed that his eyes look different, odd, reddish; curious thing, had he been crying? Then, Sit on the bed, darling, in the middle. He put around my neck a jewelled collar, attached to a chain which was in turn attached to a hook on the wall where it was kept, and looked me up and down again.

Then he did something unusual; he turned on the TV. I watched this when I was alone in bed, but rarely if ever with Teddy; we watched all sorts on the TV in the lounge, but never in bed. There were porn channels on TV, of course, but we never really got into watching it; Teddy was a doer, rather than a viewer. But here he was, turning on and tethering his smartphone to it and bringing up something to watch; I wanted you to see this, I think you might find it interesting, as I did.

I didn't know what he'd got in mind, but I played

along; and then I went weak in my stomach and felt sick and wanted to run, but I couldn't go anywhere, naked and chained as I was. So I shut my eyes as all I was able to do so as not to see the big TV screen, showing myself and Steve, in this very bed, doing it as though we were never going to get the opportunity to do it again.

Open your eyes, darling, or I'll put them out for you; Teddy's words were horrifying, the more for being said in a rational and normal tone. It was as though he was asking me to perform some everyday task around the apartment; Turn the heating up, darling, or we'll freeze. I was frozen then, with terror, but somehow I obeyed; because I was sure he'd do what he said, he seemed perfectly capable of doing so. We'd seen it done, or a simulation of it anyway, in a production of *King Lear*, and I'd had to hide my face from that. Then Teddy took my head in one hand, with a vice-like grip on my hair, and held my face towards the screen, so that I couldn't help but watch.

To watch myself, with Steve, first on my back and then, after a break filled with touching and caressing and kissing, with me on top of him, and then him taking me from behind after another break. There was even a soundtrack, so I was forced to listen to Steve's grunts and words of love, and myself begging to be taken and gasping and crying out in ecstasy as I climaxed. I tried to let my eyes glaze over and go out of focus, but Teddy was onto that as well; every time I tried it he gave a sharp tug on my hair and commanded me to Watch, Bitch. I was forced to see the whole thing, for however long it took, in this very apartment and this very bed where I'd done so much that was similar with Teddy, who watched both the screen and my face, with a terrible calm which terrified me.

As the thing ended, he stroked a finger down one of my breasts; Was this sweet paper, this most goodly book made to write 'whore' upon? He continued, speaking to himself, as if in a trance; I had been happy if the general camp, Pioneers and all, had tasted her sweet body, so I had nothing known. Then he lost the calm tone and poetic Shakespearean language and addressed me prosaically; You fucking whoring little cunt. The voice was still silky smooth and controlled, if to breaking point, but his face had gone dark, as though the blood had stopped still in the veins there. On his forehead I could see them, knotted into a clump at either temple. The previously well-leashed violence was threatening to spill out, and his grip on my hair tightened.

Her hold on Dora's hand tightened at this point, as if remembering that grip; it was painful, but Dora said nothing. I was paralysed, petrified, Mags said in a low voice, I could only think of how the plot of *Othello* continues; Strangle her in her bed, even the bed she hath contaminated. Teddy knew this, being so cultured, so educated; he'd taken me to see *Othello* once and I knew it was a favourite of his. There was no need here for an Iago to provide any ocular proof, he had it already. But Desdemona was innocent, and I was guilty as charged; and my efficient memory, automatically searching on the theme of adultery, reminded me then of Teddy telling me in Naples once of a real woman, Maria d'Avalos, also guilty when her husband the aristocratic composer Gesualdo butchered her and her lover in bed together. And I don't know if she managed to fight back, but I do know that Desdemona did, and they both died, factually and fictionally; and I, as real and alive as my namesake Maria, thought that I too might as well go down fighting.

I found my defiance, and my voice, even though it was shaking with fear; Why are you complaining? You made me a whore, I've been that to you for always. He laughed bitterly; Not without my involvement, you bitch, and as I remember you came looking for it. You sold yourself to me and I own you, I control you; you fuck anyone else it's because I want you to. I'd never seen him like this; there'd been anger obvious in his facial expression on occasions, but held in, suppressed. Now he lost the little control he still commanded and just let rip. Shagging the bloody chauffeur, of all people, the hired help; which is what you are yourself of course, contract cunt. I pay for it, he gets it for nothing; how many times, you whore? How many times has he had you only hours before I have? In this bed? In these bloody sheets? Did you even shower in between us? Have me when you'd only just had him? Dirty, disgusting little slut.

Then he really let me have it; every foul piece of language he could think of came my way, there were even some foreign words I didn't understand in there. What he'd called me initially seemed tame by comparison, as did the abuse by the uncharming Prince, which arguably had been the beginning of the road which brought us here. Teddy had always possessed a great command of the tone and inflection of his voice; he could use the most vile language and make it sound poetic, fit for a royal garden-party; but when he was angry the words sounded as blunt and crude as they were supposed to.

He suddenly spun round, away from me, like he'd heard something behind him and was maybe expecting to see Steve there; he threw his fist backwards, prepared to take a swing at him. But of course Steve wasn't there, and Teddy spun round towards me again and swung at me instead. Hard across my face, I could hear the bones in his hand crunch as the initial pain set in, then more pain as I flew across the bed and connected, hard, with the wall. I tried to rise, shaking though I was, and got halfway, but he hit me again, from the other side; and this time my journey across the bed was arrested by the collar and chain around my neck, the collar cutting into my skin and forcing me to cry out again.

Through the pain and dizziness I was aware of him, standing over me and breathing heavily, but under control once more; Do you understand what it would do to my reputation with my associates if it was known that I can't control a bloody woman? How then can I control my business activities to any great degree? And it flashed through my mind and my pain then, bizarrely and irrelevantly, that Teddy had always told me it didn't matter what other people thought. But he continued; Not to mention them laughing behind my back at how bad in bed I must be if the woman I'm keeping is dropping her drawers for my driver.

He dragged my head up by the hair, forcing me to look at him, and his face was purple and ugly and like I'd never seen it before. You'll find your level, bitch, you'll end up giving blow jobs down at the docks. He pushed my face against his groin, where I felt his hardness and thought he was going to force himself into my mouth. But he knew from experience that I'd use my teeth without a second thought; he'd taught me too well, and I'd play-bitten him enough in the past, so he didn't risk that. He smashed the flat of his hand across my face again instead; No, that's too good for a cheap whore like you, you'll be taking it up the arse in back alleys. His hand went to his fly and, sensing what was coming, I began fighting him as much as the waves of dizziness and my weakened condition would allow.

But his strength was as if the muscle-power he'd always restrained was now let loose, and I'd no chance. He threw me face-down, held one hand over my mouth, and the other hovered over the backside he had loved to squeeze so much. He touched me lightly and I winced as I struggled, expecting the worst and tensing for the pain; but he withdrew his hand and I heard him breathing heavily. He spoke then, extreme restraint obvious in every syllable; I could break our contract, as you've done, through acts forbidden therein. But I've decided to claim whatever moral high-ground could ever exist in this sorry affair. You've

168

behaved like a common prostitute, and I give you notice to quit this apartment accordingly. In other words, get out, bitch, and don't be here when I return.

He let go of me then and ran his hands through his hair, with weariness apparent in every line of his body; then, savagely, How long, how long? He almost said it to himself, but I managed to get out a reply, albeit with difficulty through the pain in my jaw and the taste of blood in my mouth; Since you pimped me to that so-called fucking prince. I saw you, going in the front door with a blonde while I was being swept out the back like dirt. To hell with your moral high ground; Steve was there for me when you should've been.

I'd rarely spoken so bluntly to him, but whatever it cost me I wasn't going to have him put it all on me. He looked me directly in the face, and his had gone from purple to pale now, but there was no acknowledgement of his own faults. I hope you'll be happy with that pimp; he always had my cast-offs, but previously he had the good manners to wait until I'd finished with them. He'll be selling you before a year is out; when he does, remember I told you so.

Then, as though as an afterthought, and in an oddly everyday manner, he took out his phone and made a call; to Steve. His voice was strained, but controlled; Shine, collect me from Bankside, would you? Come up to the apartment when you get here. He hung up; Let's see what lover boy thinks of his damaged goods. I wondered momentarily what he'd got planned for when Steve arrived, but then I stopped caring and let the waves of shivering and dizziness take me; Let him attack me or kill me, I just didn't care any more. Then I lost sight of him because I blacked out.

I came to, and it can't have been that long afterwards, because I could hear movement in the next room. I realized I was still naked on the bed, freezing cold and trembling uncontrollably, and bleeding from where Teddy had hit me. I could still taste the blood in my mouth;

it seemed to be congealing now. I forced my eyes open and saw clothes torn and piled up on the bed next to me, and the picture on the wall that concealed my jewel safe had been moved aside. The safe was open, and presumably Teddy had removed the jewels in which he'd once smothered me, as he'd destroyed the clothes in which he'd likewise covered me.

I heard him moving, but didn't see him in the room, so I risked moving my aching body and clawed the bed quilt round me in a feeble attempt to get warm and protect myself somehow. As I did so I became aware of something around my neck, lighter than the heavy collar and chain, which had gone the way of the other jewels, presumably. I tried to look down, but it was too painful, so I put my hand up to feel whatever it was. I winced as I caught the welt on my neck caused by the collar cutting in, but I realised I was wearing the chain and pendant 'H' for Harlot which Teddy had required me to wear. It spoke his final pronouncement on me as clearly as he'd done himself.

Her hands were on the pendant now, and stayed there, still, as she continued. I heard voices in the next room then, but I was on the verge of unconsciousness and they were indistinct; but the raised one was Teddy, no mistaking that voice, and the other I thought was Steve, his rougher, East London accent. Then I heard the beeps of the security system at the front door, so someone must've been leaving; Please don't be Steve, please don't leave me alone with Teddy. But Teddy, apparently leaving, suddenly had an afterthought, and I could hear his words. Have you had her in the car? I didn't hear Steve say anything, but Teddy continued. Of course you have, stupid of me to even ask. In the back, I presume, where I sit; why not? Well, you can keep it; in lieu of severance pay. He sounded calmer, more controlled, and very business-like now. Mrs Markham will sort out the documentation, log book and so forth, and forward it to you. Then he switched back to vicious mode;

So take it, and that bitch, and get out. I missed what happened next, but heard his parting shot. He spoke more loudly, he must've hoped I was conscious and wanted me to hear. You know what you'll do when you've had enough of her over-used body? You'll sell it, as I did, for your own advantage. Don't fool yourself. Now get out; and I heard him leave.

And then he was gone, and Steve came running into the bedroom, dismayed at the state of me and holding me; No need to ask what happened here; Angel, Angel, are you hurt bad? Deep concern in his voice as he held me and inspected my broken face. Nothing life-threatening, it seemed, superficial wounds physically but psychological damage obvious from my continuous trembling, which I couldn't stop, hard though I tried. Steve rummaged through the pile of torn clothes and rescued some which weren't too bad. He clothed me in them as decently as was possible, then wrapped me in the quilt from the bed, bloodstained as it was, and carried me out to the lift; not the regular lift, but the service lift, I noticed briefly. Then, mercifully, I passed out again.

She stopped, trembling with the recollection of events, and the tears began to run down her face. Dora reached across her to the box of tissues on the bedside table and put it on the bed before her, but she didn't seem to see it; so Dora took out a couple and put them into her hand. They were taken, and used, then Mags leaned back and lay down, on her back and then turning onto her side; I've made such a mess of my life. She almost whispered it, and then was silent.

There was nothing Dora could say; it wasn't her place to offer judgement on her patient, or the people who'd been in her life, although privately she'd cheerfully have strangled Mr Edward du Cain. So instead she soothed the girl, stroking her hot forehead, shushing her, Go to sleep now. Almost obediently Mags obeyed, and soon the only sound in the room was the even sound of her sleeping breaths.

Dora sat and watched over her; she would have liked to go and get Laura, or Celia, but she didn't want to leave in case Mags awoke and found herself alone. She brooded on what she'd heard tonight; Why is it that women become so dependent on men? She knew the answer, of course, it was the way societies had been organised for centuries, from the beginning of time, maybe, and it wasn't changing fast. It was changing though, albeit slowly, of course; so many women now were independent, had careers and made their own life-choices and decisions.

She included herself in this, plus her mother Rose and her daughter Ruth; they were a strong breed in some ways, it seemed, but she knew this wasn't the whole picture. Yes, she had a career, courtesy of supportive parents with a broad outlook on life (and she thought of Mags with her narrow-minded parents), and could support herself financially if she had to. But emotionally? There'd never been anyone other than Des for her, and if she were to lose him, what then? She didn't want to even think about it.

Weak, weak, Dora told herself as she drove home. She'd sat with the sleeping Mags for some time, until Laura poked her head around the door at about 5am, bringing a cup of tea for Dora and sitting by the bed while the nurse took a much-needed trip to the bathroom. On her return, Dora brought the lecturer up to speed on the girl's story and her distressed state before she'd slept, and Laura shook her head. I do wish she wouldn't do it to herself, but I can't stop her; we need to find her something positive to wake up to. And, leaving Dora alone once again with her patient, she left the room and re-entered some moments later carrying the sleeping Katie. At her request, Dora carefully peeled back the quilt to one side of Mags, and the little girl was tucked-in next to the young woman. Through some instinct they cuddled up to each other in their sleep; and when she

172

awoke the expression on the mother's face was relaxed and more peaceful than before she'd slept. She cuddled the sleeping child but said little as Dora administered her medication as usual, although she smiled and bid the nurse goodbye quietly.

By the time she arrived home, Dora had resolved to be weak no longer and find the strength to confront Des; difficult, as he'd already left for work. Frustrated in her need for positive action, Dora found herself searching his things for any sign of deviation, sexual or otherwise, from his marriage vows. The pockets of his trousers, both on the top and inside of his wardrobe, his desk in the box-bedroom he used as a home office, even the garden shed; but nothing, no notes, no suspicious phone numbers or addresses, no pornographic magazines and no porn sites on his computer. She knew his password, he made no secret of it, he'd actually given it to her once when he'd been ill and needed her to keep an eye on his e-mail; he could have changed it after that time, if he'd been intent on secrecy, but he hadn't, and surely that was a good sign? But he could have another e-mail account, more than one, about which Dora knew nothing, and the thought tortured her. Stop it, she told herself, you're being ridiculous, this has to stop; so, having taken a shower and eaten a good breakfast, she took herself to bed, resolving to speak to Des as soon as possible.

As soon as possible came that evening, with him arriving home earlier than Dora would have expected and disarming her intention to be firm with gifts; a large bouquet of flowers and chocolates, a similarly large box. What did I do to deserve this? she asked him, while, What have you been doing to feel the need to bring me these? she thought privately. Can't I treat my wife sometimes? he asked, all innocence; You've seemed a bit down recently, it can't be easy, doing the work you do, spending all that time around dying people. Well, we're all dying, you know, Dora told him disapprovingly, it's just that some are doing it sooner rather than later. Whatever; Des put his arms around her and squeezed her from behind, kissing her neck and nuzzling her ear, and Dora kissed him in spite of herself and laughed at him; Get off me now, I need to put these in water.

So he let her go and took over preparation of dinner while she saw to the flowers, and put the chocolate box in the lounge for after dinner; and when Des had changed and freshened up they ate dinner and then sat in front of the TV, where Des helped Dora eat some of the sweets he'd bought her, before she had to get ready and go to work. She was torn as she drove away; the presents were the kind of thing he'd do, he'd done it before more than once over the years, and she loved the impulse that prompted him to make such gestures; but this time she couldn't help but suspect an ulterior motive. She put these thoughts aside as she parked on Laura's drive and prepared to listen to her patient's story, the better to forget her own.

12: COMMON III

I don't remember too much about leaving the apartment, Mags commenced, semi-reclining on the bed when Dora had tended to her physical needs. I do remember my time in the clinic, though, where Steve placed me until my physical injuries were healed; the mental damage was going to take a bit longer. A private clinic, known to him through contacts from his employment with Teddy, with no questions asked about how I got in the state that necessitated my admittance. Steve visited me frequently; no-one could've been more attentive. He even brought in what he'd received of my belongings; nothing that Teddy had given me, but some books, a few old clothes from my student days and other bits and pieces from my life pre-Teddy had been efficiently boxed by someone, and an e-mail message sent to Steve to come and collect them from Mrs Markham.

He'd also gone back to the apartment to make sure nothing had been forgotten, and he was right, because there were other things he felt I had a right to, so he took them and brought them to me. I thought he was brave to go anywhere near Teddy's property, but in the event they hadn't run into each other; Steve knew all the staff well, reception, maintenance, cleaning personnel and so forth, so it couldn't've been difficult for someone to give him access to the flat (which apparently had been deep-cleaned already and advertised for rental), and Teddy it seemed hadn't been back since the fatal afternoon.

Steve also brought me a laptop so that, having no clothes, I could buy some online and have them delivered. Not too many, but enough to get me out of hospital and started in my new life; which meant putting behind me the old one, with the memories of Teddy having any number of expensive new clothes sent to his apartment from a Knightsbridge store when we were first together, so I could choose what I wanted without considering the cost.

When I was judged well enough to leave the clinic, Steve collected me in his car; a more everyday affair than the Bentley which Teddy had passed to him; it might've had good memories for us, but there were also memories of Teddy which we didn't need. And of course it was far too big for Steve's business needs; he'd had hopes of running his own private chauffeur business, but he was fairly sure that Teddy, with his considerable clout in the business world, would put the word out and make it difficult for him to operate. He was working instead as a minicab driver, so at least we had an income to be going on with. What was left over from the proceeds of the Bentley, after he'd bought the new car and paid for the clinic and the clothes for me, was saved for a rainy day which we hoped would never come. We've got to be careful now, Angel, he told me, we've far less cash than we're used to and it'll take a little time to get on our feet.

He'd had to get out of the mews flat, over the garage where the Bentley had been kept, and of course owned by Teddy, so he'd been staying with a friend while he found us a place. The new home he took me to was very different from what I'd been used to with Teddy, but somewhat better than my student digs. A long way from Bankside and Borough Market in every sense, but not far from Bow, was our new home. A flat over a shop, a little small and cold maybe, but adequate for our needs and with an affordable rent. We'll get it cosy, Angel, it'll just take a little time, he told me, but in the meantime we can cuddle up in bed if it's cold; I'll keep you warm. He certainly did that; for the first time I was the exclusive partner of one man, no sharing, no threesomes, no going with whoever Teddy needed keeping sweet, or blackmailed, or whatever. Just Steve holding me and kissing me and making love to me; it felt good and was the best part of it all.

The flat needed a good clean, and I wasn't used to housework; Teddy's pampered baby had been given paid help to clean, shop and cook, to do the laundry and so forth. But I set to work willingly, when Steve was out in his cab, to do all those things and play house in the way that ordinary people did. I didn't do too badly, although my cooking left a lot to be desired; *You'll get the hang of it, Angel, but I think a takeaway may be the way to go tonight,* Steve told me on more than one occasion. So we spent cosy evenings curled up in front of the TV, eating pizza or Chinese or whatever and drinking, white wine, or red, or either of those for me and alcohol-free or softs for Steve, in case he got a call and a fare. The wine wasn't the champagne or vintage stuff I'd been used to with Teddy, but everything was changed now. And afterwards, when Steve didn't have a late fare of course, long leisurely sessions in bed keeping each other satisfied before sleeping, and waking to do it again.

She'd brightened up now, and Dora would have liked to think that her new life with Steve had turned things around for her, but apparently not, given what of she knew of the girl's recent life. Still, Mags seemed to be having happier memories, which was an improvement, even if temporary. One weekend, she told Dora, Steve came up with a way to have fun which was a world away from how I'd lived with Teddy. *We could just stay in bed, Angel, but it'd do you good to get out and see the real world,* he told me; *there's a funfair on down Epping way and I think we should go.* It sounded good, very different to what I'd been doing, so on Saturday afternoon we set out, wearing casual clothes, jeans, fleeces and so forth. We got the Tube, which was also fairly novel to me; Steve had to rescue me from a fate worse than death when I went ahead of him into a carriage to be greeted by drunken shouts of welcome from a bunch of football supporters who'd been getting tanked-up before the match. I don't think you'd like to be gang-banged between here and Epping, Angel, as he pulled me clear and steered me to another, quieter, carriage further down the train, but they're probably too drunk anyway.

The fair was so much fun; swingboats, dodgems, the big wheel, Steve took me on every ride possible. He got a bit stroppy when one guy running the ride got chatty with me, and rather handy as he secured me into my seat; but he took himself off fast when six-foot-six Steve made it clear I was taken. He won me a mystery prize on the coconut shie; he ought to have been a cricketer, those balls went exactly where he wanted them to. The prize, when unwrapped, turned out to be a hair-care kit; brush, comb, scissors, a pack of large hairpins and a hair-band. I threw it into my tote bag and ran over to the shooting range next, where Steve was keen to see if he could win anything more, but I was struck by the urge to have a go myself. We had a sexist exchange over it first (It's a bloke's thing, Angel), but the man running the stall took my side. Let the lady have a go, winking at me, and probably thinking I'd win nothing, so it was in his interests to encourage me. He showed me where to aim and how to shoot the rifle, and I imagined Teddy's face on the target; then it was easy. I won, a cuddly toy, a teddy-bear, of all things; it went into the tote bag and the spree carried on. I pigged out, cheeseburger, chips, pizza, Pepsi, candy floss, and then threw up in the bushes behind the booths and tents and guy ropes. Steve thought this funny, as he held my hair back and then fed me bottled water to clean out my mouth. Everyone does it sometime, Angel, and you've gone for it today.

We decided to find a pub; wine would take away the bad taste better than water, Steve said. So we found one, not too far off; I was busting for the loo, so I left Steve to get the drinks and headed for the Ladies. The door to the cubicle creaked as I pushed it open, and then I froze, as did the woman inside. She wasn't doing what I would've expected; this pub had the usual Drug Taking Will Not Be Tolerated signs, but that hadn't discouraged her. She'd lain down a line on the back of the cistern and was ready to snort.

I recovered first, smiled nervously, shook my head and gestured, I didn't see anything, really, and backed away. She stopped me with a gesture, Wait; she snorted, about half the line, then came up and gestured to me; You want? Why not? I thought, very sociable of her, and if she gets caught then I'm in trouble as well. Plus I didn't know how good or bad this stuff was. But what the hell, I thanked her and indulged, and soon the good feeling was racing through me.

I went back into the bar and located Steve. The place was busy, there was a good buzz and live music, and I felt good, what with the coke and all, and a few glasses of wine just increased the feeling of euphoria. We drank, laughed, tapped our feet to the music and even had a conversation with some other people, because the place being packed it was necessary to share tables and everyone was friends with everyone else.

We seemed to fly back on the Tube, I don't remember too much about it, apart from Steve's arm around me and laughing down the street all the way to our front door. Then it was Steve's turn to get to the loo fast, so I took out the contents of my tote bag; the little box with the hair-care kit he'd won for me, and the teddy-bear. Looking at the bear I suddenly got angry; I emptied out the contents of the hair-care kit on the bed, and found the scissors and hairpins. I stabbed the scissors into the teddy, viciously, several times, then I thrust in the pins, all over its body, and left them in. Then I started laughing, and couldn't stop, and I shoved the bear on top of the chest of drawers, overlooking the bed.

What's going on, Angel? Steve emerged from the bathroom and I couldn't explain to him, so I just reached out for him and started pulling his shirt off. He got the idea fast, and we ended up in a frantic tangle of shirts and jeans, and my panties got ripped off, and we just spent the night banging each other's brains out, with the teddy-bear watching us. I'd gone a bit insane, I think, with the fun and the coke and the drink and all of it. The next morning I felt remorseful, not to mention like shit after all that booze, and coke, and junk food. I saw the sad-looking teddy-bear, mutilated by me, and the tears came to my eyes. I took all the hairpins out of the unfortunate toy, then just sat and cuddled it and cried my eyes out, I didn't know why, while Steve was in the shower.

Her bright mood had darkened now, and, strangely, her hands had gone to her pendant and stayed there as she sat, silent and brooding on past events. Needing to stretch her legs, not to mention the bathroom, Dora asked if Mags would be alright alone for five minutes, and could she get her anything while she was gone? Cake and hot chocolate, perhaps? Yes, please; Mags would find that comforting; so Dora did what she needed to and provided them both with suitable refreshments. Mags took some time over hers, then put aside her plate and cup, wiped her mouth, and went back to her story.

It didn't get better after that trip to the fair; far worse, in fact. The crying over the teddy bear wasn't a one-off; my emotions were all over the place from that day onwards, and it wouldn't take much to set me off. Neither was the being sick at the fair a one-off, courtesy of all the junk I'd consumed; I started being sick regularly, in the mornings mainly, and it didn't take much to work out why.

She looked at the understanding in Dora's eyes and carried on. I wasn't happy to find out I was pregnant, not now; all those years with Teddy, what a difference a child would've made to us. He wouldn't've made me do those things if I'd been the mother of his child, I'm sure of it; and now, with Teddy gone and me with Steve, I couldn't be sure who was the father. And it was more complicated than just the two of them.

I didn't tell this before, she said then, quietly, but there was another possibility. There was a day, while Teddy was trying hard to get us back to where we'd been before all the bad stuff, and while I was seeing Steve behind his back. Well, Teddy had to go to a meeting with someone important, in the countryside North of London somewhere; he'd been going to travel by helicopter, but the weather was terrible, we were getting the tail-end of one of those storms from America, you know? Hurricane something-or-other it was, the wind speeds were really high and conditions for flight not good. Teddy was advised not to fly, and he listened; he was very sensible about not taking unnecessary risks, so Steve had to drive him there and, as it was an overnight thing, with a dinner and so forth, Steve had to stop over as well.

On top of this, I wasn't feeling very well; I was running a temperature, hot and flushed and feverish, and Teddy got the doctor in. He couldn't find anything obviously wrong, so presumed it was the beginnings of flu and recommended rest, lots of sleep and liquids, but he couldn't really give me any medication for it. Teddy wasn't happy to leave me like that, but the meeting was really important and he had to go, for which he apologised. When I'd been ill once before and he'd had to go away his PA, Imelda Markham, had come in to keep an eye on me; but this time she was going with Teddy, as he needed her there. So he arranged for his brother to come over and look after me. James never got ill, apparently, and neither did Teddy; they were incredibly healthy and fit, they both worked out at a gym regularly, and James played other sports, squash for one, I remember. So James didn't mind being exposed to my apparent 'flu because he probably wouldn't catch it.

He came over very soon after Teddy and Steve had left, and he couldn't've been more attentive. I was all tucked-up in bed and not feeling very sociable; so having

181

checked on me, James installed himself on the big, cosy bedroom armchair with a book, so he could keep an eye on me as closely as possible. I was soon asleep; and when I woke up, about six hours later as he told me, James was still there. The thing was, I felt so much better; thinking about it later, I swear my ailment was stress-related, because I was so confused about my respective relationships with Teddy and Steve. I loved Steve, I thought, and wanted to be with him, but although I thought I hated Teddy I couldn't imagine life without him. I was constantly in fear, but whether of Teddy finding out about Steve, or of losing Teddy I don't know; and they came to the same thing, really. Whatever, I was living on my nerves, losing weight and getting pale, and maybe I was having a little breakdown.

Anyway, I woke up and stretched and James was right there, How are you feeling, darling? What can I get you? And then, as now, I had hot chocolate and cake, Dora. I felt so much better, the shivering and shaking had gone and my temperature was down; maybe because Teddy and Steve were both away and I could relax at last, albeit temporarily. I was ravenously hungry, for the first time in weeks, I remember, I felt sweaty and I wanted to wash, but I had to convince James that I wasn't overdoing it. He felt my pulse, and my forehead for heat, and let me have a shower, with the en-suite door open just in case I was taken poorly again; and when I came out he'd made the bed up, put on clean sheets, and had something cooking in the kitchen, Only soup and bread I brought with me, darling, I don't want you overeating and bringing it all back; he was so sweet.

So we ate in the lounge, me all wrapped up in a big warm robe and on the sofa with a tray on my lap, with James next to me making sure I had all I needed and clearing up when I'd finished. We agreed it was best if I didn't go back to bed immediately after eating, that I ought to stay upright for a while; so James opened a bottle of red wine and gave himself a large glass and me a small one (Don't want you overdoing it, darling, see how you go with a small one first), and we cuddled up and watched an old movie, James's arm around me protectively. I felt so relaxed from the tension of my situation with Teddy and Steve, and so warm from the wine, and so cosy and at ease with James, undemanding, asking nothing of me but to care for and comfort me, even though we had a history. So I had some more wine, and laughed and cried at the film, and old romance with a happy-ever-after ending after some touch-and-go sad stuff; and then I felt sleepy, and started to loll drowsily against James, who looked at me and laughed and rumpled my hair, and Time for bed, I think, he said.

He picked me up, effortlessly, and I put my arms around his neck, the better to hold onto him as he carried me to the bedroom; and he held me with one arm then, and turned back the quilt with the other, and put me down on the bed. And I ought to've removed my arms from his neck and let go, but I didn't, because I didn't want to lose the warmth and comfort of his presence. His face was close to mine, and I looked into his eyes as he bent forward to kiss me goodnight, and I kissed him back, lingeringly, and, I don't want you to go, I said, Stay; and he did.

So you see, Dora, there was a third candidate for the role of father to my unborn child; but actually there were only two, because when my pregnancy was confirmed, Steve got really angry and we argued. It's not like you didn't know I was still sleeping with Teddy, I told him, but I'm positive it has to be yours; I'd been with Teddy for years and it never happened, and it wasn't for want of opportunity, our relationship was based on sex and it was a very fulfilled relationship. Oh yeah? Steve was aggressive like I'd never seen him before, Well I've got news for you, Angel; and his tone in pronouncing his name for me suggested that I was anything but.

183

It can't be mine, he told me flatly; I got married quite young, I was only about twenty-two. She was a practising Catholic, she said, and couldn't use birth control; I could, though, but she felt it was cheating. So we had two kids quite fast, two girls, and then for her sake I had a vasectomy. She was really happy I did that for her, and how did she repay me? He was bitter then; She ran out on me, went off with some other guy, took the kids and just went. I came home from work one day and they'd gone, vanished, she must've planned it very carefully.

I found out what I could, it took time 'cause they'd covered their tracks very carefully, but eventually I heard they'd moved up North somewhere. I could've made a fuss, tried to get visitation rights and so forth, I mean they were my kids, but she'd make trouble, as in, how could I have time for them when I was always working? And I thought, they're her daughters as well as mine, and if they're anything like her why would I want anything to do with them? Best let them go, and I did; if they come looking for me when they're older that's something else and I'll deal with it if and when. But for now, Angel, I'm not supporting some other bloke's kid, that's up to you.

So I did, Mags said, impersonally now, I had to, and I used men coldly and hardly, the way I'd meant to use Teddy when I first met him, to get him to support me; but now to support my child, as Celia'd done. She told you, didn't she, that we were both in the same profession? Dora nodded; And your baby? Katie; you've been wondering, haven't you, but been too polite to ask? Katie's my daughter, and James is probably her father, and even if by some miracle it's Teddy instead, they're both in prison and not currently available for DNA testing. And I won't be around for much longer to look after her, not that I've been very good at that; so Laura, dear Laura, has said she'll care for her and give her the best upbringing possible. And I know she will, she'll be a far better mother than I've been, but she's the wrong side of sixty now so even if she sees Katie into adulthood she won't necessarily be around for much longer after that.

I'm sorry, Dora; Mags looked tired, worn-out, and her eyes gleamed with unshed tears. I want her with me all the time, but then I think that's not fair, she'll miss me the more when I've gone. So then I leave her to Vivie, who's so good with her, to get her used to being without me; and then I can't bear it, and need her with me right then, you've seen me have Laura bring her in the middle of the night. I just don't know what's right; I love her so much, whoever her father is, and God knows I'm glad it's not Steve.

Our relationship went downhill fast, both before and after I'd had Katie, she went on then. Steve supported me, grudgingly, before she was born, because I was paying my way in bed, as he so charmingly put it; but of course, the more pregnant I got the less I did in that department. It caused some huge arguments, because Steve wanted me to, and I'd refuse because I felt it was putting the baby at risk; he'd have been happy if I'd had a miscarriage, the bastard. But I didn't, and she was born healthy, and I've never regretted having her.

But Steve was adamant; even though I was available to him again in bed now (and he made up for lost time) he said in no uncertain terms that I needed to be earning and contributing to household costs. Not easy, with a baby to care for, but I supposed I'd have to be like other modern women and get some childcare; because, despite living with Steve, I was effectively a single parent due to his attitude towards a child which wasn't his. I wished I'd had the luxury of being a stay-at-home parent so that I could totally care for and enjoy my baby. I've never understood why, when a couple have a baby, they choose to both go out to work and get childcare. Apart from the fact that they miss so much of their child growing-up, a large percentage of what they earn goes on paying someone else to look after the child; why not just look after it themselves? One parent ought to stay at home, it doesn't have to be the mother, the father could stay if that's what he'd like.

She shook her head and pondered the matter, then looked up with concern; I hope I'm not being tactless, Dora, you're a career-woman and maybe that's what you did, and you had every right to, just as millions of other women do; this is just my opinion, that's all. No, she wasn't offended, Dora reassured her patient; her situation had been different, she'd managed to fit her work around her babies, which was partly how she'd got into working night shifts. Plus she had a supportive husband in Des, not to mention his parents, and her own, who'd pitched in to help. It hadn't been easy, but between them they'd managed it, and Ruth and Matthew were a credit to them. Mags hadn't had such support; she wasn't to worry about it.

Mags looked relieved, and continued. I thought first of my degree qualification; admittedly it was tainted in having been paid for by Teddy, but I'd earned it, even if rather questionably, and perhaps now was the time to try to put it to the use for which it was intended. To do some honest work for a change in the cause of supporting myself and Katie and shutting-up Steve, who was currently bringing in all the money and was increasingly bad-tempered because his minicab work didn't seem to be increasing very much. So I set about searching for gainful employment, but the reality was somewhat different to what I'd hoped for.

To begin with, it wasn't a good time of year; it being summer, and the universities having just released their latest finalists into the workplace, there was a glut of graduates chasing every vacancy on the market. Additionally, I'd only managed a low 2:1 and, although it was With Honours (the only honour apparent in my life to date, ironically), it was far from the 1st which might have given me an edge with would-be employers. And as to the life-skills – being part of the uni rowing team, or voluntary on-campus work at the student union, for example – which were supposed to have broadened us out, made us more rounded individuals, what was I supposed to say? I never got involved in any of those things because my focus when not studying was fixed firmly on Teddy and everything pertaining to him. So, unless I wanted to list my vast portfolio of sexual skills (which might've gotten me an interview in certain places, I reflected ironically), I'd little to put down on that section of the application form. Filling these in became depressing, especially when, having despatched them, I often didn't get even a rejection letter, never mind an actual interview.

I had to do something, so pitched my sights lower. But having the degree worked against me here, because I was seen as over-qualified to work in a shop, or a factory, for example. Care work? Cleaning? But despite Steve insisting that I work, he had a curious kind of pride over these latter; No, Angel, I'm not having you getting your hands dirty cleaning up others' shit, in care homes or public toilets or whatever, for minimum wage, forget it. I protested; We need money, you said so yourself, and at least it's honest work. But all I got was, Angel, what do you know about that? You never earned an honest penny in your life. Which was hurtful, and untrue. I did work, as a waitress, and in the campus shop, in my first year and a half at uni; and in bars too, so what about bar work now? No, he didn't want me on show, with all kinds of guys potentially chatting me up. Not without him being in control, anyway, because what he said then left me in shock; You were du Cain's girl, high-end goods. It was well-known that he only had primo pussy and there are guys who'd pay well to spend some time with you.

I managed to speak then; What he'd said was offensive, even if it was true, and he couldn't possibly mean it seriously? Anyway, I wasn't the only one, I told him,

Teddy must've had lots of women, before me and possibly concurrently. I thought darkly of the blonde I saw him taking through the front door of Lord R's, while I was being hustled out the back. I'd been jealous, which is why I was in this situation, and I'd gone off the point, probing Steve to see if I could find out some of the things I never knew about Teddy; and I did.

More than you know, Angel, he told me. Of course he had women, loads of them whenever he wanted, but he never set any of them up in an apartment like he did you, never kept anyone as permanent and bought them jewellery and clothes and whatever like he did for you. Just saw them when he wanted and gave them a kiss-off payment when he'd had enough. He kept them around, of course, and paid them to service the capable guys, the ones he didn't send to you. You he only sent the impotent old bastards, keeping your pussy for himself and making you special that way too; and that makes you the next best thing and closest he's ever had to a wife. I just looked at him; why hadn't I known all this before?

I'd questioned Steve once about Teddy and the girl I'd seen him with. Steve drove him everywhere, he must have some idea whether Teddy had other women at the same time as he was keeping me. The Prince's party, I said; he had a blonde on his arm, I saw them as we left. No, Angel, that was Imelda Markham's daughter, Ursula. She drove du Cain that night, short notice, her mother got sick and I was driving you. But Mrs Markham's got deep black hair; such a blonde daughter? It doesn't necessarily follow, Angel, I don't know, maybe Imelda uses dye; but her husband's Scandinavian, so maybe Ursula gets it from him. A Scandinavian named Markham? Imelda uses her own name, Angel, I think they're separated. Ursula doesn't drink, I know, I took her out once. I guess the boss thought it might be fun for her to go to the party that night. But my focus had shifted again; You took her out? Yeah, only the once; bit of a stuck-up tight-arse, if you want to know, nothing doing with her so I never asked again.

I still wasn't convinced about Teddy having nothing going on with Ursula, because of something her mother said once; because I'd met Imelda, I think I told you earlier, Dora? There'd been a Saturday night when I spent a couple of hours at Teddy's place with one of his old men; I'd stopped objecting by then, it was easier to just get on and do what he wanted done, and fortunately none of them was capable of doing much more than stripping and stroking, or being stroked by me, with a cane or hairbrush or whatever. This one was no different, but it took ages for him to do what he needed to, which was taxing on my body and on my nerves. What if he managed more than I wanted? But he didn't, and I spent ages in the shower afterwards, with Lady Macbeth as usual, with the water too hot and then too cold and then too hot again, and after a restless night with very little sleep I felt exhausted, as well as very hot and feverish, on Sunday morning. I suppose it didn't help that I'd come down from the coke I'd taken before the old guy. I did that every time now; Teddy didn't have to give it to me, I knew where to find it and dosed myself up before going to work.

Anyway, I wasn't well, and Teddy was concerned, but then he got a phone call around lunchtime and went into overdrive; he was onto Imelda at once to arrange him a plane and accommodation; he had to go to Paris now because the old man had come through fast (You're wonderful, darling, I knew I could trust you, he told me) and the deal was happening. But when Imelda phoned back with his journey details he asked her to come over on Monday and check up on me. I'll be back on Tuesday, darling, but Imelda will keep an eye on you in the meantime. So when Steve came to take Teddy to the airport, he dropped me off at my place on the way. I felt better in my own space, spending the rest of the day vegging-out, watching old movies, reading, listening to music and getting junk food sent in.

I felt totally recovered on Monday, although I skipped the gym and stayed sluttishly late in bed. Housekeeping could just do it all tomorrow morning, for today I didn't care. Imelda phoned me at around eleven, and I told her I was fine now. Nevertheless, she insisted on coming round, as that was Teddy's express order, and what Teddy wants, Teddy gets. She arrived around twelve-thirty, bearing an array of fast foods for me; high-end supermarket-style, of course, I couldn't see her in Tesco somehow. Pasta salads, sandwiches, sushi and so forth, and cheesecakes, baked lemon and chilled chocolate, she'd even found one with coconut; she'd certainly done her homework on me.

Curious about her, I invited her to stay to lunch and help me eat some of it and, surprise, she agreed; equally curious about me, perhaps? I opened a bottle of white wine, as Steve was ferrying her between me and her office, and we sat and ate on the sofas. But then, of course, what to talk about was a bit of an issue. We managed on small talk, at which Teddy's various drinks parties had made us both experts, TV, sport, fashion, even a bit of news and the latest politics. Then we fell silent for a moment, and she looked at me seriously; What are you doing with Edward? She waved her hand, Don't answer that, I know, but why? I shrugged; Because I love him, I suppose. She snorted, in that way experienced adults do when confronted with naïve young people; You're not much older than my daughter, and I wouldn't let her near Edward if I could help it.

I went on the defensive then; Why do you work for him, if he's so bad? She shrugged. He pays well; and I have two children in university. My husband left us, he went back to Sweden and it's not easy getting money out of him. Then she checked herself, and the time, and said she should be getting back to the office; and we never really spoke again. And on Tuesday Teddy returned, bearing macarons from Laduré, and a little gold heart brooch studded with sapphires (Not as blue or as bright as your eyes, my Baby) and our life together continued much as it had before.

But looking back on this time, I still wasn't so sure about Teddy and Ursula; clearly Imelda hadn't been able to keep her daughter away from him, and Ursula it turned out was at university. Was she Teddy's new contract courtesan, potential or actual? Students are always short of money, as I knew from personal experience; it was why I'd gotten to where I was. Imelda had said she wasn't getting much if anything from her estranged husband, which must've put the financial pressure on Ursula even more. But I couldn't really know anything but that she'd been with Teddy that evening, and helped exacerbate the situation which nudged me into Steve's more-than-willing arms. Steve, who'd claimed to love me but now suggested selling me; appalling in itself, but additionally he wanted to use my past with Teddy to increase the price he could get for me. I was fighting him, obviously, but my past life was against me and it was a losing battle.

Because Steve wasn't like Teddy. He didn't have the calm control and subtle psychological coercion that Teddy exercised and which I'd come to feel somewhat terrified of and powerless against. Steve just made plain, straightforward statements, the upside of which being that I felt able to fight him, and the downside that I rarely if ever won the arguments. So when he now announced that I was going on the game, no argument, a battle royal quickly developed from my downright refusal. What's the difference from when you fucked other guys at du Cain's behest? He couldn't see it, obvious as it was, so I made it clear; I didn't, there was only James, his brother; the others weren't capable, as you well know. But he wasn't interested in the difference. Brother, Schmother, he laughed, they had a deal going down and you were the sweetener. I didn't care though, and told him so; Whatever I may've done before,

I'm not going to do it now.

Then he got nasty; Fussy, aren't you, for someone who was putting it out whenever and wherever du Cain told you to. The first time I had you you were coming from that impotent bastard of a prince who liked to strip you and shout at you but couldn't shag you. This enraged me; How the hell do you know that? You know far too damn much. But he just nodded and continued; It must've been really hard to go without for someone who likes cock as much as you do. Flashing your snatch at me when I was driving just to get a cheap thrill, giving me a stiffie I couldn't do anything about. I had to go and pick up a tart and pay to do her in the back, and you owe me for that. At that I laughed; I've paid you in kind many times over, and you didn't need a tart, you could've done yourself, like you used to do with those panties you ripped off me sometimes. You think I didn't know you'd take them away and use them to give yourself one off the wrist later? I matched him, coarseness for coarseness, bastard that he was.

And then he hit me. Not in the face, mustn't damage the appearance of the goods and lower their potential price, but he thumped me hard in the stomach, winding me and knocking me to the floor. But I didn't care by now, and taunted him, not caring how much I might injure myself in the process. You did a tart where you did me the first time? Yes, a whore in the back of a car's just about your level. No decent woman would touch you, you're nothing but a pimp! And you're no decent woman, he shot back. Don't think I don't know that way after I'd finished with her the boss and his brother were still taking turns banging you. A real classy piece, aren't you?

I was taken aback when he said that. He knew I'd been with James, but about that particular night? The threesome? I tried to use it in my favour anyway; Well if I'm really so lacking in class, maybe your guys won't be so keen to have me. And you're a prick-tease, he continued, taking no notice; I tell you, if I'd been taking you back from him that time you flashed me, rather than to him, I'd have driven you somewhere and fucked the living daylights out of you and to hell with the consequences. And you knew I would, so when you needed it bad you turned on the tears to Steve, good old Steve, he'll finish the job for me, so you turned those big eyes to looking at me and crying, Please have me, Steve, please finish me off; and I did! A slag who was dripping wet before I even touched her; it's a wonder your cunt's as tight as it is given the amount of cock that's been through it.

Dora, despite her new-found tolerance, was wincing at some of the language Mags was using, but the young woman didn't seem to notice and continued mechanically, her eyes glazed, looking back over time. His vicious verbal assault was cut short though, and here her eyes gleamed and she smiled almost viciously, because I'd got my breath and balance back and I flew at him, I lashed out with both hands, trying to scratch his face and get to his eyes, and I did manage to take him off guard and scratch his right cheek badly.

But he was so much bigger and stronger than I was, he easily grabbed my wrists and held them in one hand; and, although I kept on struggling, he had me down on the ground. Then he pushed my skirt up and ripped my panties away and shoved one hand up between my legs; and he nodded in a knowing way, contemptuous even, like he wasn't surprised. Then he was in me, far too easily and I was responding and enjoying it even as I hated him, none the less because I knew he was right. I hated him at that moment, but my body responded independently of my mind and betrayed me once more.

When it was over, he just lay on top of me, so I couldn't move, and looked at me appraisingly; You certainly know your stuff, Angel. The thing with old du Cain is, he prefers untouched arse, when he can get it, which isn't that often, in this day and age. It's easier for me, because I prefer a bird that knows her way around a bloke's body, and you sure do. Old Eddie broke you in beautifully and I'm going to reap the benefits, as are the other blokes I've got lined up for you. And you will put out for me, Angel, like you did for him, or you'll regret it. He said it menacingly, quietly, and then he left me. It was ludicrous that, given what was at stake for me, my first reaction to his words was resentment, on behalf of Teddy, that Steve could refer to him in such a disrespectful way. But when I got past that and took in the implications of what else he'd said, I was terrified; because he'd sounded just like Teddy had, at the end.

I curled up into a ball and carried on shaking; I was trembling and I couldn't stop. My teeth were chattering and my stomach hurt from where Steve had hit me; I ached all over just from the shock. I must have lain there for ages, and then Katie began to cry in the bedroom, which brought me to myself, because she needed me and I had to go to her. It was comforting, holding her and talking baby nonsense to her, and it helped me, soothed me as well as her. As I fed her I became calmer, and I thought about what Steve had said.

Was it so different? Why had I caved in and gone with other men at Teddy's behest, but was so unwilling for Steve? Because I'd loved Teddy, I concluded bitterly, and I thought I'd transferred my love to Steve; but I was having serious doubts now. He'd just caught me at a weak moment, when I was feeling insecure and vulnerable, and I'd fallen for his lines. Had he loved me, really? Or did he just want to get back at that snooty bitch (as he'd called me in another recent argument), take her down a peg or two? She won't be so high and mighty when she's selling it to all comers because I'll make her sorry if she doesn't.

Then I remembered my jumbled thoughts on the night I'd gotten together with Steve, *Dr Zhivago* and *Rigoletto* and all the other stuff. Maybe it was a set-up;

Teddy had already passed me round his victims, and they didn't want any more, so he passed me straight on to his employee, Steve, and I fell for it. Because how did the cameras remain enabled that time, when Steve and I were in bed together, to give Teddy such infallible proof of my cheating? Somehow it seemed to tie in with Steve knowing so much. Maybe he'd had a hand in arranging the cameras for the blackmail scenarios, as Teddy's trusted employee; because when things needed arranging for Teddy I felt sure Steve Shine wouldn't be above arranging them.

I'd also thought that Teddy had given Steve the Bentley because he couldn't bear to use it again, knowing what we'd been up to in it. But it was a generous thing to do, especially in the circumstances. It would've made better financial sense to sell it, and Teddy always had good financial sense. So maybe it was the agreed pay-off for Steve keeping his mouth shut about things he'd arranged, and for taking me off Teddy's hands? I remembered one of Teddy's parting shots then, that Steve always took his cast-offs but not usually until he'd finished with them. That could be true, because Teddy hadn't finished with me when I started with Steve.

Whatever the truth, I told myself bitterly, now you can forget Marjorie Majors, forget a slow descent through the ranks of the super-rich. You dropped caste along with your drawers, when you dropped them for the driver; we can't have you shagging the chauffeur, no, there'll be a red light, a warning light over you in the upper echelons. So you've gone direct from the master to the manservant and down a different career path. The pub over the cocktail party, cheap wine over champagne, smack over snow, and a gang of guys keen for a taste of what the boss was banging before. This kind of high-end merchandise isn't available here often, but now, for a short season, they can try the crumbs from the rich man's table at knock-down prices; and did he ever knock me down. But I was so tired with it all, and my thoughts were going round and round, so I settled Katie down in her little cot, then lay on the bed and just closed my eyes; I tried not to think, and at some point I must've fallen asleep.

I woke with a start to the sound of the door opening, and Steve was standing there, with a look on his face that I couldn't make out. When he saw I was awake he bent down and made as if to hold me. I winced instinctively away from his hands, but they touched my abdomen anyway and emphasised the pain from where he'd hit me. He backed off and put them to his head in what looked like despair; Oh Christ, Angel, I'm sorry, I'm so sorry, I don't know what comes over me. I just get so angry, it's frustrating not being able to give you all you deserve, but we need the money to live, especially with the baby now, and I'm just not getting the work. I love you, I want to look after you, but it's so hard not having the cash I need to do that.

Is that more comfortable? He was helping me to sit up, piling pillows behind me to support me whilst saying all this, and it did feel a bit better, so I nodded whilst biting my bottom lip. He went and made me a cup of coffee, with a couple of pain killers and a hot-pack to put on my stomach, then sat on the edge of the bed, all attention, while I took the pain killers and drank the coffee. Then he sat and just held me while I leant against him. It was like with Teddy all over again; I needed comfort after the pain, and the only person I had to provide the former was the one who'd put me through the latter. But I was too exhausted to argue any more, so I just went with the flow.

When I felt able to do things for myself, Steve ran me a hot bath, and I slowly washed myself while I soaked, then put on old leggings and fleece and socks, round-the-house gear which made me feel warmer, because I'd been feeling cold despite the bath. When he'd got me curled up on the sofa, with cushions and the quilt from our bed, and

Katie to feed, he went out to get a Chinese takeaway, which he re-heated in the microwave and served onto plates for us, going to get me more when I wanted it, so that I didn't have to move. He even took Katie and put her back in her cot for the night.

So we sat, comfortable with our meal and an old film on TV, like we did when we first moved in here, before Katie was born and money became quite such as issue, and lack of it seemed a fair price to pay for escaping from Teddy. And later, when we were all warm and sleepy from the food, Steve picked me up, all wrapped in the quilt, and carried me to bed, and I was like a rag doll in his arms. And I didn't resist him when he told me he loved me, and put his words into practice, very carefully, on my body. You're still my girl, Angel, I'll look after you, I promise.

The next morning I was a bit stiff, and sore around the stomach, but otherwise not too bad. Steve didn't seem to be around, but he'd left a note on the bedside table, saying he'd gone to the shops, presumably so I wouldn't think he'd run out on me. I got up slowly, fed and changed Katie, then showered quickly while she was dozing, put on comfy and casual old clothes again, left the bed unmade and draped myself over the old sofa. Steve appeared soon after, with Danish pastries which he warmed while he made coffee, then brought them to the sofa and ate breakfast with me.

Then he gave me the good news. He'd stormed off to the club after our row yesterday, and in the course of a conversation Harry the owner had offered to have me work behind the bar for a few nights each week. I was looking to get someone in, he told Steve, so why not your girl? Most of the members know her by now, and she knows them, and they know you won't put up with them trying it on with her, even if you're not here; what'd you say? Steve had said Yes, because, I couldn't wait to come back and ask you, Angel, and you did say you'd consider bar work. You can take the baby with you and put her in her pram in the room behind the bar, so you'll hear if she needs you. So I agreed, considering the alternative, and as soon as I was over my soreness I became a part-time barmaid for four nights each week.

The work wasn't too hard and the clients were friendly. Steve could sit and drink with the lads if he wasn't working, or even if he was. He was very good at just drinking softs, or alcohol-free, so if he got a call and a fare he could just up and go. If he wasn't back before closing one of the other guys would give me and Katie a lift home; there were other cabbies amongst them, and usually at least one or two were in. On the downside, I wasn't sure about having Katie in the back-room of a bar, but I let it go because she was far too young to know where she was. She was near me if she needed me, was what mattered, and Harry was very understanding if she did and I had to take time out to see to her.

Additionally, the money wasn't too great, but I did enjoy getting out of the flat and seeing other people. I'd always been a bit of a loner, but these days I didn't like to be alone too much. I tended to drift into thoughts of my life with Teddy, both good and bad, but both upset me equally and I didn't like to go there. So pulling pints, even for a low wage, was a far better alternative.

Unfortunately it didn't last, because Steve was still worrying about our income, or lack of it, and his old unwelcome suggestion once again raised its ugly head. He was far more subtle about it this time around, relatively-speaking, that is. He got in Millie, the cleaner from the bar, who'd had children of her own and was very reliable as a babysitter; she'd minded Katie a couple of times before. Then he took me to a pub where we weren't regulars and brought me a decent dinner, soft drinks only for me, of course, as I was still feeding Katie. He also offered me a treat before we went out; the magic white powder, which I hadn't used since I'd got together with Steve, but which I hadn't needed to get me through Ordeal by Teddy's Associates either.

I wouldn't have touched it if it'd been available when I was expecting Katie, I wouldn't have put my unborn child at risk, and that'd also been the case since she'd been born; I was still breast-feeding her, after all. So I refused, politely, although I was suspicious as to why Steve was offering it now; but I wasn't going to be the one who raised any difficult subjects. I ate and drank and chatted with Steve and tried to convince myself that this was just him being nice, even while I doubted it.

My doubts were confirmed when we got home; Steve didn't raise the subject until then, when Millie had gone and I'd seen to Katie and put her down for the night. Then he made love to me like he used to and launched his attack when I was fulfilled and sleepy and my guard was down. Look, Angel, I know I was tactless last time, but it makes sense. Only decent guys, Angel, I promise, and it won't be for long, just until I get fixed with something more permanent and then I'll support us all, even Katie, I promise. I didn't say anything, I didn't need the fight; I just let him say what he had to.

He'd really thought this out; The thing is, Angel, how about some of the guys from the club? They all know you now, they like you, and you know them, you have a chat and a laugh with them when you're serving and I know some of them are interested in more. It wouldn't be like having strangers. I told you before, it's well known that du Cain set you up in a way he never did any other woman, and for a long time, which makes a lot of the guys think you've got something special that the others didn't, and they'd pay well for a piece of you. And you wouldn't have to do it cold, I can get snow, I got it tonight, didn't I? You'd feel good, and it'd be temporary, I promise.

I fought him then; the idea was obscene, I was a nursing mother, did he seriously think I was going to take coke and go with other men and from them to my child? He could forget it. I thought he was going to get nasty again, but he restrained himself and it was obvious he was doing so. You can put her on the bottle, she's almost six months now, it won't hurt her, and we need the money. He went on and on in this vein, and I felt my eyes glaze over and my mind remove itself from the proceedings. I just felt tired, and numb, and for some reason I remembered once accusing Teddy of putting something in my drink; had Steve spiked my tonic water at the pub? I just wanted to sleep, and I thought that, in his own way, Steve could rival Teddy for trying to talk me round; for talking me round; because I gave in.

Dora considered all that Mags had said as she drove home, and told herself she was lucky; she might be having worries about Des, but he was a prince among men compared to those who'd been in that young woman's life. She hoped he'd still be at home when she arrived, because she wanted to tell him so, and how much she cared for him and loved him; but he'd already gone to work, leaving everything ready for Dora's breakfast in his usual considerate manner, and she had to be satisfied with that. I'll tell him this evening, she told herself, talk to him, put all these silly fears to rest; but she was unable to do so because, having showered and eaten and slept like the dead, she was awoken at around four o'clock by a surprise visitor; Matthew, their son.

He'd come over on an off-chance, because he had time before doing a late clinic duty tonight, and brought her tea and biscuits to have at her leisure in bed, he informed her, because he'd brought the makings of dinner with him and would cook it and eat it with her and Des before he and his mother went to their respective work. So they all three had a good evening, with a pasta dish cooked by Matthew and a de-luxe ice-cream he'd bought for sweet, which left no time for Dora to have her heart-to-heart with Des.

Tomorrow, she promised herself as she kissed him and hugged Matthew on her way out the door, tomorrow.

13: COMMON IV

And why did I give in to Steve? Mags continued that night, Why was I doing it at all? Because I felt so alone, I had no-one but Steve, far from ideal though he'd turned out to be, and because he did look after me. He constantly reassured me, as he called it; Listen, Angel, it won't be forever, it's temporary, I've got feelers out, I'll get more steady work soon and then we can rethink. And in the meantime I had a small group of regulars. I told myself it wasn't that different from when Teddy used to loan me out to his contacts, but I was lying to myself.

Teddy wanted something from those guys, a deal, their silence, and I was the bribe, the sweetener, the reward. Whereas Steve was doing a more direct deal, payment for a prostitute; he was no more and no less than a pimp. And the guys themselves were different from what I was used to; no old, impotent ex-public school types, but fully-capable, in the main, with their own reasons for using a working-girl.

I worked during what I called my night-time world, and when I wasn't working, I had my daytime world, the light in my life, Katie and her care. I loved spending my time with her, and managed to separate the two worlds in my mind whilst holding on to the fact that my work supported my baby. I remembered then how I'd pretended to use birth control with Teddy in the early days, and eventually got pregnant when I was least expecting it, and I didn't want that to happen again. I loved little Katie so much, but I didn't want another child, certainly not under these circumstances, and although I had to use condoms I wasn't going to take chances with them, their being notoriously unreliable. So I spoke to Steve, and he agreed with me, though not for love of me (If you're in the club you're out of the game, Angel); so he took me to a clinic where they fixed me up with the pill.

Similarly, he insisted on us both having the AIDS test; there'd been no need while I was with Teddy alone, I'd been with no-one else and Teddy had been checked and anyway had been fussy about who he'd been with before he met me. I remembered his wish for oral sex only on our fateful first night, he was taking no risks with a girl he'd only just met and knew nothing about. I realised that, if he'd been seeing anyone else while with me, he'd have insisted on them being tested also. His brother James he must have known was OK, or he wouldn't have shared me with him.

To my shame I realised that I'd put us both at risk through my affair with Steve, although Steve as it turned out was clear. And, if there was any grim humour to be had from the situation, I bet Teddy got tested so fast his feet wouldn't have touched the ground, for AIDS and STDs, after he found out about me and Steve; he probably had it done before he came and confronted me. But now Steve took charge, and once we'd both been checked he insisted on a rigid use of condoms by clients, no exceptions.

Harry's bar was a good showcase for me; I dressed to show myself to advantage, and when the word went round that I was available to serve more than drinks I was in business, in a small way at first but it slowly grew. As Steve had said, I did know the members, some better than others, so they didn't feel so much like strangers. Harry would've been happy to let me use his upstairs room, for a consideration, but I wasn't keen and neither was Steve. There was Katie to be looked after, and I wasn't having her in the room behind the bar whilst I was otherwise occupied upstairs; but paying someone to babysit her back at the flat would've eaten into the money I was earning for her support.

You'll have to work from home, Angel, was Steve's solution, but I wasn't keen on that either; I didn't want to use the place we called home for the kind of work I was doing. There was a small bed-sit for rent on the floor above us, one room with a kitchenette and bed plus a small bathroom, which I thought would be ideal. But Steve said No, it meant more money outgoing, more than paying a babysitter, and I'd have to work longer hours to pay for it; and reluctantly I had to agree with him.

We had a second bedroom, a box room really, but it was adequate for the purpose. I didn't like the bathroom having to be used by clients, but there was no way round it, I'd just have to clean it each day; I was developing definite OCD tendencies over this. But it wasn't like I was entertaining a lot of guys, and I gave up my bar work, because my old sense of caring what other people thought of me kicked in. It felt a bit weird, being on show at the bar with all the guys knowing what else I did, even though they were the ones doing it with me.

I felt more secure at home, more private somehow, which was bizarre given the profession I'd taken on. Common prostitute, it was called until recently, although I don't like that word. It doesn't roll off the tongue like whore, harlot and hooker; there's no poetry in prostitute, except for the alliteration I've just used. And of course it's what Teddy called me when he finished with me. He called me all the other things during the course of our relationship, certainly, but that was just a game, sexually-exciting stuff to heighten our enjoyment. But he never called me the P-word, until our awful ending, which I hate to remember.

There was also a potential problem in working from home, as in a conflict of interest when Steve got a fare and couldn't be there, to keep an eye on both Katie and myself. I put my foot down about that, though; I wasn't going to be alone in the flat with these guys, and little Katie wasn't going to be alone while I was with them. I needed Steve, on the other side of the door, just in case, and so did Katie; fortunately he saw the sense of this, and declined fares when I was working. I guess it wasn't too bad; I wasn't walking the streets, with all the dangers attendant on that. I was at home, and knew Steve was there for me, although my feelings were mixed over that. If anyone were to turn nasty he could be there fast; but on the other hand this was the man who claimed to love me, selling me to others and providing me with the means to get through.

Because I couldn't do this without some medicinal help, as it were, any more than I'd been able to when doing favours for Teddy's associates. Then, there'd been white powder, to give me confidence and a high to help me do what I'd got to. But now the colour was darker, brown, although the shade could vary, because we weren't as well-off as we would've liked, and it was cheaper. I could take it in the same way, and it made me feel good, although in a more relaxed and laid-back way than before. I could feel more removed from the proceedings, detached, as though I were watching from the sidelines rather than a participant; which was fine by me, plus it was also easier to sleep afterwards.

'H' is for Heroin also, I thought when Steve first gave it to me, looking at the gold pendant and chain which Teddy had given me, and left me wearing when he discarded me. That must've been the last time he touched me, and I'd started wearing it sometimes since then; all the time, after Steve started me on this line of work. I hadn't felt Teddy's reasons for giving it to me fair at the time, but now I felt it provided a link back to him, which I found comforting in a weird sort of way. And at this point she took hold of the pendant and kept her hands there through the rest of her narration.

I only worked nights, and not all night, so had plenty of time to sleep and do other things that needed doing around the flat. We shopped online, and a lot of what we bought was convenience food, because cooking went by the board. It wasn't a big issue, not as healthy as it might've been, but I'd never had any issues around weight and neither did Steve; and I could give Katie commercial baby-food from jars after she was weaned. We both worked, so it was only fair we both got stuck in and gave the flat a clean each week, and as it wasn't large it didn't take long. To be fair to Steve, he did want to get someone in to do it, but that may've been because he didn't want to have to get his hands dirty doing it himself.

But ultimately he had to, because I wasn't having anyone coming in and getting ideas about how we lived. I was getting paranoid about privacy in a way I'd never had with Teddy. The housekeeping staff managed to be mostly invisible as they did their work in the Thameside and Bankside apartments, and if you don't see people you don't worry about what they think. But this place was so small the only way to avoid them would be to go out, which was OK for Steve, but where would I go? I didn't go shopping, or meet friends; not that I had any, of course. I was still mainly a loner, through force of habit acquired during my only-childhood, with no school friends, and then setting myself apart from my peers at university to be there for Teddy; and I was getting to be more and more reclusive as time went on.

Anyway, where would I find friends, given my profession? I was happier indoors, taking care of Katie, spending every possible moment with her. I never went into the spare bedroom except to work, and Steve cleaned it, by unspoken arrangement because he seemed to understand my need in this. I couldn't avoid the bathroom, there being only the one, so my cleaning it when or if my visitors had used it became a ritual, an OCD-type thing. The pre- and post-bathroom were not the same place as the during-bathroom, and I managed to divide my thinking on it in a similar way to that I used when with my clients.

I remembered how I'd managed to divide body and mind with Teddy, as I let him use my body while my mind was with Steve. So now I was grateful to Teddy for teaching me to be a good hooker. I remembered something he'd once told me, about how the sex trade had worked in Ancient Greece, Pornai being prostitutes at the lowest end of the scale, paid by the act, while Hetairai, at the top of the scale, had exclusive and long-term relationships with one man, as their companions as well as their sexual partners. Many were educated also, such as Aspasia, the mistress of Pericles, the one-time ruler of Athens, who was devoted to her, apparently. You're Hetairai, darling, not Pornai, Teddy had told me then; well, I was Pornai, not Hetairai, now that I'd dropped caste.

My body gave the men I entertained what they'd paid for, and my mind travelled elsewhere. I had to remember occasionally to say something that'd please them; but I used to do that with Teddy, too, post-prince. The sheets weren't satin, and the men weren't billionaires, or millionaires, but it was the same thing, just with less money. I remembered thinking of Steve when I was with Teddy; but now, as I looked at the ceiling, or the wall, I thought of Teddy, who'd introduced me to sex, and how I funded my degree through that; it helped, because now I was supporting my child through it, as Celia had done, but with more men than just one. One; Teddy; he came back to me far too often these days.

She paused here, and seemed to think for a few moments; but then her chin fell down to her chest, and Dora realised that she'd fallen asleep. Moving softly, for fear of waking the girl, Dora moved to the bed and carefully arranged the pillows behind her patient to provide maximum support; then she sat and thought about what she'd heard, deciding that her own life had been sheltered and protected and wonderful, compared to this girl's, despite the material luxury in which she'd lived for some years. As she sat musing she thought she heard a noise in the passage outside, and moved to the door to open it quietly, holding a finger to her lips to prevent whoever was passing from coming in and waking Mags. It was Laura, who came in and deputised whilst Dora visited the bathroom and then made coffee for the nurse before returning to her own bedroom.

Mags awakened after about half an hour, yawned and stretched and then continued her narrative as though she hadn't taken the time out: So there were some brighter moments, and some not-so-bright and, as I said, the work might've been worse. But the regular supply of heroin provided by Steve took the edge off any bad feelings I had and helped me cope, most of the time. But I was looking to the time when Steve got regular work and I could stop. Stop the work, not the stuff, that is; it helped me to block out unpleasant thoughts which I was worried would return without the drug-induced haze.

Eventually, and ironically, I got half my wish; Steve got work, but I didn't stop mine. He'd got another driving job, not in a minicab but for a private individual; taking him around, or taking others around for him, whatever the boss specified. The boss, I suspected, was a drug dealer; a shady character who I'd seen when we used to go to the club, always with lots of people around him. Not a minor dealer, but their line manager, so to speak, dishing out fresh supplies of gear or whatever to the guys who worked for him and collecting their take. Beggars can't be choosers, I thought, when Steve told me, but the downside which affected me more was the fact that there was a lot of night work involved; so Steve said he wouldn't be able to be around as my security.

I was alarmed; I can stop now, can't I, now that you've got work? But he wouldn't let me. Angel, you've built up a good steady regular client base, it'd be a shame to lose it. My work's not guaranteed, if the boss gets nicked I'm on the street again. Besides, your little habit costs enough. But my main concern was security; he wouldn't be there to look after Katie, and me. No problem, Angel, he told me, I've got someone else to fill in.

Someone else turned out to be Rocky, one of my regulars who I frankly found a little bit frightening, to say the least. So far he'd been one of the lowlights of my working week. He had a massive chest and seemed almost as wide as he was tall, and he wasn't that tall, shorter than Steve and even than Teddy, I would've said. He wasn't fat, however, but pure muscle and bone; built like a brick wall. He had curly black hair on his head, greying only slightly, and a huge amount of body hair, going grey on his back. He reminded me of a silver-back gorilla, and my secret nickname for him was King Kong, not the least because I felt tiny and threatened in his huge paws.

On his first visit he hurt me, not intentionally but out of thoughtlessness, as it happened. He put his full weight onto me, almost crushing me; he had absolutely no finesse about him. As I'm only five feet one inch tall with my weight in proportion (Teddy used to describe me as a 'pocket Venus, curvy in all the right places') and used to more consideration, I cried out in pain.

To give him credit, Steve was through the door in almost nothing flat; What the hell's going on? We got it sorted out, Rocky was apologetic and more considerate from then on, although he remained mechanical and detached. This wasn't unusual in the guys who came to me, they were paying and didn't have to be nice. Rocky thawed out a little as time went on, though; he even called me Doll, making the proceedings a little less impersonal. He went so far as to explain his cold manner to some extent, if rather crudely and briefly; he was a man of few words. He'd had a wife, apparently, but she'd done the dirty on him. It would take a battalion of Grenadier Guards to get me married again, Doll, was how he put it; so now he hated women in general and used sex as revenge. They're all the same, he'd say, basically they've all got hair round them, Doll, nothing personal intended. Charming; but was he actually any worse than Teddy, who called me every name under the sun at the end? Just because Teddy had money and education didn't mean his attitudes were any more enlightened than those of the largely uneducated Rocky, I think.

So Steve worked longer and longer hours, and it got so that I rarely saw him, while Rocky sat in the flat as my minder while I was working, and made endless calls on his mobile, apparently related to whatever he did by way of work. He also kept an eye on Katie, if she woke, which she didn't do often; it was as if she knew it'd be a bad idea. But when she did, Rocky was curiously gentle with her; I'd had misgivings, but he disproved them completely the first time I came out to visit the bathroom between clients and found her cuddled in his huge hands while he soothed her back to sleep.

I warmed to him then; any man who was so good with children couldn't be too bad, I felt, and I tried to treat him better than the others, out of gratitude. Because when I was through for the night, he'd see whoever off the premises and take his payment, in kind; after which he'd take himself off, with a Night, Doll. But one night, when Steve was going to be away till morning, he stayed while I showered, then put his arm around me and came with me into the main bedroom. He stayed all night, and I let him. I missed being held, for myself, with some affection, rather than for what I was selling; and even Rocky's rather undemonstrative embrace was better than nothing.

I was touched that he seemed to care a little. His stop-overs got to be a habit, and I even felt that Steve wouldn't much care if he knew. I was fed and clothed, as was Katie, the household bills were paid, and Steve would provide me with the much-needed medication to take the hardest edge off my working nights. He met up with Rocky on a regular basis, in the bar I presumed, for each to update the other on whatever they might need to know. In this way we fell into a routine, or sorts, between the three of us; not exactly cosy domesticity, but it filled a need for some sort of security, I suppose.

But one evening, when Steve had been gone for over twenty-four hours, Rocky didn't show up. I had to take the guy who had an appointment on trust, but he was a long-standing regular so it wasn't a problem in the event, and I managed to keep my fears about Katie being unattended to myself. When he'd gone and I'd checked on Katie (who'd stayed obligingly asleep), cleaned up, and was showered and changed, there was still no Rocky. So I took a glass of wine, and a snort, put on some background TV, then enjoyed just lazing on the sofa with the bedroom door open so that I could hear Katie should she wake. I dozed off, and then, it must have been much later, I was awoken abruptly by the door opening and the lights going on, and Rocky was there telling me that Steve was dead.

I think I'm ready … Mags broke off from her tale, stretched herself, yawned and indicted her need; and Dora realised with a start that there was light coming in around the edges of the blinds. Going to draw them back, she realised the sun was well-above the horizon now, meaning it was time to administer medication and see to her patient's other needs; a reference to her watch confirmed this. The time had flown by, she realised, and she'd been so absorbed in what she was hearing that she'd been unaware.

When she arrived home, Des had gone to work, as usual, so there was no time to affirm her love for him and speak of her worries. She looked at the neatly-made bed, the breakfast things left out for her and thought, was this not an affirmation of his love? Or was it just a habit he'd got into? He'd always done this for her, so there must be at least an element of habit in it by now, but then he didn't have to do it. Love, habit, or both? Dora couldn't think straight; she was more than usually tired, although she wouldn't have missed the story Mags was telling, night by night. She gave up on thought, freshened up, ate a fast breakfast and then went to bed, where she fell asleep almost as soon as she'd pulled the quilt over her head.

14: BREAKING AWAY II

That evening, Mags picked up the story where she'd left off, as though she hadn't spoken or moved since Dora had left her in the morning: I couldn't take it in at first, I could hardly wake up properly, but Rocky was getting me a shot of brandy from the bottle Steve kept for himself because I couldn't stand the stuff. Drink this, Doll, for the shock, just knock it back, it'll help. And I suppose it did, it woke me up and deadened the shock also; because it was a shock, even if I'd long since fallen out of love with Steve, and he with me, if we'd ever been in it.

On the M25 it was, a lorry-driver fell asleep at the wheel and crashed through the central reservation as Steve was passing in the outside lane of the opposite carriageway. He didn't stand a chance, but at least it was quick, apparently. I just felt numb, and allowed Rocky to put me to bed, with a sleeping tablet for good measure. He had the good taste not to join me tonight, but sat up in the living room with the TV on low, and I knew he'd be there for Katie should she need him.

I still didn't sleep for a while, though; my pre- and post-client snorts must still have been having some effect. At one point I thought, Did Teddy have something to do with this? Have Steve killed for revenge? And was I to be next? But as the sleeping pill gradually took over, and calmed me down, I became more rational. Even Teddy couldn't set up a supposed accident like the one that had claimed Steve's life. Arrange for a lorry to crash across into the other lane at the precise moment when Steve was passing? A suicide lorry driver? Because he'd also been killed, apparently, and some other motorists, unlucky like Steve. I was just being ridiculous, I decided, before I lost consciousness and awoke well past mid-day.

I wasn't asked to the funeral; apparently Steve had parents living, somewhere in Essex, plus a brother and a sister, and the funeral took place there. I don't know what they knew about me, and our relationship, if they knew anything at all. But if they did it must have been negative, because Rocky, who was looking after me and sorting things out, intimated that I wouldn't be welcome. I didn't really care; Steve hadn't exactly taken me home to meet the family, and I didn't need to start with that now. What'd be the point?

He was gone, it was over, and our relationship had been well past its best. He'd hardly ever been at the flat in later days, he'd turn up during the night at times, and Rocky clearly knew he'd be coming back because he wouldn't stay those nights. So Steve would arrive in the early hours, and I'd hear him making a drink, a snack or whatever, using the bathroom, coming into the bedroom and undressing. Then he'd get into bed and instigate sex, not love-making any more, those days were long gone. This was the pimp exercising his right over his prostitute, doing with her what everyone else was doing with her, but not having to pay for it. I missed the Steve I'd known when we first started, he'd been there when I needed someone, and we'd had some good times, but those were long over, and I didn't miss the later version.

While the fact of Steve being gone was still sinking in, there was the more immediate question of what I'd do now. I could stay in the flat, and continue earning my living as I'd been doing, but as without Steve's income I could only just about afford the rent, never mind paying the bills and eating, I'd have to work more; and I wasn't keen on doing that. Rocky solved my problem with a speech which was massive, compared to his usual laconic manner. Come and stay with me, Doll, till you work out what you want to do. It's my own place and you don't look like you cost a lot to feed, neither does the little one. You can do the housework for me if you want to contribute, save me the cost of a cleaner. Oh, and you can come off the game or stay on, up to you, but if it's stay I need to know so we can work something out.

He paused for breath, presumably because so many words in one go had tired him; but they pleased me immensely. Some cleaning for my keep, and my baby's, and no men to entertain, just Rocky. If he'd been Teddy I'd have thrown my arms around him and thanked him as physically as possible, there and then. But he wasn't, and he didn't expect such displays from me. So I just took his hand and squeezed it, and he squeezed mine back. Thanks, Rocky, I'd like that very much, because I haven't got a clue where I go from here.

So he left me to sort out my stuff and pack it up, such as it was, saying he'd be back in a few hours to collect me. It wouldn't even take that long, I thought; Katie and her things, my clothes, a few books, some bits and pieces I'd picked up along the way with Steve, including the teddy bear I'd won at the fair. I'd hung on to this, despite my initial mistreatment of it; I used to take it to bed with me, when neither Steve nor Rocky was with me, obviously, and it'd soaked up my tears on more than one occasion. Katie liked it too, she'd waved her little arms, gurgled and chuckled the first time she'd seen it, so I'd given it to her and it lived in her cot, except when I took it, which was when she was asleep; when she awoke she'd cry for it back. So now it went into the tote bag it'd arrived in, and when Rocky returned it went with us to his place.

I'd very little money; whatever Steve had on him when he died had presumably gone to his parents, and there was nothing in the flat apart from what was in the housekeeping jar and what I'd found in the pockets of his jackets and trousers in the wardrobe when I'd gathered his things together to be delivered to his family via Rocky. So

I'd have to come up with a way to earn something, because being without much felt precarious to say the least, and even though Rocky was being hospitable at present, I was rather at his mercy and didn't like being that way. I wasn't going back on the game, though, of that I was certain.

Rocky's flat was a bit further out of town, in a dedicated apartment block, and in better condition than the run-down over-a-shop place I'd shared with Steve. It had two bedrooms, but by unspoken agreement I shared with Rocky and settled Katie in the other. Rocky wasn't always there, he appeared to have a lot of business to do out and about in town, and when he was home he was constantly on his mobile. Our relationship contained more regular sex than it had before, and it couldn't be called love-making to any extent. I was providing a service, and paying rent in so doing; but we had a relationship, of sorts.

In his honest if unintentionally tactless way, Rocky said he preferred working girls because They're more honest, relatively speaking, there's no pretence of love, or caring, Doll, no lies, they're doing it for the money so you pay them and that's it. He was right, so I didn't have to pretend to enjoy it if I didn't, and he told me so. But I did enjoy it, sometimes, and I told him when I did, which seemed to please him. It could be exhausting, but at least I was a one-man woman again, even if only temporarily; because I'd learned by now to be wary of what life was going to hand out.

So there I was, fed and housed along with my baby daughter, but I knew we couldn't stay this way indefinitely; for once in my life I had to make a practical decision, rather than depending on the whims of so-called love. I remembered the last time I'd felt in charge of my own life, when I'd decided to go to university in the face of forceful opposition from my parents. Entering into a relationship with Teddy didn't count, I told myself, because I'd fallen in love with him and it wasn't difficult to decide to throw in my lot with him. Now, however, there'd be no man, no so-called lover to depend on; it was entirely down to me whether Katie and I lived or died.

I felt suffocated in Rocky's flat then, and thought back through the events of my life that'd brought me there, man-dependent creature that I'd become. Things were different now, though; I had a child to think of, totally dependent on me. I needed to get back to the independent young woman who'd got herself to university and feed on her energy. I'd never considered myself impulsive, but now it occurred to me that I ought to go back, physically, to the university, or at least the city in which it was situated and where I'd left my get-up-and-go self. I'd do it, I decided.

I'd gotten to know Rocky's mother, who came round regularly to check on her son (as if he was still a young child), and she adored Katie; she'd look after her for me for a couple of days, no question, she'd have happily brought her up entirely, had it come to that. I had more money now, Rocky giving me cash to buy household necessities, not to mention whatever Katie needed; like his mother, he had grown attached to her and wouldn't see her go without in any way. So I had enough, I decided, to pay for a coach ticket (that being cheaper than the train) and a low-budget hotel for the night. What else I'd do when I got there I didn't know, I just knew that I needed to go back to the place from where I'd followed my current life-path and take stock.

So arrangements were made, and a couple of days later I was on the coach heading back in space, and in time also, in an odd way. It felt strange, being out on my own, making this journey alone on a bus with a variety of strangers, without Teddy or Steve or even Rocky calling the shots; but it also felt good, which I hadn't expected. Just me, myself and I, even if we didn't know what the upshot of this trip would be. But I was making it, for better or worse, and just hoped it'd be the former rather than the latter.

Arriving in my old university city felt strange too, as I walked from the bus station to the hotel I'd booked for the night. A trip back in time, and I noticed the changes which had occurred since I'd left what seemed like an age ago. Some old shops and bars had gone, and new ones had sprung up in their place, although my memory was hazy about some of them. I hadn't ventured into town too much, in the early days, having so much to discover on campus first; but I'd started to go there sometimes, when I felt settled in my new student lifestyle, and I'd been getting to know the town. But then I'd met Teddy on that fateful night and stopped having a life here, apart from my studies and living in the shared student house when I wasn't with him.

It was just after two in the afternoon when I checked-in to the hotel, and I didn't spend long there; just enough time to deposit my overnight bag and use the bathroom, after which I took myself up the hill to the campus. I could have taken a bus, but the weather was dry, not too cool, and I needed the exercise, after sitting all the way from London. It turned out to be the best choice too, because I didn't see any buses passing me as I made my way further back in time. I stopped at the corner of the road where the house I'd shared with other students was located and walked down to take a look at it; I remembered when Teddy had dropped me off on Sundays and I'd walked down the road, to avoid my housemates seeing him. I remembered Steve picking me up outside the house and being taken for my boyfriend by them. The house looked pretty much as it had back then, maybe a bit scruffier, in need of some paint and repointing around the brickwork; landlords don't tend to do much to student lets, why bother for a bunch of transients? I left, and continued up the hill to the campus.

Once there, I walked round, blending into the crowd of students and lecturers and other staff milling around the place, going to and from their work or leisure activities. I'd half expected to see a few faces I knew, but that didn't happen; the place was a small town in itself, with thousands of people having business there in one way or another. I recalled an old saying I'd heard somewhere about seeing everyone you'd ever known if you sat in Piccadilly Circus for long enough; the same might apply here, to university-connected people anyway, but I only had a few hours and wasn't sure I wanted to meet anyone anyway. What'd they say to me, and I to them? Hi Mags, fancy meeting you back here; how are you, what've you been doing since the old days? Oh hi, good to meet you too; not a great deal, haven't used my degree really, been on the Game, actually .... No, I didn't think so.

So why had I come here now? Back then, I'd come here as a would-be independent young woman, but lost focus and become totally dependent instead on a man. How had that happened, and why? I needed to work backwards to the point of loss, and the answer wasn't long in coming; money, or the lack thereof. I remembered the bar and shop jobs I'd found to try to make ends meet; they'd been on campus, giving me less time to go into town, I recalled. It'd made sense, since I was so short of cash, to not spend it needlessly on bus fare; and, as the shared house where I lived by then was closer to the campus than the town I could walk to both my work and my studies. I recalled the fruitless trip to see Laura, try to get an extension to my essay deadline and relieve some of the tension between working for money and studying for my degree. But she'd been unable to help me, on the grounds that every other student was in the same boat as I was; and looking around me now I couldn't imagine that things had changed that much.

I felt depressed then; revisiting my youth on the campus wasn't producing any answers, and the whole visit seemed like a mad idea and a waste of money. Money; there it was again, beating like a hammer against the inside of my brain now as it had back then. I needed to find employment, some way to earn enough to feed, clothe and house Katie, and give her a halfway-decent upbringing. I remembered the answer I'd found back then; Teddy and his contract. But I didn't want to think about him, or the fiasco of our failed relationship, and I looked around desperately to distract myself. There was a bus just pulling up in the road opposite, headed for town, and I ran over to get aboard, seating myself near the back and looking without seeing at the houses and gardens we passed on the journey.

Back in town, what was I to do? It was only between five and six o'clock, and I didn't fancy an evening sitting in the hotel room. It was too early for a drink, but not for coffee, so I took myself to the outside area of the local branch of a national coffee-and-cake chain and gave my order to a waitress who was obviously a student; things don't change, I told myself once again. The weather had improved, a late-afternoon sun was doing its best to make up for the overcast day which was almost over, so it was pleasant sitting there. I'd passed such a solitary and indoor existence, in the main, that it felt good now to be outdoors, part of a crowd of people, all anonymous individuals but making up a society in our collectivity.

I hadn't forgotten the need to find an answer to my problems, but felt I could afford to let my thoughts wander for a short time and enjoy the moment; which was how I was, watching the world go by, when the voice and conversation which hadn't happened on campus interrupted me. Mags? Is that you? What are you doing back here? Or did you never leave? I didn't immediately recognise the voice, but looking up I recognised the face, and the voice slotted into place with it; Liz Needham.

After all this time; Liz, the agent of my meeting with Teddy, albeit indirectly. She of the wordly-wise attitude, the all-knowing one who'd explained to me the pros and cons of working as a hostess at the stag dinner. She saw the surprise and recognition on my face and indicated a chair at my table; May I? I nodded, too surprised to know what to say. I'd come in search of the past, but hadn't expected to find this particular part of it; the watershed moment, when I'd gone from impoverished student trying to find work to pay my way to contracted mistress of a very rich man, pampered and indulged and deeply in love with him.

For a few moments we just looked at each other; she must be in her mid-twenties, I recollected, only slightly older than me, and she didn't look bad. She hadn't changed much in the face, which I still recognised; a few lines around the mouth perhaps, but the differences in the main lay elsewhere, and from what I could see she must be prospering. Her hair was no longer the dirty-blonde bob I remembered, but a sleek cap of expertly-cut and highlighted red and blonde and black. She was wearing too much make-up, I thought, yet it was well-applied, and her fingernails obviously benefited from the not-infrequent attentions of a manicurist. The clothes were expensive too, as were the matching handbag and shoes, classic and elegant styles if in rather too bright and brash colours to be considered the epitome of good taste, and the look was completed with expensive-looking costume jewellery which once again wasn't quite the thing, being large enough in size to qualify as vulgar.

I didn't even think these things consciously, as I appraised her; in my life with Teddy I'd been dressed in, and by, the best names in fashion and design, and I'd absorbed the code of how to look expensive and yet tasteful which came to those who could afford such things. Which level, I reminded myself now, as I realised what I'd been doing, I'd fallen far below; and the result was what Liz was now seeing. A mid-twenties woman, with striking white-blonde hair still as her best feature, but changed in other ways. I'd gained a few wrinkles, I knew; the drink and drugs I'd been taking to get me through my questionable career-path had taken a toll there, and the experiences through which I'd passed had left me with a world-weariness which showed in my facial expression, I was sure. My body was outwardly still slim, and it didn't take much for me to keep it that way, but when undressed I had the usual unmistakeable marks which childbirth leaves on most women, albeit lightly in my case, barely noticeable and nothing like as bad as some. I couldn't aspire any longer to the clothing and jewellery with which Teddy had showered me; chain-store I wore now, and well-worn at that. Such jewellery as I had was costume stuff like that Liz wore, but unlike in that it was much cheaper and looked it, I feared.

I cheered myself with the remembrance that Liz had never seen me in my heyday, so the clothes weren't that much different from the inexpensive stuff I'd worn as a struggling student, and that the facial changes were similar to those she displayed. I realised that something needed to be said, but couldn't think of what to say, so I smiled and left it to her to begin, which she did once she'd finished appraising me as I'd done her. Good to see you again; and I'd have liked to return the compliment, but I wasn't sure it was. I couldn't in all justice blame her for my meeting with Teddy and the turn my life had taken since, but she was connected with it and therefore tainted by association, I felt. But then I relaxed; I'd come back here to find answers to my life-problems, and maybe Liz could provide some as she'd done before. After all, I'd had a good life with Teddy up to a point, and I was older and wiser and able to say No to anything I didn't want, I hoped.

So I told her why I'd come back. Not the details of what'd gone wrong with my life, but the fact that I was raising a child alone, unemployed, and in need of gainful employment; that I'd taken time out to come and look back at my past in the hope of finding a way to proceed in the future. She nodded, attentive and wise as always; her life, it appeared, had gone down an unexpected path also, although she was settled and prosperous and in no way regretting any of it. We should celebrate meeting up again, she said then, with something stronger than coffee; that's if you're free now? I told her that no-one at the hotel would miss me, so she suggested a nearby hotel bar to which we went, once I'd paid for my coffee.

It was an expensive establishment, several stars above that which I'd checked-into earlier, obviously well-built and insulated as the sounds of the street, loud even at that time of the evening, receded to the point of non-existence as the heavy front door closed behind us. The bar was quiet and not crowded, with tasteful music played at a level low enough for those patrons present to hear their own conversations but not those of others, the seating being well-placed to ensure a good measure of privacy.

Liz, I felt, had clearly been here before, and more than once, given how she made her way directly to a table set within a curtained alcove far from the door and ordered confidently from the hovering waiter without reference to the list; Dirty Martini, and ... ? She looked at me and, heartened by her attitude and not wanting to look like the poor country-cousin overwhelmed by her surroundings, I found a similar confidence from my old life with Teddy returning to me; Negroni, not too much soda. Liz looked impressed, and approving, and we sat down simultaneously, equals in life-experience if not in income these days.

The drinks came and I savoured the first taste of mine; my drinking for some time now had been confined to cheap wine, but this was like being back in Teddy's world, a cocktail party for the super-rich held in a five-star hotel or someone's penthouse apartment somewhere. Teddy's, on some occasions, and myself dressed in a tasteful and expensive frock, possibly the blue velvet with matching shoes which went so well with my hair ... but that part of my life was over, and I put the memories firmly aside, apart from that of the drink now touching my lips. I couldn't really afford it, but decided to think about that later and enjoy the moment; maybe this meeting would provide what I needed, for Liz at least wasn't some man waiting to take advantage of me for his own profit.

She must've read my thoughts; On me, she noted, as she raised her glass to me, and I had the good taste not to argue, although I felt this gesture (which I'd have to reciprocate) left the ball in my court to open the conversation with my own story; which I was none-too-eager to tell. But Liz was ahead of me; So I gather that Mr Super-Rich du Cain is no longer in the picture? She pre-empted me, and I only just managed to keep my cool and not spill my drink. How did you know? I put the question quietly and directly; let her tell as much of it as possible before getting involved myself; and tell she did, most frankly, from a point not long after the stag dinner took place.

The total sleaze-bucket, as she'd called him at the time, the one who'd taken her phone number, surprised her and came through with a call a couple of weeks after the dinner. Not such a sleaze-bucket, apparently, and a relationship of sorts ensued in which he wasn't slow to splash the cash in her direction. Then came the business proposition, which was nothing like the exclusive arrangement I'd had with Teddy and which Liz's new man had told her about; the parts which he knew, anyway.

Danny Martini was his name and, like the drink Liz raised to him now, he was called Dirty Martini by those who knew him on account of the porn empire he headed and which included several agencies. Escort agencies, they were called officially, arranging for good-looking young women to attend events, both public and private, with their clients, who were mostly older and well-off. Unofficially, the clients might request certain other services, of a sexual nature of course, from these escorts, who could make their own private arrangements with the men to their mutual satisfaction; sexual for him, financial for her. The agency took a 50% fee from the 'official' activities; steep, but as they didn't get anything from such other fees as the girls could make from their private activities with the clients they thought this only fair. In this way the agency distanced itself from any suggestions of their providing prostitutes and of getting into any hassles with the law, although they were well-aware of what frequently went on between clients and escorts.

So Danny had recruited Liz for one of his agencies, and she hadn't been unwilling. Imagine, Mags, I got well-paid to attend all sorts of events with these guys, drinks parties, dinners, race meetings, you name it; and if I didn't like the guy I didn't have to provide him with anything else at the end of the date. Mind you, it wasn't difficult to like most of them, they were bloody well-off and there's something very attractive about money, don't you agree? Well, as I was at that time trying to find a way to provide for my daughter and myself, I couldn't disagree with her, despite the fact that it was obviously prostitution, albeit at a more sophisticated level than that to which I'd sunk with Steve.

Liz filled me in on the details; the agency had sent her to a professional photographer, paid for by them, who took photos of her which stayed on the right side of decency – just – yet displayed her charms to advantage for those prospective clients who'd check them out on the agency's website. They'd contact the agency, who'd act as go-between and arrange the meeting between client and escort; and then it was up to these latter to arrange matters between them. Relatively safe, too, Liz told me, the agency got feedback from the escorts on the clients, and any bad-news guys were banned and blacklisted, by other agencies as well; and as Danny apparently ran several of these it wasn't difficult to spread the word. They requested too that you let them know when you arrived at the meeting, and when you left too, so they could keep tabs on you and your safety; good security, as these things went, and not every agency was so ethical, if that was the word.

She sat back and finished her drink with a satisfied air, signalling discretely yet effectively to a not-obviously hovering waiter for refills, waving away my offer for these to be on me when they arrived. Once again I accepted with grateful grace, and sipped mine while I considered my imminent entry into the conversation; I'd been going to ask her what'd been the outcome of her degree studies, work-wise, but we seemed to have gotten beyond that. I'd noticed as she spoke that she'd used the past tense when talking of her activities as an escort, so used this as a starting-point. Are you still doing it? You look like you've prospered – indicating her expensive-if-somewhat-tasteless turnout.

She smiled; Well, occasionally. I had quite a few regular clients, some of them still like to see me sometimes and it'd be bad manners and bad for business to refuse. But these days my relationship with Danny is business-only; I never expected it to last at the personal level, so I made sure I'd have something to fall back on when it finished. I made sure to let him see I'd a good head for business and, when it was obviously ending between us, I got him to take me into the business on the management side of things. So I'm not a failure as a business-studies graduate.

She looked smugly satisfied then and I thought, Good old Liz, eye on the main chance and good luck to her. So I'm in the office mostly now, she continued, arranging for the photos to be taken and posted on-line, liaising with clients and arranging the bookings, keeping in touch with the girls, getting their feedback and giving them tips, hundreds of things that I don't have time to go into now. There's so much to be done; and of course I get involved in recruiting new girls.

Which is where you could come in; Liz looked me

directly in the eye now, and meaningfully so, and I looked away first. So du Cain is in the past, and you need money; she stated it as a fact, which of course it was, and continued. I gather too that you left him for his driver, who eventually led you into work far less pleasant than what I'm proposing. I couldn't quite hide my shock then, how did she know? And I looked the question at her. She laughed; Steve Shine's activities were known to many of du Cain's acquaintances, he fixed them up with his boss's cast-offs, but you (taking pity on my wince, which she must have seen) he kept for himself initially. She stopped then; it was enough, and her offer hung in the air between us as I hesitated, not knowing what to say or do.

You ought to think about it, Mags, she encouraged me; what else are you going to do? Try to use the skills (she put little speech marks around it with her voice, amused now) your degree gave you? Join the long line of too many graduates applying for too few jobs? Been there, done that. Her tone was dismissive; Don't think I immediately abandoned myself to just such work as Danny gave me; it left me free, mainly during the daytime, of course, to look for more legitimate work, and I did try. But I rarely if ever got an interview, and when I did it was Thanks but no thanks. Just as well really, because the salaries were pitiful compared to what I've managed to make with Danny.

And you could do the same, she insisted; your daytime free (unless you get the horsey ones, who want to show you off at the racecourse, or those who engage you for a couple of days to travel with them). You can spend all the time you like with your kid, get a sitter for when you're working (I can help you with that) and, like me, only go further with guys you like. Good money, and on your own terms, she concluded.

What could I do? I agreed to sleep on the idea and meet her for brunch the next morning, before my coach left in the afternoon. Liz had an appointment to get to, so I left her then and took some supermarket sandwiches back to the hotel to spend the evening thinking over her proposal. Once there I showered, and ate, but felt restless confined in my room, so took myself to the bar for a couple of drinks before turning in for the night. I could see the street from where I sat in the bar; so many people all going about their own business, society happening, and I needed to find my place in it, in such a way that I could give my daughter a good start in life.

I didn't want Katie growing up in some run-down area, like the one I'd lived in with Steve, coming home from school to let herself in before she was old enough to be on her own, while I slaved in some shop or bar for the basic wage that barely covered the rent and certainly wouldn't extend to childcare. But what Liz was offering me would; it wasn't what I would've chosen, but I could see that it'd pay enough that my daughter wouldn't go without; and who was I to be fussy, given that I'd already been engaged in such practices, at both the higher and lower ends of the scale?

I spent a restless night, and in the morning met with Liz to accept her offer. I told myself it'd only be temporary, until I could find something respectable and well-paid to support us with. Plus it wouldn't be like being controlled by a man, as with Steve; Liz would be my contact, but I'd be free to take or leave such offers as were made to me after I'd carried out the 'legitimate' escort part of the job. I'd be working on my own terms, for a change, and I liked the idea of that.

Mags paused here and thought for a moment, while Dora took the opportunity to plump up the pillows behind her. Yes, I liked the idea, and how it panned out seemed to justify my decision. Liz made all the arrangements, got the photos taken and posted online and so forth, even pitched in and helped me find a flat; still in London, of course, that being where most of the work opportunities were, and she lived there too. She'd just been back in the old city visiting a contact for a day when she and I bumped into each other, which seemed to signify further that working with her was meant to be. So she helped me get established in a good area far from the run-down neighbourhood where I'd lived with Steve, with a reliable and highly-recommended live-in nanny-cum-home-help with whom I, and more importantly Katie, hit it off at once. Rebecca was her name, Becky for short, in her late twenties; she soon became indispensable to Katie, who was growing fast and not far off needing a nursery school. But I put off thinking about that for the present; I knew now that I'd be able to afford one, come the time.

Mags stopped at this point, apparently thinking over the memories of that time. It was good, she concluded, or so I thought. She sat thinking now, in silence, until she fell into a light doze from which Dora had to wake her gently to administer medication and see to her other needs before departing for her own home and her own bed.

Her own bed, but not her own husband, unfortunately; Des had already departed for work when Dora arrived home, which was no different to any other morning except for the rare occasion when he was late. Such an orderly routine, she mused, while eating a lonely breakfast of tea and toast at the kitchen table; each day much like the next, the same routine, laundry and housework done at set times, fitted into the work routines of this busy couple, bills paid on time courtesy of direct debits, or reminders Des had set in his computer. Everything with a place to be in and everything in that place in this clean and tidy home, thought Dora, which was satisfying, but also boring; boring, boring, boring.

Such a contrast to the chaotic existence of her patient, as she thought back over the life-story Mags had been narrating regularly; too much chaos there and too much order here, Dora decided. A balance was needed, some much-needed order in the girl's life and a little chaos in her own. Was that why Des was potentially carrying on with someone else? To relieve the boredom of their sterile, antiseptic existence? To live, for a change, through the highs and lows of passion, such a contrast to the routine of three meals a day and no sex because we're supposed to be too old for that? There was much to be said for a well-ordered life, but something was missing; Dora was too tired to think about it now and abandoned the attempt as she took herself to bed and fell asleep almost instantly.

15: INDEPENDENCE

The next evening found Dora fitting back easily into the routine which had been established by now; either Laura or Celia letting the nurse in and making her a hot drink, along with one for themselves and Mags, and passing the time of day whilst they did so. Vivie she saw less frequently, mostly when Mags requested the presence of little Katie and Vivie brought her, either awake or asleep, to be cuddled by her mother.

Tonight found Katie already asleep in Mags's arms, to be collected and put to bed by Vivie. As the sleeping child was carried out, Mags sighed, her eyes following her through the door; and Dora knew she was thinking that she wouldn't be around much longer to care for her, which must be torture. How would she, Dora, have felt had it been her, knowing her child was to grow up without parents, at the mercy of strangers? Even such good and caring strangers as Mags had here as her loyal friends? She shuddered at the thought.

I told her a bedtime story, Mags said then; 'Little Red Riding-Hood' tonight, maybe because I want so much that she'll avoid the clutches of wolves in men's clothes, unlike her mother. And for a while I thought I'd escaped from that, working with Liz on my own terms; because it was good for a while. She moved naturally back into her own story here. I made it work for me, and I felt better than I ever had, escorting the men as I was contracted to do and then deciding for myself whether or not I'd provide anything else they might request.

Some of it was great, she enthused then. There was one man, older, distinguished, he reminded me of Teddy so much that I almost refused his request because it seemed dangerous to get in any deeper with him. But I gave in; what the hell, he attracted me as Teddy had, in the early days, and that had to make what happened between us better. Which it did, to the extent that he became a regular, taking me to plush parties as eye-candy on his arm and later to a swish hotel room as bed-candy for the night.

He even took me to Paris for a weekend once; cocktails and dinner on Saturday evening and a private house-party on the Sunday, but during the day on Saturday I was free to do whatever I wanted while he was in meetings. To see the sights, get my hair and nails done, whatever, and he picked up the bill. It did remind me of having been there with Teddy though, in love with him and enjoying his company; it made me wistful, and I had to put those days firmly in the past and focus on the £12,000 I was being paid for the weekend.

Dora couldn't restrain a gasp here; so much money, plus the cost of Mags occupying herself when alone, just for a couple of days and nights; she could see how a young woman in need of money might be tempted. Mags registered the nurse's reaction and laughed; Yes, Dora, enough to pay the household costs, keep myself looking good for the clients and put a chunk aside for Katie's future; which was the most important thing, of course (she grew serious here) seeing as how I won't be there to look after her.

She put the thought firmly from her then, focussing on her story; He wasn't the only regular I found, I soon had a small stable of them, and they were all men with whom I decided I wouldn't have a problem spending the night. So it was all going well, I was popular and the agency was pleased with me; and then I met Dwayne and it all started to unravel.

There was nothing wrong with him, she hastened to explain, in fact he was one of the friendliest guys I'd ever met, with the widest and most infectious smile. He was from South London, six foot four and sporting muscles which suggested serious time spent at the gym. Long, deep-black hair braided with beads, skin the deep-brown of the darkest milk chocolate, just before it becomes plain; even darker than you, Dora.

The nurse was taken aback at this; she hadn't really thought about all the anonymous men with whom Mags had had dealings, but she realised now that she'd unconsciously expected them all to be white. Does that make me a racist? she wondered, but filed the thought for later as her patient continued.

He was young, too, in his late twenties, Mags added, which was a refreshing change for me. Laid-back humour-wise, with an infectious laugh, he didn't take himself or what he did for a living too seriously. He'd come from a not-too-great start in life and was doing the best he could to get by and, this also being the more recent story of my life, we got on well. He was an actor in porn films, she threw in casually, cashing in on the assets with which Nature had endowed him; and the old racist ideas about black men and size were, in Dwayne's case at least, very much the truth.

Has she been reading my thoughts? Dora wondered; yet it was a relief to get the racist thing out in the open. But why ...? she began, and stopped uncertainly; how could she ask the reason why a good-looking and well-endowed young man who'd got no issue with performing the most intimate acts with strangers in front of a camera would need the services of an escort?

Mags did read her mind then. I wasn't his escort, she explained, but that of another man at the party where Dwayne and I met; we got chatting at one point, when my client was talking to Dwayne's agent, and he asked me out on a date, an actual date; not a paid escort and client thing. He actually wanted to see me for my company, not to pay me for sex. Well, I accepted his offer and he bought me dinner, and we had such a good time. And, you won't believe it, he took me home in a taxi and didn't come in with me; a real gentleman, and I appreciated that.

It took a few dates before we got intimate, so old-fashioned and so unusual. I liked him for that, as well as in the bedroom when we eventually got there. We became an item; I spent a lot of time with him and we actually formed a relationship in a very loose sense. I wasn't bothered by what he did for a living, nor he by what I did, because who were we to complain, after all? He was at the top of the game in his sphere, well-known, and I attended functions with him and even got my picture in the glossy magazines; I became well-known myself, as his girlfriend. Which became a problem, she grimaced, because I started to work less; and then even less, until I'd almost stopped doing anything at all for the agency, which displeased them, and Liz in particular.

I remember her phoning to read me the riot act; Don't blow it over one guy, Mags, she told me, you've got a good thing going here, think of the dosh you're missing out on, think of Katie and her future. And I know I ought to have listened to her, to the bit about Katie at least, Mags conceded then; but I was enjoying being in a relationship again, albeit an uncommitted one, and being in it for no greater reason than that I'd chosen it for attraction rather than money.

Which isn't to say that Dwayne wasn't the most generous guy on the planet, she conceded then; he splashed so much cash in my direction. There you go, girl, buy yourself something pretty for me to take you out in tonight, he'd say, and give me far more than I needed to get myself dressed up for him; and he wasn't bothered about the change, so I'd stash the leftover money away for Katie's future, after I'd paid the bills.

We were having fun, she continued, and as I was enjoying his company I'm afraid I began to behave badly, staying at his place more and more and letting Becky take care of Katie alone. I'd paid the rent on the flat for a year up-front, so she had a roof guaranteed over her head for some time to come, and I knew she was in good hands, and well-cared for on an everyday basis; so I became careless about spending enough time with her.

She frowned then; The real problem was drugs, I'm afraid. The thing was, I'd used them with Teddy and Steve, to get myself through the things they wanted me to do that I didn't want to, and I'd managed, just about, to get off them when the bad things stopped. I didn't need them when I could pick and choose my clients for myself, and now they were offered to me purely as a leisure pursuit, to be taken just for the good feelings they provided, rather than help me be impervious to the bad things happening to me.

Well, there were drugs in good supply at Dwayne's place, not to mention a very unconventional domestic set-up which included the harem and the hangers-on. The former was explained by the fact that Dwayne, despite his good looks and good nature, had a tendency to frighten off women due to the size of his assets, well-advertised as they were. His corresponding dearth of potential female partners was compensated for by his having a close-knit live-in harem made up of some of his former on-screen partners with whom he'd had a successful working relationship. 'Whores de combat', he called them in a good-humoured way, and I was included in that; he'd read it somewhere, he said and I oughtn't to take offence.

I don't really know what the others thought about it, I never got close to them, but I personally didn't mind, and actually agreed with him; it was what I'd been doing, after all. I didn't have a problem with sharing him either, as I've said it was an uncommitted and very open relationship, and I felt like sleep and relaxation. I liked sex with him, of course, but I didn't mind not being with him every night; and as part of the harem I only slept with him occasionally.

He didn't exactly take turns, but he'd have a favourite of the moment. He seemed to sense my need to chill out for a while, however, so I got to rest and he didn't go without.

So I hung out at his place with increasing regularity; nothing heavy, just spending time and listening to music, and turning on, of course. Because as well as the harem Dwayne had his entourage, friends from his South London upbringing who lived at his place. Hangers-on, they might be called, but I suppose I was one too, so I was in no position to name-call. Whatever, they did the work of the place, so I didn't have to lift a finger for the first time since Teddy, and I wasn't complaining. They also went for food, drink and drugs, of course, so I had no problems taking myself down on smack when I wanted, rather than livening myself up on coke.

I spent most of my time at Dwayne's place resting, and it was a relief to have nothing else to do. I visited Katie sometimes, not as often as I ought to have, but she was safe and stable and didn't seem particularly bothered by my visits; but on one particular trip she cried when I picked her up and I was upset by that. I came down hard on myself for it, and rightly so; I knew I was neglecting her, but what does she need with a mother like me, I asked myself. I stayed on for a while, letting her get over her upset and putting her to bed myself, reading her a story and sitting beside her until she was asleep, just thinking about my life to date; but the thoughts weren't good ones.

When she was fast asleep I went to my own bedroom and carried on thinking. I had the few bits and pieces from the wreck of my life that Steve, with uncharacteristic thoughtfulness and braving Teddy's wrath, had retrieved from my apartment so long ago; maybe he did think he loved me at the time. Now I went through these and remembered the circumstances surrounding them. In a plastic bag I found, long-forgotten, the lace-topped stockings I'd been wearing when I first met Teddy. They

236

were stiff in places, stained with dried semen and a little blood, his and mine respectively; we were joined there, in a strange sort of way and I'd kept them for that reason. A strange love-token, I mused; but did Juliet get a better from Romeo, when he did her virgin knot untie? Maybe she would've been happy with the stockings; the first time is special, or should be. Mine was, even if ironic in that I thought I'd already had the first, which hadn't been special in any shape or form.

Bad thoughts of my early life came then, and I pushed them aside bitterly. I was fed up with the whole sordid mess and I didn't know where to go from here. I couldn't hang-out with Dwayne for ever, it was only a temporary respite and then what? Back to the agency work which paid the bills and more? It hadn't been the worst work I'd even done, I'd enjoyed much of it, and certainly the abundant money I'd earned by it. But I knew it was only one phase of my life, and I was getting older; I remembered the thoughts I'd had about Marjorie Majors, the dwindling work opportunities of the ageing hooker, which I'd had on the fateful night when I'd started cheating on Teddy with Steve. There'd got to be something better, but what?

I had no family to support me, financially or emotionally. My parents didn't want to know and as far as I knew I had no other relatives. I thought about that; other students I'd known would often speak of family members. I particularly remembered one guy, a housemate of mine, who went home one weekend and, returning, spoke of a large family gathering, the big brother back from active service overseas, the arrival of aunts and uncles, a convergence of cousins, all to celebrate Nana's ninetieth.

But this kind of thing was unknown to me; no other relatives ever visited our house, or we theirs, if they even existed, that was. It was possible that my parents had no siblings, but they must've had parents, who could still be out there somewhere. I was only in my mid-twenties, so my parents must be in their late-forties or early fifties, I calculated; so, barring some terrible accident, there ought to be four grandparents, or one at the very least, out there for me. But it seemed that my parents had cut themselves off from them, and me with them.

I didn't even have a name, not a real one, anyway, since my father had threatened to sue if I used his. I'd not really needed one, existing in the shadowlands of society as I'd been doing. I'd had a National Insurance number, when I worked on campus what seemed centuries ago, but it'd fallen into disuse; it was only when I joined Liz and the agency, where the agency salary for my official work was taxed, that I'd had to get back into the system. The other work, the private arrangements I made with clients, was all cash in hand; in Steve's hand, mostly, when I was with him, I remembered bitterly.

But I'd needed a name for the agency work, both the official and the unofficial, and something a bit more exotic, shall we say, was not unheard-of in this line of work. So the name I'd been using since my father disowned me was perfect; it came from when sex had first become mildly kinky for me, when I had the threesome with Teddy and James, so long ago, and James had referred to me as 'Ms Mystery'. I'd shortened that to Mystry and it seemed suitable, so I'd become Magdalena Mystry to the extent that I'd forgotten I'd ever been Maria Manville.

I felt very alone, thinking about all these things, more so than I ever had, and not much good to my daughter in that frame of mind; so I paid Becky a good bonus, made sure the bills were paid and that she knew where to find me, and left them to it. Katie was better off without me, I thought, and I carried on thinking when I got back to Dwayne's place. My future and fate lay in my own hands, just as when I'd gone to university, but I'd made a mess of it back then and was in a far less favourable position to make a better decision now.

I felt despair then, and took a long, hard look at myself in the mirror. The body which I'd put to such a use disgusted me, and the idea of self-harm occurred to me. Cut off my long, white-blonde hair, cut and scar my soft and supple skin, and my breasts, which had all helped to get me into trouble. But I'd already been harmed enough, by myself and others, and I didn't want another stay in hospital. At least at Dwayne's I could please myself how I spent my time. I took a snort of snow to try to lift my mood, and decided I'd think about my future tomorrow. As was becoming the norm in my life, though, my immediate future was decided by an agency other than myself.

Mags stopped at this point, frowning at the memory of her behaviour at that time. It was a bad time, she concluded, and I paid for it, ultimately; but Katie was OK, she was looked after, though small thanks to me. Then she sat, brooding silently, until she fell into a doze, from which Dora had to wake her gently to administer medication and see to her other needs before departing for her own home and her own bed.

The usual lonely daytime bed it was for Dora, left neat by the good offices of Des, along with all the other routine little gestures he'd carried out to make her homecoming easier, and she appreciated them, boring as they might seem in the light of her recent evaluation of her home routine. She'd thought that Mags had arrived at some kind of order in her life, given where she'd gotten to in her story the night before last, but now she'd abandoned that idea in the face of the drug use and thoughts of self-harm which had taken over. So Dora felt safe in her own well-ordered life, tedious though some might think it; and, when Des came home to spend the evening with her before she returned to Mags, she put aside her misgivings about him and was just grateful to have him there.

16: ARRESTING

The story didn't improve when Dora was back seated at the bedside and Mags had resumed her narrative. I was in a deep sleep, she recounted, when the banging and smashing noises started, and then chaos ensued. Shouts of Police, Open up, the sound of heavy boots running up the stairs and along the corridors of the house. Only half-awake, I just managed to grab a robe and throw it over me before the bedroom door flew open and I was blinded by the torchlight before the light was switched on. Things were very confused after that, but I remember being allowed more clothes before they hustled me out and down the stairs, where the other residents were in like situation. I saw Dwayne; What the hell is going on? It's a raid, Girl, we're busted, was all he managed before we were bundled out through the front door and into the back of a van in the street outside.

The nightmare continued at the police station, although fortunately Dwayne had a good firm of solicitors who'd represented him before, so there was legal representation for me when I was interviewed. I was bailed, pending further enquiries, along with everyone else who'd been brought in; I was being charged with possession of more than one Class A drug, because they'd found large quantities of both coke and heroin on my bedside table. I was luckier than Dwayne and his friends, who were being charged for supply as well as possession, the stuff found on myself and the other girls being taken as evidence of this and given that both Dwayne and his friends had previous.

Then it was back to Dwayne's place to take it all in and await court attendance and my fate, whatever that was to be. Probably prison, from what I gathered from my experienced housemates; it might've been my first offence, but I'd been in possession of a lot of stuff and that counted against me. A fine as well, most probably, and I didn't have much money to spare because I'd been saving every penny for Katie's future.

Katie! In the shock of everything that'd happened I hadn't thought about my daughter, so used was I to knowing her well-cared for by Becky; but now I became frantic. What'd become of her if I went to prison? I was out of the house so fast, half-running in the direction of my flat, which was too far to reach quickly, but I'd have run all the way if I'd had to. The other half of me was checking the road for taxis, so I could flag one down, and fortunately I found one quite quickly. I had to get the driver to trust me and wait while I went indoors and got the fare from Becky's housekeeping cash, but then I was there with Katie in my arms, holding onto her for dear life while she complained that I was squashing her and Becky looked at me in amazement, wondering what'd happened to bring me there, scruffily-dressed, on a Saturday morning.

She knew better than to ask immediately, though, given my obvious state of distress, and contented herself with getting us both coffee, and milk for Katie, before taking charge of the situation. Mags, you need to calm down, you're hurting Katie; she prised my daughter from my arms gently and sat her at her little table and chair, in front of me where I could see her, giving her the milk and biscuits she'd bought, plus a colouring book and crayons to keep her occupied. Katie thus engrossed, Becky took me to sit at the breakfast bar to drink coffee and interrogate me in a low voice; Mags, what is it? What's happened? Tell me.

I told her it all, in a voice as low as her own, and Katie looked over at us from time to time, visits by her mother having become a rare thing; but she couldn't hear us, and even if she did hear the odd bit or piece she wouldn't have understood anyway. Becky was marvellous,

241

and non-judgemental; no point crying over spilt milk, was her outlook on life, far better to deal with what's happened as best you can. My own solicitor would have to be brought in, and fast, we agreed between us. Becky had no problem with continuing to live with Katie, although financial arrangements needed to be made so that the rent was paid and she could pay the bills. I reckoned I'd enough put by to keep the household going for maybe two years, and hoped fervently I wouldn't be going away for that long. I'd just have to do what I could, including taking out some form of legal guardianship for Becky, who was willing to assume the role, because I didn't want Social Services getting involved and taking Katie away from me; if that happened, I might never get her back.

I started getting panicky again then, at that awful thought; I started shivering all over, and trembling, I think I was in shock. Becky calmed me, soothed me as she must've done for Katie when she had bad dreams, and suggested I try to sleep for a while. I didn't think I could, but I let her lead me to my hardly-used bedroom and help me to bed where, totally overwrought and exhausted, I soon slept.

I awoke in the late evening in a panic; where was I? I didn't recognise my own room at first, expecting to be at Dwayne's place, but then I remembered. I shook myself awake and left the room in search of Katie, finding her in the kitchen with Becky, drinking hot milk. She was more accepting of my presence now, I'm sure because Becky had talked to her about me while I was sleeping; so she allowed me to hold and hug her and read her a story when she was tucked-up in her little bed.

When she slept I returned to Becky, who informed me that she'd let Dwayne know I was here, so he wouldn't worry about me, and also contacted my solicitor so I could make arrangements with him as soon as possible for Katie and herself. Then she made me something hot to eat and gave us both a glass of wine as we settled on the sofa together and I poured out my worries. She sensibly pointed out that I could only do so much at this time; we'd have to deal with whatever happened in the order in which it happened and hope we could get through; and I couldn't argue with her.

I was feeling pretty low, and there was of course nothing in the house to help lift me back up, so I started feeling desperate. The idea of prison terrified me; I'd heard stories about life inside, and didn't like them at all. But then of course things got worse. My solicitor, Charles Manners, duly got in touch, but before we could meet I received the unwelcome news that the police wanted to talk to me again. Why, I couldn't imagine; they didn't want anyone else from Dwayne's house back, apparently, and some were on far more serious charges than I was. But Charles came to see me at home, and we worked out the arrangements for Katie and Becky's immediate future before we attended as requested to help the police with more talks, which sent me further on my downward spiral.

Apparently someone (identity not revealed) was being blackmailed. He'd been sent film showing him engaging in bizarre sexual activities with a woman with long, white-blonde hair, something which it was assumed he wouldn't want made public. The film wasn't of the best quality, but he knew where he'd indulged with a woman like that, the place being my old Bankside apartment and the woman being me. The blackmailer it seemed hadn't calculated that his target would go to the police; but the man's wife was dead and his grown children estranged, and he didn't care what anyone else thought by this stage of his life. Which meant that whoever was behind this blackmail had seriously misjudged the situation, and that person, he said, was Edward du Cain; Teddy.

Apparently my erstwhile lover and keeper was known for some decidedly dubious dealings and murky manipulation if things didn't go the way he wanted. Not the criminal underworld exactly, but the shadowlands where honest dealings meet the margins of illegality. And I'd been aware of this.; I might once've been immensely naïve, but those days were long over. I'd known that both my apartment and Teddy's had been filled with security cameras, and when Teddy asked me to entertain other men in either of those locations I'd known the cameras would be recording everything. He had reasons of his own for this, obviously, but he didn't tell me in so many words and I didn't ask him. Not just because asking Teddy what he didn't want to tell never led anywhere, but because I really didn't want to know; which didn't mean that I couldn't work it out for myself, and words like sweetener and reward, bribery and blackmail had more than once gone through my head.

But it's not difficult, when in love, to make excuses for the bad behaviour of the loved-one or, if excuses are impossible, to ignore the behaviour. And if ignorance is impossible, active participation being required as in my case with those men, then put up a losing fight and go along with it; do what's required and say you're doing it for love. Soak up the misery, deal with it, and when it all gets too much, find another lover, as I'd done in Steve; who, along with his associates at Harry's bar, had given further hints of Teddy's questionable business activities which had fallen on my willingly-deaf ears.

It was no surprise to me therefore to be told these things, and that the police were investigating Teddy with a view to charges on a range of white-collar offences; insider trading, money laundering, bribery, false accounting and so forth. Apparently they could only get him imprisoned for about ten years at absolute maximum for these, and in the event he'd be out in half that time with good behaviour, as was usual. But if they could get him charged additionally with attempted blackmail, which attracted a maximum term of fourteen years, and the sentences ran consecutively, rather than concurrently (which they'd push for), it'd mean that with the maximum term for both they could put him away for twelve years, even if he only served half of each sentence; and, as he appeared to have made some enemies high-up in the police force (sweeteners and bribes will only get you so far, some officials being incorruptible, apparently), they wanted to put him away for as long as possible. My own involvement being known, as Teddy's former lover and the woman in the film, this made me an accomplice to blackmail (if it could be proved) and liable to another criminal charge for this; thus potentially extending my own time in prison. But that doesn't have to happen, Ms Mystry, if you will agree to testify against du Cain.

It was all too complicated, too much to take in, especially coming so soon after my own arrest and my concern over potentially losing Katie, and I felt faint. I was allowed a break, but afterwards they continued, trying to persuade me in a supposedly-sympathetic way. Come on, Magdalena, you were just a girl when you met him, weren't you, young and inexperienced? He picked you up at that dinner and threw money at you, blinded you with luxury, love-bombed you; then manipulated you to do these things with the guys so he could blackmail them, and you found it hard to refuse? Pity you weren't a few years younger, we could do him for child abuse as well.

They'd done their homework and were at their persuasive best; You go into court and tell it that way, you were young and naïve and he abused your trust. Help us nail him and we'll go easy on you over the drugs. They made it sound so bad, like I was Monterone's daughter and Teddy the depraved Duke, I thought, remembering *Rigoletto*. But that wasn't my Teddy. He hadn't used me briefly and passed me on to his entourage to take turns with me. He'd kept me with him for years, lavished luxury and love on me, because I was sure he'd loved me; if we hadn't lived together under the same roof that was just his preference for living alone. I knew I still loved him, despite all the bad stuff, and there was nothing I could do about that.

Charles Manners got me out of there at this point, and my torturers agreed; Perhaps you need time to think about this. Which was all I did, when I was back at the flat with a large drink to help me cope. I was being offered a deal; testify against Teddy and put him in prison to save myself from going there for longer than I had to. Sacrifice Teddy to save myself; I thought about it long and hard. First I remembered the bad things; giving me to those other men (one of whom had put me in this situation), the way he'd beaten me when he found out about Steve. Revenge for those things would be sweet.

But then I thought about all the good things; his extreme generosity to me, his loving behaviour, his care for me, so much that was good between us until the deterioration of our relationship and the catastrophic end. I remembered then his self-control at that end; true, he'd beaten me but hadn't sexually assaulted me as he so easily could've, even if he'd claimed the moral high ground for that. And I knew that, whatever he'd done to me, I couldn't do this to him; I too could claim some moral high ground and display dignity rather than wreak revenge.

What to do? I could straightforwardly refuse to help and let them do their worst without me. But they'd probably find a way to make the charges stick, because who else but I could stand up to support Teddy and say, No, there was no blackmail attempt? So I made my decision; I'd agree to help, go in as a witness for the prosecution, but then not help, in fact do what I could to hinder their case. And afterwards they could do what they liked with me. Prison's prison, however long you're there for, so I might as well be hung for a sheep as a lamb.

Then I remembered Katie; what if they tried to take her away from me, despite the measures I'd put in place to keep her away from Social Services? I called Charles

Manners in a panic; but no, he assured me, he'd already taken steps to prevent that; without my permission, which he regretted, but he'd felt the need to act with speed.

It turned out that, rather than pay the rent on my current apartment for another year, he'd taken a smaller one in a quiet area of my old university city, away from the glare of publicity which would soon surround me. I'd always kept Katie in the background of my life, and as she hadn't yet started school, her entries in the computers of the Establishment were limited to her birth and use of the Health Service. And, as I'd used my real name, Maria Manville, and missed out the 'Magdalena', on her birth certificate, it'd be hard to link her to Magdalena Mystry, which I'd been using ever since my father had disowned me. Additionally, as I was unsure who her father actually was, I hadn't named anyone in that role on the certificate.

So Katie was quite well-protected from anyone making a link between her and myself, and there was of course Becky and her application for legal guardianship. She'd become devoted to Katie, and was prepared to go to great lengths to keep the little girl with her; even to the extent of claiming to be her mother, should the need arise; but we'd cross that bridge when we came to it, Charles said. For the time being, though, he'd established a distance between Katie and myself which ought to keep her safe, and we'd look to the future once my more immediate fate had been sealed.

It was settled in my mind then; I'd help Teddy whilst pretending to revenge myself on him. I'd attend court as a prosecution witness and present myself as a well-experienced woman; not a girl who'd been young and in love and therefore able to be controlled by a coercive lover, but a hard-faced female with both eyes firmly on the main chance, aiming to find someone to pick up the bills for her lifestyle and not too fussy about what she gave in exchange. I won't pretend I wasn't frightened, but I'd got to forget that and do what I had to; and the deal was duly done.

Mags closed her eyes here, and fell into a light doze; Dora took the opportunity to get up and stretch her legs and, hearing someone passing lightly on the landing, opened the door and asked Laura (for it was she, on her way from the bathroom) if she would watch Mags for a few minutes whilst Dora made a similar visit. On her return, Mags had woken again and requested hot chocolate, which Dora went to make along with coffee for herself. When Laura had gone back to bed, and they'd refreshed themselves, Mags took up her tale again.

The court was packed on the day of my appearance. It was crowded most days, this being such a big case, and Teddy the figure at the centre of it. But today the police outside were pushing back the crowds. Everyone it seemed wanted to see me; as the girlfriend of a well-known porn actor I'd attracted some publicity, and that'd helped the blackmail victim to identify me as the woman who'd been filmed with him. The ex-mistress and accomplice of Edward du Cain, who'd taken part in kinky sexual scenes to entrap all those men over whom Teddy wanted control; and a few others it seemed had come clean about their own involvements with Teddy and their sexual scenes with me, because it looked as though everything would come out anyway in the course of the investigation, and it'd look better if they owned up willingly rather than being outed unwillingly.

So there was a ghoulish need by many to see me in person. Some of the less-reputable tabloids had been digging around and found out about the end of my relationship with Teddy, the way Steve had put me on the game and my more recent escort activities which had led me to Dwayne. My face was all over the papers now, but the public wanted more; what more did they expect? To see me in the flesh and hear my voice admitting my crimes, they hoped; to see me publicly shamed, talking in a tearful voice, hiding my face, humiliated. Well, I wouldn't give them the satisfaction; let them see that I could go down fighting, to hell with them all.

Finally I didn't care what other people thought of me, only what Teddy thought, and I wanted him to think better of me than he had when he'd finished with me. This could be my only chance to see him, to show him a penitent Magdalena. It ought to have been in private, but it was in public, and that seemed par for the course because so much of my life had been on public display. What did it matter?

I'd prepared as well as I could for what was to come; I wasn't expecting a good outcome from this day's work. I'd ignored my defence counsel's instructions to put my hair up and dress soberly, to look respectable; This is who I am and I'm not going to try to work that old ruse, it's so transparent, I told myself. So although I took some more sensible clothes in a bag, not expecting to be released, I went in with my colours nailed to the mast. Long white-blonde hair flowing as usual, high-heeled shoes and short, tight-fitting skirt, blouse with V-neck plunging to my cleavage and showing clearly the 'H' pendant (which she now took hold of); my message to Teddy, which hopefully he'd interpret correctly. I'd also taken on board a little Dutch courage to help me through the thing; I'd have preferred the Colombian kind, but Dwayne and his entourage wouldn't dare touch the stuff at present, with their own criminal charges hanging over them. So gin had to do.

There was a buzz from the public gallery as I entered, but I took no notice. I was trying to get a surreptitious look at Teddy before things started, because I wouldn't look at him during the proceedings, I'd decided. I saw him, looking so alone; it was so long since I'd seen him, that awful day when he'd beaten and discarded me, and understandably he hadn't looked too well then. Now he looked worse, very tired, with a yellow-and-greyish tinge to his skin. He'd lost weight, but he hadn't really had any to lose so looked too thin; and his beard wasn't as neatly trimmed as it used to be.

He'd know what I'd agreed to say against him, my signed witness statement having been made available to his counsel in the lead-up to the trial so they could object to anything which appeared inaccurate, or whatever, to them. So I didn't want to meet his eyes and the coldness which I knew would be there for me, treacherous bitch as he'd think me. I wanted to take him in my arms and comfort him, tell him I was on his side, but instead I took the oath. I used my false name, the one everyone now knew me by, thank goodness, for Katie's sake, and possibly that negated everything I said. I don't know, but it was as good as my real one to perjure myself with; and I took my seat in the witness box.

I wasn't educated in law, and it was a complex process for me; so if I get some of the details wrong you'll have to forgive me, Dora. The nurse smiled; I probably know even less than you. Well then; and Mags smiled back. I'd been called as a witness for the prosecution, and Mr Maxwell, their counsel, got to question me first to gain the 'evidence in chief' as it's called, to provide maximum support to their case. I could tell by the frown on his face that he didn't approve of my clothing, which wasn't what'd been dictated. I was supposed to look respectable, and innocent, which was a laugh; the jury wouldn't be fooled, they'd all read the scandal-sheets and knew the kind of woman I was. So the hair put up and the skirt let down and the neckline filled in wouldn't change a thing, Mr Maxwell; what you get is what you see.

He started with the usual preliminaries (which I assumed them to have been) of who I was, relationship to the accused and so forth. Then, Ms Mystry, How would you describe yourself as a person when you first met Mr du Cain at the age of 18? To which it'd been agreed, and I'd signed my witness statement to this effect, that I'd present myself as naïve, young for my age, easily-manipulated by the much-older man I'd fallen in love with.

I changed my story almost immediately, however; I'd say I was fairly confident for my age, I told him, I knew what I wanted out of life and was prepared to go and get it. Maxwell looked even more uneasy, but continued with the agreed script until the unscripted answers I was giving made it clear I'd reneged on the deal. So, Permission to treat the witness as a hostile witness? he asked of the judge. And permission was duly granted, after some conferral, and sending the jury out and bringing them back in again after agreement was reached that I'd obviously changed my story.

So Maxwell got to ask me the kind of leading questions that Teddy's defence counsel would've asked me; as in, You were a student, in need of money, and you went to work at the charity dinner to make some, because it paid well? I agreed to that, and he continued, You were a naïve young girl, Ms Mystery, weren't you, and you fell in love with Mr du Cain and he took advantage of that?

I had my contrary answer ready now; time to think Picasso; time to think hard-faced whore. I went to the charity dinner to find a sponsor, for want of a better word, a man who'd undertake to support me financially in return for my sexual services; I knew what I was doing. Maxwell wasn't happy; And you met Mr du Cain? Yes, I did. And he suited your idea of a sponsor? Yes, he did. But you fell in love with him? And allowed him to manipulate you as his accomplice because you loved him?

Cue my key statement: I suppose you could call it love, Mr Maxwell, but my kind of love is a business, and for me the business of love is to be bought and sold, subject to contract. I signed a contract with Mr du Cain; his financial support in exchange for my exclusive sexual services, and that included sharing me with his friends and family if he so wished. And he did so wish, regularly. That was what I signed up for, of my own free will, and my counsel has a copy of the contract if you wish to see it. I broke it, ultimately, but that was my fault and responsibility, not Mr du Cain's. So there was no blackmail intended, Mr Maxwell, and no accomplice; just security cameras in every room of an expensive apartment block that was full of them, and two consenting adults in a bedroom together.

Mags intoned the words as though she was still in the courtroom; she must've rehearsed them many times before her day in court, Dora thought, and clearly remembered them as a key moment in her life. She couldn't have stopped listening if she'd wanted, hooked into the story as she was, and after a pause Mags continued in a lighter tone.

Teddy's defence counsel must've been rubbing his hands with joy, under the table, because I was doing his job for him and there was no need for him to cross-examine me after Maxwell, who couldn't do much with me but did his best. Then how would you account for the blackmail attempt that has been made on Mr X?

I was ready for that also; Well, I saw some of the security-camera films in Mr Shine's possession when I was living with him. Maybe he took them in a misguided attempt to protect me, or maybe he enjoyed watching them himself, or maybe he thought he might use them for gain in the future if his financial situation warranted it. But I don't know, and I never saw them after his death. One of his friends gathered his possessions and took them to his family, so anyone could've got hold of the films and used them. It looks as though someone has, but not Mr du Cain; he had no need to, because he always told me why I was to spend time with these men, who'd always kept to their side of the deals they did with him; I was a reward, not a means to entrap them.

I looked coolly at the helpless Maxwell, as hard-faced as I could be; I thought then, I'm sorry Steve, because you were good to me for a time. But I have to blame you now because you can't go to prison, you can't go anywhere, because you're dead.

I was dead too, for that matter, metaphorically-speaking. I'd made a deal with the prosecution and broken it in court. Breaking contracts it seemed was becoming a habit with me, and I knew I'd be made to pay for this as surely as the last one. Maxwell was trying to regain his poise but he was angry now, and losing his judgement, it seemed to me. Even though he must've known it wouldn't do any good, he tried to humiliate and embarrass me by going into the immorality of my lifestyle since Teddy; Ms Mystry, your profession, in all its different manifestations, is one that until recently would have been called that of a common prostitute?

I'd had enough by now, I'd done what I came to do and didn't want to answer any more questions; and he'd given me the opportunity to leave with a flourish. Anyone who has known me in the Biblical sense, Mr Maxwell, knows that I'm a very uncommon prostitute.

OK, my words weren't original, a paraphrase from the uncommon thief Hans Gruber, a.k.a. Alan Rickman, in *Die Hard*; but they did the job. There was laughter from the court, and the judge calling for order, and the upshot was that I was held in contempt and remanded in custody pending my own drugs trial. As I was taken down I allowed myself a fleeting last look at Teddy. He understood what I'd been doing; there was warmth in his eyes and the ghost of a smile around his lips and even maybe a miniscule nod. I thought then, See, Teddy, I finally got over caring what others think of me, except you; and then I lost sight of him.

I heard eventually that they couldn't make the blackmail charge stick, but they took him down on the other charges anyway. He got eight years, and he'd be out in four if he behaved well, but it could've been so much worse. My own trial was smaller in every way, much lower-key, although there was quite a smattering of press outside after my performance at Teddy's trial. I got four years for possession of Class A drugs, plus four months for direct contempt of court for my disrespectful behaviour at Teddy's trial. With good behaviour and luck I'd be out in two years for the drugs, plus two months for contempt, as I'd got to serve both sentences consecutively rather than concurrently. So with two months of my life I'd bought Teddy possibly eight years, I calculated. It didn't feel like too high a price to pay.

She was silent then, her hands playing automatically with the pendant around her neck until they stopped, and Dora realised that she was asleep. She stayed that way, until it was time for Dora to attend to her needs before making her way home to her well-worn routine of eat, shower, sleep, shower, eat and return to work. Even the presence of Des during the evening seemed routine to her now, preferable as it might be to him going out with who knew who. The interest in her life these days seemed centred in the tale told by Mags and, even if it was outrageous, chaotic and ultimately tragic, at least it was a life being lived, Dora felt.

17: INCARCERATION

Mags didn't give much preamble before recommencing her story that night, and Dora didn't mind; she needed to hear it as much as Mags needed to tell it, apparently, and the longer it went on the better, as far as she was concerned. She knew it had to end, as the life of the teller had to end, which after all was the reason for Dora's nightly presence here; and in a strange way she couldn't explain, Dora felt that the end of her night-time visits here would be the point at which she'd have to face the problem of Des and confront him, for better or worse. So she was glad when Mags began telling her tale each night, and tried as she listened to ignore what would come when it was over.

Prison was a world of women, Mags went on now, and alien to me in the main; ironically much like a convent, if what I've heard about the latter is true. The residents of both live in cells, only this was an anti-convent, full of sinners rather than saints. There were other women like me in there, all on the game at different levels; it's just a matter of degree. Their falls had been from lesser heights, but I'd started at the top, then suffered a spectacular fall from penthouse to bargain basement. I'd recovered slightly, it's true, but I'd still ended up here with the rest.

I'd never had girlfriends, not close ones; Becky was the closest I ever came, with her selfless devotion to Katie, and I wish I'd gotten to know her better. Liz Needham was next, and I wondered only idly what'd happened to her because I never heard from her again; some friend, but I'm sure she's still out there, recruiting the innocent and the experienced alike to make a living out of them in her so-called escort business. A product of my isolated childhood, I was never totally comfortable with crowds or even smaller groups of people. Teddy was the first person who became close and eventually everything to me, and he was the first in a line of male companions. So in a world totally composed of women I felt like a fish out of water.

Being admitted to prison was interesting, in an ironic way. I had to sign loads of forms. Compacts they called them, which told us what we could and couldn't do; contracts, of a type, and I didn't have a great history with those. What I found particularly amusing was that there wasn't too much time to read them before signing; déjà vu, back to the charity dinner contract which I wasn't allowed to read or take a copy of. The contract which allowed me to meet Teddy, leading to my contract with him which ultimately set me on the road to where I am today. Or did it? Would I have got this cancer that's eating me if I'd had a completely different life? I really can't say.

I prefer to forget other parts of the admission process though, because being a drugs offender I got the full strip-search; twice, actually, being re-categorised from my initial prison and moved after a couple of months, so I had to go through all the checks and inductions again. But I was lucky to be moved, it having been decided that I wasn't an escape risk. Where on earth could I have gone, even in the UK? And as to overseas, I didn't even have my passport any more; Imelda Markham used to keep it in a safe in her office, so she could use it to book travel for Teddy and myself. I wonder what became of it, and of her for that matter, once Teddy was imprisoned.

My second prison had a much more relaxed system, but the initial search was identical to that in the first. I hated it, but possibly other inmates liked it, because some of them had apparently gone Gay for the Stay, as it's called, for the cuddles as much as anything else, from what I heard, but I was off sex in any shape or form. It'd become bad enough with men, and as women had always been distant creatures for me I preferred to keep them that way. There was one who tried it on with me, but I fended her off with a bravado

I was far from feeling. Fortunately she was relaxed about it; No need to be hostile, just asking, don't ask don't get.

But I was glad I'd been assigned to a two-person cell rather than one of the dormitories, and the presence of Celia there was very reassuring to me. Yes, Dora, our Celia, of sturdy farming stock, and who assured me that she could handle herself if it came to a fight. Not that it ever did, because the women in there with me were categorised as non-violent and wouldn't want to get themselves re-categorised and moved elsewhere.

So there was a possibility of women friends for me, and something went right for me when I got her as my cellmate. Big, motherly Celia, always there to comfort and hold me when the nightmares came, and they came often in the early days, when I was so frightened of it all. They started in the first prison; I couldn't sleep most of the time, but I remember one particular night. Along the landing somewhere a woman was repeatedly kicking the door to her cell and shouting; probably the junkie new-arrival they'd brought in that day. I just lay on the hard single bed and remembered my king-size bed with the satin sheets at Bankside, as well as my comfortable bed at my new flat, probably re-let now that Becky and Katie'd moved away. But I did sleep, eventually, fitfully, and then the nightmare came for the first time. Making love with Teddy, and then there was someone else there and I thought it was James, so I turned to him but it was Steve, then Rocky, then Dwayne …

I woke up in a cold sweat. I didn't need all the others too, but the woman along the landing wasn't the only one having withdrawal symptoms. By the time they transferred me I was supposed to have stabilised, but even after the move I seemed to go up and down for some time after I'd come off the stuff. Cocaine; Heroin; at least prison had the positive effect that I was weaned off drugs, although seeing life in its true colours, especially in those surroundings, was a very negative experience to live through. I felt isolated, but then I'd started life feeling that way so it wasn't totally alien to me. But the depression, panic attacks, headaches and so forth took some coping with, and Celia was there for me. She became my first really close female friend, possibly my first friend period; because with men, as *When Harry met Sally* puts it, and if you believe it (which I do), men and woman can never really be friends because the sex part always gets in the way.

We formed a bond, Celia and I, and that wasn't really surprising given the similarities between us. She turned out to be as big a victim of a religious upbringing as I was; for I'd come to believe that my isolated, cuddle-less childhood, lacking in siblings or schoolfriends, had let me down badly in my formative years. Celia's only about five to ten years older than me, I've guessed from what she's said, although physically she looks older, I suppose due to her hard life. Don't tell her I said that, Dora, Mags interrupted herself, I wouldn't hurt her for the world. Dora felt that Celia had such a thick skin it would be impossible to hurt her, but she shook her head rapidly to reassure Mags, who continued.

Well, Celia hadn't been told anything about the facts of life and, far less lucky than I, she fell pregnant out of wedlock in her mid-teens. She did tell me, Dora interposed then, one night when you were sleeping and she sat with me. Mags nodded; So you don't need me to tell you. Well, she had a tough life raising Vivie, and when things got as bad as they could get, she sold the only thing she had to feed her child, and she carried on that way. She was walking the streets below to feed her baby, picking up kerb-crawlers, while up above I was in Teddy's penthouse apartment, selling my body in satin sheets for champagne and lobster and velvet frocks and jewels and the price of a degree.

My degree; a BA, and a joke. Teddy used to laugh and say it stood for Big Arse, and I admit I was a little broad in the beam. He loved it, as I think I've said already, and liked to have me wear skirts and dresses a little tight, to emphasise it and make other men jealous of what he'd got. I remember the blue velvet he bought me the first week we were together. Virginal blue, he said, yet tartily tight-fitting over the tits and arse; a paradox, like my name, like me, Maria Magdalena. I remember thinking that my Bankside apartment block was probably full of the mistresses of the men who lived in Teddy's Thameside one; I used the gym in the basement regularly and there were only ever women there, young and good-looking ones, all very made-up and groomed even though they were only working-out. If I was right, the building was as much a brothel as the small flat in which Celia and her friend worked.

That's what she was inside for, this time around; because, as I'd learned, prostitution itself isn't illegal, but how you go about it can be. More than one woman working in the same residence constitutes a brothel, which is illegal; so when cash-strapped Celia and another working-girl pooled their limited resources to live and work in the same flat, they broke the law. She didn't like having to do it, especially as Vivie had to live there too, but it was a case of needs must. They'd have been OK, she said, because the neighbourhood had a lot of questionable activities going on in it, and most people minded their own business and looked the other way. But one neighbour got snotty about the amount of men coming and going at their flat, and contacted the police, so there they were, arrested.

As far as I can remember, she said that the friend was a first-time offender so didn't receive a custodial sentence. Celia'd been in trouble before, though, and more than once; persistent loitering to solicit in the same area, despite repeated warnings, advertising herself by putting cards in telephone boxes. That's all they're used for, these days, she told me, no-one in this day and age uses the phones any more, and they've all been vandalised anyway. If they wanted to stop us they ought to take down the phone boxes.

Whatever, as a repeat offender with quite a bit of previous to be taken into consideration she was given three years custodial this time, and she'd probably be out in eighteen months. Having arrived only a couple of months before me, also having been re-categorised and moved from another prison, she and I'd have about ten months together, with luck. I wondered how I'd manage when she left, but tried not to think about that.

Vivie was a resourceful mid-teenager by then and managed to go and sofa-surf with a school friend who'd got a sympathetic mother. Celia obviously missed her, despite the regular visits, so maybe I was some kind of surrogate. Whatever, I was really glad to have her in my cell and on my side, and not just for the night-panic comfort but because she helped deflect other negative attitudes held against me. The majority of the women were OK, mostly victims of domestic violence who'd had enough and fought back, I assumed from what I could gather, because it was an unwritten rule that you didn't ask and didn't tell the reasons for our stay inside.

But there's always at least one, and in my case it was Siobhan, a hostile young woman who took against me. My case was better known than many, or more correctly my part as witness in Teddy's trial was well-known; but I wasn't regarded as at risk in any real way. Strangely, Siobhan thought she was being funny, but she'd an odd idea of humour. She regularly taunted me with my past life, such as loud comments at meal times; No lobster for the duchess today?, that sort of thing. I usually ignored her, and the others didn't much like her either, so I felt some safety in numbers. But Celia took a firmer line, telling her to Piss Off, Fuck off, and so forth, and protected me generally.

Fortunately Siobhan was moved elsewhere after a couple of months, to everybody's relief.

As to the rest of life inside, there's very little to tell; monotony, mostly. Eating, although I didn't eat much, the food being dreadful as far as I was concerned. My taste had descended of necessity from the rich food Teddy always gave me, but this was far below even the worst take-aways I'd shared with Steve, and I frequently felt hungry. I got work of sorts, in the laundry; it was that or the kitchen, and as the food was bad enough already and I'd never been noted for my cooking skills (I never did get the hang of it, despite what Steve had said) I thought it'd be better for us all if I stayed well clear. I wanted to be a library orderly, I was qualified for it through my degree, but it was seen as a cushy post and, although I applied to be transferred, there was always someone ahead of me on the list and it never did happen.

We got some fresh air in the exercise yard daily, but what was there to do apart from walk around and talk? It was only for just over half an hour, but was a welcome break from being inside the rest of the time, so I shouldn't criticize it. There was a gym too, but a waiting list, so it took some time before I could get to use it. It reminded me of the days when I had the private one in the basement at Bankside, but it was very different to that, as were the women working-out there.

I checked out the education programme, but they didn't really want me there and I didn't want to be there either, so everyone was happy when I stayed away. For one thing, the skills they'd got to teach were far below the level of the degree I already had; for another, I was a living contradiction to the message they were trying to pass, that education could turn around the lives of those who'd gone wrong, like us. Because here I was, with a BA which ought to have been my passport to a great life, yet I'd been a sex worker in various ways and arrested for drug possession before getting sentenced for the drugs plus the contempt of court I'd shown at Teddy's trial; and ended up here with no life and no hope.

So one way and another I spent a lot of time thinking about the past, which wasn't necessarily the best thing for me, but what else was there? Swapping life stories with Celia took us so far, but about the particulars of our previous careers we were sparing; they weren't careers to be particularly proud of, and we avoided as much as possible talking about the less-savoury characters who'd passed through our lives. So the past couldn't be avoided; there was a lot to think about, and Teddy had a way of making his way to the front of my mind.

It'd been hell in prison at first for me, but for him? His OCD tendencies, for example, I didn't feel would mix well with prison life. But I couldn't help coming back to his sexual appetite, which had been vast. Because if, as Steve had so crudely put it, I'd loved sex, so had Teddy, and neither of us was getting any now. That wasn't an issue for me, because I'd had enough to last me a lifetime, and it was frankly a relief to be without for the foreseeable future.

But Teddy? Was he really going without? What Teddy wants Teddy gets, as James would say; not that James had been saying much, recently, from what I'd heard. He'd been jailed himself as the city trader arranging dodgy insider doings for Teddy, and he'd steadfastly refused to add anything to what they'd already got on his brother, despite being offered a deal. So they'd jailed Teddy anyway, and when I thought about it more I realised that he was probably King of the Heap by now, and able to do what he wanted, as he'd shown through his generous offer made to me early on in my first prison.

Because I hadn't had to go through the pain of getting off drugs. An approach had been made to me, early on, with the offer of coke; not a huge amount but free, and on a regular basis, and courtesy of Mr du Cain. If I hadn't loved him already I would've then; he was acknowledging my service at his trial, and thanking me, and it would've been so easy to avail myself of his generosity in that way. But I'd made the difficult decision to get off the stuff, and besides, I had to take a voluntary drugs test each month. So I'd be caught, and bang would go my good behaviour record, and my being re-categorised to a somewhat better place and getting out in half my time. And while I'd no idea of where I'd go or what I'd do when released, apart from finding Katie and Becky with her, it was still preferable to staying inside. So I sent my thanks, emphasising my deep and lasting gratitude for the offer, but declined as gracefully as possible.

I speculated then that if Teddy could get coke into prison to me he could get a woman in for himself, no problem; smuggled in via the grocery van in the evening, out via the laundry van in the morning, or vice-versa. He might have to drop his standards a bit, though, it wouldn't be as easy as on the outside to tell where she'd been or who she'd been with. I remember Steve saying how it was always the best for Teddy, which without boasting was what I was; a virgin, no wonder he hadn't been able to believe his luck. Men pay a lot for virgin arse, as the Engineer says in *Miss Saigon*, and Teddy paid handsomely; my fees, my living expenses, clothes, jewels, the high life with him. He only gifted me to those he judged as deserving of me, and for as long as he thought; and never all the way, except with brother James, under his supervision, as it were, the first time, and for only a few hours alone with me later. The others, for whatever period was necessary to honey-trap them, and film them for his purposes. It was only when I tried to take control, as with James, that he punished me, lightly, as I now realised. Then my affair with Steve, my total fall from grace and expulsion from the Eden of Teddy's territory into the Hell that my life became.

I mused on this a while, and then came back to the

point, realising that I was most likely over-estimating Teddy's abilities. To get a woman smuggled into prison? That sort of thing only happened on TV, or in the movies, both of which admittedly I had watched too much in my former life. No chance of that now; I didn't have a TV, and neither did Celia, and I thought it'd do my over-active imagination good to break that habit too.

I thought about the offer Teddy had made me, though, and wondered if I dare ask him for an alternative. Charles Manners, my lawyer, had helped me put measures in place to keep Katie safe, but they wouldn't last forever and it wasn't fair to expect Becky to give her life over to my daughter, devoted to her as she might be. I needed to put something far more stable in place until I got out of prison and could assume responsibility myself. I agonized over the idea, but I didn't have much time; Katie's future was at stake and I needed to ask Teddy for help soon, while his goodwill towards me lasted. I couldn't be sure it would, and I also worried that he might reject my request out of hand; was I willing to put myself through the humiliation of a rejection?

For Katie, yes, I decided, I was. So I put aside my pride and worded a careful request, in all humility, explaining that I'd got a child now and was anxious about what'd become of her while I was in here. I realised I had no right to ask Teddy for help, I explained, but a mother's love … and so on and so forth. I didn't go into the whys and wherefores of Katie's possible father, but kept it as short and simple as possible while not downplaying the importance of the matter to me. The warder who'd made the approach to me with Teddy's initial offer provided me with a pen and paper, when I explained to her, and undertook to see that the message got through outside official channels. And then I waited.

It didn't take long; Charles Manners requested a visit, and gave me the news that he'd been summoned to a meeting with one of Teddy's legal advisers with the aim of putting in place a generous financial package for Katie, so she wouldn't go short or suffer materially while I was away. She'd be allowed to stay living where she was, to keep things as stable for her as possible, and Becky would continue to care for her; everything would stay as it was, apart from the fact that Teddy would pick up the bills. He'd even got a private school lined up for her, if I wished, and I had to think about that.

Apparently they took children as young as two years old, which I thought far too early, and even though Katie was older than that and would be of school age before too long I wanted to keep her safe with Becky for as long as possible. However, who knew what might happen to Becky, or to me, for that matter. It was as well to have something in reserve just in case and, although I felt my daughter too young to be boarded just now, beggars couldn't be choosers. So we left things as they were, with the boarding-school option available if required.

There is just one more thing, Charles asked me, after I'd signed such papers as I needed to, and Mr du Cain's generous provision for the child is not dependent upon this; but he would like to know who is the little girl's father … He paused, and the words 'if you know yourself' hung in the air between us. This was no time for false pride, so I wrote a short note (not allowed officially, but the bribed warder would help Charles see that it got to Teddy) outlining what I knew. Which was, of course, that it was unlikely to be Teddy himself, given that I'd never become pregnant whilst living with him, that it was also unlikely to be Steve Shine, given the vasectomy he'd claimed to have undergone (and, although he hadn't been the most truthful man on the planet, his antipathy towards Katie and unwillingness to support her suggested that in this instance he'd been telling the truth), so the most likely father was James, Teddy's brother. And I briefly explained about the night when I'd been unwell, and neither Teddy, nor Steve, nor even Imelda Markham had been available to look after me, so that James had leapt into the breach and matters between us had gone further than we'd intended.

Having to tell Teddy that must've condemned me in his eyes as a total slut, I felt, but as he was now going to support Katie I felt I needed to be totally truthful. Besides, I told myself, at least it shows a family link which must work in her favour; an uncle is more likely to look after his flesh and blood than a stranger is, and even whilst incarcerated Teddy was a powerful and protective connection for Katie to have. It'd be a load off my mind to feel that he'd be looking out for her, whatever happened to me.

I didn't feel so good when my first Christmas inside came around. I hadn't been transferred long before, and was still feeling unsettled and emotional and dreadful, partly due to coming off the drugs. Unfortunately the attempts of the prison staff to inject a little seasonal cheeriness into the place made me feel worse. I remembered past Christmases with Teddy, on the terrace of either his or my penthouse overlooking the Thames. We could see the fireworks from there on New Year's Eve, drinking bubbly and then going inside to make love as the first thing we did in the year. Even later, when thing were still good with Steve, I went with him to a pub and tapped my foot along to the Christmas music, had the regulation turkey and all the trimmings on the seasonal menu, then went home and to have ready-bottled mulled wine and mince pies and watch old Christmas films on the TV before going to bed and making inept and drunken love before sleep.

Things couldn't be more different now; Steve was dead, and Teddy and I were both inside, but apart, not together. The Pogues' 'Fairytale of New York' playing over the intercom seemed appropriate for our story; I could have been someone; Well so could anyone. And I'd been his someone, and he mine, but we'd both blown it. The bells are

266

ringing out for Christmas Day? Yes; Five minutes to lights-out.

Would you mind if we put the light out in here now, please, Dora? It's hurting my eyes and I need to rest them. Dora hastened to oblige, and helped Mags into a comfortable position under the covers where the girl closed her eyes and was soon asleep. She was certainly getting weaker, Dora thought, as she sat in the darkened room with only the moonlight coming through the almost-drawn curtains to illuminate the room and the girl on the bed. Ghostly she looked, pale with a slight bluish tinge, as though she were already dead, and that wasn't far off, Dora feared. She sat, thoughtful, enjoying the quiet and calm of the not-quite-dark room, and achieved an almost-meditative state, trance-like but with no hint of falling asleep. She lost track of time and, when Mags awoke, stretching her arms and asking how long she'd been out, she had to consult her phone to find that it was 2am.

Plenty more time then, Mags commented, so where was I? Dora reminded her, but mindful of her charge's weakened state also suggested that she leave off the story for tonight and get some more sleep, which she clearly needed. No, Mags countered, I need to get this told; there'll be time enough for sleeping soon; and she picked up the thread with a sigh.

I wasn't expecting much from the new year, but it dealt me a surprise present. Laura Hogarth, my old university tutor and mentor, our Laura, Dora, had apparently found me via the Prisoner Location Service and was asking to be allowed to visit me. Obviously my agreement was required for her to do so, and I didn't dismiss the idea out of hand. Why on earth would she want to see me, after all this time and what I'd done in the interim? Did I really want to see her? I couldn't bear the idea of her coming to be mean to me, but she'd always been fair as far as I remembered. What the hell, let her come, it'd be something to ease the boredom and monotony of my existence. I could always take her off my visitor list if I didn't like what she'd got to say.

My visitor list; that was a joke, insofar as it was non-existent, because who was there to visit me, apart from Charles Manners, for the business meetings I'd had with him? My parents had kept to their decision to disown me given at my graduation, and would I was sure treat me like a leper should I approach them; which I wouldn't, obviously. I remembered what Teddy had once said about them, that they weren't as forgiving as the Son of God they claimed to revere; and He treated lepers a lot better too, I thought bitterly. But I put those thoughts aside and the first visit I'd had was duly arranged, with me prepared to get what I could out of it.

When Laura and I were seated opposite each other, in the row of other prisoners and visitors which included Celia and Vivie to my right, she came straight to the point. Oh God, Mags, how I wish I'd given you that essay extension. Bless her; I couldn't resist an ironic smile. I think it would've taken a lot more than an essay extension to keep me out of the trouble I've landed myself in, Laura. It's not your fault. She smiled then, and we got into the questions of How she knew I was here (silly question, it'd been all over the media, but I felt I had to ask), Why she wanted to see me, and so forth.

I had to smile ironically again when she told me she'd initially tracked down my parents in her attempt to find me, and that they hadn't wanted to know; true to their word. In a nutshell, she wanted to help me. Students were under such pressure these days, look at my own case (Sorry, Mags, that was tactless but you know what I mean), which meant I was the obvious candidate for her attention: Where will you go, and what will you do, when they let you out?

Good question. I had nowhere to go and no-one to go to, apart from Katie, and the need to support and protect her would be the obvious focus of my life, but how? I couldn't really expect Teddy to continue supporting her once I was released, and I'd got a criminal record now, one that would stay with me for a long time; about twenty years, from what I'd been told. So my employment opportunities I felt were zilch, to say the least, and the open-armed shrug of the shoulders I gave Laura said it all, apart from the issue of Katie, which I told her about then.

Well, maybe that's what I can help with, she told me without hesitation, bless her. I have a granny-annex going begging, no rent required as the mortgage is paid off and the household bills aren't large. Apparently Laura's elderly widowed mother had lived with her, until she'd passed away recently, so I was welcome to go and live in the annex while I got on my feet again. Laura would help me, she said, it'd be just a question of time and looking around. Maybe at the university, she obviously had some influence in her department; or maybe the probation service, they took ex-prisoners to help others not to re-offend. There must be a niche for you somewhere, Mags.

Doing what? I wondered. Being a mother to Katie, a real mother this time, I told myself; earning a respectable living away from the emptiness of my former career, and the lure of drugs to get me through it. That was the only meaning in my life, but I'd no clue what in the world I'd find to do to make a success of it. But that never became an issue, as matters turned out.

For the time being, though, it was good to know someone cared about me enough to visit me in here, and Laura continued to do so. She also met Celia's daughter Vivie, having got talking to her as they both left on the day of her first visit to me; and it turned out that she could help her too. Vivie was a student by now, going into nursing, and at my old university, which of course was Laura's. It wasn't such a coincidence really, I'd gone to the closest university to home as a condition set by my parents to my going at all, and it was the nearest that carried nursing courses for Vivie.

Of course, she'd got financial issues, and wasn't happy about the idea of starting life with a massive debt around her neck. It was all depressingly familiar to me as the beginning of my route to the life I'd led, and to prison. But Laura offered Vivie accommodation free of charge in the annex she'd offered me; I'd accepted, but I wouldn't be needing it just yet, so Vivie accepted too, but only on condition that she be allowed to do the housework for Laura. She could fit it around her studies and not lose too much time at the latter, she thought. So that was settled.

Unfortunately good news is often followed by bad, and about six months later Celia was released. I was pleased for her, but anxious about how I'd get by without her, not to mention who they might put in to share my cell now, or even worse, put me into one of the dormitories. I didn't want to be mentor to some new first-timer, or intimidated by some old timer, but even less did I want to be at the mercy of half-a-dozen others in a dormitory. I wasn't feeling great, I was tired, most of the time, and my appetite was non-existent. But what was there to wake up for, and why would I feel hungry for the slop on offer there? I spent most of my time lying on my bed thinking over my past, both good and bad.

Teddy was on my mind again; why wouldn't he be? He'd been such a large part of my life, for better or worse. I kept remembering the hard sell the police had given me in trying to get me to turn on him, to get him sent down for much longer. They'd said he was rotten to the core, which I thought harsh, but I'd still considered it. Teddy's core, his hard core of bribery, corruption, blackmail and extortion, and I was part of them all, for politicians, police, judges, anyone with any influence; there was even rumoured to be a royal, who I'm sure was the Prince who'd been instrumental in the ending of my time with Teddy. All in his pockets, and he'd got deep pockets; not deep enough, it appears, as there were some, the incorruptible or the dissatisfied, who'd been gunning for him and eventually put him away.

But despite all that he was the love of my life, and still is, because I don't believe it to be that simple. Yes, he did bad things, and I should know because I was on the receiving end of some of them. But he also did good things, and I was on the receiving end of those also, such very, very good things that make me believe he really did love me, in his own way. So I reject most of what they told me, because he was my first and only love and, if it could ever be said that I had a husband, he was mine. I fell hard for him, and I'm not the first woman, and won't be the last, who's gone that way. You see them on TV, and in films and books, but real life must've had many, and reality is where I'm at, now, I think. I'm rambling and raving now, aren't I? My thoughts are jumbled, anyway, and it isn't snow or smack now, because it can't be. It's the other stuff, the legal stuff.

Dora wasn't sure about that. Obviously the medication must have some effect on Mags, but right now her cheeks were red and she did appear feverish; the habitual and automatic playing with her pendant and chain had speeded-up alarmingly. Dora moved in to feel her pulse and take her temperature, both of which were slightly higher than was ideal. So, in no-nonsense professional mode she insisted Mags rest for a while, after a cooling drink of squash from the jug on the bedside table and the administration of her medication. This latter was earlier than normal, but not much, and Dora's shift would soon end; but Mags seemed determined to tell as much of her tale as possible before that time came and, after closing her eyes and resting for ten or fifteen minutes, reopened them and continued in a weak but resolute voice.

Whether or not Teddy is rotten, and I don't believe he is, I certainly am, as it turns out; or rotting, from the inside out. Cancer, not AIDS though, and I wasn't expecting that. Given how I've lived I would have thought AIDS, or some other STD, was a certainty, condoms being so unreliable. But this is another favourite, cancer of the cervix; that little piece of me that's been sitting there all this time taking quite a beating, and now it's had enough and given in. Ironic, isn't it, Dora? It's unusual in women below the age of 30, so cervical screening isn't offered until the age of 25, but of course you know that. I was of age to have the test when I went inside, but the admission medical was basic so I told them I'd had one privately not long ago, and they didn't check. I'd heard what the test was like from some other girls, at uni and in Teddy's crowd, and I wasn't keen; I'd had enough men sticking things in me and I didn't need any more.

Although, of course, sexual activity can be a factor, apparently, and I've been nothing if not sexually active. It also seems that there was some drug which could affect babies in the womb, if their mothers had been taking it. Diethyl-something, I can't remember exactly, but Laura looked it up for me, and you'd know, wouldn't you, Dora? The nurse had to admit that she couldn't bring the name to mind immediately, but Googled it quickly and came up with Diethylstilbestrol. Mags nodded; It was discontinued, though, and from what I can work out that was before my mother was expecting me, so it's unlikely to be that.

I wouldn't mind asking her, though, but there's no way I could; she wouldn't speak to me, and what'd be the point anyway? It wouldn't change anything. But I do wonder if the cancer had been there waiting to get me from when I was young; it might've been something to do with my inability to have a child for so long, although eventually I had Katie so maybe that was down to Teddy. Maybe things would've been different with him if we'd had one early on; I always seem to come back to him.

Whatever, back in prison I'd been feeling tired, but I put that down to feeling stressed in general since being locked up. My appetite had gone as well, but I put that down to my dislike of the food. Siobhan may have been a bitch in calling me the Duchess and joking about the food not being good enough for me, but she was right. I was spoiled, eating with Teddy, and even if I ate junk food with Steve it was at least food that I chose and liked. So my weight loss I put down to my lost appetite and low food intake.

It was only when I started having what I thought were extra periods that I went to see the doctor, who referred me to a gynaecologist for testing. It was at least a trip outside, if under guard; but the cervical screening didn't give a good result, so I needed further tests and I got the lot. Blood tests, scans, biopsy and something I'd never heard of before, a colpo-something; Colposcopy, Dora was able to supply this time, as Mags looked enquiringly at her; anyway, the upshot was that I'd got advanced cancer which had spread.

You know the rest, Dora; Stage 3 Cervical Cancer and chemoradiation the treatment. I remember the regular trips out to the hospital to receive it; they were the best part of the process, something to relieve the monotony, because it was all a waste of time. The cancer's won, although to be fair it wasn't much of a contest. They'll say I lost my battle with cancer, they always say that, don't they, and in my case it'll be true, even though there's little fight left in me now. I used to put up a fight, when it seemed worth it, like when I wanted to get out from my parents' strict regime; my back was against a wall and I won.

But I seem to have been beaten whenever I've fought since then. By love, when the need to keep Teddy won over my wish not to do the things he wanted me to do, and I lost. By fear of the future, when Steve also wished me to do things I didn't want to, and I lost then also. I fought in court, though, for Teddy, and arguably I won then, because it was he who got the positive result and I the negative. But now I'm fighting for Katie, because I so want to be around for her, to give her a better life than I've had, to see her grow; but it's a losing battle because I can feel myself getting weaker by the day.

She was close to tears now, tears of frustration though, and she waved away the arms which Dora extended to put around her, instead taking and holding onto one of the hands in a strong grip which belied the weakness she was apparently feeling. My body's wasted, my hair's gone, and I'll be gone too before long. I could've stayed in prison to die, and I accepted that because where would I've gone? To Katie? I couldn't feel that I'd be any good to her in this state, and Becky had enough on her hands caring for her, never mind a terminal invalid.

She smiled then, through the tears which had sprung to her eyes, wiping them away with the tissues which Dora offered and continuing in a choking voice. But Laura had other ideas, she paid me another visit and persuaded me; Mags, I want this, let me make a home for you, just for the time you have, you must come, you and Katie. Celia will be there too, I've spoken to her, she wants to care for you, let us both care for you. So I agreed; Celia, good, motherly Celia, my cellie who comforted me when I had nightmares, and wanted to care for me at the end. Laura, my ex-tutor and mentor who wasn't under any obligation to re-enter my life but did so anyway because she cared. Both of them such good friends, so late in life.

Late? Relatively speaking, I suppose, as I won't be around much longer; I'm only 28, but I do feel so much older. Celia's only about ten years older than me, maybe less, but she seems much older too; not surprising, given how hard her life's been. But mine was easier than hers, at least for a while, and we both ended up in prison; but now at least she's going to live and I'm not.

I was given a compassionate release for my last few months, and installed in Laura's house much sooner than anticipated, so I'm in the main house rather than the annex, where Vivie's living. Celia being here helps her as well as me, as it turns out; Vivie started out doing housework, laundry, ironing and so forth for Laura as a way of paying some kind of rent, but trying to fit it around her studies caused some conflict, so her mother's pitched-in and taken it on. She's housekeeper to Laura, organising everything, the shopping, repairs and so forth. Laura's working at the uni part-time now she's getting older, but she's mainly writing, essays, articles, even a book, so being able to leave the mundane stuff to Celia frees her up to do what she wants.

Celia gets on well with Laura, they have a wonderful relationship. It's great to see the way Vivie is so non-judgemental about her mother's former career too; as far as she's concerned Celia did what she had to in order to keep her, rather than give her up for adoption, and the bond between them is really remarkable. So Celia's staying in the annex with Vivie, and she won't take any money from Laura, who's recommended her to various friends because her housework is good, so she's working full-time between them all. That way she makes some money which, with living rent-free, means she can get by. She's by no means making a fortune, but she's got bed and board and her daughter with her, so she's happy; she's had enough trouble in her life to know when she's well-off.

Between them they look after Katie, who seems to have coped with moving here and losing Becky, who was sad to lose her in turn; but she'd met a young man, the old story, and wanted to get married and have children of her own. So Katie came here, and Becky broke the bond slowly, visiting often and gradually lessening the visits; and Katie's gotten used to Vivie and Celia and Laura, and me, of course, for the time I have. But when I've gone the others'll be here and hopefully Katie won't notice too much that I'm not. She brushed more tears from her eyes then, but smiled through them. I could've been so much worse off, but I've got the three of them looking after me as well as you, Dora. Between them and their work or study commitments there's usually one at home, and then you come in for the night, and I'm grateful for the care you all give.

She paused, unable to speak for the emotion she was feeling, but then collected herself and continued quietly. Sometimes, when I'm calm enough, I try to get used to the idea of death, and the hereafter, if it does exist. When I knew I was going to die sooner rather than later, I thought about religion. I hadn't been exposed to the best bits of it, my parents who didn't practise what they preached, and those later churchgoers who wouldn't go out of their way to see a teenage girl home safely on a dark night. But could there be something else? Something they hadn't discovered? I don't know, so I'll just have to wait and find out when the time comes.

I remember one story from the Bible, a comforting one for me, about two men in the temple. One made a big show of his prayers because he thought he was righteous and bound for heaven; the other, though, was of some disreputable profession, I think, though I can't remember what it was. Anyway, he just stood and bowed his head and said, God have mercy on me, a sinner. It's like he was saying, My life's too complicated for me to understand myself, so trying to explain it to you is beyond me, God. But you don't need me to, you know all about it because you've seen it unfold, so I'm putting myself in your hands and it's up to you what you do with me, and whatever it is, I'll accept it.

And I suppose that's pretty much my situation, Dora, she said then. I have up-days and down-days, you know, you deal with them every night. Once, when I was down, I looked at my lack of hair, courtesy of the treatment, and got upset, thinking how it used to be. I remembered a trip to Florence with Teddy, seeing a wooden statue by Donatello of the penitent Magdalen, in the wilderness in the later part of her life, gaunt, emaciated, with uncut hair which had grown so long it covered her body. I wished I'd hair like that now, to go with my emaciated body, and then I remembered my hair-bereft childhood, the pudding-basin haircut, and the bad that came from it. I felt so odd then, a freak, and I'm very glad on that count that I didn't go to school, like other children, because I probably would've been teased and bullied unmercifully.

I did go to Sunday School though, every week, after the morning service when the adults stayed in church to listen to the sermon and the children were taken into the church hall to be taught Bible stories. One little girl, more fortunate than I, regularly came on Sundays with her hair hanging around her shoulders, held by a ribbon on her head, tied in a bow on top. Well, one day, going to find my parents when Sunday School was over, I visited the toilet on the way and found a ribbon on the floor. Pink, it was, and satin, and it fascinated me. I picked it up and ran it through my fingers, sensually and no doubt sinfully also, then put it in my pocket and carried on my way. Outside the door I met the long-haired girl, going back the way she'd come and crying. I've lost my ribbon, she told me, I didn't notice until my mum saw me.

I could've given it to her then, because it had to be hers, and I should've, but I was full of the idea of sin and thought she'd think I'd stolen it. So I said nothing, and let her go on, knowing she wouldn't find what was burning a hole in my pocket, because now I had stolen it. And when I was back home, and my father had lit a fire, my mother called him out into the kitchen to do something or other, and he went. So I was left with the fire burning, taking hold of the paper and kindling and logs, and I put my hand in my pocket and took out the ribbon and quickly put it into the fire, right into the part where the flames were thickest and it'd burn quickly. Because there wasn't anything else I could do with it. I couldn't have worn it without being discovered as a thief, and even if I could've it would've looked ridiculous in my monk-minus-the-tonsure hair. It crackled, and sizzled, just for a moment, and then it was consumed totally, so there was nothing left of it by the time my father came back.

It's tortured me at regular intervals down the years, how I let that little girl cry, and how bad I'd been. The bad feelings have never stopped, even when I realised much later that what I really wanted was the long hair to wear the ribbon in. So I'd grown my hair, and worn it loose like I hadn't been able to as a little girl, and become Daddy Teddy's Baby, and worn it loose for him also because he liked it that way. But now it'd gone, and thinking about the Donatello figure I thought, If I could go into the wilderness and do penance instead of what's waiting for me, would I? But I think I'm already in a wilderness of sorts, and being hairless is my penance, an appropriate one.

I can't pretend it doesn't bother me, the idea that there might be something after, and that I'll go downwards rather than up, penitent or not. I remember once when Teddy took me to see *Don Giovanni*, you know, Dora, the womaniser? Otherwise known as Don Juan? Yes, that's him, seducing every woman he came into contact with. Well, this was a production with the stage arranged near the end with a sort of basement level below the main stage; and when Giovanni'd gone down to Hell, a curtain opened below to show him there, with a naked woman in his arms, totally at home and not seeming punished at all.

It comforted me, in a way, and then I remembered seeing Marlowe's *Doctor Faustus*, which ought not to have been comforting, given what happened to him for his contract with the Devil to sell his soul. But when Mephistopheles, on Earth, is asked by Faustus why he's out of Hell, he replies, Why, this is hell, nor am I out of it. And if that should be the case then maybe I've paid my dues here and I just might be cleared to go upwards instead.

She was quiet for a few minutes then, seeming exhausted with the effort speaking had taken, but apparently determined to go on as soon as she was able, and Dora respected this, sitting and thinking in her turn. She hadn't heard of Faustus, but this didn't seem the time to ask for more details; instead she made a mental note to look him up later. When Mags spoke again it was with a frown and a concerned tone; Vivie's having money troubles, Dora, even living rent-free with Laura, because she's a student and it goes with the territory. Celia came to talk to me, when Vivie was out at uni, and she's worried from what Vivie's been saying that she might be considering questionable methods of making some money.

It's depressingly like my own story, and Celia feels guilty, of course, because Vivie's accepted her former career with such relative ease that she's frightened she's given her daughter all the wrong messages and is responsible for what she's considering doing. I started thinking about it, when she'd gone, and it took me back to where it started for me, the charity dinner to try to make some immediate money and maybe find a sponsor. Meeting Teddy, everything that followed, good and bad, my fall from love and the high life with him to the low life. I thought I could help, perhaps, or at least try to, and not just Vivie but others. If my experience won't put them off going the same way I don't know what will; at the very least the attempt'll give my life some meaning. So I asked Laura to let me use her little recording machine.

She showed the nurse then, the small, slim machine on the bedside table which Dora had assumed to be a phone. It's been here all the time, Dora, recording whatever I tell to whoever's in the room; I sit and tell my life to Laura's machine, as well as Laura, Celia, Vivie and you, mostly, Dora, whenever any of you is around to listen. When the time comes Laura'll take it, transcribe and edit it and then use her contacts to try to get it published; I'm known, through my relationship with Dwayne and Teddy's trial, and that ought to help.

Don't worry, Dora, as she saw the look of concern on the nurse's face, she won't use anything you've said when I've been talking to you, and she'll delete everything when she's got all she needs; you can trust Laura. Dora did trust her, and relaxed; Why not use it, she thought, do some good when you've gone; for that alone you deserve the best of whatever's waiting for us afterwards.

Mags stopped then, the colour gone out of her face and the strength, such as she had, out of her voice; she closed her eyes and gradually went to sleep. Dora was glad she'd administered the medication early, because it would be a shame to wake Mags now, when she was resting. When Celia arrived, bringing coffee, Dora filled her in on how weak Mags had become, and the housekeeper assured her that she'd see to washing and dressing her when she woke. Feeling exhausted herself, Dora drank her coffee and then drove home carefully, to go straight to bed and sleep like the dead, without either breakfast or a shower.

18: LIBERATION

Mags was looking brighter when Dora arrived that evening, even though she was clearly getting weaker and required more help with basic needs. Her skin was glowing, slightly tinged with pink, rather than her usual indoor pallor. I had an up-day today, she told Dora, as the nurse helped her to the bathroom and assisted with what she needed to do there. I felt more energetic when I woke, she continued when Dora had got her back to bed, so Celia helped me into the garden, because it was warm and sunny and I wanted to feel the sun on my skin and fresh air on my face. The energy didn't last, though, and I soon felt weak again, but I enjoyed sitting in the garden chair, waking and dozing by turns; then I woke suddenly and looked around, because I felt someone behind me.

It was James. When did he get out? He's done his time, and it showed, even through the big smile he gave me. He was more grey of hair, more lined of face and much thinner; prison must've been a huge change for a privileged city trader, but it's what he got for doing dodgy insider deals for Teddy. His resemblance to his brother is still very evident despite the changes, and I felt a pang of longing; I hoped prison hadn't been too hard for James, but I remembered the other brother, still inside, and hoped for him too.

I wanted to kiss James, but I hesitated. My condition isn't catching, obviously, but I didn't want to risk a rebuff, given how awful I look. It could be a problem for some people; but not for James, it seems; he and Teddy shared much, myself included, but not the OCD tendencies. He hugged me and kissed me on both cheeks, Magdalena darling, then helped me carefully back into the chair.

You've come on a good day, I told him, usually I have trouble getting out of bed in the morning. He looked at my face, and he must've been shocked by my appearance, but he hid it very well. I can't be bothered with wigs, I won't need one for long, it'd be a waste of money; so James got the full force of my baldness after last having seen me with my hair long and flowing.

Celia was home today, ironing and minding Katie, so she brought us tea; we sat drinking it, a rather sedate activity for us compared to the old days. I didn't ask why he was here, and he didn't tell; we both knew he'd come to say goodbye. There was one issue before that, though; Katie. Teddy had told his brother of her existence, together with the information that James was most likely her father, and of course he wanted to speak about her and see her if possible. So Celia brought her out and sat her carefully on my lap before leaving the three of us alone together.

She looked at James solemnly, and he looked back equally so; I told her he was her daddy, but I don't know if she really understood. She sat on his lap, though, when he asked to hold her and I made sure she was happy with the idea; but then she got bored and agitated to get down, so we let her go and explore the garden, keeping an eye on her the whole time. James was pleased, and anxious to let me know he'd get involved with her upbringing now that he's at liberty; Teddy's been great, supporting her, but now it's my turn, he told me; he was really keen on the idea. Apparently he didn't have any issues with the small possibility of her being Teddy's, but was prepared to assume full responsibility as her father; and whichever of them really is, I was reassured that both will see she doesn't go without.

We spoke of other things for a while, and I became more tired, and James said he really ought to be leaving and let me get some rest. He took a thick envelope from his jacket pocket and gave it to me. I looked at it, and at him; You must need something to live on, Magdalena darling, and even living with friends costs, so you must let me help you. The financial authorities would be straight onto any accounts I opened, so I'm afraid it has to be cash. A bit tasteless, but there it is.

I smiled and thanked him; he was right, I couldn't afford the luxury of refusal. I do have some money put by, but I need to leave everything possible for Katie's future; even if Teddy and James are supporting her, I think it's only right that her mother do something for her too. Plus, I need to give something to Laura, who's gladly supporting me, and Katie, but it isn't right to let her assume the total financial burden.

James stood, and helped me up, then took me in his arms and held me hard against him. He kissed me full on the lips, a long and lingering kiss full of real feeling; I kissed him back in the same way. Then he apologised, clumsily, for our first time, for sharing me with Teddy; It was unbecoming and wrong. No, I told him, I wouldn't have missed it for the world, no apology necessary; if it hadn't happened we mightn't have got together later and made our child.

He smiled, and nodded, and then he left; on his way he scooped up Katie, who didn't seem to mind, and carried her inside. I saw him through the window, talking to Celia, and I knew what he was saying; Let me know when it's happened. I sat and thought about him, and I wondered how it would've been if he'd got to me before Teddy at the fateful dinner. But it didn't happen and I don't think it ever would've; somewhere it must've been decreed that Teddy and I were meant for each other.

I asked Celia after James had gone and Yes, he'd asked to be notified and left his contact details, for arrangements about Katie also. I thought for a while and then wrote a letter; two letters in fact, and it took ages, given how weak I felt. One was to Teddy, so difficult and so personal; I tried to keep it as short as possible, there was so much I wanted to say, but I didn't want to ramble. I didn't accuse him, or blame him, or say anything negative about his own conduct; he did share responsibility with me for our break-up, but what'd be the point of dragging all that up?

Beside which, he'd been so forgiving after the trial, offering to help me and assuming care of Katie; I wanted to leave him on a positive note and try to encourage the good memories. So I thanked him for all his goodness, apologised for my own bad behaviour, asked for his forgiveness and told him I loved him; all as simply and straightforwardly as possible. It was something like,

Dear Teddy,

I know I've no right to approach you or address you so familiarly any more, but there are things I need to say before I go so I hope you'll forgive me. I've given this letter to James to pass to you when that's happened, so now you're reading it that means I'm no longer around.

I want to thank you for taking care of my daughter, who has to go through life without a mother now. I'd no right to expect that, especially in the light of my bad behaviour towards you, I've no excuse but that I was very silly and jealous and confused and I made a bad decision. You were right to break with me for hurting you, and my life's become worse since and that's my punishment. But it'll be over soon and I'll never see you again, and that's the worst of all. I'll never know, but I hope you'll find it in your heart to forgive me for everything bad I did. I hope you'll be able to put your own life back together eventually, maybe with someone who deserves you.

Thank you for all your kindness.
I love you.
Mags.

She paused for a moment then; she'd clearly memorised every word, and her hands were playing with her pendant again as she continued; Thinking about how I wouldn't see Teddy again, not on earth anyway and maybe not afterwards, I felt it'd be some comfort to know he felt something similar; but I'll never know now. I wish I could see him.

There's no point wishing for the impossible, though. I put both letters into envelopes, Teddy's inside a covering one for James, asking him to pass it on when I'm gone. I put James's name on the outside envelope, then gave it to Celia and asked her to let him have it when she notified him, afterwards. When she'd gone back to her housework I opened the envelope James had given me; there'd been an unspoken understanding that I wouldn't open it in front of him, to leave some dignity for both of us. Used notes, it was, wrapped in paper with the amount written on it, because James had sensed that I wouldn't be up to counting it.

Twenty thousand pounds! I'd have been happy with less, or nothing at all, because he owed me nothing. Or is it all from him? I'll never know, but it's too much, I think. I can't insult either of them, or both, by sending it back though, and James was right, I do feel the need to pay my way. Now I can give Laura something for my living costs, and for my dying costs, as undertakers don't come cheap. Something to Celia to help her get by, and thankfully something to Vivie to help with her study costs. They deserve it for their care of me.

She stopped here, clearly exhausted, and for once acknowledged the fact; I don't think I can go on. There were tears of frustration in her eyes and, apart from trying to sooth her and make her as comfortable as possible in her bed, Dora didn't know quite what to say. Would Mags last long enough to tell all of her story? There didn't seem any more to tell, really, she'd told the events of this day, today, so that had to be it. Dora felt deflated, somehow, that there wasn't some other ending, happier, but this was it; reality.

Mags slept then, and didn't re-awaken until about an hour before Dora was due to leave. She didn't say a great deal, apart from thanking Dora after the latter had administered her medication and helped her to the bathroom and back, and the nurse wondered if she'd last the day. But Dora returned home as usual, to eat and sleep before preparing dinner to share with Des; and as she began to do the latter, the phone rang.

It was Des; he hoped he'd caught her before she started cooking? Which Dora assured him she hadn't. That was good, because he'd decided to go straight to the pub from the office with the others, it was someone's birthday and they'd decided to make an evening of it. So if Dora didn't mind (she did, but couldn't bring herself to say so) he'd get something to eat there and save her the trouble. He was sorry to miss seeing her, but it was the weekend soon and they'd have loads of time together, so it was only a few hours they'd miss tonight.

When Dora had put the phone down she couldn't resist the impulse any longer; she walked rapidly out to her car, switched on the ignition and drove to the pub where Des had started going out drinking with his so-called colleagues. She knew which one, he hadn't hesitated to name it when telling her of his evenings out. Arriving, she parked without too much difficulty, thank goodness, on the opposite side of the road, a short distance away but in a space from which she could see the entrance. Being a town-centre pub it didn't have a side entrance, or rear car park, so anyone entering or leaving would have to use the front door.

She turned off the ignition and waited; and waited; and waited, eyes on the front door, until her impulse was rewarded; or punished. Because eventually she did see the unmistakeable figure of Des walking along the pavement,

286

heading for the pub door; with his arm around a woman. That was all Dora was able to ascertain, before they were in through the door and lost to her sight. She couldn't make out much else, but what she'd seen was enough; she put her head down on the steering wheel and sobbed as though her heart was breaking; which it was.

When the storm of sobs had subsided, Dora wiped her eyes and thought; what to do? Go into the pub and make a fuss? An undignified row, in public, in front of that bitch who was making a play for her man? No; not yet, at any rate. She had to think it out; plus, there was her shift to go to, and get through, and she couldn't let her patient down. She drove slowly back home, deflated and defeated; her worst fears were coming true, and she wished for all the world that she didn't know. To have continued in ignorance, if hardly blissful, would have meant she could have braved the thing out, until Des had had his fling and finished it.

Which wouldn't necessarily have been the case, Dora reminded herself; what if he came to her and asked for a divorce? She'd have to cope with it in that instance … She couldn't think straight, so pulled herself together firmly, as firmly as she could, at any rate, and prepared for her shift; that would take her mind off her own troubles.

She felt terrible when she arrived at the house, and looked it too, apparently; because Mags, when the nurse had administered her medication, washed her, changed her clothes for a nightgown and made her comfortable in bed, looked at her closely and said quietly, Dora, what's wrong? You don't look good, are you ill? Dora waved a hand deprecatingly to dismiss the idea, but couldn't stop the ready tears which started from her eyes at this gentle expression of concern.

She sat and sobbed, trying to get control of herself whilst rubbing uselessly at her eyes with a tissue; so undignified, and so unprofessional! The girl watched her closely and, as the tears flowed, reached out her arm and took the nurse's hand, squeezing it reassuringly. Then, as Dora got herself under control, Tell me, maybe I can help you for a change. I don't have any more to tell myself, she continued, as Dora shook her head, and I don't have the energy for it anyway; so do tell me, Dora, please.

Dora couldn't help herself, in the face of this generous offer; and who else did she have to talk to? Professional colleagues? The nature of her work meant she spent her time largely alone, caring for patients like Mags, rather than in a ward, with other members of staff in close proximity all the time. Her children? She wouldn't confide in them, even if they weren't so busy at work to have enough time to spend with her. Des was their father, why potentially lower him in their esteem, damage their loving relationship, over something which could turn out to be nothing? Her own parents? No, for the same reasons as for her children. The bottom line was, there was no-one else.

So she opened up to Mags, who sat and listened to all the doubts and upset and lying awake, to the undignified search for signs of another woman, checking her husband's desk, his shed, his clothes, their sheets. All of that, and then sitting in her car outside the pub, and seeing him entering with another woman; leaving Dora where she was now, paralysed with uncertainty, not wanting to confront Des, to potentially find out what she'd rather not know and have to act on that information.

Mags, although obviously weakened, listened intently from her reclined position against her pillows, then spoke when Dora stopped. The other woman, she mused slowly; That could be innocent, you know, a colleague who remarked that it was cold, and Des putting his arm around her in a friendly way, or joking, maybe. She saw the disbelief on Dora's face, but continued nevertheless; Look at what happened to me; I've told you how I saw Teddy with a blonde girl, taking her to the party I should've been going to, and assumed the worst. But it was innocent, as it happens, for reasons I'd never have guessed, and so could this situation be with Des.

Her voice was weak, and she spoke slowly, but persevered as the nurse continued to shake her head in disbelief; Look, Dora, How well do you know Des? I mean, as much as anybody can ever know anybody else? Have you met his family? His parents, his sisters and brothers, his friends? Does he confide in you, tell you his secrets, talk to you about things he'd never talk to anyone else about? You know what I mean.

Dora knew, and answered in the affirmative; she'd met his family, all of them, for they were a large and close family, since before she and Des were married. And yes, he did tell her the things closest to him, and he'd started doing so even before they'd been married, it was one of the reasons why they'd married. Soul mates, that's what they were, Des had told her one day in a moment of extreme happiness, because she'd told him her innermost thoughts also; and now here she was, imagining her Des up to all sorts of things which were totally out of character for him, and frightened to speak to him about it.

Mags must have read her thoughts in her face, because she spoke before the nurse could. You must speak to him, Dora, even if the outcome isn't good, although I suspect it will be, from what you've told me. The thing is, she continued, I never really knew Teddy. Although we lived in separate apartments, at his wish, we had the most intimate relationship; but it was really only physically-intimate. I never met his parents, or uncles or aunts, and it's possible they were already dead by the time I met him, given his age then; but he never spoke about them, or whether he'd ever been married, or had children, and he made it clear he wouldn't go there, when I tried to ask him about them. The only family member he ever admitted to was his brother James, and I've told you about the night we all spent together, and my other times with James; but I sometimes wonder if I would've even met James, if he hadn't happened to drop in on Teddy one Friday evening just before I arrived for the weekend.

And, she continued, obviously very tired by now, Teddy never really opened up to me in any other way. There was just the one time, I told you about it, when we spoke in the night, about going to live simply on an island, and he told me about the stars, do you remember? Dora did, and also how Mags had remarked that it had been the closest she and Teddy had ever been. Well, Mags continued wearily, and it was more than just the need for sleep that was tiring her; I lived with a man I didn't really know, and I played it his way and didn't ask him about what he didn't want to tell, so much so that I became frightened to ask him anything, eventually. And it all went wrong, and he's in prison and I'm going to die soon; but you, Dora, you've such a rich and full relationship with Des, in so many ways, and with children to show for it. But it's going wrong because you're worried about something and frightened to speak to him about it, which doesn't sound right; what's really bothering you, Dora?

She fixed Dora with a searching look then, intense eyes looking bigger through the thinness of the face into which they were set and the lack of any hair surrounding it. She startled the nurse, who hadn't expected such insight from this girl who was gradually fading out of life. She knows, Dora thought, the things I haven't mentioned, my loss of interest in physical intimacy, my worry that Des is going elsewhere; but she couldn't speak and just stared silently back at her patient.

When I was with Steve, Mags began after a long moment of searching Dora's face, I had a regular, Mike, one of the brighter spots of my life post-Teddy. He was a market trader, in his mid-forties, I would've said. He loved his wife, and enjoyed sex, actually he couldn't get enough of it; the problem was that his wife was incredibly fertile, and they'd had ten children in twelve years. They were Catholics, so you see their problem. Apparently his wife was worn-out and weary by the time he came to me, and I'm not surprised; but she'd decided that the only permissible and effective method available to them was also the last word in contraception; No.

Mike could see her point of view, all these pregnancies were making her ill; but he needed to relieve his natural urges somewhere, which is where I came in. He'd had a few regular girls over the years, but they'd all disappeared for one reason or another, and another man had sent him to me. He was as faithful to me as to a wife, which was a bit weird given the nature of our relationship; but he matched his visits to me with visits to the confessional, and his wife knew what was going on, so the situation was as open and above board as it could be and, from my point of view, Mike was about as pleasant as things got.

And of course, she added, he could do things with me that he wouldn't ask of his actual wife. Some men are funny that way, I've found, and I guess some women are too; marriage seems to put certain sexual activities out of bounds, which is a pity. If all married couples could have an open and experimental sexual relationship, what couldn't they do?

Dora nodded, bleakly; not that long ago she'd have said that Mike ought to have resisted his natural urges, but now she wasn't so sure. Everyone was different, and he'd loved his wife, it seemed; he'd just come up with the best solution to the situation in the circumstances. It didn't completely fit Dora's situation with Des, there being no fear of any more children for them, but it made her consider her own case more deeply. Would Des go elsewhere for what he wasn't getting at home?

You need to have it out with him, Dora, rather than ignoring it as I did for most of the time, until I thought Teddy was about to finish with me. I spoke then, and I was so frightened, but it was business worries that'd been keeping him from me and he still wanted me with him; even if it was to help him sort out his problems by seeing the Prince, which really finished us. But you and Des aren't like that, Dora, your relationship isn't complicated by bad things like those Teddy asked me to do, which I should've refused if I'd had anything about me. Talk to Des, Dora, have it out openly and honestly; and even if the outcome's bad, you won't be alone in the world. You've got your children, they'll be supportive, and you've got your work, your career, you'll be able to support yourself in a respectable manner. And it sounds cold and hard to say it, but you'll learn to live without Des, as I did without Teddy.

Mags laughed bitterly as she said this last, a harsh sound that quickly turned into a hacking cough, and Dora's professional side kicked in. She was meant to be making this girl's last days as pleasant and painless as possible, but here she was wallowing in self-pity while her patient re-lived things unpleasant to her and made herself miserable. Without thinking, she stood up and approached the bedside, her arms outstretched; and the girl went into them, receiving the proffered hug and winding her own arms around the woman. No more now, Dora told her, it's tiring and upsetting you and I oughtn't to have told you; it was unprofessional of me, and I apologise. But Mags continued to hold her, and in the same way that Dora had intended to comfort her, the patient now comforted the nurse.

They stayed like this for some minutes, before Dora suggested some refreshment, and Mags accepted; so, having made her comfortable, Dora went and made hot chocolate, less strong than usual and, finding cake in the kitchen, cut a small piece; she didn't want to make the much-weakened girl ill. Comfort food prepared, along with tea for herself, she returned to the bedroom and was rewarded by the girl's obvious pleasure in what she brought. She ate slowly, being visibly weaker than she'd been, Dora noted, but enjoyed what she ate, and then lay back against her pillows.

I'm very tired, she explained, if explanation were necessary, as Dora drew the quilt over her. She slept soundly while Dora sat beside her and felt exhausted herself; with everything going round in her head she could easily have slept too, but that wasn't allowed. She focussed on the sleeping girl; Mags was getting weaker every hour, no doubt about that; it couldn't be long now, her professional experience of these cases told her.

19: ENDING

When Dora got home in the morning, she considered the conversation she'd had with Mags. She's right and I've known it all along; I must speak to Des, she told herself firmly; but what would the outcome be? That would depend on him, and how he feels about me; does he still love me? she wondered fearfully as she removed her coat and shoes and went up to the bedroom to shower and change. She saw the bed carefully made, the shower cleaned and dried after Des had used it, the clean towels left for her; then turning around she went straight back downstairs to the kitchen and saw the breakfast things laid ready for her, flowers bought for her by Des in a vase on the windowsill and reminding her of the chocolates he also brought sometimes, and relief flooded through her.

Of course he loves me; the knowledge dispelled the doubts she'd felt. All the little acts of domestic thoughtfulness weren't just things Des was doing to assuage his guilt over having an affair, but real things, caring and loving. And do you love him, Dora? She knew she did, of course she did; so why was she denying him the physical expression of that love? Because of some prissy notion of respectability? Or perhaps because even she, the self-sufficient career woman, could feel insecure in middle-age about her own attractiveness to her husband? She resolved to speak to Des soon, and this time she meant it.

The opportunity came much sooner than she'd expected, in the form of a phone call, about mid-morning, rudely awakening her from the fitful sleep into which she'd fallen after lying awake considering her soon-to-be-talk with Des. I'm sorry if I've woken you, it was Celia on the other end of the line, picking up on the sleep in Dora's voice, but I thought it'd be best to speak to you as soon as possible. It was OK, Dora assured her politely, I'd only just gone off, no harm done, and what can I do for you?

Could they make a change to Dora's next shift, please, Celia requested; I should've rung the agency but you're one of the family now, so I wanted to speak to you directly. Touched, Dora said that of course she'd make the change. The thing is, Celia continued, would you mind taking tonight off and coming in tomorrow morning, about 7 o'clock until lunchtime, maybe? One part of Dora welcomed the change, the other, weaker, part didn't, knowing what she would have to do during the unexpected evening and night off. But she'd already agreed and wouldn't go back on that; so, when Celia had hung up after thanking her profusely, Dora lay and thought with fear about the coming confrontation with Des.

Thankfully she fell asleep soon, worn out with worry as well as with the physical fact of having been awake the entire night; but the thoughts came back to her as soon as she awoke around 4pm, and wouldn't go away. She prepared dinner for herself and Des as she usually did, but her heart wasn't in it. If she confronted him before eating, she felt sure neither of them would feel like eating afterwards, whatever the outcome; and if they ate first it'd be all the more difficult to maintain her nerve to confront Des afterwards. What to do? She hung around the kitchen in an agony of indecision, so unlike her usual efficient self.

The decision was made for her by Des himself, as it happened, in another phone call. He'd had a late offer to go to the pub, it was a special occasion, someone had been promoted and wanted to celebrate, which made it difficult to refuse, so would Dora mind too much if he didn't come home for dinner, eating at the pub instead? Two nights in a row, Dora thought; she wanted to say that Yes, she did mind very much, and needed Des to come home because she had to talk to him about something very important. But her nerve failed her and she found herself telling him that it was OK, he'd saved her the trouble of cooking; she could have something easy and quick herself, and hoped he'd have a good time at the pub.

When he'd expressed his gratitude at her understanding and hung up, Dora found herself standing looking at the phone in disbelief. How dare Des, how dare he take the initiative out of her hands like this, and how dare she give in so weakly! She fumed around the kitchen then, automatically doing sundry jobs that needed her attention; emptying the tumble dryer (and slamming the door), folding the laundry (haphazardly) and putting each item in its appointed place (but getting some wrong); washing the dishes which awaited her in the sink (almost breaking some as she slammed them down on the draining-board); checking the fridge and larder and making a shopping list from what she found, or didn't find, in them (missing quite a lot of items).

She did these things automatically (and angrily), gritting her teeth as she tried to distract herself from her thoughts. The dinner she'd made went into the fridge, to be reheated tomorrow, before she set-to and made herself a snack, cheese on toast, which she didn't really want in the slightest apart from the fact that she hadn't eaten since a small breakfast when she'd arrived home early that morning. So she ate, reluctantly, but didn't really feel any the better for it; she'd burnt the toast, and the whole thing tasted like ashes in her mouth.

Throwing most of the inedible food in the bin (and Dora abhorred waste), she slammed the lid of that also and stood, impatient and unresolved. She didn't know what to do with herself, with the whole evening alone ahead of her; she looked at the clock and thought about Des. He'd probably be leaving the office soon, en route to the pub and … what exactly? What was he up to? What he'd told her, or something, or someone, else? That girl she'd seen him with? Suddenly her anger re-ignited, as she thought again about all the things Des might have been doing while she was on the night shift and unable to do more about it than imagine what he was getting up to. Well, tonight that wasn't the case; tonight Dora was a free agent, able to do what she wanted; and what she wanted was to finally have things out with her husband. Her husband; that was the point, and she was his wife and he owed her an explanation through the commitment they'd made when they married.

The hell with it, Dora thought then, and she couldn't believe herself, using such an expression, but there it was; on the impulse of the moment she put on her coat and outdoor shoes and left the house, having to remind herself to watch her speed as she drove to the pub and parked; on double yellow lines, as it happened, with the attendant possibility of getting clamped, towed-away, or fined at the very least.

But Dora was beyond caring about such things; all that mattered now was confronting Des. She didn't bother to wait for him to arrive; if he wasn't there already she'd sit somewhere near the door, the better to see him when he did, and who he was with, and deal with him. She was breaking another taboo now, going into a pub alone, which would have been unthinkable for Dora in the past, but she was beyond any thoughts apart from those centred on Des.

So she pushed open the door, more forcefully than was ideal in the heightened state of her emotions and in the process attracting the attention of more than a few people standing at the bar or sitting; one of which latter was Des. He was in a booth, back to the wall and facing outwards, directly opposite the door and looking at his wife as she burst through it; and in front of him, back to the door, a girl, possibly the one from the other night, with her beaded and braided hair visible as it fell down her back. Public row or not, Dora was decided, and walked with firm steps now, directly towards them and the smile which had broken on her husband's face.

This threw Dora; no guilt, or panic, no falseness about the smile, the better to brazen out the situation in which he found himself? She checked her stride, and stopped, as she saw him say something to the girl; then resumed her walk towards them, preparing herself for the excuses which must come. And then the girl turned in her seat to face Dora, who nearly collapsed from her nervous exhaustion as she recognised their daughter; Ruth.

Dora could hardly hide her relief, but from somewhere found the control to make it look like surprise at finding Ruth here with her father. I didn't recognise you, you've had your hair braided, she got out, holding the girl at arm's length to inspect the new hairdo after the mother-daughter hug. Then she made some excuse, loosely based on the truth; I was given the night off at short notice, after your father had phoned, so I decided to come and have a drink and a meal here with him. I was going to surprise him but I'm the one being surprised. Not quite a lie, she decided privately, more some economy of the truth, but added to near-speeding and illegally parking … Oh, she exclaimed at this last and, Des asking what was wrong, offered to go and move her car. We don't want to spoil the occasion with a ticket or worse, as he headed out the door, leaving Dora and Ruth to catch up.

While he was gone, Dora ascertained that he'd been seeing Ruth on more than one of these occasions, having a drink with her and going back to her place afterwards because he was feeling a bit lonely all alone at home. He's not blaming you, Mum, Ruth was quick to reassure Dora, he understands the needs of your work and knows he's had to leave you alone in the past when it couldn't be helped; but he can't help feeling lonely either, and he's been missing you. Us too, she added, by way of mitigating any sense of guilt her mother might be feeling, Matthew and I; between

298

us we're all so busy with our work that family time seems to have gone by the board.

As if reading her thoughts, Des reappeared at this point, bearing not just the welcome news that Dora's illegally-parked car had gone unnoticed and was now legally parked further up the road, but the equally-welcome information that he'd just phoned Matthew, who happened by lucky chance to be free and was even now heading over to join the rest of the family for a long-overdue get-together over a meal.

The next morning, after a rare and precious night cuddled up with Des, Dora rose quietly, so as not to wake him, showered, ate and woke him when she was ready to leave. She drove through the light early-morning traffic thinking about the previous evening, buoyed-up and secure in the knowledge of being part of a loving family and of the good time they'd had together, with promises to make the time to do it again, and soon.

She was feeling lighter of heart and happier than she had for a long while, but her good mood turned serious when she was let into the house by Laura, in a dressing gown and looking as though she'd been up for a while. She's not good, she told Dora with concern, and the nurse saw what she meant upon entering the bedroom while Laura made coffee for them both.

Mags was awake, lying flat on the bed, obviously exhausted and weak, feverish too, with a flush on her face; but glowing also, with a light in her eyes which Dora had seen there before, usually when the girl had been recounting the good days, when she was in love with, and living for, Teddy. There was another difference about her, but which Dora couldn't immediately put her finger on, and forgot about as Mags grasped her hand firmly when Dora prepared to administer her medication, looking searchingly into her face. You look happier, Dora, are things better with you? I'm so glad, when Dora smiled and nodded, squeezing the girl's hand in turn.

Guess what happened to me last night? Something so wonderful; and Mags was trembling with scarcely-suppressed excitement. To you and me both then, Dora told her, but let me get this done before you tell me; she finished seeing to the medication before propping Mags up on pillows, ascertaining that she was as comfortable as was possible, and seated herself beside the bed. She didn't like the agitation Mags was exhibiting, an indication that the end wasn't far away? But she clearly was impatient to tell Dora something, so the nurse took her hand and asked, So tell me, what's happened?

It started yesterday, Mags told her, I didn't really believe it'd happen, or could happen. You'd gone, and I was dozing lightly before Celia woke me, coming in as usual but this time without my tea or any of the comforting things she usually brings with her. She just stood there looking like she was trying to work out what to say, but couldn't, so I asked her, What is it? She looked me in the eye then and just said, He wants to see you.

I didn't need to ask who and Celia dropped her eyes. It's my fault, she said, I phoned James when you'd given me the letter and told him I'd got it. He'd asked me to let him know when – she hesitated, and I knew what she meant, so I just nodded – and of course I will. But I thought … she hesitated again, and I knew she meant it wouldn't be that long, so I just nodded again and so did she, and continued, and he drove back here to get it – you were asleep by then – and he opened it while he was with me, and found the other one. Well, I don't know quite how, but there are ways, you know, and James must have passed it on to him immediately, and now he wants to see you.

Well, I couldn't speak at first; I was so happy just with the thought that Teddy wanted to see me, but I didn't think it could happen, of course. How could it? I thought maybe Celia'd just told me to make me happy by knowing, and she must've read my thoughts, because she shook her head; Officially it can't happen, you're not family, not a blood relative, and you weren't ever his wife. Maybe if you'd been his partner immediately before he went inside it'd be allowed, but you'd been split up for a while, and there were the others.

Yes, the others; and Mags was sombre then, in recounting the dark parts of her immediate past. Steve, who went from supposed loving partner to pimp; Rocky; my work for Liz, the men I met there, and Dwayne as one of these, of course. So many since Teddy, and I didn't give a damn now about any of them, but they were an obstacle to my seeing him at the end, and I felt despair.

So that was that, I thought, and I knew Celia meant well, but I wished she hadn't told me. She came in close though, pulled up a chair in front of me and took my hands as she sat; It can happen, but you'd have to go to him. Do you think you could be strong enough, physically? Well, we both know I'm getting more and more tired and weak and worn out each day, not to mention the pain that's getting more frequent; you know too, Dora. But I decided I'd find the energy and manage this if it killed me. which it probably will. But I'm dying anyway, and soon, so what do I care? I wanted to see Teddy again, so I told Celia Yes, as strongly and firmly as I could; but we both knew it'd have to be soon.

She made me as comfortable as possible and told me, You need to rest and save your strength. Then she left me; and I don't know for how long I dozed, but I woke again when she came back in to tell me that it was on, for last night. That's why I didn't need you here last night, Dora; I rested and slept all day, and by the evening I was a nervous wreck. I tried to stay calm and composed, because it'd got to happen, because I'd got to make it happen.

Laura was working from home during the day, and came to sit with me, but she could see I was distracted, and

I told her I just felt like sleeping all the time; so she put it down to my weakened condition. We hadn't told her what was arranged; Celia'd said, Keep it between ourselves, and I'd agreed. Laura didn't need to get involved in illegal activities, with possibly a criminal record if things went wrong. Vivie'd been drafted in to get her out of the way during the evening; there was a play on at the university theatre and Vivie got hold of tickets for them both, by way of thanks to Laura for all her help, she told her. So they'd gone out earlier, and by the time they returned I'd be on my way, hopefully, with Vivie taking Laura for a late supper afterwards, and she could be trusted to string matters out.

I felt terrible; my immune system's broken down, you know, and I could catch any coughs or colds or whatever bugs are going round, but I was determined. I held on, Dora, and when you'd given me my meds and gone home I drifted in and out of sleep. Celia woke me at around nine in the evening, giving me hot chocolate, to soothe me, she said, and then helping me to put on men's clothes, prison uniform I think, and a woolly pull-on hat to keep my head warm and cover my lack of hair. Ironically, I felt like Cinderella, with Celia as my fairy godmother dressing me for the meeting with my prince. She helped me slowly downstairs, half-carrying me, and into the back of a van parked outside; a laundry van, I think it was, my pumpkin coach. Celia was dressed in a uniform with some kind of logo on the breast, and she helped me into an identical shirt, as insurance, she said. She was coming with me; I couldn't manage alone and I didn't argue.

We left at ten, in the back, she sitting with me lying against her, on what I assumed were laundry bags. They made a soft bed on which I dozed, in and out of consciousness, and lost track of time; but it did seem ages, a couple of hours, maybe? I don't know. Eventually Celia woke me gently and I felt the van slow down; I heard the clang and clatter of gates opening, we turned in and stopped, and the driver spoke to someone. We drove further, stopped again and I was helped out, held up by Celia and someone else unknown. We went through a door, down corridors with that prison smell I remembered so well, musty, with not enough fresh air circulating, then through another door and I was deposited on some kind of seat by Celia and her unknown helper. She hugged me before they left, the door closed and locked behind them. I got my breath, looked up, and saw Teddy.

He was standing there before me, just as he'd been in the early days, although older, more weary and strained-looking, thinner. The prison clothes he wore were about as far from the Italian tailoring of old as they could get. I realised that I must look as bad, far worse, in fact; I'd wanted to see him so badly I hadn't considered that I didn't want him to see me; not like this, anyway. His beautiful Baby, with the big booty and boobs, abundant blondness above and below, sexual and sensual; now become this worn and wasted woman, bone-thin and bald, all desire drained from her. Not quite all; I still wanted him, as he'd been in the beginning, but he couldn't want me, not like this. I looked at him, ashamed to be there now.

He looked back at me, as controlled as so often in the past that I couldn't tell what he was thinking. Then he smiled; Really, Baby, I thought I'd taught you better fashion sense than this. I tried to smile too, with relief and happiness and a whole load of other things I couldn't identify; but my mouth wouldn't do what I wanted it to and all I could manage was a little twisted grimace. He looked at the floor then, and started shaking, and I realised he was crying, something I'd rarely if ever seen him do before. I wanted to go to him but I didn't have the strength to get up; he came to me and I dissolved in tears too. His arms were around me, and mine around him, and I felt motherly towards him then, like I had in the past when he'd looked tired and careworn, and I wanted to protect him; but I

303

couldn't do anything but cry.

Then he was under control again, and shushing me, soothing me, just like he'd done at the beginning when I was a virgin and frightened because I didn't understand what he wanted from me. I realised then that I was sitting on a bed, old-style prison issue, metal frame, thin mattress, scratchy blanket on top and very uncomfortable; but Teddy was there and I'd rather have been there with him at that moment than anywhere else in the world. He held me, calming me, Hush, love, hush, we don't have long, and somehow I managed to control myself; I didn't want to waste this precious time.

He turned my face up to him and stroked my cheek, and his hand went to the woolly hat, but I shook my head and turned my eyes down in shame for being so vain; I didn't want his pity. Your hair? Chemo, I got out; I wanted to say more, but I could feel my voice going again, so I stopped and just looked at him and shrugged. He smiled; Let it go, it doesn't matter, his face seemed to say. I took his hand then and covered it in kisses, I controlled my voice but all I could say was I'm sorry, I'm sorry, over and over.

He hugged me even closer to him, so I couldn't see his face but I heard his voice, unsteady as mine. No, Baby, it was my fault, my responsibility, I should have known not to treat you as I did. I behaved badly, I got out, bitterly, I didn't have enough faith in you, I behaved like a whore. I felt so ashamed, but he shook his head and looked at me directly. He opened up to me then, as he'd never opened up in the past; If you did it was my fault, I treated you like one, I used you like one. I didn't need all the wealth and the power, but I made you do those things because I wanted it and I couldn't get it honestly. I started with very little in life, and it was enough for me; but it was taken from me, even my own country. So I couldn't get enough, I thought; but it's no excuse for my behaviour towards you. I punished you too much, and for things that weren't your fault. You were a child when I found you, Baby, and if you punish a child when they don't deserve it they'll misbehave all the more, because they might as well do something to merit the punishment. I shouldn't dare ask you to forgive me, but … He trailed off and I smiled through my tears; It doesn't matter, let it go. He kissed my hands; You're still my Baby.

I did forgive him, I'd already forgiven him long ago, but I wasn't ready to be so forgiving of myself. A common prostitute, more like, I told him, remembering what he'd called me when he'd broken with me, and his eyes threatened tears again; So much to forgive me for; I shouldn't have said it, I was bitter and hurt, because I loved you, even if I never said it; and I still do. You did say it once, I thought, because I'm sure he did, but I didn't say so because I didn't want to bring up any more old, unhappy things, and there'd been too many of them in our life together. I just told him, I loved you too, I still do.

But when he said, I ought to have made you my wife, I stopped him. No, not marriage, it would've been just another contract, on another piece of paper. The only real contract of love isn't written down; we should be with people because we care about and love them, and treat them well, that's the only reason. He held me closer, if that was possible; I'm supposed to be a businessman, I should've known love's not a business with contracts and waivers and so forth. But you're my wife, you've been that since I met you, you always will be.

He kissed me then, full on the mouth, laid me gently backward on the bed and began to undo the buttons of my borrowed shirt, but I stopped him. I remembered his old OCD tendencies. You know what I've been … what I've done? He shrugged, It doesn't matter any more, I don't care, anyway, when was I ever a saint? Certainly not since I lost you. He continued to remove the shirt, and the T-shirt, and found the chain he'd given me, in anger, what seemed like so long ago, with the 'H' pendant. You still wear this? I never take it off, I told him. Well, he must've known that I had to in prison, when they took it and put it with my other things, to collect when I left; but he understood. You don't need it any more, you never did. So much to forgive me for; may I?

He reached round and undid the clasp, looking at the 'H' as he took it from me. 'H' for Helen, I think; as beautiful as Helen of Troy, Baby. You used to call me that sometimes, I said then, remembering; not that you'd know it now, thinking of my extreme skin-and-bone condition. But he leaned over and kissed my well-pronounced cheek bones; Whoever and whatever, you're still my Love. Then he put the chain and pendant in his pocket and it was gone; he kept it, and I'm glad he's got it, to remember me by, but I miss it too, as my link to him.

Dora realised the difference about Mags then; the pendant was gone, although her hands were automatically moving at her neck, gently stroking the place where it used to sit, unceasing as she went on. He kissed me then, and I wanted him, but I was so frightened it wasn't possible, because of the pain and weakness and side-effects of my treatment. But he understood, and just held me close, and soothed me and caressed me. It was like our first night, again, and it made me cry more, that the end should be so like the beginning and yet so different.

Somehow, though, despite my weak and withered body, and the thin, hard mattress and inadequate single bed, we managed; and if it was over too fast, and was far from what we'd achieved in the past, it was the most full of mutual love, and mutual forgiveness also. We sat, and held each other, and I remembered our music, the Romanza, the Bacarisse. It went through my head and I told Teddy so; he smiled, Mine too. I knew he wasn't lying.

Afterwards, when our time was running out, lying in each other's arms, I wanted to know, What will you do, when they release you? He didn't hesitate; There's an island, fairly isolated, I always meant to take you there eventually, but it never happened. I've enough put by, where they can't find it, to see me through. He grinned devilishly at this; still baulking authority and doing things his own way. A simple life in a simple place will do for me, he said then; maybe James can come too, if he wants. It was just the two of us, from his teens, I've always tried to look after him. I never knew anything much about Teddy's early life, and I felt deep sadness about that, but it was too late now, so I just said, James looks after you too; we wouldn't be here now if it wasn't for him.

And you've been looking after his child, or possibly your own; she's your blood, anyway, I told him then. I had to mention Katie, thank him for his care of her, which would be ongoing, he assured me now; I once said that any child you had would have two fathers, you remember? I did, but felt myself blushing in remembering the circumstances. Teddy hugged me to him then, to help me hide my blushes; You've nothing to feel ashamed of, it was my responsibility, as the child is now. She could be mine, and between myself and James she'll never go without. I was relieved, and said so, but I moved on then, there was so much to cover in so little time.

Do you think there'll be anything afterwards – you know, after I've ...? I felt him stroke my cheek, gently; There has to be, for you; you're proof that angels exist, so there must be a heaven for them to exist in. I wasn't so sure about that, I hadn't been exactly angelic as he well knew, but I let it go; If there is, and I'm allowed to, and able to, I'll find you. It must be easier as a spirit, no heavy body to drag around. I was trying to lighten the mood, like that time he showed me the stars in the early hours. I'll search every island if I have to, and watch over you, I told him; then he told me the location and name of his island and I committed it to memory and hoped.

He remembered the night of the stars too, then; Do

you remember the constellations I showed you? And the star? Ursa Major and Ursa Minor and the Boötes, and Arcturus? I nodded, because I was feeling so weak now I could barely speak, and he held me even closer, if that was possible. Maybe you can find them, and I can look up and hope you're there. We both smiled at our own ridiculousness, but it was all the hope we had.

Then our personal midnight struck, far too soon, and the bribed guard was there, saying I had five minutes and then I'd got to go. Teddy held me tight like he never wanted to let go, and I did the same, and I was crying but trying to smile. Then I was picked up bodily from behind, and I looked back helplessly over the unknown shoulder as I was carried through the door. I saw Teddy's face and he'd recovered his old iron control, he was managing not to cry. I saw his eyes and they looked bleak; but he managed a weak smile and I tried to do the same.

He was lost to me then, and it was a blur of corridors, no time to lose any glass slippers, and being bundled into the back of the van, where I curled up and cried weakly. Celia held me but held off from comforting me with words because she knew it wasn't possible. I hate that I'm going to lose him again now I've won him again, but at least I saw him, and that's a comfort, if a small one.

I thought about religion again, then, and I prayed; If you're there, please be there, I want there to be something, even if I'm to be punished. Because I've seen him again and I want to be with him again, and I know it's not possible here, but afterwards? You know me, what I am, what I've done, and why, and it's up to you what you do with me. You pardoned the other one, the other Magdalen, because she loved much, and so have I. I've got him back to lose him again, and maybe that's my punishment; but if it has to be him or me, let it be him, please look after him because he's still here and he needs it. I knew I was being illogical, over-emotional, but it didn't matter now.

She stopped then, obviously exhausted and in pain, and Dora helped her drink some water. When she'd recovered her breath, she continued: When I got back, at about 5am it must've been, Vivie was up, to help Celia get me inside and into bed. It'd been physically and emotionally taxing all around, and Celia was tired too.

Laura had gone to bed without coming to see me beforehand because Vivie'd suggested, in a very determined fashion, she told us, that it would be better to wait until morning, and Laura had accepted this without question. Vivie thought Laura'd got an idea that something was going on, but didn't ask; so if questioned, she could say honestly that she'd gone straight to bed on her return home and that in the morning I was in bed as usual.

Celia and Vivie made me as comfortable as I could be, but I couldn't sleep. There'll plenty of time for that afterwards; and afterwards won't be long in coming, I think. I just lay there and held my fairground teddy, and thought about it all, remembering his face, his body next to mine. I wanted to go over every second of it all again and again, but eventually I slept because I couldn't stay awake.

I woke, eventually, and I felt weak, and I thought, It must've been a dream, I must've dreamed the whole thing because I'm far too weak to have gone like that and been with him like that and made love with him like that. It must've been a dream, mustn't it, Dora? She was insistent, and the nurse realised that she was worried for Teddy, for Celia and Vivie, even for Laura; and for Dora herself now, because she'd heard about what happened, which was illegal, and she might be classed as an accessory after the fact, or something like that, based on what she'd read in the newspapers and seen on TV, if they got found out. But equally Mags could've imagined it, morphine being prone to cause delirium; so, Yes, it was a dream, she agreed, and thought, it could have been, but it might also have been true, and that's what she'd have wanted it to be, for her patient's sake.

Mags dozed then, fitfully, and Dora kept watch, drinking the tea that Laura brought her with concern in her eyes; Can it be long now? The nurse shook her head and promised to call her if, or when, things took a turn for the worse. But Mags awoke soon, seeming a little stronger as she stretched her arms and wiped the sleep from her eyes, and turned her attention to Dora. How are things with you, Dora? Have you found any answers to your issues? And the nurse told her what'd happened the previous evening, how because she'd been given the night off she'd gone to the pub and found Des with Ruth and her fears to be groundless.

Mags smiled, and sat up, wearily and with some difficulty; I'm so pleased, Dora, but it wasn't for nothing, was it, all the worries and fears you had? It looks like you've been given another chance to get it right with Des. Remember where you began and get back there; Don't be a white Baptist, Dora, be yourself and dance. I danced with Teddy again last night, the last dance, the smoochy one, just before they close the hall and turn off the lights. So live, Dora, and dance again with Des.

She stopped, taken by a coughing fit, and fell back weakly on the bed when it was over. The end was coming soon, Dora was sure; she summoned Laura, who was sitting on a chair on the landing, not far away, and Laura went for Celia, and Vivie, and little Katie, who was put into her mother's arms. Maybe she sensed the gravity of the occasion because she didn't struggle, as she usually did when awoken rudely, but accepted what was being done with her and cuddled up to her mother, who kissed her and spoke to her with difficulty. Mummy loves you very much, but she's got to go away for a while now; Auntie Laura and Auntie Celia and Vivie will take care of you. The little girl looked bewildered then, and she looked angrily at her extended family; She's like him, isn't she, Mags managed weakly, looking at Laura, and Dora knew she wasn't talking about James, and neither was Laura; Yes, Mags, she's his, I'm sure.

Is she? Laura asked herself, because Mags has forgotten that I've never met Teddy, and I'm just trying to tell her what she wants to hear, at the end. Don't worry about her, she told Mags, she'll have the best upbringing love can give, we'll all see to that, Celia and Vivie and myself, and James, and Teddy ... Her voice trailed off as Mags nodded and closed her eyes, before falling into unconsciousness. Celia made as if to take the child away, but Katie turned and scowled at her before snuggling up against her soon-to-be-dead mother.

They prised her gently from her mother's arms, and to distract her Celia put the fairground teddy into the little girl's arms as Vivie took her and held her. When it was over, when Mags had breathed her last, her female family laid their last kisses gently on her face and Vivie carried away the bewildered Katie, who understood that something bad was happening but not exactly what; they could hear her crying, and Vivie's soothing, as she carried the little girl away. They were followed by the stoical Celia, who squeezed Dora's hand before she half-led, half-carried the distraught Laura out of the room. Dora, left alone with Mags, held her close, just as all those men must have done, and when she first came to this house that would have repelled the nurse. But now she held the still-warm body and kissed it gently, and thought the girl one of the most beautiful things she'd ever encountered.

When Dora had done what was needful, done what she had to and initiated the necessary procedures, she was seen out of the house by the ever-practical Celia. Laura, it appeared, had been the most grief-stricken of all, so Celia had given her a sleeping tablet, which had taken effect quickly. She thanked the nurse for everything she'd done and went to shake hands with her; but Dora, on an impulse, opened her arms and gave the woman a hug, which was returned with some surprise but real warmth. Dora then asked, Would they call her, when the funeral had been arranged? She'd like to attend, if they didn't mind.

Of course not, she'd be welcome, was the reply, although it would be a small affair, a direct cremation with no service; Mags had requested this, to keep costs down and for the money to be used to raise her daughter. Dora was saddened by the lack of religious rites, but understood the dead woman's issued with religion, as well as the mother's concern to leave as much money as possible for the benefit of the child she was leaving behind.

20: NEW BEGINNINGS

When the day had come and gone, and Magdalena's earthly remains decently disposed of, Dora took a few days off just to settle herself, she told her supervisor. It was all they could manage, busy as they were now becoming, and they were also keen for her to resume working the late shift, possibly even another all-night care slot. Dora wasn't sure how she felt about that, but she'd see; she'd been giving a lot of thought to the difference between her mother's career, aiding birth, and her own, aiding death. We haven't done much between us for the part in between, she mused, the actual living of the life. She'd practised other forms of nursing early on in her career, community nursing and so forth, but she'd quickly gravitated to the palliative care sector. Maybe it was time she did something about that and moved back into helping people live their lives, while they had them before them to live.

She'd heard of a centre not far away, not in the leafy suburb where she lived, but close to the town centre, where the homeless and rough sleepers, the addicts and the prostitutes, were to be found. They were always glad of volunteers, she'd been told, whether to serve soup or tea, or help find somewhere to sleep, or just to provide moral support. There must be something a trained nurse could do there, Dora was sure; some kind of clinic, because where did the homeless go when they needed medical care? Maybe Ruth and Matthew could play a part? Steady on, Dora, she told herself, one step at a time; but she was excited by the idea and knew that Des would understand if she decided to follow it up. Not if, when, she told herself; it was going to happen, she'd make it happen.

In the meantime, she treated herself to a lie-in and didn't get up until seven; not late by many other people's standards, but late for her, this woman who'd always been up and doing by six and never in bed until the last dish was washed and dried and placed in orderly fashion in the kitchen cabinet designated for the purpose. Having done what needed to be done around the house, she took herself into town and went shopping; for food, as usual, but into the clothes shops as well, unusually, and came out with several interesting-looking carrier bags. She found her way into a hairdresser's, where they could manage to squeeze her in if she didn't mind waiting for half-an-hour? She didn't, and in fact filled the time with their manicurist, who'd just had a late cancellation. Passing a travel agent's as she left, Dora did an about-turn and went inside, to issue forth again bearing several travel brochures focussed on the Caribbean. She knew Des had some leave due, which he'd been planning to use to sort out the garden, neglected for some time due to pressure of work. That could wait, Dora decided; time to visit Jamaica, time to get back to their roots, feel the sun, drink the rum, dance as they hadn't done for so long and live again.

The upshot of all this unusual activity was that Desmond Stuart-Frazer came home that evening to a house with the lights turned on and heating turned up, so much more welcoming than the dark and lukewarm place he usually found waiting for him. There was music playing in the kitchen-diner, flowers in a vase on the table, which was laid for two with the Sunday-best cutlery and crockery, and a delicious smell of goat curry, rice, peas and sweet potatoes in the air, reminding him of his youth. Best of all, there was Dora, hair trimmed, neatened and done up in the kind of highly-impractical style which she disapproved of in others most of the time and in herself all of the time, and wearing the best dress that a well-known high street store had to offer in a pink and purple pattern which suited her warm dark skin admirably.

Hey, what's all this? Am I in the right house? Des was delighted and, when his wife assured him that he was indeed in the right house with the right woman, he grabbed hold of her and danced her round the kitchen like they hadn't done since they were young, possibly not since the time of that church youth gathering where it had all started for them.

Much later, after dinner and wine and more dancing, smooching to something slower and more sensual, had led them upstairs to their bed, resplendent in new crisp sheets in warm tones of terracotta and pink and orange, he held his Dora close and asked, Is it my birthday and I just forgot? Or have I died and gone to heaven? Dora, wiser now, told him enigmatically, No, someone else special died and went to heaven; and that was my birthday, so I thought I could start over and live it all again with you, if you don't mind? He didn't mind, and he didn't totally understand what she meant, but their life had just got a whole lot better, and he wasn't going to argue with that.

BIBLIOGRAPHY AND AUTHOR'S NOTES

FILM AND TELEVISION SOURCES

Die Hard, dir. by John McTiernan (20th Century Fox, 1988) [on DVD].

Dr Zhivago, dir. by David Lean (MGM, 1965).

Four Weddings and a Funeral, dir. by Mike Newell (PolyGram Filmed Entertainment,1994).

Gigi, dir. by Vincente Minnelli (Warner Brothers, 1958) [on DVD].

Jesus Christ Superstar, dir. by Norman Jewison (Universal Pictures, 1973).

Shirley Valentine, dir. by Lewis Gilbert (Paramount Pictures, 1989).

When Harry met Sally, dir. by Rob Reiner (MGM, 1989) [on DVD].

MUSIC AND MUSICAL SOURCES

Alain Boublil and Claude-Michel Schönberg, *Miss Saigon*, dir. by Nicholas Hytner, The David Geffen Company, ENCORE CD5 (1990) [on CD].

BIBLIOGRAPHY AND AUTHOR'S NOTES

Salvador Bacarisse, 'Romanza' from *Concertino for Guitar and Orchestra in A minor, Op. 72,* on Guitar Moods – The Ultimate Collection, Deutsche Grammophon, Deutsche Grammophon, UPC 00028947912811 [on CD].

Janis Ian, *Between The Lines*, Spasm, Inc., EDSX 3005 (1975) [on CD].

Roy Orbison, *Mystery Girl*, Virgin Records, Virgin 86103 (1989) [on CD].

ONLINE SOURCES

Cover design by Alice Alinari at:
https://unsplash.com/photos/MS371wlcGPo

http://www.astro.wisc.edu/~dolan/constellations/constellatio ns/Bootes.html
[accessed 17 November 2018].

http://ukcriminallawblog.com/concurrent-or-consecutive-sentences-sentencing-for-multiple-offences/ [accessed 14 December 2018].

https://www.doingtime.co.uk
[accessed 14 December 2018].

Dumas, Alexandre, fils, *La Dame aux Camélias,* Project Gutenberg eBook, 15 December 2018. Available online: www.gutenberg.org/files/1608/1608-h/1608-h.htm
[accessed 28 December 2018].

https://www.gov.uk/
[accessed 14 December 2018].

BIBLIOGRAPHY AND AUTHOR'S NOTES

https://guide.iacrc.org/step-eight-obtain-the-cooperation-of-an-outside-witness/
[accessed 14 December 2018].

https://www.ifagiolini.com/betrayal/gesualdo/
[accessed 12 January 2019].

https://www.macmillan.org.uk/
[accessed 15 January 2019].

https://www.naxos.com/sharedfiles/PDF/8.573147-49_sungtext.pdf
[accessed 12 January 2019].

https://www.pitt.edu/~dash/perrault03.html
[accessed 28 January 2019].

https://www.sentencingcouncil.org.uk/
[accessed 14 December 2018].

https://www.talktofrank.com/drugs-a-z
[accessed 11 December 2018].

https://www.thoughtco.com/pornai-the-prostitutes-of-ancient-greece-120997
[accessed 17 November 2018].

https://www.vice.com/en_uk/article/exqk3j/we-found-out-what-happens-if-you-get-caught-with-drugs   [accessed 11 December 2018].

BIBLIOGRAPHY AND AUTHOR'S NOTES

OPERATIC SOURCES

Verdi, Guiseppe, *Rigoletto*, Libretto by Jules Barbier and Michel Carré, dir. by David McVicar (Royal Opera House, London, 2000) [on DVD].

Gounod, Charles, *Faust*, Libretto by Jules Barbier and Michel Carré, 1859.

Mozart, Wolfgang Amadeus, *Don Giovanni,* Libretto by Lorenzo Da Ponte, dir. by Francesca Zambello (Royal Opera House, London 2002) [on DVD].

Verdi, Guiseppe, *La Traviata*, Libretto by Francesco Maria Piave, 1853.

TEXTUAL SOURCES

Margaret Atwood, *The Handmaid's Tale*, Vintage, London, 1996.

Giovanni Boccaccio, *The Decameron*, Penguin Books Ltd, London, 1995.

Angela Carter, 'The Bloody Chamber' in *The Bloody Chamber*, Random House, London 1995.

Geoffrey Chaucer, 'The Clerk's Tale', in *The Canterbury Tales,* J. M. Dent, London, 1999, pp. 223 – 256.

John Cleland, *Fanny Hill*, Sidgwick & Jackson Ltd, London 1989.

BIBLIOGRAPHY AND AUTHOR'S NOTES

Wendy Doniger and Sudhir Kakar, eds. Trans., *The Kama Sutra of Vatsyayana,* Oxford University Press, New York, 2009.

John Donne, 'The Flea' in *Love Poems,* Orion Books Ltd, London 1996, pp. 1 – 2.

Nathaniel Hawthorne, *The Scarlet Letter*, David Campbell Publishers Ltd, London 1992.

Christopher Marlowe, *The Tragical History of Doctor Faustus (A-Text),* in David Bevington and Eric Rasmussen (eds.), Doctor Faustus and Other Plays, Oxford University Press, Oxford & New York, 1995, pp. 139 – 183.

Eric Partridge, *Shakespeare's Bawdy*, Routledge, London, 2000.

Prévost, Antoine François, *Manon Lescaut*, Oxford University Press, Oxford and New York, 2004.

William Shakespeare, *Hamlet*, in Stanley Wells and Gary Taylor (eds.), The Oxford Shakespeare: The Complete Works, Clarendon Press, Oxford, 1988, pp. 653 – 690.

William Shakespeare, *Macbeth*, in Stanley Wells and Gary Taylor (eds.), The Oxford Shakespeare: The Complete Works, Clarendon Press, Oxford, 1988, pp. 975 – 999.

BIBLIOGRAPHY AND AUTHOR'S NOTES

William Shakespeare, *Othello,* in Stanley Wells and Gary Taylor (eds.), The Oxford Shakespeare: The Complete Works, Clarendon Press, Oxford, 1988, pp. 819 – 853.

WORKS OF ART

Donatello (Donato di Niccolò di Betto Bardi), *Penitent Magdalene,* 1453 – 1455, Wood, 188cm, Museo dell'Opera del Duomo, Florence.

Pablo Picasso, *Head of a Sleeping Woman*, 1907, Oil on canvas, 61.4 x 47.6cm, The Museum of Modern Art, New York.

Pablo Picasso, *Les demoiselles d'Avignon*, 1907, Oil on canvas, 243.9 x 233.7cm, The Museum of Modern Art, New York.

Author's Notes

1. Magdalena was born in 1984 and went to university in 2002, aged 18, when fees were not yet extortionate, relatively speaking. She met Edward du Cain in her second year (2003) and left university in 2005, aged 21. She spent 3 more years after this with him, making her 24, and then spent 2 years with Steve Shine, being 26 when he died. She then spent 3 months with Rocky and 9 months with Dwayne, taking her up to 27. At this age she was sentenced to 4 years and 4 months in prison, and would be out in 2 years and 2 months with good behaviour. However, her cancer was diagnosed when she'd been in for about 1 year and a few months. She underwent treatment in prison for

some months, but when this failed she was given a compassionate release, aged 28, for what was judged to be the last three months of her life, making 28 her age at death.

2. Dora is 48, this being 2012. She was born in 1964 to Jamaican parents who came to the United Kingdom in the early 1960s. She met and got engaged to Des at 17, in 1981, and went to train as a nurse at 18, in 1982. Des was himself climbing the career ladder and agreed to wait for marriage until Dora had completed her training. They got married when she was 20, in 1984, and she had her son, Matthew, at 23, in 1987 and daughter, Ruth, at 25, in 1989. Matthew went to university in 2005, and Ruth in 2007. Matthew graduated as a doctor, and Ruth as a dentist, and both are working by 2012.

ABOUT THE AUTHOR

Laura Lyndhurst was born and grew up in North London, England, before marrying and travelling with her husband in the course of his career.

When settled back in the UK she became a mature student and gained Bachelor's and Master's degrees in English and Literature before training and working as a teacher.

She started writing in the last couple of years in the peace and quiet of rural Lincolnshire, and published her debut novel, *Fairytales Don't Come True*, in May 2020. This book forms the first volume of the trilogy, *Criminal Conversation*, of which *Degenerate, Regenerate* is the second. The third volume, *All That We Are Heir To,* is in the process of being written.

Laura has also published *October Poems*, to which *Thanksgiving Poems and Prose Pieces* is a follow-up. She has also written a psychological suspense novel, *You Know What You Did*, which is awaiting publication.

OTHER BOOKS BY THIS AUTHOR

Degenerate, Regenerate,

the sequel to *Fairytales Don't Come True* and Volume 2 of
Criminal Conversation,

published January 2021

…

October Poems

published November 2020

…

Thanksgiving Poems & Prose Pieces

published December 2020

…

You Know What You Did

due publication 2021

…

Coming Winter 2021

Volume 3 of *Criminal Conversation,*

All That We Are Heir To

Printed in Great Britain
by Amazon